P9-BYV-028

DISCARD

The
YEAR
OF THE
LUCY

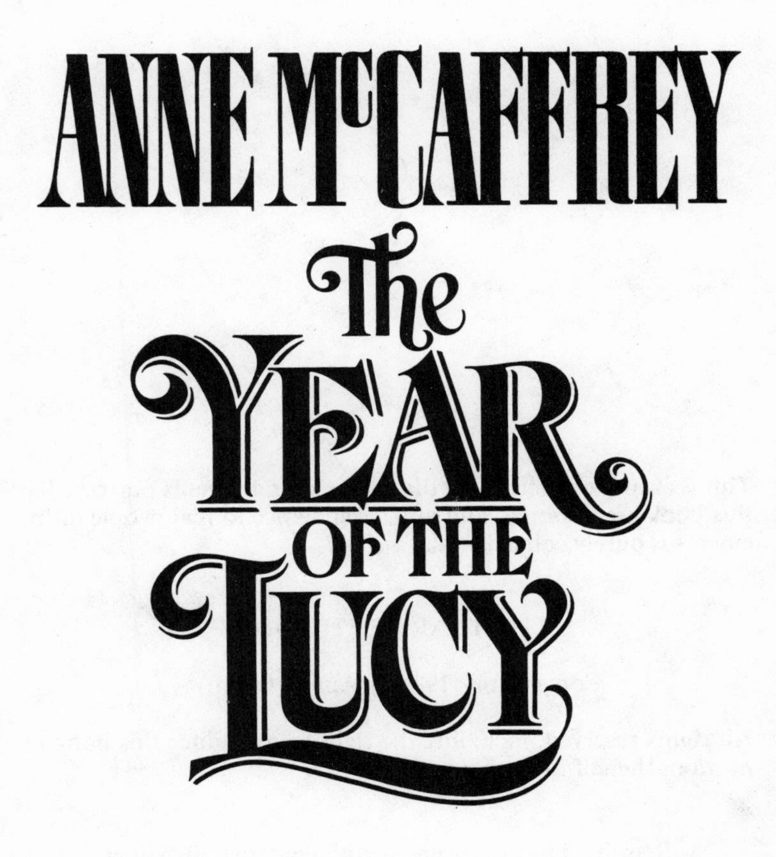
ANNE McCAFFREY
The
YEAR
OF THE
LUCY

TOR

This is a work of fiction. All the characters and events portrayed in this book are fictional, and any resemblance to real people or incidents is purely coincidental.

THE YEAR OF THE LUCY

Reprinted by arrangement with Underwood/Miller

First Tor Printing: September 1986

A TOR Book

Published by Tom Doherty Associates, Inc.
49 West 24 Street
New York, N.Y. 10010

ISBN: 0-312-93981-7

Library of Congress Catalog Card Number: 86-50316

Printed in the United States of America

0 9 8 7 6 5 4 3 2 1

With great friendship for my Wilmington Cronies

Isabel Worrell   Betty Philips   Dorothy Rathje

and to the memory of
Elsie Watson

The
YEAR
OF THE
LUCY

CHAPTER ONE

The Year is 1961

MIRELLE STRUGGLED against returning consciousness because it would end the delightful sequence of dream. Eyes half-opened, she lay on her stomach, feeling out the day ahead of her as she often did, trying to decide if getting up was really worth the effort. Sometimes she knew in advance that it wouldn't be. Today, the coolness from her open bedroom window, a patch of brilliant blue sky seemed propitious auguries. Something else, however, niggled and she cast her mind back to the lingering aura of the dream that she had been so reluctant to leave.

She mumbled with pleasure to herself as she recalled a fleeting part of the sequence. It was a dream that she had often had before, reaching only a certain point before wakefulness dissolved it. When Steve had been away on a long swing around his territory, or when she was particularly annoyed with him, she would deliberately conjure the opening scene of that dream in erotic revenge.

This morning it had merely arrived within her unconsciousness. Mirelle closed her eyes, hoping that she had not passed sufficiently into the day that she could not return to the dream. She imagined herself back where she had left and tried to progress to the next episode.

"Mom!" A strident yell shattered her efforts. "Where are my clean socks?"

"That tore it." She rose to her elbows, turning her head over her shoulder toward the bedroom door. "In your drawer. Probably under the school pants you crammed in there yesterday when I told you to straighten your room."

"They are not . . . oh, yeah," and Nick's voice, starting from a roar, dwindled abruptly to a chagrined mutter. If Nick were dressing, she'd better rise.

Well, thought Mirelle, *I'll pick up the dream tonight where I left off.* She threw back the blankets, grinning at her reflection in the mirror over the double chests. Seeing Steve's unused bed in the reflection, she wrinkled her nose at it. *Never around when you want him. Why can't he have a promotion into the main office?* She sighed, turning on the hot water tap to soak her cloth. Grumpily, she regarded herself in the cabinet mirror.

The face that returned her sleepy stare had a livid crease mark across one cheek where she had lain on a blanket fold. She rubbed at the mark with the hot cloth, reddening her prominent and slightly slanting cheekbones. Subjectively she hated this inheritance from her Hungarian father. The clear ink-blue eyes and corn-silk hair were also his legacy but these were common enough. She wore her heavy hair straight, just below shoulder length, clipping it back from a center part with barrettes. No hair style, elaborate or plain, would ever soften the set of her eyes above those distinctive Magyar cheekbones.

When she reached the kitchen, the floor and cabinets were already awash with mushy designs of cereal and spilt milk. She blinked furiously, trying to clear sleep from her eyes as she filled the kettle, measured coffee into the pot. She could hear the TV set going and only hoped that the troops were well supplied so that this morning, at least, she might have the first cup of coffee in quiet.

She was not, by nature, an early riser like Steve and Roman, her eldest son. Fortunately Steve enjoyed puttering bright-eyed by himself in the morning and Roman was now old enough to use such energy delivering morning papers. When Steve was away, as he was so often, Roman could be relied on to wake the children in time to dress for school, now that all three went full time. The years of dutiful rising with alert babies had been endured and were now behind her. In Mirelle's estimation, the luxury of an extra half hour's sleep was well worth the messy kitchen. And there were even mornings when riot and rebellion did not erupt before she had consumed the first of her many morning cups of coffee.

"I want Channel 3," screamed Tonia in a piercing treble.

"Well, you can't have it," replied Nick in a bellow which provoked Tonia to repeat her order an octave higher.

Will he never learn to handle her as Roman does? Mirelle squirmed, wondering how long she could ignore the wrangling.

"No one can hear a thing," cried Roman, loud enough to make himself heard, but in a placating voice. "Tonia, you have fifteen more minutes to watch than we do. You sit and eat."

"But that isn't fair."

"Eat," Roman repeated authoritatively.

He sounds just like his father, Mirelle thought, holding her breath, wondering if Tonia would subside, and adoring her diplomatic Roman. *If Nick will only keep still, all will be well.*

The kettle whistled inopportunely though she got it off the heat with amazing speed. Not quickly enough, however, for she could hear footsteps on the TV room steps: Tonia to deliver her complaint in person now that Mommie was among the living.

As she poured water into the drip pot, Mirelle realized she had hunched her shoulders in anticipation of Tonia's demands.

"Not a word, Tonia," Mirelle said, taking the initiative. The injured expression on Tonia's pretty face altered to incredulous. "You do have more time before school so they have choice of channel now!"

Immediately her daughter's face crumbled but seeing that Mirelle regarded her with stolid impassivity, Tonia retired in sulky tears to the TV room. Apprehensively, Mirelle held her breath but all she heard was the scuffle as Tonia arranged her chair. She wondered if Roman might be gagging Nick with a firm hand or a subtler form of fraternal blackmail.

There was something to be said in favor of the English system of nursery and nanny, Mirelle told herself. Something, the sane observer in her mind replied drily, but not too much, ducks. Mirelle's nanny had been a Yorkshire lass, stern, impartial and unaffectionately devoted to her charges. As Mirelle raised her own children, she'd often noticed, with grim amusement, her tendency to do the diametric opposite of what Nanny would have done. Abruptly, Mirelle cancelled this train of thought, as she always did when vagrant thoughts brought back associations with that period of her life.

The coffee had dripped down and, as she carried pot and mug into the dining room, she caught the flash of yellow between the houses on the crest of the hill two blocks above their house.

"Bus, Roman!"

Her summons precipitated a thudding on the steps, a slap-slap of hands on the wall by the closet door, more thumps culminating in a rattle and the decisive bang of the front door. From her view out the dining room window, she saw the lanky form of Roman charging down the lawn. He and the bus converged on the corner of the street. There was no perceptible halt in the bus's movement as Roman swung through the open door and the bus maneuvered past the stop.

"Well, he never does miss it." Half an hour more and the house would be hers until 3:30. The joys of motherhood consist mainly of the times the children are NOT in evidence. "Not precisely true," Mirelle amended candidly because she did enjoy her children's company: only not all three at once.

"My hair won't part," sobbed Tonia from the doorway. Automatically Mirelle held out a hand for the comb and concentrated on Tonia's hair, as thick, silky and tawny as her own.

"Wear the corduroy jacket, duckie, it's chilly," she said as she fastened the heavy barrette in place.

"It'll be boiling by lunchtime and then I'll have to carry it home," said Tonia in a petulant voice.

"So be hot by noon but wear the jacket now when you need it. 'Sides, the day I see you carrying anything home . . . " Mirelle leaned around to glance at the pert face and smiled. Tonia tried to glower but failed. Exuberantly she threw her arms around her mother's neck, kissing her cheek. Some of Mirelle's irritation with the early morning hassle vanished with the sweet pressure of her daughter's arms.

"There. You're groomed and lovely. Go watch Channel 3. NICK!" Mirelle raised her voice in a tone loud enough to pierce the canned laughter of the TV. "The bus'll be here any minute."

"Aw, Mom, Roman's just left."

"And if Roman's just left, can yours be far behind? Get going."

Another sequence of clatter, thud, slap, rattle, bang and Nick, sauntering indolently, made his way to the bus stop.

"Two down, one to go," said Mirelle in an effort to rouse herself. The coffee was just cool enough to drink. The morning paper had been strewn over the dining room table by either Nick or Tonia because Roman always left it folded for her. She managed to restore the sheets to order and started leafing through as she sipped her coffee. Another flash of yellow through the trees, a grinding of gears and Nick was off.

Mirelle blinked again and again, trying to clear her eyes of sleepy winkers, enough to see the print. Nothing horrendous caught her attention in the main section. She arrived, unstimulated, to the funnies and forced herself to read all the comic strips. Thus she saved the daily horoscope till the last. A bad forecast would spoil the lingering pleasantness of her dream. She grunted over the ambiguity printed under her zodiacal sign, and decided that her initial impression of a nice day was not going to be star-crossed.

"Tonia, turn off the TV and get out to the bus stop. Now!"

"Aw, Mother."

"I am not, I repeat, I am NOT driving you to school again this week."

"Gee, Mother, in the middle of such a good cartoon." But the fact that Tonia's voice was coming toward her indicated that the child had given in to the inevitable with only a token struggle. Mirelle caught a glimpse of Tonia in her jacket, heard the door politely closed and then saw Tonia, skipping across the lawn. Her bosom girlfriend of the moment waited at the bottom of the hill and the child's wide-armed gesture of greeting proved that TV was already forgotten.

Mirelle poured herself more coffee, flipped the paper over and started to re-read it with considerably more attention and understanding than her initial attempt.

There wasn't much of interest in it and she sat brooding over the classified section. Maybe, Mirelle mused, she should have taken on that substitute art teacher's job. She'd have got used to being stared at by the children in time. She might even learn how to talk in front of groups. The hours were compatible with her desire to be home when her children were, and the salary was tempting. But—there was the other side of the coin: the necessary 'education' courses to be taken at night to qualify for Delaware teacher certification, the tales of the rougher elements in all the high schools, her own antipathy to large groups and its necessary social involvement. She didn't need to work: they were finally solvent and there was always her inheritance which Steve would only let her spend on herself anyway.

Let's get away from that topic, Mirelle told herself sternly, wondering why her mind kept wandering into controversial areas this morning.

No, she didn't need to work. She needed to get to work, down in the studio. There was no excuse for her malingering. She had promised herself all during their early infancy and childhood that, once the children were all in school, she would spend some time each day in her studio. Here it was spring of the second year in which Tonia was a full time student and she had turned out no more than a few soup bowls, some figurines for the family creche scene and obligatory gifts.

All those years when she had had to balance duty and desire, when she had had no special place to work in or to store incompleted pieces, those times accused her of present procrastination.

Mirelle looked out the window. The day with its fresh lovely blue sky, the burgeoning chartreuse of leaves filming the woods beyond and the young trees of the development, the moist freshness of the air, was not to be wasted on brooding. Mirelle rose with a sigh and went down the steps to the lower corridor. The lefthand door opened to the TV room; the right one to her studio was ajar. The unfinished clay bust on the potter's table accused her, too. How long ago had she started that? She grimaced. It was not a day to cope with 'him'. 'He' was not behaving. When inanimate objects of your own creation flout you outrageously, let them sit neglected until they have learned the error of their ways and become pliant.

Mirelle flexed her long fingers thoughtfully as if they were shaping the recalcitrant material and then she shook them to get rid of the unconscious urge. She knew this was not a day for modeling. Her inner restlessness was not in that direction.

"I'll go horseback riding," she announced to herself out of a totally unsuspected longing and realized that physical exertion was exactly what she needed.

"Of all the half-baked procrastinations," she was exclaiming in disgust a few hours later. She was sprawled on the ground, looking up at the chestnut who had just managed to shed her. "I might just as well have fought the clay all morning instead of you, you clayhead," she told Boots.

She got up slowly because the toss had knocked the wind

from her. The chestnut eyed her coolly, shifting his front feet and snuffling as he jiggled the bit in his mouth.

"It isn't as if we didn't know each other well, Boots, or maybe that's why," Mirelle said, half-scolding. She gathered the reins, pleased that she had at least remembered to hang on to them when she felt herself tumbling. "You might warn me that this is your week for shying at logs you know as well as your own stall. Come on, Boots."

She reached for the stirrup iron and the gelding sidled away from her, but she had her fingers round the metal and, with a quick forward step, she vaulted up, only then aware of a lack of resilience in her left ankle. But she was mounted and quickly jammed her feet into both stirrups.

On her way back to the stable, she concentrated on Boots' behavior, bringing him on the aids in every pace, making sure that he played no more silly tricks on her. He was fresh, having had no exercise since the previous Sunday and he was still young enough not to be as jaded as most riding school hacks. Mirelle was a capable rider, and thoroughly enjoyed the tussle of skill over brute strength. When she dismounted at the stable yard, she realized that she must have wrenched her ankle badly in the toss, for it would barely support her.

"Boots shed you?" asked Mac, the stableman, without a trace of sympathy. "You're all covered with leaves," and he obligingly started to brush them off. The operation took longer than Mirelle felt necessary.

"Thanks, Mac," she said, adroitly turning. "This is Boots' week to spook logs."

"He's fresh, he is," Mac agreed while Mirelle mused that the chestnut was not the only one. She fished in her jodhpur pocket for her money and paid Mac.

"Be back again soon, Mrs. Martin. You haven't been as steady as you used to."

"Takes money, Mac, and I prefer to see Roman and Nick riding. I'm getting too old to risk the occasional toss now."

"Pay attention, then," said Mac with a snort.

"I know. My own fault. See you."

He waved her off as he led the gelding into the dark barn. She limped over to the Sprite.

As she eased herself into the seat she grimaced at the thought of having to shift with the bad foot. She drove out of the stable yard, evading the muddy pits and enjoying the Sprite's light handling.

At least you can't throw me, she thought and just as instantly regretted the statement. The sudden sharp crack and explosive whistle could mean just one thing. She grabbed the wheel tightly as the car, which she was swinging onto the highway, bucked against the deflating tire. She fought the wheel, slowing down on the shoulder of the road. Swinging her legs out from under the steering wheel, she stood up, immediately losing her balance as the weakened ankle collapsed. Swearing under her breath, she limped back to look at the flat.

"Of all the unkind cuts." She appraised the damage with disgust. "Well, pal, we're both lame." She balanced herself against the low chassis and began to unscrew the spare tire.

The sound of crunching gravel attracted her attention and she was startled to see a blue Thunderbird coming to a stop just behind the Sprite.

"Hi, there. Saw the tire go. Then, when you started hobbling, I realized that the female was truly in distress," said the driver as he got out.

In a slim-cut, finely tailored black top-coat, a jaunty snap-brim Stetson on his head, her rescuer looked an unlikely type to respond to her situation.

"I'm usually a disgustingly competent female," she said, grinning in appreciation.

The man was taking off hat and coat, poking them into the opened window of his car.

"Such independence puts Boy Scouts out of business," he said goodnaturedly. He crouched down by the damaged tire, trying to determine the point of puncture, then straightened, dusting his hands off. Instinctively she glanced at them, noticing the very short clipped nails, the blunt tips of the long fingers. "The wheel's covering the puncture. Nail probably, because your tread is still good. Where do you hide the jack for this overgrown bathtub?"

"Boy Scouts are supposed to be polite, not condescending," she said, grinning maliciously, "not that you should talk with that overbuilt, overpowered, overpriced. . . . "

"Yah, yah, yah," he said, laughing back, his eyes crinkling at the corners, his grin boyishly lopsided.

Steve's eyes used to crinkle like that, Mirelle thought irrelevantly. But Steve used to laugh a lot more than he does these days. She silently cursed competitive business and sales quotas.

"I'll get the keys," she said, shifting balance so she could make her way along the side of the Sprite to the driver's side. Her good Samaritan touched her shoulder lightly.

"Get off that ankle and make like a lady executive," he said. He took her by the hands and assisted her to the grassy bank above the shoulder.

Her laugh turned to a groan for an injudicious movement tweaked her foot as she sat down. It took her a moment's hard concentration to fight back the tears. When she looked again, he was opening the trunk and getting out the necessary tools.

"You don't seem to need directions," she said.

"Oh, I had one of these runabouts. Surprising how quickly one remembers the idiosyncrasies of the beasts."

"I see you've also graduated to the tender supervision of the AAA."

He glanced up startled, and then looked over his shoulder at the telltale emblem on his car license. He grinned.

"There's a difference or two between this bathtub and that behemoth. Particularly when it comes to wrestling jacks and tire lugs." He had removed his suit jacket and, although Mirelle thought he must be in his forties, he was lean and quick of movement. "It does me good to recall, however briefly, my lost and carefree youth."

He made short work of loosening the bolts, raised the car on the jack, and removed the flat. Mirelle's sculptor's eye noticed the play of muscles across his back, the long line of his leg in the stretched fabric of his pants. A receding hairline emphasized the shape of his handsome head. His dark brown hair was worn long in the back and showed silvery at the temples and above his well-shaped ears.

"Do I pass, ma'am?" he asked and she realized that he had become aware of her scrutiny without being embarrassed by it.

"I only patronize well-dressed mechanics . . . "

"One does have confidence in the dapper workman . . . "

" . . . Who uses Brylcream . . . "

" . . . Smokes filter-type cigarettes . . . "

" . . . Brushes when he can with Gardol . . . "

" . . . And drives a wide-track Pontiac . . . "

They laughed together. Then, with a flourish, he released the jack and the Sprite settled to the ground with a puff of dirt. Mirelle tried to rise, struggling awkwardly. He was at her side in one long step, holding out his hands.

"You really have wrenched it," he said with a low whistle.

Suppressing an irresponsible yearning that he'd sweep her in his arms and deposit her, preferably in his car, Mirelle allowed him to help her limp to the Sprite. When she started to swing her legs under the wheel, he caught her by the knee and, over her protests, deftly removed the jodhpur boots. She pressed her lips against the pain. Under the heavy athletic sock, the swelling was apparent.

"I got tossed," she said ruefully as they both examined the injury.

"The beauties of spring, no doubt, distracted you," he said, grinning up at her, his lean attractive face alive to the humor of her situation. His eyes, she noticed, were grey blue and he was tired.

"No, it was Boots' week to spook at dead tree branches."

He rose in a lithe movement and retrieved his coat from the back of the Sprite. He took the handkerchief from the breast pocket, a large red silk square. Deftly folding it into a length, he tied it in a brace around her foot.

"That's a good handkerchief."

"We Knights of the Road use nothing but the best," he

said glibly, fastening the knot securely. He rose, brushed off his dusty knee and regarded her expectantly.

"It does feel better strapped this way."

"Do I give the old Scout Master's words of wisdom on sprains?"

"Hardly necessary," Mirelle said with a laugh, suddenly at ease again with his flippancy. "One of my favorite pastimes is ankle-bending. I'm surprised they bother to swell anymore."

She swivelled around and put her foot gingerly on the clutch pedal.

"Your boot, madam." With a cavalier bow, he presented it.

"Monsieur, vous êtes un vrai chevalier," she heard herself saying.

"Enchanté," he replied and his lips twitched as he noticed her flush. "Seriously, though, shouldn't I follow you to make sure you can drive all right?"

"Oh, I haven't all that far to go," she said hastily. "I'll make it. But your handkerchief . . ."

He waved aside that consideration. "Remember me the next time you play tisket-a-tasket."

Before she could protest, he had turned and strode back to the Thunderbird. Gingerly she started the car, wincing with pain as she pressed the injured foot down to shift to second.

He did follow her down the highway, all the way to Silverside Road where she turned off. She saw his farewell salute as the Thunderbird proceeded straight on, toward town.

CHAPTER TWO

ALTHOUGH SHE ALLOWED Roman to practice first aid on her and was grateful for the strapping as she hobbled about, Mirelle made light of the incident. By Friday, when Steve returned from his trip, the swelling of the ankle had subsided, leaving a high tide mark of deep purplish blues and yellow-greens from instep to heel. Prompted by the children, she gave the now equally colorful version of the spill, flat tire and the courtesy of her Knight of the Road.

Passive with the fatigue of the long train trip home and well-fed, Steve listened politely, amused by her narrative, but disgusted by her injury. A natural athlete, Steve had a curious attitude toward physical injury of any kind. In the fifteen years they'd been married, Mirelle had yet to see him cut a finger on his tools, bang his thumb with a hammer or fall heavily when he played touch football with the boys. On their family camping vacations, he had always emerged unscathed and disdainfully insisted that the cuts, bruises, sprains and abrasions suffered by everyone else were due to unnecessary carelessness or ineptitude. Steve was a slow and deliberate workman, possessed of great patience in contrast to Mirelle's mercurial work habits. Yet his craftsmanship, his intent on perfection appealed to the artisan in Mirelle.

One of the reasons they both hated the constant long business trips was the impossibility of starting any of the mutual projects they had both enjoyed during the earlier years of their marriage, when Steve's territory had been smaller and he'd been home every night. The price of promotion was less private time.

Mirelle had known by Steve's face and his lingering welcome kiss that his trip had been successful. He was tired, yes, but neither defeated or frustrated. The same conscientiousness that he turned to private projects was given to every one of his clients, often involving him in unnecessary research to satisfy the particular needs of a special contract. This perseverance was annually rewarded by the Company with a bonus. Mirelle never felt that that compensated for the hours which Steve devoted to a small account or the frustration he suffered when, for no reason, he failed to get the contract and took an official reprimand. Nor did that bonus compensate Mirelle when Steve took his irritation and disappointment out on her and the children.

Lucy Farnoll, with her marvelous earthy humor, had taught Mirelle that this was part of a wife's function: to bear the brunt of her man's irritability, redirecting it if possible, but always recognizing both his need to sound off and the source of his frustration. Sometimes though, Mirelle cringed at the prospect of Steve's temper: he could be vicious, physically and mentally, wounding her where she was most vulnerable. Sometimes, despite an intellectual understanding of his need, it took Mirelle a long while to reconcile his rash angry words and actions. Now, as she roused him to laughter at her caricature of her Knight of the Road, wielding the lance of a trusty tire-jack. she was unbelievably relieved that he was in a good mood. He'd feel like getting out into the yard this weekend, instead of poring over reports and analyzing old orders. They wouldn't have to spend Saturday wrangling over decisions that she'd had to make in his absence, decisions which he'd sometimes insist could have waited for his return. They could putter amiably in the yard, clear away the winter mess from the new growth. There might even be a movie in town which he hadn't seen. Sunday, instead of being a day of apology or brooding, would be pleasant: church, a leisurely dinner, a comfortable evening. She'd feel at ease with him, not having to watch every word she said for fear he'd take exception. The children wouldn't be clumsy with nervousness, or disappear all day to escape his unpredictability. Tonight had gone well: the weekend would be fun.

"That was a good dinner, hon," Steve told her as she shooed the children away. She poured more coffee, enjoying his company without the distractions of the youngsters. He stretched luxuriously, grimacing abruptly as a muscle tightened across his back. He rotated the shoulder against the cramp.

"Have time to get into the yard this weekend?" she asked.

"I need to. I'm winter soft." He groaned, rubbing his shoulder, looking up as she laughed.

"You? Never."

At forty, Steve was as solidly muscled as he had been at twenty-four and he looked scarcely a day older. He had the type of facial structure and regular features that would retain a boyish quality when he reached seventy. Not so much as a single white hair grew in the thick brown wavy crop that he kept brushed back from his high, broad forehead. Any extra flesh that he put on during the winter, and he tried to stay in hotels featuring indoor pools and gyms, was burned off on the family camping jaunts. The only signs of ageing were the minute lines around his green eyes and the slight grooves which disappointment had traced at the corners of his full-lipped mouth.

"By the way," Mirelle added, "I'm afraid the white azalea by the northeast corner is winter-killed."

"Damn," Steve said irritably, sitting up, "I'll check that first thing tomorrow. He swore all those plants were field grown."

That next week, Mirelle washed and ironed the red silk

handkerchief and absently put it in Steve's drawer when she sorted the laundry. Between getting the yard ready for summer, getting out lighter clothes and planning weekend camping trips, Mirelle had no occasion to recall her Knight of the Road until late June when Steve discovered the handkerchief in his drawer.

He'd had an inconclusive and hurried trip south, missed a plane connection on the way back. He'd arrived late in the office and had been called down by his immediate superior for some insignificant detail. The appearance of a strange handkerchief had shattered his tenuous self-control and he had flared up at Mirelle with a ridiculous accusation. Mirelle knew, as well as he did, that his boss's wife slept around constantly, brazenly enough to have once flirted with Steve, but for Steve to accuse Mirelle of infidelity was outside of enough.

With resigned patience, Mirelle defended herself, trying to keep the incipient brawl under control. She succeeded only in goading Steve into a full-fledged scene. He denied that she had ever mentioned a sprained ankle or a flat tire until she retorted with the menu of the meal they'd eaten that night, the discussion of the winter-killed azalea, and forced him to admit he was mistaken. And that was equally a mistake.

"I don't need to fool around just because that's the current suburban pattern," she'd flared. "I've got better things to do with my spare time."

"Yeah, yeah," and he was snarling with frustration, "you and your cultural superiority over we poor colonials; but you can't tell me you take all your frustrations out in that muck . . . "

"I'm not frustrated, Steve," she interrupted hastily, wearily. When he started to drag her sculpting into an argument, he wanted to hurt her because he was hurt.

"Don't take that long-suffering attitude with me," he'd cried, grabbing her. He used her that night with the bruising urgency that was his custom when he was troubled.

He needs me, she consoled herself the next morning, not entirely displeased. At least he hadn't stalked out of their room, which would have meant that the matter was serious. As long as she could get him in bed with her, things would work out. But oh, how Mirelle hoped he'd get rid of the notion that she'd ever even been tempted to be unfaithful, Barnhill's sluttish wife, notwithstanding. Probably, thought Mirelle, Barnhill got feisty because his wife had taken a new lover whom Barnhill hadn't had time to identify. He'd taken it out on Steve. But for Steve to accuse her of infidelity? That was a revolting development.

Despite her disclaimer, Mirelle knew that she did take out her frustrations in sculpting, but she also got rid of them in a positive, creative fashion. She'd always considered that preferable to the usual activities open to suburban housewives with time on their hands. Constant transfers from town to town, eight in the fifteen years with the Company, had made Mirelle very chary of forming close attachments to anyone. There was always the painful break when they had to move away. At first she had tried, but after they had been transferred from Ashland and her deep friendship with Lucy Farnoll severed, she had given up. Naturally introverted, Mirelle had ceased to make even casual acquaintances, pleading the care of her family as an excuse against the desultory attempts in each new neighborhood to involve her. She spent her free time worrying over and perfecting the few pieces of serious sculpture she attempted.

Fortunately Steve was a home-abiding man. What entertaining they did was limited to fellow salesmen visiting the main office to whom Steve offered hospitality, knowing how sterile a hotel can be and how much a few hours in a home can mean to the transient. Mirelle enjoyed cooking for any reason and Steve was proud of the fact that invitations to his home were eagerly sought. Otherwise, she and Steve were content to stay at home, listening to music, reading and working on family projects.

After the Great Handkerchief Debate, Mirelle brooded over his accusation all day. She was utterly disjointed by his joviality when he got home that night. All his dissatisfaction with self and circumstance had dissipated.

"Management broke its heart and anyone who's been

with the firm ten years or more gets a huge four weeks' vacation," he announced at dinner, his eyes sparkling.

The kids let out a concerted shriek of triumph. Roman broke into a wild war dance around the table, scaring Tasso out of several of his remaining lives, while Tonia's piercing treble rose to the coloratura octave. When Steve finally got them under control, there was a scramble for the touring maps, pencil and paper. As Mirelle listened to the scope of the intended trip, she irrationally realized that she would have no time whatever for the studio until August at the earliest. It would take her from now till they left in late June to prepare for the trip. The sane observer reminded her that she'd had all winter in which to work, undisturbed. It was neither Steve's fault nor the children's that she'd made no use of that time. She resolutely thrust aside her irritation and took an active part in the discussions.

She and Steve had designed and built the interior of their Volkswagen camping bus. Two years later in Canada they'd been offered double its cost by another camper, struggling with his more expensive, less efficient equipment. He'd suggested that Steve patent some of his innovations and sell the plans to one of the camping magazines but, to Mirelle's disappointment, Steve had never done anything about it. It had been very hard for her to refrain from calling his attention to the commercial imitations of some of their bus's unusual features when they were camping last year. Cleaning and stocking the bus were her responsibilities: the others organized the details of the trip. And this year's plans were well-laid, avoiding some of the fiascos of the previous year and inaugurating no new ones. They had a marvelous trip.

Halfway through the projected traverse of the country, they had blithely discarded the rest of the itinerary to settle in a wild Wyoming valley. A torrential summer storm had forced them to seek refuge in a valley ranch north of Caspar. By the time the roads were passable two days later, Jacob Overby, the rancher, had hinted broadly that there was no need for the Martins to take off in such an all-fired hurry. Plenty to see and appreciate right there in the valley. His two boys, providentially the same ages as Roman and Nick, clamored enthusiastic seconds to the invitation. Overwhelmed by the genuine welcome, Steve and Mirelle had accepted.

For two ecstatic weeks, Roman and Nick had their own horses, and Tonia a stubby-legged pony. When Mirelle wasn't lending Lena Overby a hand with cooking or cleaning, she sketched every aspect of the valley ranch and all its inhabitants, fowl, equine, bovine, canine and human. She had ridden, too, with a fleeting memory of Boots' insurrection and a determination to avoid a repetition. A toss on the mountain meadows or rough trails could spoil everyone's holiday. Mirelle, trained by an English riding master, found the relaxed western posture hard to imitate at first. Steve, disgustingly at ease on horseback, laughed her out of her self-consciousness until she was as comfortable sitting the jog trot of the quarter horses as everyone else.

But mostly, Mirelle sketched: especially Jacob Overby whose weather-beaten face fascinated her. The craggy nose, the brow-hidden eyes, the gaunt cheeks stained deep brown by wind and sun, the jutting jaw and the curiously mobile mouth were translated into endless studies. Perhaps this was the face for the unfinished head that languished, unfeatured, in her studio.

Steve, with Jacob, Roman and Roger Overby, had gone off on two pack trips, business for the Overbys, pleasure for Steve and Roman. Steve was beginning to realize that Roman was rapidly approaching manhood. Nick was left behind, disconsolate. Unfortunately Nick tended to irritate his father with his darting shifting ways. Mirelle had always seen the similarity between Roman and his father: a preference for method, a delight in physical prowess. Nick, on the other hand, wanted to do a thing immediately, too impatient to develop necessary skill. Nick was apt to be wild to finish a project in the morning and by mid-afternoon forgot that he had started something at all, a tendency which infuriated his father and weighed against his joining a camping trip which had certain hazards. Yet Mirelle recognized, even if Steve hadn't yet, that Nick was the more imaginative of the two boys, often providing the inspiration for many of the projects which Roman, in due course, finished. This summer was Roman's, not Nick's. He'd have to wait to find a basis on which he and his father could meet. And Roman needed his father's companionship now.

For Steve and Roman, the vacation was an unqualified success. Tonia was oblivious to everything once she was introduced to the grey pony, so Mirelle and Nick were odd-men out. If she managed to cajole Nick into a semblance of good nature, she failed to lighten her own inner discontent. She held herself sternly in check, trying not to dampen the others' pleasure, hoping that she didn't seem aloof. She had the most curious sense of disorientation, as if she were marking time. She was extremely careful to pretend indifference which only underscored his hopefulness. "We'll see what happens when the old boy retires."

Mirelle gave a deep sigh and Steve reached over to pat her hand reassuringly.

"We could stand a little settled family life, hon, couldn't we? The last weeks were just great. Improved the old man's temper no end, didn't it?" When she laughingly agreed, he threw an arm around her shoulders and drew her closer to him on the wide front seat. She snuggled into him willingly. "Take Jake Overby, now," he went on, "there's a man who knows what settling down is." Steve clicked his tongue in a wistful manner.

Carefree, relaxed, boyishly hopeful, Steve was recreated in the image which she cherished from their early months of marriage.

Fundamentally, he is just too good and honest, she thought, looking sideways at his clean-cut features in bold profile against the sulphur-blue hot sky. *He should never have followed the lure of big business, big money and all its big headaches.* The war had given Steve what peace would never have offered, a chance to go to college and a compulsion to produce on a higher level than his parents. But Steve worried too much, straining against management directives that shaped policies which were repellent to his basic integrity. Unable to reconcile inconsistent attitudes from his management and still represent his customers' needs to the Company, Steve took unnecessary blame on himself that other, more calloused or diffident salesmen ignored. Steve would have been happier running a small business just as he wanted to, or a ranch, like Jake Overby. Then he'd've been at peace with himself. But he kept insisting that he had to make something of the opportunities that he'd been given. Mirelle knew the source of that compulsion, and though she was powerless to counteract the basic fallacy, she tried her best to buffer its effects on Steve.

And here he was, having thoroughly enjoyed his vacation, optimistically returning to what would no doubt turn into another illusion-shattering disappointment, all in the name of Big Business. Mirelle ached for him, loath to try now to temper his hopeful approach with her cynicism. Grimly she began to steel herself to cushion his inevitable disenchantment. The sane observer reminded her that Steve was a very capable man, that same honesty appealing strongly to many of his customers. There was always the chance that his abilities would be recognized by management in the fall. *There was that chance,* she told herself, unreassured.

The prospect, however remote, of remaining in one town, even Wilmington, for longer than two years was unbearably tantalizing. To settle, to dig down roots, to develop continuity had assumed the proportions of discovering El Dorado to Mirelle. In their courtship, Steve's reminiscences of his childhood, comfortably spent in the Allentown, Pennsylvania house that his grandparents had built, had cast the rosy glow of happily-ever-after on her future as a wife. They'd join his parents in that huge rambling house, and she'd finally know what 'belonging' felt like. When her mother had sent Mirelle to live in America with her childhood friend, Mary Murphy, to escape the bombings in London, living and life had assumed a quality of all things good and wonderful to Mirelle the child. But Mary Murphy had lived in a succession of comfortable rented apartments. And Mirelle had never thought to discount a European-based generalization of the American smalltown life, nor the exigencies of an increasingly transient, technological business age, and the happily-ever-after-in-the-family-home was an exploded and explosive myth. When she had unexpectedly confronted the reality of a basically conservative, narrow-minded settled community outlook, Mirelle had bitterly discovered that transiency could be preferable to mental stagnation.

She had also assumed that Steve's broad-mindedness was deeper and that his cultural base had been firmer. His sophistication turned out to be a thin veneer, actually little more than contempt for every aspect of his small-town upbringing whose limitations he had realized during two years in the occupation forces in Vienna. Close brushes with death as an infantry officer had sent him in desperate search for an anodyne to the horrors of war. He'd found this in Vienna in the beautiful works of art, the opera, classical music, all removed from the ugliness that he had to erase from his mind.

After his Army discharge, a return to the pattern of his youth had been abhorrent to Steve, and he had welcomed a job that took him to new places constantly. It didn't matter to him where he lived geographically, nor how often he moved. His job was the constant, and his family the anchor: or so he thought. Mirelle had painfully come to accept that: she had no alternative. But if they could and did stay in Wilmington . . .

What could be, would be, Mirelle told herself. But Steve's announcement thoroughly dampened her spirits. The sense of marking time all summer now developed the cadence of uneasy anticipation, off-beat, agitated. The prospect of fall assumed a gloomy aspect.

CHAPTER THREE

ONCE THEY WERE HOME, Mirelle had to clean the dusty house thoroughly. The yard required considerable work after a month's neglect. That done, she found the kitchen had to be painted and was consequently able to push aside the tentative desire to coax Jacob Overby's lined features from the plasticene head. Of course, by then, it was time to get the children's school clothes ready and that chore made it necessary for her to reorganize the attic storage space.

When Steve mentioned a Labor Day weekend jaunt up to Cape Cod, she enthusiastically agreed, physically tiring herself so thoroughly that she had no time left over to upbraid her sane observer.

Then, abruptly, she was left in the quiet of a childless house, ordered, clean, painted, without a single excuse for further procrastination. Steve departed on the first of the fall business trips and the accusing anonymity of the unworked head drew her to the studio.

Stolidly she took out her mass of sketches of Jacob Overby and arranged them on the wallclips. She stared at them. Thoroughly disgusted with her perversity, she forced her hands to the tools, digging out the eye sockets, shaping the brows above them, excavating the jawline from the material. Dutifully she worked all morning, covering the still impersonal head with unexpected relief when she heard her next door neighbor calling her children in for lunch.

The next morning, once the house was picked up, she took herself firmly in hand and resolutely strode into the studio. Critically she reviewed yesterday's effort. Somehow, it was easier to start today and she hopefully assumed that it had been simply a matter of getting back into a routine which included studio time after the casual living of the summer.

Suddenly she realized that the face which was emerging was not Jacob Overby's at all. Surprised, she flipped through the rest of the summer's sketches. The features were familiar but she couldn't identify the face which was emerging from the clay. She sat, hands idle in her lap, staring at the head, entreating the resemblance to assume identity. Until she knew who the man was, how could she continue? Disgusted with herself and the recalcitrant plasticene, she left her stool so abruptly that it clattered to the linoleum. She'd put some wash on, and if that head didn't cooperate then, she'd. . . .

Her jodhpurs, hanging on the door of the laundry room since the previous spring, for she'd worn jeans like everyone else in the valley, slapped about her face as she jerked the door open. The sight of them provided her with an excuse. What she really needed right now was an outlet for her pent-up physical energy. She'd go riding, and show Boots she'd learned a thing or two over the summer on the willing, eager quarter horses of Wyoming.

"Besides," she told herself as she collected car keys and enough money for the ride, "I'll want to do a horse for Jake Overby to ride. So this is study."

The first fifteen minutes on Boots' back made her laugh for her balance had been subtly shifted by the weeks of western saddle riding and she had to reseat herself, legs in a proper position for the English saddle. She stopped slouching and sat straight, repositioned her hands and took up more contact on Boots' bridle. No more sloppy riding now! Or Boots would dump her.

At her favorite long stretch on the bridle path, she gave Boots the aids to canter and, settling her hips into his smooth rhythm, she allowed him to slowly increase his pace until he was at a hard gallop. Then she eased him back to a walk, with him snorting and having a bit of a blow, tossing his head. She patted his neck, soothing him to the slow pace, feeling the shift of muscle tissue as he tossed his head. Then she smelled her palm for the marvelous pungent odor of 'horse' lingering on her skin.

As she rode on, the dissatisfactions of the morning faded. When they reached the crest of the hill and the natural opening in the trees, she reined him in. She looked down into the dip between the hills where the trees were still sparklingly green after the rainy weekend. The russet of the sourwood trees and the yellow of the ground honeysuckle emphasized the different tones of greens: the whole scene was composed and serene to her artist's eye.

"If I were a painter," she told Boots, "this scene would be a nice change to the mossy millstone school. But . . . that brilliance would be so hard to capture. Maybe some pure research egghead will find a way to put odors in paint and you'll have to sniff paintings, too."

Dissatisfaction returned. Broodingly, she turned Boots away from the view and down the hill. He minced his way, snapping his feet into place, crunching the pebbled surface under his rear hooves. He tried, once, to break into a run again. It gave her distinct pleasure to rein him in smartly and feel that she had the strength to control something so strong and massive. She took perverse delight in the resentment she felt through the reins. With his hocks under him, he was almost bucking, to have a run up the next slope. When she did let him out, clapping her heels to his ribs, she seemed to sink into the ground as he surged forward. They were both breathless when she pulled him up.

"And I take it all out on you." She stroked his now moist shoulder. He snorted companionably, jiggling his bit.

The feeling of loneliness—alienation, rather, since she

was used to being lonely—and depression seemed to intensify. The immediate future, with Max Corli's retirement approaching, held no prospect which might lift her spirits. If she could only get down to some solid work on that damned head. Then she remembered her chevalier.

Boots' ears wigwagged at her chuckle.

"I'll call it a tribute to a flathead cavalier." She laughed again, wishing there were someone, anyone whom she could laugh with, and talk to. Someone like Lucy.

" 'But she is in her grave, And oh, the difference to me.' "

Even after seven years, thoughts of Lucy and what their relationship had meant to Mirelle brought a lump in her throat.

There must be someone else in this god-forsaken town that speaks and understands the same things I do. There must be. There must be some other company wife who can't tee off on the Greens and bid slams daily at the Clubs because such activities revolt her. They can't all want to be ticky-tacky. There must be someone else who doesn't fit in. Somewhere for me to belong.

She kicked Boots into a hard gallop on the flat stretch ahead, furious with such rampant self-pity. Boots was cool enough when she finally brought him back into the stableyard but Mac's eye didn't miss the sweat line of roughened hair. He ran a hand under the girth.

"Yes, we motored on a bit. He was fresh," Mirelle said.

"You're not the kind that misuses a horse, Mrs. Martin," Mac replied as he took her money. "If you did, you wouldn't ride here, let me tell you."

"I had a grand ride, Mac."

"Come back soon."

She caught herself gunning the Sprite excessively when she started it. She couldn't spend the entire day venting herself on everything she used. She down-shifted at the stop street that fed into the highway and the Sprite stalled. When she turned the ignition key, nothing happened.

The bloody generator brushes must be jamming. She yanked on the brake and jerked the door open. She propped up the hood and stood looking in at the engine, completely disgusted.

"Anything I can do, lady?" asked an amused voice and Mirelle stared up in amazement at her Knight of the Road.

"You remember me? You had that sprained ankle?" Embarrassed by her lack of response, he added, "You'd been thrown and then you had a flat tire . . . "

"Oh, I remember. Very clearly and gratefully," she said, shaking her head at her gaucherie. "I still have that red handkerchief, all neatly pressed. I put it in my husband's drawer and . . . " She broke off, appalled at what she had been about to admit.

"Tsk! Tsk! You really must keep better track of lovers' mementoes. Complicates relations," he began and then stopped as he looked at her face. "I'm sorry," he said quietly, no longer amused. "I didn't mean that. My tongue runs away with me. But it was such a coincidence to see you in much the same spot again."

"I didn't get tossed today," she said, smiling in hope of retrieving his engaging smile, "but this beast won't start. The generator brushes have a tendency to jam."

"Try starting her again."

"Nothing'll happen," and her gloomy prediction came true.

They stood side by side, staring at the sportscar's engine.

"As you do not apply to the nearest AAA when in trouble, would a lift to the service station at the crossroads be of any assistance?"

"It certainly would." But, as they started toward his car, she stopped. "Is that out of your way? I can walk up to the stable and call from there."

"It's not out of my way and, if I'm going to make a practice of halting here to rescue you, let me finish what I start," he said, opening the door of the Thunderbird with a flourish. *"Votre chevalier à votre service!"*

As they drove off, Mirelle suddenly remembered with chagrin that she had brought only a dollar above the cost of the ride.

"Would you be an absolute angel and finish at the Flying

A station? There's one a little further on and I have a credit card. I was only going riding and didn't bring much money with me."

He flashed her a grin. "I'm rarely an absolute angel but in your case I'll make an exception."

"That is such a stupid phrase. Be an absolute angel . . . what's absolute anyhow?"

"What's an angel for that matter?"

"I think perfection would be utterly dull."

"Perfect hair with Brylcream . . . "

"Perfect teeth with Gardol . . . "

"Oh, no, I've switched to Crest." He grinned in a toothy parody of commercial grins.

They laughed together easily. Mirelle found herself contrasting the incident with the summer's moments of easy laughter between herself and Steve. They had almost revived the sweetness of their early months of marriage. Soon, too soon, the strains and tensions of every day would dull that fragile fabric of summer respect and understanding.

"Here we are, ma'am," and the voice of her good Samaritan broke into her speculation. They had pulled into the Flying A station.

The attendant sauntered over, jutting his head down to hear the driver's request. Her Knight explained the situation, where the Sprite was located and asked how soon it could be attended to.

"Wal, now, it's lunchtime, y'see, and the boss ain't here, and I'm alone on the pumps, y'see, so I can't leave."

"How long before the boss is back?"

"He left about twelve and should be back 'nother half hour."

"I'll get some coffee at the diner," said Mirelle, starting to open the door.

Her Knight leaned over quickly and took her fingers from the handle.

"We'll be over at the diner," he told the attendant. "Can you pick up the Sprite the first thing after the boss gets back?"

"Sure. Guess that'll work out all right."

"Oh, now really," Mirelle said in protest as they angled across the highway to the diner. "This is far beyond the call of duty, you know."

He pulled on the brake before he answered.

"Let's say that I would be very pleased if my favorite lady in distress would help me kill a few hours which I'd despaired of murdering alone."

Mirelle temporized with a laugh. There was no reason not to accept, after all, and if it would repay his consideration. . . .

"Misery loves company," she said as they left the car. She noticed his quick glance. As he carefully locked the car up, she berated her thoughtless tongue. If he wanted to kill an hour with her, she could at least act graciously.

"I'm scarcely a soignée companion," she said, indicating her jodhpurs as he guided her towards the steps of the diner.

"I think it is too shocking of you not to have brought along a change."

"I'll see to the horses," she said, holding up her hands and heading toward the ladies' room at the side of the diner.

"Do," he advised and she heard the rippling undercurrent of amusement in the one word.

As she stepped into the restroom, she realized the *double entendre* of the euphemism and grinned into a mirror that reflected back her blush. He was quick, that man. She washed hands and face, combed her hair and fussed with her lipstick.

"The trouble with diners," he said, rising from the booth as she approached, "is that they lack a bar. Such catastrophes as visit a traveler are often eased by a jolt or two. Or do you drink?"

"Invariably, after catastrophes."

"Your ankle, I trust, is fully recovered."

"Except on rainy days."

"Did your ride stimulate your appetite?"

"Not half as much as it relieved my inner tensions." Instantly Mirelle damned her tongue and wondered what on earth was possessing her to blurt out what was at the top of her mind to this complete stranger.

"You're lucky then," he said with sudden gravity. They looked at each other then, trapped. Neither made an effort to break the gaze or distract the other from the mutual, searching appraisal. His was a very interesting face, lined and tired, but alive: his gaze was direct and uncritical.

"I . . . like to sculpt," she said, speaking softly and earnestly, "and I've been working on a bust recently. It's daft, I know, but this morning when I passed the place where you helped me with that flat, I realized that I'd been trying to sculpt your face."

"Highly flattering to think that flat-changing can lead to immortal clay," and though his face remained serious, his eyes danced with laughter. Not laughter at her: with her. Mirelle had been right: he also appreciated the humor. "My name is James Howell," he said, rather formally extending his hand across the table to her.

"I'm Mirelle Martin," and his fingers were very strong.

"Mirelle?" he asked and then, to her surprise, spelled it correctly.

"I was christened Mary Ellen but it got elided into Mirelle."

"Distinctive. And it suits you."

"I've always felt more Mirelle-ish than Mary Ellen-ish."

"Mirelle goes with the Sprite, horseback riding and sculpting."

"Oh?"

Her fingers had been nervously spinning the salt cellar. He reached across and spread them flat on the formica. They both looked down at them, as if they were the hands of a stranger. The long tapered fingers that never fit into gloves, the very square palm, the arching thumb. Then she noticed that the webbing between his long blunt fingers was well stretched.

"You're a pianist."

"You're observant!"

"Necessary for a sculptor."

The harried waitress swooped down on them, poking menus impatiently at their hands.

"Are you a concert artist?" Mirelle asked when the woman had left with their orders.

"A concert accompanist. A highly specialized variation." His eyebrows quirked with inner amusement.

"Indeed it is. My mother was a professional singer. I've had chapter and verse on accompanists."

"Your mother . . . was?"

"She died . . . twenty years ago now. She sang in Europe. I don't think her name was ever known in the States. She was Mary LeBoyne."

"Irish, I deduce." He was honest enough not to pretend recollection.

"Do you live in town?" she asked, to change the subject.

"I do now." He made a grimace. "My very old and very comfortable apartment house in Philadelphia was condemned and torn down for the much vaunted urban renewal. After a very discouraging search, I gave up and headed south. I've been teaching here at the Music School for the last two years so this seemed a logical relocation. Also the connections to both Philly and New York are good."

"True." He didn't like the town any more than she did.

"However," and he sighed, "owning one's own house has advantages. No one can complain about practicing at all hours."

Mirelle grinned. "Sculpting is a silent profession."

"Don't you cast in bronze or work stone? No tapping of hammer and chisel?"

"You don't cast in bronze in your own house. Too costly. You send the piece out to be cast, to Long Island, if you can afford it."

"I'd no idea."

"Modern technology."

"With us everywhere. What about plaster? Or wood? Or . . . whatever it is that some sculptors use for raw materials . . . metal scraps, tomato cans and stuff. No blow torches?" His expression was comically wistful and Mirelle was sorry she'd agreed to lunch with him.

"None," she replied, trying to control her exasperation.

"You just pat the clay and turn the wheel?"

"Sometimes I whittle."

His eyebrows flew up in mock astonishment. "I wondered who supplied wooden nutmegs these days. Tell me, do you whittle to you, or from you?"

"Neither."

"How is that possible?" And Mirelle realized that he was deliberately baiting her.

"I scrape back and forth, like so," and she demonstrated. "I get fascinating textured effects."

"Where are these chefs d'oeuvres to be seen?"

"Nowhere locally. I've some things placed in museums and a small gallery on 50th and Lexington used to handle my work. I still get occasional commissions . . . " She broke off because his mobile face registered astonishment when she mentioned museum and gallery. "And yes, there is a kiln, but it's a commercial one and takes up half my studio. And nary a single panther on the mantel comes out of it."

"I most sincerely and abjectly beg your pardon, Mirelle." He caught her eyes but she looked away, despite the contrition in his expression. She regretted accepting assistance from him and violently wished that she could just walk away from the table. She had met such condescension all too frequently but somehow, had not expected it from him and she was disappointed.

At this point the waitress came and slapped their lunch platters down, deftly if noisily.

"Coffee, with or later?"

"Later," they both said in a mumble.

When she had marched off, James Howell reached across and captured Mirelle's hand as she reached for a napkin.

"A talent is never an easy gift," he said.

"How would you know if I have any talent?" she demanded, sullen with her disillusion.

"Because of your attitude toward it," he replied, as if that answer were obvious. He turned his attention to his lunch.

She forced her resentment down. They talked of any number of inconsequential subjects until she noticed with surprise that the tow truck had retrieved the Sprite.

"He'll need the keys," she exclaimed and started to rise.

He took the keys from her and delivered them across the street. Mirelle watched his long figure and noticed, too, something to spring on him when he returned. At the station, he stood for a few moments, hands on his hips, in front of the Sprite, held nose-up by the tow truck. He talked to the mechanic, grinning, amused by something the man was explaining with many gestures. Then the matter appeared to be settled and James Howell sauntered back across the highway. In his short absence, Mirelle had seen him in another perspective.

"How long were you in the infantry?" she asked and was rewarded by his surprised exclamation.

"How the hell did you know that?"

"The way you walk," she said, grinning at the accuracy of her observation.

He tipped his head back and laughed.

"Not much escapes you, does it?"

"Nope."

"Except remembering to check your battery."

"Oh, no. No. No. I checked it yesterday when I got gas. I know that car. It's the generator brushes. They jam."

"Yes, that does seem to be it," he agreed blandly. "It'll take another half an hour or so, he thinks."

"Are you sure he does? Think, that is?"

"There's always that interesting possibility, isn't there?"

"Look, you've been a very good Samaritan . . . "

"But you don't need to hang around any longer," he finished for her.

"But you don't."

"All right, if you object to my company so much," he said with mock petulance and made a great show of getting to his feet. "I've got more than two hours before the first lesson and the only occupation I can dream up to fill that outrageous length of time is to buy something for my lonely bachelor supper tonight. That cannot take upwards of fifteen minutes, no matter how long I dally."

"If you stand in the longest line at the check out, you could stretch it to half an hour."

"Hmm, with steak juice dripping down my hands? The piano keys will be gory with beef blood."

"Never happens. Everything is all prepackaged with cellophane."

"It isn't cellophane anymore."

"Well, whatever it is."

"Such antisepticism takes all the charm out of shopping," he said wistfully. "Now, in Europe, where prepackaging has not yet spread its plastic aura, they wrap things up in funny paper triangles . . . "

Memories flashed across Mirelle's mind, accompanied by appetising smells and a tactile memory of texture, of rainy mornings spent shopping with the bustlingly efficient hausdienst . . .

"And by the time you get home everything crushable is, and everything cool isn't."

"You've lived abroad?" He was surprised.

"Yes," said Mirelle in as flat a tone as she could to discourage further questions.

"That's a definitive answer," he remarked, clearing his throat and adjusting his tie knot. "Remind me never to broach that subject again."

"I'm sorry," and her contrition was sincere. "Some of my bleakest moments were spent in Europe."

"Mine, too," he said, looking her squarely in the eye. "But mine happened years ago now. Yours must have, too."

She nodded. "I'm quixotic company. I'm sorry."

"I understand," and he leaned forward conspiratorially, "that every well-built Wilmington development has its own windmill."

"Are you sure you're a concert pianist?"

"Quite sure," he replied with a sniff, settling back. "Matter of fact, I was practicing my trade the last few times I rescued you. One of the artists with whom I'm under contract lives out Lancaster way. We've been rehearsing before going out on tour."

"Do you tour often?"

"Sometimes too often, I think." He sighed and signaled the waitress for more coffee. "I presume that coffee is as essential to you as it is for me."

Mirelle nodded.

"I've had the house here now for a year," Howell went on, "and I still can't find my way around the inner city. I've not been in it often enough."

"When we get transferred, I throw the kids in the car, take a road map and drive around, getting lost until I find my way home from any quarter of the map."

"In that car you threw kids?"

"No, I only got the Sprite last year. We've been here in Wilmington almost two years."

"You sound apprehensive."

"Longest time in one place yet."

"D'you mind the moving?"

Mirelle shrugged. "It wouldn't do me any good to mind. But then, I've always been on the move."

"Yes, you would, if your mother was an opera singer."

Mirelle could feel the muscles along her jaw tighten.

"Did I put my foot in it again?" he asked plaintively.

"No, my own private road to hell is paved with such potholes . . . "

" . . . And other people's good intentions?" One eyebrow raised, giving his face a cynical cast.

"What's the fee, doc?" She grinned at him in wry apology.

"For analysis? Free with every act of knight errantry."

The sound of a racing engine split the air. Mirelle saw her Sprite being backed out of the garage bay.

"My word, they've done the trick." She rose.

"The hour's over?"

"Midnight hath struck and voilà! my pumpkin!"

He paid the check at the cashier's desk and then, clipping his hand under her elbow, he guided her across the highway. As she gave the mechanic her credit plate, she caught James

Howell's unguarded face. There was a quality of sadness and she wondered if she had underestimated his age. As he turned to regard her, a vivid smile dissolved the pose.

"I'll away now, milady, and purchase me dinner steak, begging always to remain your respectful servant." He opened the Sprite door with a superb flourish of hand and arm.

The mechanic came back with her receipt and card, and so she was obliged to end the interlude. With a farewell wave, Mirelle eased the Sprite out into traffic.

When she got home, she sat down immediately and sketched his face as she remembered it during that unguarded moment. She filed the study away carefully but the warm feeling of their second meeting stayed with her. That night, before she went to sleep, she rummaged in Steve's drawer until she found the red silk handkerchief. She put it at the bottom of her own.

CHAPTER FOUR

THE BRONZE PIG arrived late one afternoon so Mirelle had to wait until the kids were in bed before she had time to put the finishing touches on the metal. She then placed the pig on the wooden pedestal, standing off to appraise her efforts.

In a way, it was like seeing him for the first time. She'd finished the piece last February. The foundry in Long Island was good but she was scarcely a prestige customer so she had to wait until they had time to cast her small statuary.

He was good all right, she allowed to herself. The head was angled so that the hoof could scratch under the ear: the expression on the porcine face was one of ecstasy.

Well, there is nothing so satisfying as catching an itch on the exact spot! She was very pleased with him. Very pleased. She put him next to the bronze horse which was modeled on Boots, in much the same pose as the day he had shed her. The horse was staring down at the ground, presumably at the unshown rider, legs braced after a sudden halt, ears pricked, chin tucked back, the long horse face wearing an expression of comical dismay and great delight.

"It'd be great to be able to do a really big piece instead of paper weight sizes," she said out loud. "Only where would I put one?"

She stroked the flank of the little horse affectionately and then turned around in her workroom toward the covered bust. She had ignored it pointedly over the last few weeks. Now she walked over and resolutely transferred it to the wheel. She pulled back the cloth and gazed critically at the head. She revolved the wheel slowly, standing back at each turn to examine the work.

Not a bad likeness without the model. But the angle of his jaw, just below the left ear, was not correct. She had got the right side in sketch from that unguarded pose of his, but she had the feeling that the jaw was still wrong. It disturbed her that she had been so unobservant.

"Too bad I can't put that walk in clay. By God, I will!"

From the storage shelf she grabbed the small wire armature made for some other abandoned project and gleefully slapped on a coat of clay.

It was not unlike her to work through an entire night when a concept had crystallized for execution. She was carefully stencilling the last details in the ground around the booted feet when the children came down in the morning.

"Hey, gee, ma, that's keen," Nick said, walking around and around the sixteen inch infantryman. The soldier was trudging from one battle to another, desperately weary, but somehow still upright and moving. "Whyn't you ever make me a lead mold for that type soldier?"

"I will. I will." Mirelle promised, gathering up the magazines and books which she'd consulted during the night on infantry impedimenta.

She made pancakes for the children's breakfast and got coffee into herself.

"You ought to work more nights," Roman said through the cakes he was stuffing into his mouth before running for the bus.

"Wait'll Dad sees him," Nick said, as he poured half a bottle of maple syrup over his pancakes.

"You didn't leave enough for me," Tonia said in a wail as

Mirelle snatched the bottle from Nick, tilting it back and proving to Tonia that there was plenty left.

Nick's comment echoed in her mind. Candidly, Mirelle didn't want Steve to see either the small figure or the almost finished head. She'd reviewed that second meeting with James Howell frequently in the past few weeks. One sees oneself so clearly in the mirror of the casual observer. In an hour and a half, that man had made her re-examine a lot of her attitudes.

"Is that enough reason to immortalize him in plaster?"

"Immert-all what, Mommie?" Tonia asked, startled.

"Did I say something?"

"You're at it again, Mommie," Tonia replied in a curiously adult long-suffering tone of voice. "You're talking to yourself."

"Well, at least I usually listen to what I'm saying which is more than you kids do. How many times have I told you, out loud, not to use more syrup than your pancakes will absorb? Just look at the waste."

"No time for the lecture," and Tonia grabbed up her jacket and raced out of the house for the school bus.

There was no chance to reprimand her for her insolence.

Just as well, thought Mirelle. *She'd spot my lack of guts.* Blearily she read the first page of the morning newspaper and then decided that she simply could not cope with the day without a few hours' sleep.

She covered the statue and the bust. Suddenly the studio couch was much nearer than her own bed upstairs. She was asleep, deeply, a few moments after she'd pulled the lap rug over her shoulders.

The sun woke her, slanting through the window into her eyes. Although the clock read just before noon, she felt refreshed by the four hours' rest. Tasso, who had a most unfeline yen for cantaloupe, had evidently chewed a corner from each piece of melon rind still on the table. He was now curled up in the wing chair in the living room. She cleared the breakfast dishes and then returned to the studio. Uncovering the statue, she was relieved to see that it was as good as she'd felt it was, with one or two minor corrections. She draped the towel back tenderly.

The mail had come but, apart from one for Steve, was all direct mail advertising which she threw out. She made more coffee and was attacking the newspaper again, getting past the first page with comprehension, when the phone rang.

"Mirelle?"

"Yes?" She couldn't place the man's voice.

"Have you ever counted how many Martins there are in the phone book of this Smith-forsaken town?"

"Many more than James Howells," she replied, placing the voice.

"That's A for effort. Have you any idea how many Martins I've had to call?"

"No," and she couldn't help giggling, "why?"

"Because, young lady, I want to apologize to you."

"To me? Why?"

"Despite my high sounding reassurances the other day, I didn't really think you were any good. I must profusely apologize. I saw an exquisite little bronze figurine in the Stamford University Museum of, no less, Fine Arts."

"Oh, my cat."

"Yes, your cat."

"I hated to sell it. Tasso's a member of the family, even in bronze. But you always sell to museums when they ask."

"At first I didn't realize whose it was. But the name LeBoyne finally rang its appointed bell. I gather you do use your mother's maiden name professionally."

Mirelle closed her eyes against the stab of pain. You don't ever escape who you really are.

"Mirelle? Are you still there?"

I won't close up on him, she told herself. *I won't. I'll throw those damned sensitivities back into the closet where they belong and slam the door hard!*

"Mirelle?"

"Sorry, I had a mouthful of coffee."

"Are you sure I didn't have a mouthful of foot?"

"Any foot of yours is welcome."

"Seriously, Mirelle, that was a lovely affectionate piece. I'm just back, you know."

"No, I didn't."

"Well, I am."

"Was it successful? The tour?"

"Very, but I am exceedingly glad to be back standing in line with dripping steak in my hands. Hotels! Yechkt!"

She couldn't help laughing at the contrast of that sound and his normally correct tones.

"How's the Sprite? Behaving herself?"

"Better than I am. I've been up all night," she blurted it out, "finishing a statuette."

"You have? I thought that sort of round-the-clock activity was limited to the Left Bank."

"Look closely at the address, pal, left side of town."

"Depends on where you're situated. Mirelle, are you free for lunch today?"

"I haven't even had breakfast."

"Tsk. Tsk. Our starving artists, oblivious to earthy requirements. I'll meet you in half an hour . . . for lunch, I might add . . . at the so originally christened Road House."

"That's not much time for a gal who hasn't had breakfast."

"That's quite enough time for a gal who's going to get lunch."

"Don't let the steak drip."

Without stopping to check her horoscope, Mirelle dashed up the stairs, showered and dressed in fifteen minutes. She made up at the hall mirror, catching a glimpse of the draped statuette as she did so, ruefully envying the playwright or poet whose works of art were rather easier to transport. Five pounds of plasticene perched on a hip was a trifle ostentatious.

She spun the Sprite out of the development in the best of good spirits, unaccountably pleased with the world, the day and its bright prospects. Not even Steve's expected return that night could mar her pleasure.

"That did it. Oh, well, I'll forget about him for the afternoon."

Easy, gal, she cautioned herself. *Forgetting the husband to lunch with another man?* She snorted at the whimsy, impatient as the cross-highway light held her up. As if Howell were that type. He was only interested in her work and that part of herself was completely divorced from her family or her marriage, for all the overlapping. It was the as yet unhampered, unpossessed soul of her that she had refused to relinquish to Steve's possessiveness. She had told him, early in their marriage, that she had given him her body, her worldly possessions, obedience and loyalty: she had given him all her love and devotion but that inner part of her that was unalterably Mary Ellen LeBoyne was not his. By the same token, she did not expect to possess his innermost secrets and soul. She doubted if Steve had any conception of such basic privacy. Very often he acted as if that final reserve were an offense against him, instead of her defense against the world. He was always striving for complete capitulation.

She got so engrossed in this subject of identity that she nearly missed the turn into the Road House.

"At least he knows where the good steaks are," she told herself as she deftly parked beside his blue Thunderbird. It was rather a shock to glance over and see him watching her, a broad grin on his face, from inside the T-bird.

"It was two to one you would park beside me if the space stayed open long enough."

"Where did you call from?"

"Inside, of course," he said, getting out and locking his car.

"What do you keep in there? Crown jewels?"

"Irreplaceable accompaniment scores," he replied, opening her door and handing her out. "Have you grown?" He looked down at her in surprise. "I'd remembered you much shorter."

"Heels." What a good dancing height he is.

"You have been rather informally dressed before." His eyes twinkled. "Seeing to the horses."

As the hostess led them to a wall table towards the rear of

the dark wood-panelled room, Mirelle was conscious of his hand at her waist, guiding her. Casual physical contact was not agreeable to her: she often could not bear to be touched, even by her children. There had been times, early in their marriage, when the feel of Steve's hand had been immensely thrilling. *Comparisons! Comparisons!*

"I beg your pardon?" and James Howell bent his head closer to hers.

"I have an extremely bad habit of talking out loud to myself and, if you make the usual comment, I'll eat by myself."

"I would never be guilty of banality," he replied disdainfully. "Besides, I've been known to carry on lengthy conversations with the bust of Mozart which leers at me above the piano. Yes, miss, we'd like a drink before lunch. What's your pleasure, Mirelle?"

She declined and he ordered a bourbon on the rocks while Mirelle scanned the faces in the restaurant, to see if there were any interesting ones.

"Any gossipy neighbors?"

Mirelle flushed at the sly taunt. "No. I don't know many people in town anyhow. But I always keep on the lookout for grist to my potter's wheel."

"Anything of interest here?"

"Nothing inspirational."

"Ever done a self-portrait? Yours is an unusual face. Those cheekbones and . . . am I intruding again?" he asked. "I can just see the little clam shell closing up."

"My stock answer is 'artistic temperament'," she said, leaning forward across the small table in her urgency to make him understand. "But you don't deserve the stock answer. I could give you a wheeze about a grim childhood. . . . "

Howell, too, leaned over, taking her hand in both his.

"I'll come clean, Mirelle. One of my artists remembers your mother, and you. Don't pull away, my dear. Madam Frascatti gave me an enchanting picture of a thin child with long tawny braids, playing with a collection of tiny toys which she had brought with her in a wooden box. The child endeared herself to Madam because she sat in the chair she was told to take, talked very softly to herself as she played with her dolls for nearly two hours."

Mirelle saw that scene again: a memory, like so many others, that she had deliberately inhibited. Now, she had a sudden total recall of that Victorianly busy room, with *objets d'art* jostling each other on every inch of table space, photos, etchings, watercolors covering the walls. She could hear her mother cautioning her not to touch anything, to play quietly so as not to disturb the adults. It had been a hot summer day but the parlor, for all its clutter and dust, had been cool. And she had been with her mother. Those times were to be cherished.

"The chair was covered in horsehair and it itched," she said with a laugh.

Howell kept watching her and she wondered what he had expected her to say.

"How is Madam Frascatti?" she asked experimentally. "She must be ancient now. She was positively creaking then."

"Oh, she does creak but what a zest she still has for life and living."

Whatever it was he had hoped to hear, Mirelle had not said it for Howell leaned back.

"Did you mention you'd met me?" asked Mirelle, trying to keep anxiety out of her voice. Howell seemed to be withdrawing from her. And now she did not wish to lose contact with him.

"No. I didn't. Because I don't feel that I have met you. I've had two amusing encounters with a young housewife and mother who drives a Sprite, rides horses, sprains ankles and mucks about with clay."

"I don't 'muck about' with clay, as you put it," snapped Mirelle.

"Easy, girl. Now Mirelle LeBoyne is talking and she's the girl I'm taking to lunch. You see," and he leaned forward again, "I saw something enchanting in that cat which stayed with me the rest of the tour. Oh, it's not great sculpture . . . you're artist enough to appreciate my distinction without taking offense because none is intended. . . . But there was a quality of serenity, of permanence, of . . . " He shrugged as the exact word eluded him, " . . . of homeliness and belonging, I guess, that struck an answering chord in this particular wanderer.

"Essentially, when I moved here from Philadelphia, it was not so much the need for new living quarters—God knows I'm not home enough to do more than 'reside'—as the need for some kind of roots for myself. Oh, it's fine when I'm at liberty and when Margaret, my daughter, is home from college. Yes, I was married," he interpolated with a sour grin, "and divorced Shirley years ago. Margaret prefers her father's company and I hers, at intervals and for not too long a period.

"It was a sense of permanence that I was groping for. And your cat symbolized it to me."

Mirelle dropped her eyes in embarrassment and delight.

"I wondered if anyone else would ever notice that in him," she said in a low voice.

"Then my interpretation was correct?"

"Oh, yes." Mirelle looked up with earnest assurance.

A drink was suddenly placed in front of Howell and he drew back. Mirelle could have wished the waitress stuffed into concrete. Howell appeared to take no notice of the interruption.

"I asked the curator if the Museum would consider selling the cat . . . "

"You what?" She was dumbfounded.

He grinned. "Oh, yes, I really did. That's how much of an impression the cat made on me."

Mirelle continued to stare at him, incredulous.

"I got the same reaction from him, too," he said with a chuckle. "But I'm sincere. I also presume that it is impossible to duplicate that bronze nor would I want to. What I want to know is, do you have anything else from your home-loving period that I could buy?"

Mirelle couldn't stop her gyrating thoughts long enough to get one out and the little soldier was the pivot.

"I seem to have stumped you."

A pressure behind her eyes warned Mirelle that she was about to disgrace herself in tears. She snatched up his drink and took a stiff gulp.

"I can't imagine what possessed you to call me today of all days. . . . No, don't interrupt, Jamie," and the nickname came out spontaneously, "but you wouldn't have said just that sort of thing if you didn't mean it. Nor would you have seen the Cat in just that way . . . I mean, superficially that's not the impression it conveys . . . I don't sell much and I can tell myself it's because I don't produce enough but that isn't the real reason and I don't fool myself that it is. But each sale means more. Each piece is a part of me . . . of my creativity. It's all the rearranging, the household things left undone that I'll have to race like mad to do later: it's screaming at the kids to leave my work alone. It's fear that somebody will knock a model over, destroy hours of work . . . or crack a cast . . . or . . . It just isn't easy to have a talent and be a wife and mother, too. It's fighting even to get into my studio. Well, not that so much anymore," she interrupted herself honestly, "but in any case, every little . . . "

"Pat on the head?" he supplied when she faltered.

"Yes, every pat on the head is precious. So you simply cannot know . . . " She spread her hands in a futile gesture at her inability to express herself. "Sometimes I feel like chucking the whole thing into the disposal and taking up tatting. At least that's considered a respectable feminine occupation."

"I am not remotely interested in buying your tatting. At least, not until I work my way through the supply my maternal grandmother left me . . . "

Mirelle found herself laughing until the tears rolled down her cheeks at her vivid mental image of James Howell patiently replacing torn tatting from a box reeking of lavender sachet.

"You're far too intense, Mirelle. Here. Finish my drink. I'll get another."

He signalled the waitress and ordered two more bourbons on the rocks.

"How old are these cast-cracking kids of yours?"

"Roman is fourteen, Nick ten and Antonia is seven."

"Prolific!"

"I wanted children."

"Having been an only child."

Mirelle looked quickly, nervously at his face but he only returned her gaze politely. She wondered exactly what he had heard from Madam Frascatti but decided that it was more likely that he was only baiting her.

"I shall either fall asleep or disgrace myself completely," she said as the waitress served the drinks.

"I never allow my companions to disgrace themselves OR," he said with massive dignity, "me!" He raised his glass in toast. "Besides, you'll shortly be packing away a huge steak, potatoes, salad and dessert before you leave and that will sop up the alcohol. Now, may I or may I not commission you to do a work of art for me?"

Mirelle hesitated, thinking of the bust and the soldier.

"Yes, I would be glad to do something for you. But I'm not sure what you want. The Cat was a twenty-two inch bronze but it isn't a specific size you're after anyhow, is it?"

He shook his head.

"Have you a special place in your home where you'd like a piece of statuary?"

He let his jaw drop mournfully. "Actually the place is quite bare of decoration, apart from a few small paintings I've picked up."

"I can't fill a gap unless I see the hole first."

"Perhaps you have something finished at home now?"

Mirelle laughed nervously. "I just did a little pig," she said to give herself time to think, "but he's not your type."

Howell laughed and thanked her for a backhanded compliment.

"Besides, he amused Tonia. I really made him for her, to remind her to stop standing in the middle of her messy room."

"Wouldn't a swat on the rear accomplish the same end?"

"No, because the pig makes her laugh and then she gets it all done in a good mood instead of turning the air green with her whines."

"Good point."

"Good pig. So you may come and see what I have and maybe you'll get some ideas."

He cocked an eyebrow and his eyes started to twinkle. "Sort of the reverse position?" he asked cryptically.

"Oh, you mean, come see where my etchings aren't and make me one?"

"Exactly. And you've nothing more than the pig?" He looked disappointed.

"Well," and honesty made her hesitate, wondering how she could avoid showing him either the bust or the soldier if he came to the house. Maybe, if she left him in the living room with the Running Child . . .

He was thumbing through an engagement book.

"Hmmm. I'll be back in town in three weeks."

"Oh?" and she was as dismayed as she was relieved.

"Yes, I'm just here overnight before the southern part of the tour. Didn't I mention it?"

"I don't think you had the chance."

"Have you any plans for October 26th? That's a Wednesday." She shook her head. "Then, if I may, I'll come to your home at eleven, assuming that is where you have your studio . . . "

"Yes."

" . . . And I'll be completely famished by twelve and you can suggest any place in town except this one for lunch afterwards as a reward for my good behavior."

"I'll keep that in mind," she said with mock severity. "The 26th it is."

"Now, aren't you at all interested in my fascinating experiences as a peripatetic piano player?"

Mirelle sat back, smiling, only then aware of how tense she'd been. She listened to his amusing narrative, needling him where she could, knowing from the twinkle in his eyes that he appreciated her jibes even when he ignored them. He used his hands expressively and she watched them almost as much as she did his face. *More distinguished than handsome, actually. And the trouble with his jawline is that the left side is slightly longer than the right. That was the disparity.*

He stopped midphrase and jabbed a finger at her. "I suspect the sculptor's eye is pinioning me. There's a glazed and calculating look on your face."

"Occupational hazard. Of course, yours is such a well-used face . . . "

"Thank you, madam." He inclined his body in a bow.

"They are more interesting to work with."

"As I was saying . . . " and he continued his tale.

It was two-thirty before they finished lunch and she reluctantly suggested departure.

"The school bus returns at 3:00 and I should be home when Tonia gets there. It's not that she isn't capable of taking care of herself," Mirelle added hastily, "it's just that . . . "

"You take being a mother seriously, don't you?" There was no barb in his words. "More than my ex did."

The sunlight was blinding as they stepped out of the darkened room. It was that, Mirelle was sure, which contributed to her fall. As she stepped aside to make room for him, she caught her heel on the uneven paving and lurched backwards. He caught her arm and pulled her sharply toward him so that she fell against his chest rather than back onto the sidewalk. Her head gave his jaw a crack and they both stood still, his arms around her: she with an aching ankle, he with a sore jaw. He reached up to his chin and looked disgustedly down at her.

"Oh, Jamie, I am so sorry. The sun blinded me and this ankle of mine is not all that reliable in heels."

"Excuses, excuses," he mumbled, rubbing his jaw but grinning. "I retract what I said about not letting my women disgrace me."

She stepped back, feeling the warmth of his hand at her back long after he had dropped it to his side. Someone opened the door behind them and there was a brief spate of apologies and jockeying of positions. Howell took her firmly by the arm and led her to her car.

"I shall be glad to take the road again," he said drily. "Most of the singers of my acquaintance can keep their feet under them. I suppose I'll have to use a different rule for sculptors."

"Think of us as chips off a new block," she suggested.

He grimaced.

"It was a lovely lunch, Jamie. Thank you very much."

"Till the 26th then."

He gave her a lopsided grin, rubbed his jaw once again before he went around to his own car.

She hurried home, with twenty minutes to spare before Tonia's bus came. She threw a smock over her dress, got out the plastic bucket and mixed up plaster of paris immediately, dashing green dye in for the color coat. While the plaster was setting, she cleared the rest of the breakfast dishes, groaning as she picked up the tepid bottle of milk. She put it carefully at the back of the refrigerator. Roman hated to get warm milk.

She raced back to the studio and tested the plaster. Just right. She took one long last look at her little soldier, comparing it in her mind with Jamie and finding it true to the model. She slathered plaster over the figure, building up between the legs, working deftly so that the soldier was completely anonymous by the time Tonia came in at the door.

"You covered him all up!" Tonia complained. "Why'd you do that?"

Mirelle cocked her head at her daughter. "There was a very pretty little deer which I'd made for a dear of my own. It stood on this very same wheel and certain small hands wanted to see if it felt soft. I believe that was the excuse. Well it was soft, and it was pulled all out of shape by the grabby little paws."

"Ah, I was a baby then, Mommie." Tonia pouted. "I didn't know any better."

"On the contrary, you did. Because you'd been told, as I told the boys . . . "

"Lecture . . . lecture . . . "

"Yes, it is! You know how little time . . . all right, no lecture. But from then on, every time I have a piece finished, I keep it safe in plaster."

"Is it a model of Daddy as a soldier?"

"No. Just a soldier."

"I know. You were watching *Combat* the other night. Is it the sergeant or Caje?"

Mirelle pretended to consider. "You might say Caje. He's the tall one, no?"

"Yes."

Tonia settled on the stool to watch her mother work.

"You starting on a work toot, Momma?"

She sounded so mature that Mirelle turned objective eyes on her child. The last lines of baby fat were gone from face and body. The nose was lengthening from a snubbed stump. The little child whom Mirelle had captured in the running figure had been superseded by a leggy pre-adolescent. A new beauty was emerging slowly.

"I'll have to do another one of you soon, hon," Mirelle said with a smile.

"Then you're on a working toot," Tonia said happily. "I'll help with things now. I wasn't big enough before."

"Why so helpful if I'm on a toot?"

"Because," and Tonia's face was contorted with the pronunciation of that invaluable conjunction.

"Why 'because'?" Mirelle insisted.

"You're all different," and the thin shoulders shrugged as the mind made the body express words which the intellect still lacked. "It's like this," and Tonia cocked her head, "you forget all the silly things . . . "

"Like rooms being picked up and meals on time?"

"Well . . . "

"And you guys watching TV till you fall asleep . . . "

"Oh, Momma, that's NOT what I mean."

"Come, kiss me, hon. And watch out for the plaster on my hands."

Tonia jumped off the stool and hugged her mother tightly about the hips. Then she skipped to the steps before she made her parting shot.

"When you see, we all get presents."

CHAPTER FIVE

MIRELLE THOUGHT she could tell how Steve's trip had been by the way he closed the car door on his return. If the omen was bad, she'd quickly send the kids to the TV room and let him vent the first wave of dissatisfaction on her. Tonight, when she heard the door slam, she read a pleasant oracle in the sound.

"It would've been a bit much if he'd come home seething today," she told the oven as she peeked in at the casserole.

"Hi, honey," he yelled jovially, struggling in with his suitcases. "Roman! Nick! Give me a hand here!"

They came bouncing in to help him, Tonia on their heels. "Bring me anything? Whaddja bring the boys?"

"Not gone long enough, baby," he said as he gave her a mighty hug. With the delightedly squealing child in his arms, he leaned to kiss Mirelle warmly. "Miss me?"

"Now that you're home, I believe I have," she said, teasingly, knowing that he wouldn't deliberately misinterpret.

"Oh, yeah," and Steve ducked his head, suddenly remembering the way in which he had stormed out of the house three days earlier. "The bogeys are off my back, the stars in favorable conjunction, the weather superb, my reservations weren't snafued and I have more than enough large orders to please the bossmen and no problems to report."

"Momma's got a commission," Roman said.

Mirelle nodded affirmation.

"And she made the keenest soldier last night," Nick added.

"On account of she watched *Combat* with us," Tonia could always find a last word or two.

"Oh, off on another toot?" Steve asked, putting Tonia on her feet.

"Guess so," Mirelle said, keeping her voice as neutral as possible. She could have choked Roman for starting the subject. She'd wanted to introduce it more gently in privacy to judge how Steve was really taking the news.

"It paid the back bills last time. What're you aiming for this time, honey?"

With relief, Mirelle saw that he was not going to start off by resisting her work-urge. She would have troubles with him later, she always did, but once she got underway, her capacity for ignoring interruptions was unlimited. Steve had once compared her to a lady steamroller.

"Trim on the house could stand repainting. I'd love to get rid of that hall wallpaper. You said something about a new suit and snow tires. . . . "

"All that with one commission?"

"You know me once I get started."

"Tonight?" he asked, slightly aggrieved.

"No." She grinned. "Tonight you and I will have some time to . . . talk." She raised her eyebrows, rolling her eyes suggestively.

"I'm hungry," he replied with a leer.

It was a happy dinner. Mirelle, feeling slightly guilty over having lunched out, had cooked a complicated casserole, a family favorite, for dinner. It had always been her policy to feed Steve well when he came in from a trip. Consequently, serving her family second helpings, she felt mellow and serene, instead of rebellious and frustrated.

It would be so much nicer, she thought as Steve and she sat over their coffee in the living room, *if I could always time my work jags with successful road trips. But you can't have everything.*

"Say, where's the soldier Tonia mentioned?" Steve asked suddenly.

"Oh, him? I've plastered."

"Without my seeing him? You only did him last night." Steve frowned.

"Well, you remember that marvelous deer . . . "

"Are you never going to forget that?"

"No," she replied tartly. "But you can scarcely blame me for wanting to avoid a repetition."

"No, I guess I don't blame you. Did you really use Caje as a model?"

"As much as anybody, I guess. It's the posture . . . you know, the broken-legged, sore-hipped, swung from the knee walk of the infantryman?"

"I always said," and Steve leaned back with a smug expression on his face, "you married me for that walk."

He bent over and kissed her.

"Why do we nag at each other, Mir?" he asked softly. "I love you, hon, but you get in one of your bitchy, untouchable moods and I'm teed off with those bastards on my tail, and we wind up at each other's throats like we hated."

Mirelle wondered if he was reading her mind.

"We've been married fifteen years, Steve. Perhaps we're just wearing away another level of petty irritations."

"Before we're deeper in the marriage rut?"

Mirelle was glad that she was serene inside or surely she would have bridled at that.

"Rut, schmut, so long as you love your wife."

"Get the kids sacked out early, will you?" he suggested, his eyes intense with desire.

"Don't you just know it!"

The next morning, because they had had the most satisfactory sex in months, Mirelle went through the business of tidying up the house, feeling slightly like Scarlett O'Hara. She loaded Steve's laundry into the washing machine and sorted out what had dried the previous day, before she allowed herself to pause in the studio.

The plaster cocoon on the soldier, now a formless blob, was cool under her hand. She envisioned it already cast in bronze but had no desire to finish plastering beyond the color coat. He was safe there, from curious fingers and eyes.

Idly she picked up her file of sketches, a rather awkward collection as she used whatever came to hand when she saw a face or a pose she liked. There were old deposit slips, shirt cardboards, programs, menus, even two match covers. She riffled through the file, selecting one or two for closer inspection, until she came to her original sketch for the Bronze Cat which Jamie Howell had admired.

She looked at it a long time, her mind's eye taking her beyond the two dimensions to her vivid recall of the finished statue. She had sculpted Tasso washing a paw, his tail carefully curved around his bottom, tail tip slightly raised. He had been sitting in the sun, she remembered, and he'd remained on the windowsill for a long time, just as if he realized that he was posing for posterity. After the session, when she'd stroked him, he'd arched his back under her hand, purring roughly. They had only been in the Spartanburg house for three weeks. Nick was an impossible yearling, Roman running wild and Mirelle was violently bitter at having been uprooted from Ashland. She'd been so happy there for she'd met Lucy Farnoll and there were few women like Lucy anywhere.

How much that sketch of Tasso evoked! Mirelle thought with a long sigh. Three weeks in a new location and already Tasso knew where the sun would be for his morning bath: where, aloof and contained, he could observe the neighborhood animals on their rounds. How she had envied that adaptable complacency. How horribly she had missed Lucy.

"Ah, she dwelt among the untrodden ways . . . " The verse popped into Mirelle's mind. How she and Lucy had laughed about it, the winter they were snowed in and the road to Lucy's house, set far back from the highway, had been impassable. They'd had to backpack supplies in.

Mirelle had actively hated Steve for accepting the transfer from Ashland to Spartanburg. She certainly had railed at the Company, slamming in the vilest of tempers around the little new house which Steve had bought before she'd seen it. Steve had been tolerant with her for a long time. But that was before management had begun to pressure him. He'd been so keen, so eager: he'd lived enthusiastically and completely in his work so that he'd been able to regard her disillusion with detachment and tenderness.

Life in Ashland had been full for Mirelle: in Spartanburg, it was impossibly tedious. She knew no one and had never made friends easily under the best conditions. In Spartanburg, the full brunt of her natural introversion pressed her into a masochistic reclusion, and the care of two young children had left her with no energy at all for sculpting. In Ashland, Lucy had often taken Roman and Nick off her hands for a day or an afternoon, allowing Mirelle uninterrupted time to work. Lucy had understood completely Mirelle's compulsion to create and her conscientious devotion to her children. Lucy had talents of her own, being a poet whose work often appeared in the literary reviews as well as the slick women's magazines. Lucy maintained that if her husband, Fred, complained about her being lost in creative trances, he never complained when the checks came in. However, Mirelle was not blind to the fact that Lucy ran an exceedingly well-organized house, kept tabs on her four children in an off-handed manner, and lived up to every duty of marriage and motherhood. She could afford to tell her husband off. Mirelle felt no such freedom.

"I run like hell to stay in one place sometimes, cookie," Lucy said one day as Mirelle watched her bake three pies at once. "Now I freeze the other two and then, when I see the old man getting feisty, I shut off the growl at the stomach level. A tip I pass on to you at absolutely no extra charge. There are ways of working the jungle we call life, but don't you ever, ever leave off that," and Lucy pointed to a doughy fork in Mirelle's hands, restlessly forming minute animals out of scraps of pie dough. "God gave you stewardship over your talent. It's HIM you answer to, not that overgrown sex-addict who sleeps in your bed."

"God doesn't have my bills to pay," replied Mirelle.

"Ask and you shall receive but remember, the Lord also helps him who helps himself." Lucy paused to brush hair from her eyes, flouring her forehead liberally in the process. "I mean it, Mirelle. The parable of the talents can refer to creative gifts as well as old coinage."

It was Lucy who provided a direction to her efforts when she realized that Mirelle had little time to complete any ambitious work. It was Lucy who discovered the answer in Mirelle's creche figurines and forced Mirelle to take time out from her frenzied endless housecleaning to make Christmas figures for the church bazaar. Mirelle had managed three dozen various animals, shepherds and kings before her cranky kiln broke down. She had the satisfaction of seeing every one sold the first day of the bazaar. It was Lucy, however, who insisted that she give only a percentage of the additional orders to the church. There hadn't been much profit but there had been enough for a book on furniture refinishing which Steve had wanted, and a new sweater for herself. And the following year, she'd had to start work in October to fill orders for her creche figures.

Lucy had sought and found an answer for her, and that year Mirelle had broached her much-hated inheritance to cast a bronze figure. She'd done a woman sitting, leaning on one straightened arm, her feet drawn up under her skirt. The dreamy face was upturned as though the woman were watching something in the sky.

" 'Beside the streams of Dove,' " Lucy had said with an embarrassed laugh when Mirelle had presented it to her friend.

Mirelle had had to turn away, deeply touched, that Lucy would perceive so accurately the thought in her mind when she'd done the figurine.

"Mirelle, it's the loveliest thing I've ever owned," Lucy had murmured.

"It's 'thank you' for blasting me out of the slough of despond."

"Just 'thank you' the girl says, with a masterpiece." Lucy's voice was unsteady. "You funny, funny kid. If you don't look like Mrs. Average Dumb Housewife, and you can turn out . . . ach, go away."

Mirelle had, almost on wings, she was so pleased with the reception of her gift. It wasn't as if she'd been afraid that Lucy wouldn't understand, but because her friendship with and affection for Lucy was such a fragile thing.

"You can't ever rush a friendship," she'd tried to explain to Steve. "It can flop, all of a sudden, like a souffle."

"Oh, Lucy's all right," he'd replied sourly. "Fred's my sort of guy, though. Sure knows his mulches."

Mirelle never tried to explain again. She often wondered if Steve hadn't been a little jealous of their friendship, and annoyed because Lucy encouraged Mirelle to be independent.

In her own way, Mirelle had quietly followed Lucy's advice: she ran like hell to keep up with the children and her housework, and always found time to work a little each day. Until they'd left Ashland.

" 'But she is in her grave, And oh, the difference to me.' "

Mirelle quoted the last lines out loud, carefully putting Tasso's sketch back in the file. "Let's face it, there aren't many Lucys in the world for Wordsworth or Mirelle. But then, how many are needed?"

She took down the photo album and thumbed through it, snapping out four photos of Lucy at various summer parties. Reluctantly she took out the obituary clipping, with its dull-looking, full-face portrait of Lucy.

The sense of loss had not diminished. Mirelle swallowed against the tightening of her throat at remembered grief. Lucy had not been much of a letter writer. There had been only two brief notes between Ashland and Spartanburg. The last one had told Mirelle of the cancer which Lucy had known was poisoning her body even before Mirelle moved away. Then Reverend Ogarth had sent Mirelle the newspaper clipping and a personal note. She could remember every word:

Lucy asked that I write you when the funeral was well past, his letter had started. *She said that she'd told you of her illness but not that the cancer was inoperable nor that her death was only a matter of months away. She was like that, giving unceasingly of herself.*

I know how close you were to her. Nothing I can say can ease this blow for you, Mirelle. But she gave me a message for you. I was to remind you that you must keep running, as hard as you can. She made me promise not to write you until after the funeral.

The tears rolled down Mirelle's cheeks onto the clipping. As she brushed them aside, she knew what she was going to sculpt next.

She had used the only prepared form she'd had for the soldier. It was infuriating to have to make a new armature with this concept boiling up inside her. She compensated by making the frame much larger.

Work big, bigger. Lucy was bigger than life anyhow. Well, Lucy was practical, too. Mirelle thought as she prepared the wires.

The thing with working small is that you finished quicker. But I don't want to finish fast. Not this time.

Mirelle made four attempts in the next two weeks before she was satisfied with a pose that expressed her conception of Lucy. She wanted to capture a certain attitude. Lucy had had a habit of finger combing her short front locks out of her eyes. She was constantly in motion and constantly losing hair pins, always pushing the lock back from her forehead as she moved restlessly from one task to another, too busy to take time to find or replace the pins. Mirelle put the figure's right hand up, in Lucy's gesture. The skirt was flying, to express the vitality and energy of the woman. Lucy had worn her hair either in a chignon or a pony tail, long before that style became popular. Mirelle chose the pony tail to express youthful exuberance. For some time, she toyed with idealizing Lucy's unexceptional features but finally she decided that it had to BE Lucy to make the work successful. Lucy's vital inner self must spring through the bronze, fleshed out in beauty so that one could almost see the marvelous snap in the eyes: hear the rough-edged contralto voice, see all the intangibles that had made Lucy beautiful.

Can ye not see my soul flash down/A singing flame through space?

Mirelle chanted the old poem to herself as she thumbed a line down the skirt. For three weeks she had spent most of her time on the Lucy. During the two brief respites when plasticene had resisted her, she had done a rough plaster of the soldier and another happy pig figure to mollify Nick over Tonia's prize. Otherwise she had Lucied.

The doorbell rang and she damned the intrusion because she was so close to finishing the statue. As she went up the stairs to the door, she looked back at her work, highlighted by the sunlight. And sighed with satisfaction.

"Expecting someone?" asked James Howell facetiously.

"Is it the 26th already?" she cried in dismay, acutely aware of her clay-smeared face and dirty smock. She stepped back so he could enter. He placed his hat on the hall table.

"It most certainly is and it is obvious that the passage of time which I marked in dragging tempo, has flown by you in industry."

"I have been working. I'm sorry. We have a lunch date."

"I also have a commission with you, or has that flown your recollection?"

"No, it hasn't. But I have to confess that I've really done nothing on it. I started out to. But then, well, I had to do a pig for Nickie when the Lucy wouldn't work, and the soldier . . . " She stopped because she realized that the soldier was in plain sight on the workshelf. And that soldier was more James Howell than the man himself.

"The Lucy?" he asked, his eyebrows rising.

She stepped aside so he could catch a glimpse of the statue down the stairway. Before she could divert him to the living room and the Running Child, he was down the steps and circling the statue with a half-smile on his face. And, of course, when he had made a half circuit, he saw the soldier.

"Ah ha," he exclaimed dramatically, striding over to pick the statuette up. He did a double-take as he recognized the features. "And when did you do this?" His expression was both startled and amused.

Mirelle wet her lips, searching for an answer as she walked jerkily towards him, twisting her hands together.

"Well . . . I . . . "

"Is . . . this soldier figure the one you mentioned?"

She nodded, unable to meet his eyes. He leaned towards her so that she couldn't avoid him.

"You have a very accurate memory, or you've been housebreaking into my war mementoes. If I didn't know absolutely that I hadn't posed for that, I'd've sworn that I had."

"You're not angry then? I mean, I have a nerve. I didn't really mean to put your face on it . . . "

"Angry? Hardly!" He shook his head. "I'm overwhelmed." He held the statue away from him, laughing at its mimicry of himself. "I still catch myself standing that way, you know, and wonder where my rifle is." He gave a short bark of a laugh. "And you'd seen me just twice before you did this?"

Mirelle sat down, nervously twisting spare globs of plasticene out of her smock.

"Here is one time I can say, without fear of contradiction, that I have made an impression on someone."

"Oh, no," Mirelle spoke up quickly, trying to keep a straight face. "I made the impression."

He looked at her blankly for a second and then menaced her with the soldier.

"You certainly cut a guy down to size."

"I surrender." She held up her hands, laughing, and was comfortable with him.

"Seriously, Mirelle," and he turned the statue over in his hands, one thumb smoothing the lifted thigh, "this is a masterful little vignette, if one can have vignettes in plaster. It makes me tired just to look at myself. But . . . "

"Oh, that isn't for the commission," she said as she sensed the reason for his hesitation. "Anyway, you couldn't have it for a while. I've promised Nickie that I'd make some models of it for his army. And it ought to be cast in bronze. Here's the pig I did, and that is, of course, the Lucy."

He examined the pig carefully, its expression bringing a smile to his face. Then he turned his full attention on the Lucy.

"A particular reason for her?"

"Yes."

He grimaced and made a motion with his hands, closing his fingers into his palm like a clam.

"No." She smiled. "No. Lucy was a special friend of mine. A staunch supporter."

"Was?"

"She died of cancer when Nick was two. Seven years ago."

" . . . 'But she is in her grave, And oh, the difference to me.' "

"You read Wordsworth?" Mirelle blinked back the tears that threatened to embarrass her.

"There are times when Gideon does not supply the traveler's reading needs."

"When did you get back to town?" she asked, remembering her manners. He looked tired, she thought, particularly about the eyes.

"Last night."

"You look it."

"Your compliments are going to my head." He accented the phrase histrionically.

"I'll change. I'll be very quick. Oh, there are more bits and pieces in the living room. They might give you some ideas," she told him as she ran from the studio.

Humming to herself as she fumbled in her closet for a dress, she was pleased that he wasn't annoyed about the soldier. She'd worried that he might be annoyed. When she came back downstairs, he was critically appraising the Running Child.

"That's Tonia at three," she said.

For a long moment, he regarded her through half-closed eyes before he smiled.

"Not bad. I timed you at just twelve minutes. I've been kept waiting longer with less result."

She dropped him a mock curtsey. He extended his bent arm.

"To lunch, madame?"

"To lunch, monsieur."

She directed him to the only other restaurant of which she had any knowledge. Over two drinks, she tried to get a rise out of him and managed not to fall for his little ploys. He told her of his trip, four good jokes that he'd picked up and one hilarious incident with a pompous ladies' club chairwoman. He didn't once mention the commission or her work but it did not seem to her a deliberate evasion.

After their lunch, however, he turned north, away from her development, then eastwards.

"I'm taking you, little spider, to see the web," he explained when she pointedly refused to ask where they were going.

"A bold course to direct my over-fertile imagination in appropriate directions."

"My dear girl, I would not for an instant consider directing *your* imagination. What impudence."

She caught a subtle undertone to his voice, but then he was turning into the driveway of a two-storey house.

"You don't know a good gardener, do you?" he asked with a weary sigh, gesturing at the neglected lawn and seared shrubbery.

"The exercise would do you good," she said with a heartless laugh.

"I'm a pianist, not a planter. I don't know a petunia from stinkweed."

"Sniff!"

"You are unkind," he said with mock petulance.

"Completely, but, at one dollar an hour I might lend you a knowledgeable yardboy."

"Robbery!"

His house, however, showed every evidence of order and attention. The entrance hall was attractively papered in a large black and white scroll design, and led into a white living room, carpeted with a rich, predominantly blue oriental. A white concert grand piano of a rather old-fashioned style dominated the room. A low, long sofa, upholstered in blue brocade, was opposite, a low coffee table, also of the Queen Anne style, in front of it. A second Queen Anne armchair completed the furnishings of the room. Over the fireplace was an excellent impressionistic painting with a predominance of reds. The dining room, seen through the archway from the living room, was also furnished elegantly in the same period, blue carpeted, with gold brocaded chairs around the table.

"It's a beautiful web."

"But sterile," he said, bluntly critical.

"I'm not sure I sculpt Queen Anne, though."

"No, Mirelle," and again he favored her with that quizzical look, "you are not the nymphs and shepherds type."

He guided her back to the hallway and opened a door that in most houses of this type would have led to a family room. It housed two more pianos, and an extensive library of music folios, books and albums was shelved on one wall. On the other, shorter inside wall, were photographs, autographed by the artists to Jamie.

"My artists," he said with a facetious bow to the display.

Several faces were immediately familiar to her. One of them was unquestionably Caruso, yet the inscription was also to Jamie.

" 'Friend of my early struggle'?" She translated from the Italian and stared at Jamie. "Surely not you?"

Jamie laughed, delighted by her confusion. "No, my linguistic sculptress, my father. He was concert master for many years at the Metropolitan. A good deal of the music here is his, and many of the photos. Unfortunately I never had the pleasure of accompanying Caruso or Gallicurci as he did."

"So you come by your musicianship second generation?"

"Yes, and I discovered who you've been reminding me of when I was browsing through some of Dad's old programs . . . "

He moved to reach an album down but she grabbed his arm.

"I don't want it rubbed in," she said.

"You come by your art second generation, too," he said, mildly surprised by her reaction. "Did it hurt so badly, Mirelle?"

She turned away from him.

"Perhaps if I'd been a boy. As always for a man, it's not socially inelegant to be different. But conformity is required of women and it's . . . it's goddamned hard to be a bastard and a girl."

She snapped the phrase out, wrenching her body towards him to see the effect of her words.

He regarded her calmly. "Madame Frascatti told me. But your mother was married at the time of your birth."

Mirelle let out a bitter laugh. "And *he* would have thrown Mother out of his house if his family hadn't convinced him that that would have given the scandalmongers a field day. So Mother was permitted to remain . . . but don't think that she didn't pay for it, day after day. And don't think I didn't. Oh, not physically. That wouldn't be in the well-bred tradition of the Barthan-Mores. Oh, why did you have to bring it up? It has spoiled a perfectly lovely day."

She turned from him again, crossing her arms on her chest, glaring out the window.

"Actually, I hadn't meant to mention it, Mirelle. I hope you believe that."

He waited for a reply. Then she felt him move to stand right behind her. From the corner of her eye, she could see his hands rising to curl firmly about her shoulders. She jerked her chin up in rejection of his apologetic gesture.

"Sometimes the very devil gets into my tongue when I'm with you, Mirelle. I knew you'd be sensitive to your parentage. I wasn't even looking for the picture when I ran across it. I had every intention of forgetting that I'd ever seen it except that you look so much like him, it's hard to ignore. He was scowling in the photo, much the same way you are right now."

The contrition in his voice had blended into amusement at the comparison and she jerked her chin higher. Then he reached for the album. She heard him shuffling the thick pages. And, although she had a tremendous desire to look, she averted her eyes when he first put the photo in front of her. One glimpse undid her resolve, because it was not only her face that stared back at her, but Nick's, when he got in one of his rebellious sullen moods.

"So that's where Nickie gets it," she said. "See, the brow-line here," and then she remembered, "but you haven't met Nick. Oh, Lord, what time is it?"

"Quarter to three?"

"I've got to get home. Tonia'll be there any minute."

He looked down at her for a long moment, then took the photo which she had thrust at him, not so much because it was of her father but because it still belonged to Howell.

"Well, you've seen the setting now," he said as he ushered her out, "although I'd prefer something to go in the music room. I'll find space for it, believe me," and he grinned as she glanced back at the crowded room. At the front door, he took both her hands in his. "Believe me, Mirelle, I didn't mean to open up old wounds."

"It's all right, Jamie."

"Now what settled you on 'Jamie'?"

"You don't like it?"

"Indeed I do but 'Jim' is the logical nickname."

"Who said I was logical? And you're just not a Jim or Jimmy," she said as she slid into the passenger's seat.

Tonia was just descending from her bus as Mirelle and Jamie drove up. The child's eyes widened at the sight of the Thunderbird. She behaved creditably during the introduction and then went obediently to change out of her school clothes.

"You have a calming effect on my daughter," Mirelle said with a laugh as Jamie followed her into the studio.

"She doesn't resemble you at all."

"No, she takes very definitely after her father's mother. A bit of astute genetic foresight on my part, I assure you."

Tonia bounced promptly back into the studio and right out again.

"Mr. Howell is here about the commission he asked me to do, so this is business, not social. Food, which is your current order of business," Mirelle said firmly, "is located in the kitchen. Do not, I repeat, do not, eat the icing without eating all the cake underneath it."

Jamie chuckled when the child had left.

"If I don't make the instructions explicit, the next thing I know the damage is done and I get the wide-eyed stares of outraged innocence and 'But you didn't say not to, Mother'." Jamie laughed outright at her mimicry. "Then there was the time," Mirelle went on, grinning over the incident, "when Steve came down late one Sunday morning and found Roman and Nick playing football with the breakfast honeydew melon. Only it was very ripe and did not drop-kick well."

Jamie roared.

"I'm not the avuncular type and your children sound more than this semi-bachelor can take in one afternoon. I'm in town for a while, so if you have any ideas, may I come over and watch you work? Or do observers make you nervous?"

"Hardly," Mirelle said, waving a hand in Tonia's direction, "the kids have even charged admission to watch the real live sculptor at work."

She waited at the door until he had driven out of sight and then turned thoughtfully back to the studio. Tasso was on his windowsill, old now and very grey about the muzzle. She stroked him, smiling over his violent purring response.

It had been such a shock to see a picture of her father. She hadn't thought of Lajos Neagu for years. Not since the terrible bitter battle with Steve and his parents over her bastardy. When they were first engaged, she had told Steve because she felt that he deserved to know the truth. He had been a little taken aback but had laughed it off. He had assumed that both her parents were dead. It hadn't occurred to him until then that her surname and her mother's stage name were the same. (Mirelle had stopped using Barthan-More when she was sent to the States in 1940 to escape the bombing of Britain. By then, Mirelle had known the full story, and had refused even the legal fiction of her mother's husband's name.)

Mirelle had seen her natural father only once, at a distance, when he'd been attending an exhibition of some of his portraits, donated by their owners for this charity showing. Mirelle had been intensely surprised, therefore, to benefit under his will along with his legal heirs. It had been that reference to her legacy in the newspapers which had touched off the nightmarish scenes with Steve's parents and, later, with Steve.

Roman had just been born so the inheritance ought to have been very welcome. Steve refused to touch a cent of it. He tried to make her refuse the bequest. He'd accused her of ruining his chances of success with the Company with the publicity of the announcement accompanying the will. He had requested a transfer from Allentown to escape what he termed the unwelcome notoriety and what he was certain was derision from friends and neighbors. It had been a cowardly and silly act on his part but his parents had made him feel unbearably ashamed of his choice of wife.

It had taken Mirelle nearly a year to recover from the shock and hurt. She had felt so betrayed by Steve's inexplicable disloyalty. If only Mother Martin had not made so much of it . . . If only Steve had stuck up for *her* . . . To prove to him, his parents and herself, that she was not at all like her mother, Mirelle had redoubled her efforts to be a perfect wife and exceptional mother and, to achieve those ends, turned into a cleaning shrew and an inflexible disciplinarian.

They had moved from Allentown to Ashland and there Nick had been born. She'd never told Steve how much Nick resembled her infamous father, but Mirelle regarded that as a bit of compensatory justice and had treasured Nick all the more.

Then Mirelle had met Lucy, and Lucy had helped mend the breach between them. And then kindly bullied Mirelle back to sculpting. When Steve saw how much Fred and Lucy Farnoll evidently admired and respected Mirelle, he began to forget the *bar sinister.* The stone of social ostracism dropped in the small puddle of Allentown had sent out very few ripples, despite what Mother Martin had shrilly asserted. No one in Ashland, had they noticed the small newspaper item, ever connected the infamous Lajos Neagu with that nice Mrs. Martin who did creche figures for the church.

Her father's bequest had been a substantial fifteen thousand dollars and a self-portrait, a small part of his total estate. Lajos Neagu had come from a wealthy Hungarian family who had circumspectly departed from their homeland before wealth had been nationalized. The family jewels had been collectors' items: his paintings had been, and still were, extremely valuable. When the crated self-portrait had arrived, Mirelle had stored it, unopened, in the attic, nor had she mentioned its arrival to Steve. She'd set aside five thousand dollars for Nick's college since Steve's parents had already started a fund for Roman. Occasionally she broached the balance for casting in bronze, or emergency money and, when they'd moved to Wilmington, indulged herself with the Sprite.

The noise of Roman and Nick arguing furiously over an incident on the school bus roused her. She threw a protecting cloth over the Lucy and went to deal out justice.

The mellow mood which had hung over the house for several weeks was abruptly shattered by Tonia's chance reference that night at dinner to Mother's boy friend.

"My what?" Mirelle asked aghast, for Steve had turned white, clamping his lips in a thin line as he stared accusingly at her.

"The man who brought you home in that beautiful car, Mommie. He's a boy friend, isn't he?"

"No, he is not," Mirelle said firmly, hoping vainly that Steve was not going to let his imagination run away with him. "Mr. Howell took me to lunch today to discuss the commission he gave me several weeks ago," she told Steve as diffidently as possible.

"What commission?" Steve's voice was sharp.

"The one that started Mommie's work jag," Nick said as if there couldn't be any other.

"You weren't asked. Clear out of here."

Mirelle seconded that with a jerk of her head which included all three startled children. She rose from the dinner table to clear the dishes but Steve reached out and pulled her down into her chair again.

"What's this all about?"

Mirelle sighed, trying to frame a satisfactory explanation. Steve jerked at her arm.

"Don't patronize me with those long-suffering sighs."

"I am not patronizing you. You are taking undue exception to a child's phrase. Mr. Howell is a male, he is a friend. To Tonia he is a boy friend."

"I'm not a child."

"Then don't act like one. I told you three weeks ago at dinner that Mr. Howell had offered me a commission. We spent the money . . . in talk . . . that same night. It was a very pleasant evening."

"Why did he have to discuss it at lunch?"

"Why not? If he hadn't taken me out to lunch and you had heard that we stayed here, talking in the studio, you'd've made another of your snide allusions to the 'casting couch'. Mr. Howell is close to fifty and has a grown daughter in college."

"Never heard of him."

"Oh, for God's sake, Steve. You're making a mountain out of nothing. Go to a movie. Go bowling. Cool down. Let me get on with the dishes."

"Don't put me off!" Steve yelled, jumping to his feet, his fists clenched at his sides.

Mirelle returned his glare coolly. "I am not putting you off and you know it."

She saw his hand come up in time to ward off the blow. She flung away from her chair, putting the table between them.

"Steven Martin, you listen to me. Your sick jealousies are ridiculous. You have, never, never had any cause to doubt my fidelity. I was virgin when I married you and I've had no affairs. If you're feeling guilty because you got laid on your last road trip, don't ease your conscience by accusing me."

"Like mother, like daughter," he shouted, thoroughly

enraged now. And she knew that her random thrust was accurate and wished that it hadn't been.

But the violence in him was looking for an outlet and she did not want to be it. She whirled, running down to the studio and trying to close and lock the door before he could storm his way through. She wasn't quick or strong enough. The door hinges ripped the wood at the force of his entry. She retreated as far as she could across the room. He advanced on her, one arm pulled back across his shoulder to slap her but his hip caught the platform holding the Lucy, and it tipped over.

As Mirelle saw the statue fall, she tried to save it but the soft plasticene flattened on the vinyl tiles just as Steve struck her. She straightened up, scarcely feeling the blow in the cold of her anger at the terrible destruction. She just looked at him. Until she caught sight of the children, peering anxiously down the stairway, their faces white and scared.

"I'm sorry, Mirelle. I'm sorry," Steve blurted the words out. He whirled, saw the children and wheeled again, wrenched open the door to the laundryroom and slammed out into the night.

Mirelle couldn't move. She was unable to look at the smashed plasticene at her feet, or say something reassuring to the children. She was aware, dimly, through her shock that they finally went whispering away. Her neck and shoulder burned from Steve's blow.

Slowly she got hold of herself. With jolting, uneven steps she walked out of the studio. She told the boys to do their homework and sat like a stick at the dining room table until they had shown her their completed assignments. She sent them to bed. She loaded the dishwasher and then returned to the dining room table.

It was insupportable that the Lucy should suffer from his unreasoning jealous anger: that was the only thought in the leaden sorrow of her numbed mind. She kept reviewing the incident: her words, Steve's irrational replies. She saw him rise again, and again, and wondered if she'd let him hit her then, instead of running, if he'd released that senseless violence in the dining room. . . .

She was suddenly aware of being cold. She looked at her watch and realized that it was close to one o'clock. She rose and went to bed. She heard someone moving around in the house and decided that it must be Steve. He didn't come up to their room. It wouldn't have mattered to her at that point if he had, but he didn't.

When she woke, still locked in numb withdrawal, she noticed that his side of the closet was open, the suitcase gone and two of his suits. Well, he'd've had sufficient clean shirts. He wouldn't be able to complain that she skimped on his ironing.

The children had got their own breakfasts: Roman had made coffee for her and set up a single cup and saucer at her usual place at the dining room table. There wasn't a sound from the gameroom but the asinine giggle of a TV cartoon character.

It took Mirelle several moments to realize that Tonia was standing in the archway, her eyes red, her mouth in the pout that precedes tears.

"It's all right, Tonia. Daddy had a bad day at the office. . . . "

"He had no right to ruin Lucy," and Tonia dove for her mother's arms, sobbing.

"That's not for you to say, dear." Mirelle found it hard to comfort her daughter because she seemed unable to soften her arms to embrace her. The boys were standing, solemn-faced, across the table. "What have you been saying to her?"

"If she hadn't mentioned Mr. Howell," Nick began, his eyes flashing, emphasizing his relationship to his grandfather, "Daddy would never have . . . "

"You have no right to . . . " and Mirelle broke off, startled by the look of hatred on Nick's face.

"I hate him."

"That's enough of that, Nicolas. You don't hate your father."

"He ruined your Lucy!"

"That is ENOUGH, Nicolas. Each of you has ruined models . . . several models, so . . . "

"You're always standing up for him, even when he's so wrong, it's pathetic," said Roman, disgusted by adult criteria.

A tardy anger roused Mirelle enough to put a stop to the remarks.

"That's enough from all of you. The incident is closed. Do you hear me?" They nodded, startled by the tone of her voice. They were afraid, Mirelle realized, to alienate her as their father had alienated himself. This mustn't continue, she told herself sternly. "You had no business listening."

"Who could help hearing?" Nick demanded, again explosive.

"The bus." She snapped her fingers at them, shooing them all out the door, disregarding the fact that the younger two would have to wait at the stop.

She watched them go, conscious that she should have countered their arguments, excused Steve's behavior. But that would have been hypocritical, she thought. She ought to have said *something*.

She drank the coffee, more out of habit than desire. She seemed to have no emotion, not even regret, nor a trace of anxiety over what was surely a critical point in her marriage. She sat there, trying to sort out her thoughts, unable to concentrate on any line. She was conscious that Tasso came up to her chair, weaving himself around her legs, purring loudly. He was hungry, she thought, and lacked the energy to remedy the problem. Then he leaped to the table and she watched him without rebuke as he lapped milk directly from the pitcher.

She wished that she still had Lucy to talk to. She censored that idea.

She was mildly surprised to see a car drive up and stop. In a passive way, she recognized it as James Howell's. As he strode past the dining room window, he saw her there, and frowned when she gave no response to his cheerful wave. She heard his knock at the door and could do nothing. After a long pause, he stood in the archway, concerned by her lack of recognition.

"What's wrong, Mirelle?" As he turned to close the front

door, he caught a glimpse of the studio, the damaged door and the statue on the floor. He went half-way down the steps as if he couldn't believe his eyes. "What on earth happened to that lovely thing?" he asked as he came back to the dining room. "Mirelle, what happened?"

She looked blankly up at him, until finally the sense of his question registered in her mind.

"Steve . . . Steve . . . he . . . " she began and was choked by the sobs that were released at this attempt to voice an explanation.

Howell reached out to her, at first sympathetically, and then in alarm as Mirelle seemed to dissolve into hysterical weeping. When he tried to comfort her, she pushed him away and ran down into the studio. He followed and found her on her knees by the statue, sobbing Lucy's name over and over, patting the flattened head.

He watched her for a moment, then went into the laundry and filled a pail with water which he threw on her. He half expected her to attack him from the savage look on her face. Instead, she gulped and made a determined effort to get control of herself. He found a clean towel in the laundry room and handed it to her.

"Thanks," she said weakly as she mopped her face and shoulders, and pushed her soaking hair out of her eyes. She got up stiffly, still swallowing sobs. "Sudden Storm, Chapter Five," she said in a rasping voice, walking unsteadily to the couch. Her knees buckled and she sat heavily. "There's bourbon in the cupboard over the fridge. I need it."

He brought back the bottle and a glass, and poured a healthy shot. She was shaking so badly that he had to hold the glass while she drank but the straight alcohol did steady her. In a moment she could hold the glass by herself.

When he saw that she was shivering now, he went up stairs and grabbed a blanket from the first bedroom. He wrapped it firmly around her, disregarding her soaking dressing gown.

Mirelle could not, or would not, look at him. She kept sipping the bourbon, waiting for it to penetrate the numbness. The phone rang, a startling sound since she was right by the extension. Howell picked up the receiver and held it to her ear. It was Steve.

"I have to be away for the rest of the week, Mirelle. It's useless for me to say that I'm sorry about the Lucy, but I am. I didn't even see it. Mirelle, are you listening?"

"Yes." Her voice was flat.

"I don't know why I do things like that. Want to lash out and hit you, I mean. But I can't seem to reach you sometimes. And I have to . . . " he broke off and there was a long pause. "When I've finished this trip, can I come home, Mirelle?"

"Yes. Come home, Steve."

She motioned for Howell to replace the headset and took another sip of bourbon without looking at him.

"I've no desire to involve myself in your affairs, Mirelle, but I cannot leave you in this state."

"I'm not the suicidal type."

"I didn't imply that you are," he said smoothly, "but you are in no condition to be left alone."

She drank the last of the bourbon and he took the glass from her hand.

"Do you have a good friend . . . " She shook her head violently, averting her eyes from the mess on the floor. "Not even one who is slightly sympathetic?"

She did look at him this time and he was surprised by the bleakness in her face and eyes. "No."

"I'm going to make you coffee and something to eat. Go get dressed," he said, rising to his feet.

She nodded, like an obedient child, and got up, wondering why there suddenly seemed to be so many steps from the studio. Or was it that they were so hard to climb with wooden legs? But she dressed in whatever came to hand. And she drank the coffee and ate the breakfast he put before her. When she had finished, he collected the dishes and took them to the kitchen. She watched him moving about, thinking that she ought to protest but no words came.

The next thing, he was holding out her coat.

"You've got to cultivate some friends, my dear, for I'm

simply not around very often to provide this type of service," he said drily as he guided her out to his car.

He drove steadily for a while without her marking which direction so she was a little puzzled when he pulled into a crowded city parking lot. He handed her out and, as she watched bemused, carefully locked the car. They were in the center of town, she realized, and found herself being led up the street to the open-air farmer's market.

"I found this the week before I started the tour," Jamie told her, "and I've had it in mind to come back when I got the chance. Let's see what's new and different to supermarket homogeneity."

In spite of her self-immolation, Mirelle was amazed.

"A walk in the woods, perhaps, or a cozy head-shrinking by your fireplace. But a farmer's market?"

"I'm always open and above board, m'dear. Any objections?"

"No, Jamie. None. Only thanks. Thanks so much."

"Let's see if you know your apples, lady," he replied, taking her arm as he saw tears start in her eyes. He propelled her firmly towards the rows of apple-crammed baskets around the nearest truck.

He bought more apples then he could eat by himself, and country sausage and scrapple, a wild-looking homemade cheese, baking potatoes, dead-ripe tomatoes and leaf lettuce, fresh basil and dill until neither could carry anything else.

Then he drove her back to her house, pressing an apple into her hand as she got out of the car. He drove off with a friendly wave.

With a deep sigh she pulled open the front door, looking resolutely down the steps. At some point, Jamie had removed the Lucy from the center of the floor. She closed her eyes, profoundly grateful to be spared the sight of the ruined statue.

Tomorrow, she thought, *tomorrow I'll go down and see exactly how much damage was done. Tomorrow I'll be able to start all over again if I have to.*

She was sagging with fatigue. She left a note for Tonia on the floor in the hall and went upstairs to bed.

The phone's shrill ring woke her around five. When she got the receiver to her ear, she heard Roman's voice, whispering on the downstairs extension so she hung up. She got out of bed and went to get supper. Then she sat and watched TV with the kids until it was time for them to be in bed.

The next morning she felt less exhausted but still detached from life. The children had already forgotten some of the tension of the previous day and she envied them their resilience. She did all the necessary chores but she wouldn't walk through the studio so she left the dirty clothes basket at the bottom of the steps. She was sitting down for another cup of coffee when Howell's car turned up the driveway. His reappearance did not, somehow, surprise her.

This time she mustered a smile as he passed the window and gestured him to come on in.

"The Madonna of the Sorrows is better, I see," he said.

"Coffee?"

"Thank you and don't get up. I know where the cups are. The bourbon, by the way, is not over the refrigerator. It is in the dining room closet. That's why I know where the cups are."

"Oh."

He sat down at the corner of the table at her right, pouring out his coffee.

"I said some selfish things yesterday about not getting involved in your marital problems. On further reflection, I have the nagging suspicion that I might have been the cause of one."

She looked him squarely in the eye for the first time since their pleasant lunch so long ago.

"I can almost set the scene," he continued, gesturing expansively in the air, "small child makes comment about Mommie coming home in a big beautiful car . . . Hubby asks sternly whose big beautiful car . . ."

"Yes, you can set the scene. But *your* entrance is the climax of Act Two, not Act One, or should I say Act 22."

"You've a jealous-type husband?" He leaned back to scrutinize her, his expression neutral. "Has he any reason?"

"In spite of my parentage, none. Maybe, *because* of parentage, none. But he feels that the sins of the mater, in this case, are indeed likely to crop up in the daughter. And right now," she turned to Howell with a brazen smile, "if he's giving me the name, I might just as well have the game. So, how about it, big boy, shall we adjourn to the 'casting couch'?"

Mirelle ruined her bold effect by bursting into tears, hiding her face in her arms on the table. Howell let her cry and when her sobs had quieted, he gave her his handkerchief.

"It would be a red silk one," she said, drying her eyes.

"I buy them by the gross."

"As if anyone would have any interest in a dragged out schlep like me," she said, pushing back her chair to get the comb and lipstick from the hall table drawer.

Howell poured fresh coffee in her cup when she returned so she sat down again, flipping her thick hair back over her shoulder.

"You have a certain *je ne sais quoi* about you even now," he said blandly. "However, I prefer to be loved for my own sweet self rather than be used in a masochistic spirit of revenge."

"You certainly deserve better. I mean . . . " and her voice trailed off. She bent her head and busied herself in rubbing off the lipstick mark on the cup rim.

"What do you do now?" he asked in a quiet kind voice.

"Oh, I pick up the pieces and try to put them back together again."

"The pieces of the statue . . . or your marriage?"

"Both, I guess. Ironic though that it's Lucy. She kept my marriage from cracking up once before and over a much, much, much more basic problem. It's funny. I know he's been unfaithful to me. And that doesn't bother me. Honestly! Because, well, infidelity is simply not worth getting upset about. I mean, I had an idea of certain qualities that would be essential to me in a husband. Steve has eight of the twelve so I figured that I was ahead of the game. Sexual fidelity was not one of the twelve. I know that isn't the usual priority . . ."

"Certainly it's not prevalent in suburbia," Howell interjected with sour amusement. "As a matter of fact, if you'd stop being such a paradox, you'd probably be better off."

"I don't understand."

He grinned at her reassuringly. "Think it over. Later. When you've started thinking again. But you are a paradox, my dear."

"What's paradoxical about not worrying if your husband is sleeping with other women? That's on his conscience, not mine. And good Lord, the man's away so much, it's only natural to . . . to do what's natural."

"You are either remarkably well-adjusted or incredibly naive."

She didn't know whether or not he was laughing at her.

"I shouldn't have brought that up, his sleeping around, the other night. But he was accusing me of it, and I haven't."

"Thus spake outraged virtue!" There was a damnable twinkle in Howell's eyes.

"I'm not being outraged virtue! But he'd no right to blame me for the sins on his conscience. And he was sorry about knocking the Lucy over. He really is proud of my work. Lucy did that for me. Maybe he doesn't understand why I have to sculpt, but he likes the money it brings in. I don't care which just so long as I have the chance to do it and he doesn't complain too much.

"Oh, don't misunderstand me, Jamie. I'm no undiscovered Michelangelo, but I've been well trained. And if there is such a thing as inherited instinct or talent, I have that, for all that my father worked only in oils. But my work is solid, competent and sometimes provocative."

"I'd employ different adjectives," Jamie said, clearing his throat hastily. "I rank 'provocative' with 'interesting' as damning adjectives. In sculpture, I put the wire-crate junkyard variety in the 'provocative' category."

"I just have to sculpt," she ended lamely.

"Then you won't give it up because of this brouhaha and the damage to the Lucy?"

"No," she said, shaking her head for emphasis, "especially because the Lucy was involved. So you will have your work," she added quickly.

"That was furthest from my mind," he said in acid annoyance. Then, seeing his reaction distressed her, he took her hand in his. "I want a LeBoyne, believe me I do. Besides," and he grinned wickedly at her, "I feel I've earned it."

"I apologize for involving you in this *crise des nerfs*. I see now that it's been building up. I can usually sidestep them but I was happy and I didn't keep my eyes open."

He shook his head disapprovingly and pursed his lips. "I don't see, myself, why you should have to keep your eyes open when you're happy."

"You're most vulnerable then," she replied as if he should know.

"No wonder you close up so tightly, Mirelle." He rose to his feet. "You have no reason to apologize to me. In an obscure way, I was glad to be here with you yesterday. You needed someone. I suggest, most sincerely, however, that you cultivate a female friend. Actually I dropped by yesterday to say that I've been called to substitute for another accompanist who's ill. I'll be away until the 14th. I'll call you when I get back."

At the door, he turned.

"Find Lucy in someone else, Mirelle. Clay has no opinions and makes a damned clammy shoulder to cry on."

She watched him stride quickly to his car, his left shoulder hiked up, his gait that of the foot-weary infantryman. For all that caustic tongue of his, James Howell was a kind man.

CHAPTER SIX

THE DAY AFTER Howell left on tour, Mirelle found the courage to go down into the studio. Howell had righted the stand and replaced the cloth. Dispassionately Mirelle stripped the statue and regarded the unnatural, misshapen twist of the mashed plasticene body. The aluminum wire of the armature showed through as a grotesque fracture through the clothing clay across the thigh and down one leg. Little suggestion was left of the personality she had brought out of her material. Tentatively she twisted the head-high hand back to its position on the forehead, then she reset the position of the body frame, obliterating the remaining details of the draping. Snorting to herself, she used both hands to gouge the plasticene from the frame, and begin afresh.

To her surprise, the reworking of the statue took a shorter time. There was a different feeling about the Lucy when she got it to the same stage it had been at the time of the accident. Mirelle tried in vain to define the subtle alteration because the result was a more powerful representation of the woman Mirelle had loved. Some of her unwitting sentimentalization had been stripped from the new concept, making it a more candid portrayal of Lucy Farnoll.

She was fussing over a minor drapery detail when the doorbell rang.

"I ought to disconnect that damned thing," she muttered as she reluctantly left the Lucy. The bell clamored a fourth time. "Just a living minute!" She wiped her sticky hands on her smock front. "Never have callers when I'm clean, do I?" She threw open the door.

"Mrs. Martin?" asked the woman standing there. She was clutching the strap of a shoulderbag, balancing a thick notebook, a packet of forms, and trying to talk intelligibly around the ball-point pen between her teeth.

She wasn't even vaguely familiar to Mirelle: not a face seen at church or the Food Fair or school and community meetings. In a stylish grey jersey dress with matching coat, her dark brown hair smartly coiffed, she was an attractive woman. Her even features were carefully made-up, lightly but expertly so that with animation the lines of age and dissipation were not immediately apparent. The mouth was wide and thin-lipped: the smile which the pen bisected was winningly apologetic., Only the expression of the large, slightly protuberant grey eyes belied the total impression of the suburban type. The eyes, quick, darting, shrewd, were mocking and critical.

"I'm Sylvia Esterhazy, your ward-heeler."

"My what?" Mirelle laughed aloud.

Sylvia Esterhazy repeated herself good-naturedly, her husky voice playing with the laugh inside her. "Your county committee woman."

The notebook was slipping from her grasp and so was the strap of her shoulderbag. Before Mirelle was aware of her intention, she had taken the notebook from Sylvia's hand and was shepherding her into the living room.

"Ward-heeler is what I am though, despite the politer title on the election ballot. We're having a registration unit at the elementary school on Saturday and I'm trying to get all those eligible down there to register. That includes dispensing Girl Scouts as baby-sitters if necessary. You and your husband have been here over the statutory year, haven't you? Good, we want your votes . . . either way . . . because the next election is going to be a bitch."

"I'm afraid I'm an Independent."

Sylvia's carefully delineated eyebrows rose mockingly.

"Don't be afraid of independence, dearie. It's better than being a Republican," and her eyes glinted with repressed malice.

Mirelle laughed. "You mean, there actually are Democrats willing to come out in the open in this state?"

"That's part of the fun of being a Democrat in Delaware," Sylvia replied with a triumphantly wicked laugh.

Mirelle grinned back.

"By any remote chance, is your husband also an Independent?"

"As much as anything." His parents had been Republicans but they hadn't often discussed politics.

"Now, may I count on both of you to come and register on Saturday?"

The thought of going anywhere with Steve on Saturday was not comforting to Mirelle. Sylvia was watching her face and abruptly altered her expression.

"He's out of town right now," Mirelle explained as smoothly as she could. "I expect him home on Friday but . . . " She shrugged.

"Company man, huh?" Sylvia asked, making a notation. "Your occupation is . . . ?"

"I'm a sculptor," Mirelle said swiftly, to forestall the onerous housewife. Then she realized that Sylvia's pen had been poised: the woman was asking, not assuming.

Sylvia rolled her eyes now, at the defiance in Mirelle's voice.

"I like decisiveness," she said with a chuckle as she wrote. "I put 'politician' down for myself," she added, looking up as she finished writing. It was then that she saw the Running Child.

"You did it," she said with agreeable surprise and absently disengaged herself from her impedimenta, walking over to examine the figure closely. "Your daughter, too," she stated.

"Yes, Tonia was three when I did it. She's seven now and grown so unlike this that I'll have to do another of her. Whining!"

Sylvia chuckled, turning the statue carefully on its base to get the full effect. "You sculpt with a great deal of love, don't you?"

The phone's summons saved Mirelle from having to answer. She excused herself quickly. The call was from a telephone solicitation for magazines so she hung up more rudely than was her custom and returned to find the living room empty.

A sound told her that Sylvia had found the studio, and when Mirelle joined her, Sylvia turned from the Lucy, her face white with shock.

"You knew Lucy Laben . . . Lucy Laben Farnoll?" she whispered hoarsely. "Where? When? She's been dead for years!"

The two women stared at each other until Sylvia laughed unsteadily.

"I didn't mean to be nosey. No, I tell a lie. I did. Then I saw the statue and . . . " Sylvia shrugged, swallowing hard. "Curiosity is the bane of my existence. But you can't imagine what a turn it gave me to see Laben to the life. Why, that's just the way she'd stand . . . we were classmates at Duke . . . when she couldn't make up her mind to shower or play bridge. We used to call her PM . . . perpetual motion . . . the way you have her feet, almost not touching. It's uncanny, that's what!" Sylvia gave an embarrassed bark of laughter, shaking her head over her reaction and shock. "Life's little surprises! You know, when I said you sculpt with a great deal of love a moment ago, I didn't realize how accurate I was. Martin. Martin." She ran the name through her mind. "Mirelle Martin!" Her eyes widened with astonishment and something else. "But, on the list you're Mary Ellen . . . "

"My baptismal name . . . "

"Mirelle. Mirelle Martin. Of course." Sylvia clapped a dramatic hand to her forehead. "In one of those Christmas letters Lucy would deign to write, she mentioned meeting a young woman who . . . " Sylvia paused, obviously hesitant with the truth.

" . . . Was a very mixed up little fool," Mirelle supplied with a self-deprecating laugh to put Sylvia at her ease.

"No, that wasn't what Lucy said," and Sylvia shot Mirelle an appraising look. "But she did mention your . . . and the adjective she used was 'lovable' . . . " Sylvia waggled a finger at Mirelle, "pieces that she bludgeoned you into doing for a church bazaar she'd got herself involved in."

Mirelle laughed as a series of happy memories from that year crowded into her mind.

"Come. Come have coffee with me," she urged Sylvia.

"Oh, Lord, girl," and Sylvia rolled her eyes heavenwards beseechingly, "I've got the whole damned street to canvass. But I'd much rather have coffee with you. You're the brightest spot in a weary dreary day. Okay! The Democratic Party owes me a coffee break at the very least."

It was two hours later that Sylvia, explosively resisting her own inclination, gathered up her paraphernalia and whipped from the house, promising in no uncertain terms to return very soon.

She was like a private hurricane, Mirelle thought, leaning weakly against the door when Sylvia had left. The vitality of the woman, different from Lucy's, had a contagious strength about it. For the first time in ages, Mirelle felt disappointment in a guest's departure. They could have talked for hours more without scratching the surface of a hundred points of common interest and disagreement. What was even more flattering was Sylvia's obvious reluctance to leave.

Mirelle caught herself up sharply. What was the use? As soon as she had got half-way friendly with Sylvia, Steve would undoubtedly be transferred. They'd been in Wilmington for over two years already, a record stay in one place. What was the sense of involving herself with all the contingent sense of loss when they moved away? A little piece of herself bestowed and unreclaimable.

That afternoon she received a phone call, from June Treadway, the chairperson of their church's women's association. Mirelle was not of an organization temperament: she joined neither bowling leagues, bridge clubs nor women's associations, resisting with inverse ratio to the amount of pressure put on her to join. Early in life, Mirelle had learned never to be dependent on the social support of other women.

In Ashland, it had been Lucy who had stimulated her interest and sponsored her at the easy geniality of the church women's groups. She had not felt like participating in that climate again. As a matter of fact, they had not sent for their letter of transfer from the Ashland church until they moved to Wilmington. Steve had initiated that action, for obscure business reasons, and Mirelle had complied because she hadn't cared one way or another. She went to a church anyway, Steve's because he had a definite preference and because she wanted the children to have consistent religious instruction until they were old enough to sort that problem out for themselves. But she had never repeated her enthusiastic participation of Ashland days. It was therefore slightly surprising that she should be approached at all by the Concord church.

"I'm afraid we keep a file on all our members, Mrs. Martin, and Reverend Ogarth from Ashland mentioned your talent for sculpting so it's down on your card. We're in need of one creative booth," June Treadway's pleasant drawling voice explained, "and I was wondering if you would consider bringing your wheel and clay, and making things right at the Bazaar."

Almost, Mirelle rudely interrupted the woman to say that she would not consider whipping up some clever little pots that would sell.

"I don't mean," June Treadway went on as if she might have sensed Mirelle's refusal, "please understand me, mass produce anything. Bob Ogarth—we were once in Ashland, too . . . " and there was such a wistfulness in the woman's voice that Mirelle's cool rebuke died a-borning. "Bob said that each of the Christmas figures which you created were unusual and imaginative. We'd really like to have more originality in our exhibits and offerings. Quality rather than quantity. I'm so bored with standardization and badly finished gimcracks. When you think of the individual talents in this congregation, I'm just certain we can do better than doilies and pot-holders!"

"In that case, it would be a pleasure to contribute."

"Oh, would you? Really? How kind you are!'

And Mirelle was astonished at the genuine ring to the banal phrases. She was also chagrined at her initial uncharitable thoughts about June.

"No, I'm not kind," Mirelle replied honestly. "I'm extremely selfish or I'd have volunteered to help when the notice came out in the church calendar."

"My dear girl," said June Treadway in a warm throaty chuckle, "that notice just gives you warning to think up good excuses. Seriously, you know how hard Ken O'Dell is working to get us all to re-evaluate church life. And that means every facet, especially Christmas. The way Bob Ogarth spoke of your creche figurines, I'm sure we want them. But I thought it would be even more interesting if people realized how much skill and work it takes to create the finished product. So, if you could be there, actually working on something . . . or would you feel . . . inhibited? Is that the word I want?"

Mirelle laughed. "That's supposed to be the word. But observers never bother me." After all, one doesn't feel inhibited about breathing.

"Might you possibly have something which you'd consider adding to the saleable articles? And I mean at the price it ought to bring, not a charitable give-away."

"I may by the end of November," Mirelle said, responding to the woman's diplomacy. She hated being pressured into selling or donating. Sylvia Esterhazy's appraisal of great love in her work had something to do with her unwillingness to squander her production on the unappreciative.

Adroitly June Treadway received an invitation to come to Mirelle's house one day the following week and left a very pleasant feeling of anticipation with Mirelle when the phone call ended.

Stimulated by the notion of working a booth for the Bazaar, she was looking through unused sketches when she heard the sound of Steve's car in the driveway. It was only 4:00 and she wondered what brought him home so early. She stood waiting for him at the door. His head was down, his hands thrust deep into his pockets as he came up the walk.

It was so unlike him to use the front door that Mirelle wondered what could have gone wrong at the office. Then she recalled that he was probably not sure what his reception would be. He didn't know that she'd reworked the statue so successfully: he couldn't know how indifferent she was to whatever emotions he might be entertaining: remorse, regret or revenge. He stopped short when he saw her standing in the doorway.

"Are the kids home?" he asked.

"Out playing," and she swung the door open for him.

He hesitated before he stepped in. Then he stood in the hallway, hands still thrust in his pockets, one shoulder higher than the other. She felt as awkward, suddenly, as he looked, and moved briskly towards the dining room.

"A drink?" she called, fixing him one before he could answer.

He stood in the dining room archway and accepted the drink. But, as she moved to pass him, to go back to the studio, he reached for her arm. She stiffened but didn't pull away. His hand relaxed.

"I hate it when I can't reach you, Mirelle, when you withdraw like that. You're like two different people. You drive me to hurting you physically. But I didn't . . . honestly . . . I didn't mean to damage the statue. I was fond of Lucy, too."

"The statue was not irrevocably damaged, Steve," she said, trying to put a little warmth in her voice.

"Mirelle!" This time his voice stopped her. "The boss called me in when I got to the office this morning."

Mirelle turned around. Could their bickering have affected his work? Or were they to be transferred . . . again! She felt sick.

Steve began to smile, self-consciously, and with a return of the boyishness that had so often made her feel tenderly toward him.

"I'm off the road. I got a raise and I'm to take over Jerry

Cathcart's job. He got a boost to district manager in the Southwest."

His face was lit now with pride in his promotion and, Mirelle sensed, relief at the reprieve from the grind of constant travel.

"I've hated the road. You know . . . " he said, turning away from her and looking through the window to the front lawn. "I did it because I had to, and I guess I've been taking my resentment out on you and the kids. You could get your work done but I couldn't even be home long enough to weed the lawn or plant a decent garden."

"It is a big relief," Mirelle said, "to think we'll be staying here awhile. I'd dreaded having to uproot the kids but two years has been our limit in one town over the last twelve years."

Neither of them was touching the core of the problem, but Mirelle didn't want to talk about that even if Steve had the guts to bring it up. She needed much more time to analyse how she did feel about Steve right now. She didn't want to be forced to voice any sentiments at the moment. She was empty emotionally, indifferent.

Perhaps his being home would help heal the rift. Surely their marriage had once had a firm footing, even after the disastrous episode over her father's bequest. Divorce did not enter her solutions nor did an empty relationship, but it was obvious that their marriage was shifting its emphasis and they would both have to feel out the new balances and checks.

Rather than precipitate any further mention of this dangerous area, she told him of Sylvia Esterhazy's visit and June Treadway's call.

"Ironic that," Steve said with a wry smile.

"Why?"

"That both were somehow connected with Lucy Farnoll."

"Oh? Yes!"

"Lucy's still got her eye on us."

"You could say that," Mirelle replied in such a way that Steve would not expand that coincidence. He flushed with angry hurt but said nothing more.

As Mirelle lay down for sleep, her mind returned again and again to the enticing prospect of staying in Wilmington, in this house. Of knowing that she could develop the friendship which Sylvia Esterhazy seemed to be offering. The woman would be good for Mirelle. It would be impossible to resist her ebullience.

She excels each mortal thing, Upon the dull earth dwelling. Mirelle snickered at her sleepy thoughts, from Wordsworth to Shakespeare. *Backward, oh time, in thy flight.*

Unbidden the dream sequence started its remembered round to fall apart with the alarm clock and the morning's reluctance to begin a new day.

CHAPTER SEVEN

ON SATURDAY, Mirelle and Steve did go together to the registration at the elementary school. Sylvia Esterhazy was very much in evidence and introduced the Martins to her husband, a tall extremely attractive leonine man, with the slightest trace of an accent.

Mirelle was disconcerted when George Frederic Esterhazy held onto her hand in a lingering fashion. Steve would notice such attentions and bring them up the next time he was consumed by jealousy. Esterhazy made her slightly nervous anyway, with the all-knowing scrutiny of rather penetrating cynical eyes. He reminded her of the actor George Saunders, not altogether a compliment to Esterhazy. Mirelle wondered what Sylvia had told him of her. Fortunately two women swept up to divert George Frederic and she took the opportunity to get on with the business of registration.

"Esterhazy seemed taken with you," Steve remarked when they were leaving the building.

"No more me than anything else in skirts in his vicinity," Mirelle replied with a scornful laugh.

"I guess you're right," was Steve's rejoinder as he noticed Esterhazy ingratiating himself to another female arrival.

The rest of Saturday passed in a similar state of truce. Sunday was placid and Mirelle didn't really have any sense of change in their routine until Monday evening when she realized that she'd be cooking full dinners every night. When Steve was on the road, she and the children generally made do with pancakes, scrambled eggs or hash, saving the big cuts of meat for the times when Daddy was home. These evenings, Steve would be home in time for a drink. The children did less fooling and more eating at the table and, as Steve was engrossed in his new responsibilities, the family dinners were downright enjoyable.

Steve made no overtures to Mirelle, for which she was thankful. She really did not wish to rebuff him openly. She had no warmth left toward him to dissemble. Only the habit of fifteen years of marriage sustained her.

On Thursday morning, she answered the phone to hear Sylvia's bright and challenging 'hello!'

"How did the registration go?"

"Ninety percent of all eligible voters," Sylvia was chortling with understandable pride. "I am assuming, of course, that the reluctant and un-American ten percent are all Republicans and we can do without *them*. Say, you made quite an impression on my husband."

"Nonsense."

"Not nonsense at all."

"He was doing the gallant with every . . . one." Mirelle nearly said everything in skirts.

"He breathes, too," Sylvia replied with a kind of sardonic undercurrent in her voice. "But he doesn't remember doing it. It's when he talks about a certain female hours later . . . I have never argued with his taste. However, that wasn't what I called to say. Would you join us for dinner at the Country Club tomorrow evening? And no wheezes about not belonging or not dancing. I have to go because G.F. is entertaining business associates, but I held out for a couple of my choosing to make the pills palatable. You and I can have our heads together all evening because people are accustomed to me behaving rudely or in other bizarre fashion. Part of my democracy."

"I'll have to ask Steve . . . "

"Don't ask him. Tell him. Oh, all right, then. Do the wifely and get permission of your lord and master, so long as the answer is 'yes'."

"Let me call you back tomorrow."

"If you don't, I'll be over there."

Sylvia gave Mirelle her unlisted number. Surprisingly enough, Steve didn't hesitate a moment, remarking that they hadn't had any evenings out in a long while. It occurred to Mirelle that Steve would have agreed to anything she suggested right then: an advantage which she'd had rarely and wasn't certain she wanted. His compliance emphasized his remorse over Lucy. Perversely Mirelle wished he'd had to be persuaded against his will. However, Roman agreed to babysit if he could stay up as late as he wanted, watching TV. As Tonia was apt to fall asleep whenever she got sleepy, Roman didn't fuss when she said that she was going to stay up all night, too. Mirelle and Steve left the kids, eating hamburgers, eyes glued to the predictable pattern of a Western.

The Esterhazys were waiting for them in the gold and white open hallway of the new clubhouse.

"The McNeills and the Clarensons are being fashionably late," Sylvia said to Mirelle.

"Steve has a thing about being on time, a hangover from the Army," Mirelle said with a smile.

"Mine comes from difficult judges insisting on punctuality," Esterhazy said as he deftly relieved Mirelle of her coat. He and Steve moved off to the checkroom, leaving Sylvia with Mirelle.

"Oh, he is giving you the treatment," said Sylvia with a laugh. "Don't blush. He'll do much the same to Fritzie McNeill and Adele Clarenson but without the extra flourishes. Or is your husband the jealous type? G.F. takes getting used to."

"Oh, Steve fancies things," Mirelle replied, astonished to hear herself making such a casual admission. But then, perhaps Sylvia would kindly drop the word to G.F.

Sylvia snorted, glaring over her shoulder at Steve's broad back. "Then he should have married a plain woman instead of an exotic one. That shade of red is superb on you. How do you keep your figure? Oh gawd, here comes death and boredom," she said *sotto voce*, switching almost instantly to smooth cordiality as she greeted their other guests.

No sooner had the Clarensons been introduced around than the McNeills arrived and the party went in to the bar. Mirelle saw an imperceptible sign pass from G.F. to Sylvia who deftly herded the three women to one side, allowing the men to do a bit of pre-dinner business. Watching Sylvia as a hostess, Mirelle was a little awed. She would never have guessed that Sylvia privately held the women in good-natured contempt. She was graciousness personified: seemed to recall every detail of their domestic routine and recent tribulations. She listened with every appearance of concentrated attention. Only the slight glazing of her stare told Mirelle that neither Adele's latest servant trials nor Fritzie's dietary restrictions were registering. What, wondered Mirelle, was Sylvia's private opinion of Mary Ellen Martin then, vouchsafed at another time to other, more vivacious companions?

Two cocktails later, G.F. seemed to have concluded his business talk and the women were drawn into general conversation. They adjourned to the dining room to a reserved window table and G.F. began to carry on a flirtation with Adele who was taking it as no more than her due. Fritzie McNeill got herself seated between Bob Clarenson and Steve, across the table from her husband whom she watched even as she coyly chatted with her seat mates.

They aren't even subtle about it, Mirelle thought, more than a little disgusted. Sylvia, at least, was witty and funny but the general atmosphere depressed Mirelle, who was not at ease in social chitchat, and unable to act the coquette, the role in which she was generally cast at first encounter.

They were waiting for dessert and coffee when Mirelle noticed G.F. Esterhazy squinting at someone on the other side of the room. Steve also concentrated in that direction so noticeably that Fritzie turned around to see what they were staring at. She gave an exasperated snort.

"Men!" She rolled her eyes. "Always an eye for pretty girls." In that tone of voice, girls was synonymous for children.

Mirelle, whose back was to the rest of the room, refrained from turning but Sylvia craned her neck, raised her eyebrows appreciatively and made a little moue with her mouth.

"G.F., especially," she laughed, flicking a glance at Steve. "That one appears to be fair game. And such a handsome escort. I'll take him any time! *Très distingué*. Whoops, they're coming this way."

Someone brushed against Mirelle's chair and as she moved it to let them pass, she inadvertently looked up. She was startled to see James Howell behind her. He smiled, wished her good evening and passed by with his companion.

"Who is he?" asked Sylvia in a hoarse whisper at Mirelle.

"James Howell," Mirelle replied, glancing apprehensively at Steve. He was still following the girl with his eyes.

"Why, he's old enough to be that child's father," Adele remarked tartly.

"Your claws are showing, dear," her husband remarked. "For my part, I'd say he had damned good taste."

Mirelle hoped that her face didn't show her annoyance but she didn't feel that she ought to mention that Howell had a daughter: Steve might wonder that she was so knowledgeable about the affairs of a man whom she was supposed to know only casually.

"Who is he?" Sylvia asked, insistent.

"He's a concert accompanist."

"The one who played for that soprano in last spring's Community Concert?"

"I wouldn't know that."

"Fancy your recognizing his face," remarked Fritzie in an insinuating drawl.

"We've met a couple of times. He helped me change a

flat tire once last spring," Mirelle said and then some perverse whim prompted her to add mendaciously. "Then he was dripping steak juice on my toes one day at the Food Fair. He was very apologetic and we got to talking in the line. He introduced himself."

Sylvia slid into the rather awkward pause with a 'sick' joke about supermarkets and the subject of James Howell was dropped. Later Mirelle glanced unobtrusively towards Howell's table. The girl's profile was turned towards her and it was immediately apparent to Mirelle that the girl was his daughter: the jawline and the set of the ears was unmistakable. She was lovely, young, and very pleased to be dining with her father. She was teasing him, leaning across the table, waggling a finger at him. He laughed and grabbed the finger.

"I promise not to drip steak juice on your toes," said G.F. in Mirelle's ear, startling her. "Will you dance with me?"

"Certainly." Charm-vendor or not, G.F. had an unembarrassing way of flattering a woman.

He was tall enough to be a good partner, and led easily and well, holding her firmly but not objectionably against him.

"You're deceptively tall, Mirelle."

"All legs."

He gave her a searching glance. "To descend to the banal, your face is strangely familiar."

"And you'd be originally from Austria?"

He laughed at her evasion. "Very good actually. But off-putting. I've prided myself that I've lost all trace of my accent." He said the last in a very broad musical comedy inflection.

"Almost. It's a game I play," and she glared at him for the mischief in his eyes, "that I can place people's accents."

"And mine to identify ethnic origins. I'd say," G.F. went on relentlessly, "that you are at least partly Irish."

"Correct. The rest is nondescript."

"My dear girl, the rest is Slav. To be precise, Magyar."

" 'Hungarian and a princess'," Mirelle retorted, quoting Professor Higgins from *My Fair Lady.*

"No," G.F. contradicted her, suddenly and unexpectedly very serious. "Not a Hungarian princess." There was a bitterness and anger in his eyes which faded instantly as he looked down at her. "Sylvia tells me that you've done a very fine statuette of Lucy Farnoll."

"It isn't finished."

"You don't look like a sculptress."

"How should one look?"

"Bulging with proletarian muscle?"

"I might if I worked in stone but I don't."

"Have you shown anything around here?"

"No. My production is limited."

"If your work is as good as Sylvia thinks, and she's astute in her artistic judgments, you at least have settled on quality rather than quantity."

"No paths to my door."

"What? No revolutionary plaster mousetraps?"

"Not even a plaster mouse. My *specialité* is pig paperweights."

G.F. threw back his head and guffawed just as the music stopped. Mirelle felt all eyes on them and tried to move back to their table, but G.F. had not let go of her. Out of the corner of her eye, she saw James Howell watching.

"What's so funny?" Adele demanded, dragging Bob out on the floor to them.

"Mirelle plays with words nicely."

"Is that all?" Adele asked in an arch fashion that set Mirelle's teeth on edge.

She rather thought that G.F. found the attitude trying as well. Fortunately the music started and G.F. swung her off. She was grateful that he had limited his remark to Adele. She had already displayed the sort of condescension which Mirelle would not have tolerated for any length of time.

When the next set of dances started, G.F. traded her off to Steve, who'd been dancing with Sylvia.

"We haven't done this sort of thing in a long time, have we?" Steve said, tucking her head against his cheek as he used to do.

"Did you try that last twist?" she asked.

"Not me," he said with a rueful shrug. "Sylvia was game enough but I begged off. She's a good dancer, though. Nice woman."

"Yes, she is."

"You could do with a friend like her, Mirelle. You've needed someone ever since Lucy died." Mirelle agreed with him. "You ought to get out with other women. Go bridging or take up tennis."

Mirelle shook her head vehemently. "And you won't find Sylvia doing that sort of thing either."

"Nonsense," he said, holding her off and looking at her rather angrily. "She did the registration canvass."

"That's not bridge or tennis. That's politics."

"It's getting out and not sticking to four walls and . . . " He broke off suddenly and pulled her close to spin to the music. As they started the pivot, her heel went down on someone's foot and she broke from Steve's grasp to apologize.

"It's perfectly all right, Mrs. Martin," said James Howell, grimacing manfully and making a great play of tentatively putting weight on his injured right foot.

"Well, you did drip steak juice on my feet in the Food Fair," she said.

"Our account is now squared then: blood for blood."

Steve cleared his throat and Mirelle hastily introduced them.

"And may I introduce my daughter, Margaret? Mr. and Mrs. Martin."

Margaret Howell shook Mirelle's hand warmly. "You must be the Mrs. Martin who sculpts. Dad said how much he admired your Cat. And to think that you live right here in Wilmington."

"And dripped steak juice on strangers in an ordinary Food Fair," added James Howell. Only Mirelle could guess at the deception behind his bland expression. "Let's see if any permanent damage has been done. May I? Thank you." And he had his arms about Mirelle and was leading her off before Steve could form a protest. "Mind you, Martin, Papa's got an eagle eye."

"You're incredibly cheeky," Mirelle said as they whirled off.

"Who's talking cheek? Steak juice on your feet, indeed! Pure fabrication!" His eyes were dancing with mischief. Nothing was wrong with his foot from the way he moved. He was a more daring and flamboyant dancer than Steve, and Mirelle was intensely aware of his strong hand on her back. He was taller, too, and as her forehead came to his jaw, she couldn't see over his shoulder. She craned her neck to see how Margaret was doing with Steve.

"Margaret will be keeping him much too busy to watch you. Dancing with her old father is not her idea of a thrill although I believe that she's a credit to me on the dance floor."

"You are a marvelous dancer."

He looked down into her eyes, grinning. "Except when a foot has been skewered by three inches of stainless steel."

"I am sorry, Jamie. Really."

"That's better," he said, smiling and pulling her closer. He rested his chin against her hair. "You're like fine wine and velvet—which reminds me. Have all the King's horses and all the King's men . . . "

"Put Lucy back together again?"

"Yes, her, too." His eyes lost the laughter as he stared down at her gravely.

"An ill wind blows no good," she said as lightly as she could for his stare was disconcerting. "I think it's a better statue now. It's more Lucy. The other was very sentimental."

"Sentimental? Hmmm." He pulled her close again to execute a complicated turn. "Maggie goes back tomorrow to college. She came down to rob me of my pelf for fine feathers. She'll leave poor Robin poorer by far, I fear."

"All in a good cause."

The music ended and he led her back to Steve, claiming his daughter with appropriate light banter.

"Nice guy," remarked Steve.

"He has a good-looking daughter, doesn't he?"

"Yes, he does," Steve said in an absent fashion, staring after the two in such a way that Mirelle knew that his suspicions about James Howell had been removed.

CHAPTER EIGHT

IN RETROSPECT the next morning, Mirelle realized that, while the evening had had its shallow pleasures, it had only served to emphasize the broadening and apparently unbridgeable gap between Steve and herself. Fifteen years of marriage provided patterns to follow and routine exchanges filled awkward silences.

Steve plunged into a backlog of projects, rewiring the hi-fi equipment which had never been properly installed in the Wilmington house, repairing furniture, refinishing the boys' dressers, painting Tonia's bookcases and starting garden beds for planting the following spring. He joined the men's group at church and had time to enjoy home and community.

Mirelle cooked, kept the house tidier during the week than she had when he was away so constantly, and spent every other moment in the studio. The children were well accustomed to such absorption and, because they knew that she was busy on creche figures and items for the Bazaar, they never noticed that she and Steve were rarely together.

Yet, despite her ability to concentrate on sculpting to the exclusion of all other thought, Mirelle was constantly having to turn her mind away from the estrangement. Fortunately Sylvia got in the habit of dropping in for morning coffee, a practice that Mirelle had never encouraged before in anyone. A visit from the often caustic, always interesting Sylvia was bracing.

"If you mind my dropping in like this, I wish to God you wouldn't mealy-mouth around, but just say so," Sylvia said on Friday. "I've been here every morning this week . . . "

"Except Monday . . . "

" . . . Which might be stretching my welcome a bit. I think you once mentioned that you didn't go for the coffee break routine." Sylvia cocked one eyebrow quizzically. There was a tautness in the cords of her neck and an undercurrent in her sardonic manner that alerted Mirelle.

"No, I don't mind you dropping in, Sylvia. For one thing, you always make the coffee yourself."

"G.F. says I'm a managing type, but I must have my daily gallons of coffee . . . "

"Which you supplied the last pound of yourself, you nut . . . "

"Why not?"

"You don't expect me to stop what I'm doing . . . "

"God forbid! It's therapeutic watching you—better you than me—muck with that filthy stuff and turn out something repulsively human . . . " Sylvia gave a delicate shudder at the grinning Dirty Dick on Mirelle's wheel. This particular model was of Nick on the memorable day when he and Roman had come home, their best clothes covered with mud, carrying a pailful of tadpoles. Small Boy Triumphant Over Odds.

" . . . And you don't natter on and on . . . "

"I don't?" Sylvia was outraged. "I talk your bloody ear off."

"Yes, but you've a style of talk that's fun."

"Good time gal, that's Sylvia Esterhazy. A laugh a minute."

Mirelle looked up anxiously.

"I talk your bloody ear off because you *listen*, and you hear, and you do me the extreme courtesy of NOT offering predigested woman's magazine drivel as advice!" Sylvia's fine eyes were troubled but she turned her face away from Mirelle. Mirelle dropped her eyes back to the Dirty Dick, stenciled over a line unnecessarily. "I've got problems," Sylvia said in a tough voice. "You've got problems. All God's children got problems. Even if I could explain mine . . . But there are some days when I've simply got to talk AT someone." Sylvia gave a shuddering sigh. "Because I *can't* vocalize what is really . . . is bothering me. Talking AT someone like you is a helluva lot of help!" Sylvia made a sound that was half-gasp, half-laugh. "God, sometimes if you can just get the words out, you realize how silly it all is. Of course," she added in a brisker, Sylvia-ish tone, "this sort of talking-at is reciprocal."

Mirelle shot a quick glance at Sylvia, wondering if she'd guessed how shaky the Martin marriage was. There was only a mute appeal in the woman's posture.

Mirelle recalled all the times when she had unburdened herself to Lucy Farnoll, monologues that often proved to herself in the hearing how trivial her problem was, receiving the compliment of sympathy and practical advice. If by providing Sylvia, who'd known Lucy, with the specious solace of being her sounding board, she could repay her debt to their mutual friend, Mirelle was more than eager to oblige.

She smiled at Sylvia, prodding the plasticene in the bucket.

"I'm not the vocal type, Sylvia, but my ears are available."

Sylvia chuckled, her whole body relaxing suddenly. "No, you're not the vocal type, but it's another mark in your favor, m'dear. I simply cannot abide women who incessantly talk about themselves." She caught Mirelle's startled look and grimaced in self-deprecation. "Oh, yes. I obviously can't stand myself by the same token." She gulped the last of her coffee, gathered up her jacket and bag. "Monday? Same time? Same coffee station?"

"You'll always be welcome, Sylvia," Mirelle said as warmly as she could.

"Thanks, kiddo." And Sylvia was up the stairs and out

the door.

As Mirelle finished the Dirty Dick, she couldn't help wondering what could be troubling a woman like Sylvia, who outwardly had all the essentials and many of the luxuries of life, was active socially and seemingly satisfied professionally since Sylvia insisted that she was a professional politician. Their relationship had not reached an intimacy at which anything deeply personal could be discussed, but Mirelle was oddly flattered by Sylvia's request.

Sylvia was not Mirelle's only visitor. June Treadway had come not once but three times, each time phoning to make sure of her welcome. Mirelle felt more formal with June but no less at ease. In her late forties, with all her children at various levels of college education, June enjoyed her involvement as volunteer secretary for the Church, organizing the social activities, assisting the very busy minister and his curate in all secular particulars.

"I'm the model of a modern matron," she told Mirelle, "and I shall thoroughly enjoy being a modern grandmother. Someone once told me that there are compensations for every age. It's a consoling notion if you examine it in any depth, and a damned good excuse, too. If I'd been born in the era when it was done, I should probably have embroidered a sampler with that motto. Matter of fact, perhaps I should anyway. Only being modern, I'll use one of those felt-tipped marking pens and have it done in five minutes instead of five weeks."

"Plan ahead," laughed Mirelle, printing the infamous sign in the air.

"That's how mine would probably look, too," June said with a chuckle.

A memory, forgotten like so many parts of her childhood, leaped to mind in unbidden association.

"When I was a child, about eight or nine," Mirelle began, "I was taken to see the Martelet at Loches. It had a horrible dungeon . . . " and she shuddered at the recollection of the cold clammy smell of accumulated fear and terror in that dark place, " . . . where the Duke of Something had been imprisoned for twenty years. He'd painted a sign on the curve of the wall. You could still see traces of the paint. The reds held up best. He'd written *'celui qui n'est pas contain'* . . . "

"How apt," June interjected drily.

"Very. The *'celui qui'* was huge and the *'n'est pas contain'* progressively smaller until it got crammed in a corner. The guide didn't say whether he ran out of paint, energy or light. But I suddenly realized that's why the Plan Ahead sign always fascinates me."

"I didn't go down in those dungeons. I'd had enough of them," June surprised Mirelle by commenting. "The children chattered all afternoon, I remember, about how hideously dark and scary it had been and so cold underground. Although it was July and warm for France. We were there in '58. Marvelous trip. But you said you were eight or nine? Were you raised abroad?"

"No, just visiting." Mirelle tried very hard to keep her answer casual, remembering how she had answered Jamie Howell.

"I guess at that age you weren't taken to any of the museums or galleries?"

"I was, but I got my training here in the States. At Cooper Union."

"But that gives excellent training. My grandfather went there. He was a printer and engraver."

"So that's why you know about the mechanics of sculpting."

"I don't know anything, my dear, but I can appreciate the result."

June was a comfortable personality and Mirelle found herself wishing that the woman would stay longer. June always seemed to have another appointment that she had to get to on time. She never appeared hurried, however, for her energy was not obtrusive, yet she apparently accomplished a great deal for the Church.

"I've got to go, Mirelle," she said now with a groan and rocked herself up out of the spring studio couch. "I should spend more time walking than 'going'," she added, smoothing her skirt over her plump hips. "Oh, well, who wants a bony grandmother?"

She grinned down at the unpainted Dirty Dicks in their various postures.

"Have you ever seen Dr. Mason's six year old Tommy? I could wish that you'd put his face on one like this fiend," she said, indicating the one with Nick's face. "But that wouldn't be very good public relations, would it?"

That Sunday Steve entered the studio for the first time. He made an exclamation at the sight of two rows of the glazed, finished Dirty Dicks.

"How many of these are you donating to the Bazaar?" he asked.

"I'd planned on sixteen of these, some of the cat poses and animals to add to Christmas scenes."

"Done anything for that Howell guy?" The question was casual.

"No. Not yet."

"What did he want?"

Mirelle decided to take the question at face value.

"He saw the Cat in the Stamford Museum. He wants something with that kind of feeling."

"What? Washing its paws? Wasn't that Tasso?"

"I should pay the cat a percentage of what he's earned for me," Mirelle said with a laugh.

"Howell doesn't strike me as the kind of guy who'd go for cats."

"On the contrary," and Mirelle regarded Steve's frowning face with bland amusement, "he's so constantly on the concert circuit that the at-homeness is very much what he wants."

"Funny he should see that in the Cat. That wasn't what you intended at all, was it?"

Mirelle looked Steve right in the eyes. "As a matter of fact, it was. I did it just after we left Ashland."

Steve flushed and Mirelle held her breath, wondering if yet again her errant tongue would precipitate an argument.

"You were pretty torn up then, weren't you? And I was so

damned glad to have a territory of my own after two years of being overruled by that paper-assed Patterson."

It was Mirelle's turn to feel chagrined. She had been such a bitch then, and Steve had been so elated by his promotion. He'd done very well and the bonus that year had been substantial.

"I got two hundred for that Cat," she said. "It isn't everyone who can make money out of being homesick."

Steve snorted. "I guess not."

He went off to bed while she put her tools away. It had been a tranquil weekend, she reflected gratefully. And he hadn't taken exception to the extent of her proposed donation to the Church, or Jamie Howell's commission. If only he would not say something, or if I can just hold my tongue, if only this truce will last a little longer, maybe I can find my way out of this impasse.

She took a shower because plaster dust was gritting between her breasts and sticking to the fine hairs on her arms. When she came back into the bedroom, Steve was lying naked across her bed. The sight of his well developed arms, his heavily muscled chest tapering to a still trim waist no longer aroused her as once it had done. There had been a time when she had risen from love-making to sculpt his relaxed and satisfied body. Plaster replicas of every portion of his physique gathered attic dust. She knew each tendon, muscle, bone and plane of his body: a knowledge that had thrilled her as lover and sculptor.

She understood what had prompted his generous attitude in the studio. Did he honestly think that a passing interest in her work constituted an apology? Or the reminder that she, too, had been at fault in their relationship?

Peace at any price, she told herself. She felt neither desire nor revulsion as she joined him on the bed.

CHAPTER NINE

THE NEXT MORNING Steve went off to work in high good spirits, kissing her soundly in front of the kids. She stared after him, mildly astonished that he actually thought last night's performance had mended all.

She had been completely uninvolved in the love-making, responding out of habit. She wondered vaguely if that's how prostitutes felt, amused at such a thought—amused in an unfunny way. Why Steve hadn't felt her unresponsiveness, she couldn't guess. He hadn't wanted to? Had there really been a time when she had adored Steve and his body, and the expression of their healthy appetites?

No bang, no whimper, not even a gasp. Was that how a marriage ended?

The question, popping unbidden into her mind, was startling enough. She rose quickly, busily clearing the breakfast table: anything to keep from thinking. She filled her coffee cup. None left for Sylvia!

God, how she hoped Sylvia would be early this morning! Talk about needing to sound off . . . just to hear how silly a notion was . . . Mirelle gulped. How could she talk around something as devastating as this? You simply don't just up and discount fifteen years of marriage one morning. And you sure as hell don't bring it up as a subject of casual conversation.

Rather desperate for diversion, Mirelle looked around the studio. She didn't have anything to glaze or fire. She had nothing started on the wheel. Her eye caught the Lucy. Okay, rub salt in. That might do the trick.

The Lucy had been relegated to a corner so she pulled it out into the center of the room and uncovered it, backing off until the couch caught the back of her knees. She sank down.

Lucy would have had an answer, at least a solution, or an idea. She wouldn't have wanted me to quit, not when I'd come so far. She never disqualified the hard work required in any marriage: hard work on both sides. But, what do you do, if there's nothing . . . nothing . . . there anymore?

Despair, like a cold wave, swept over Mirelle. She began to cry, in gusts that came from deep in her guts. She drew her legs up against her stomach against the racking spasms. Her body was suddenly more committed to the exertion of weeping than it had been to last night's sexual act.

In one sane compartment of her mind, she was appalled at the intensity of her hysterics, yet unable to control herself.

Oh, God, make the phone ring. Let someone come to the door. I'll have to get control then. I'll have to calm down. Someone! Help me!

The door was flung open and Sylvia came bursting in. The shock stilled the next sob in Mirelle's throat. She held her breath with every ounce of strength, determined not to let the sobbing resume. Sylvia! Thank God. Then Mirelle panicked. Oh, my God, what do I say? I can't . . . I can't talk. She'd know.

"Any coffee left, Mirelle?" Sylvia asked, half-way to the kitchen even as she called.

"Make more." The two short words came out just as if Mirelle was concentrating on a vital detail. She struggled up from the couch and lurched into the laundryroom. She grabbed the first towel in the basket, turned on the tap and started slapping water in her face, still gulping back the remnants of the hysterical contractions.

"You sure are eager-beaver in the studio this morning," Sylvia was saying cheerfully from the kitchen.

Oh, please, stay there a little longer, Mirelle silently entreated as she grabbed a clean bra and pants from the dryer. Yesterday's jeans were gritty with plaster and caked with paint but with a clean shirt over them . . . She even found a piece of broken comb with enough teeth left to get her hair into some kind of order. She dabbed at her eyes again with cold water but her hands were trembling badly. So were her knees.

"Got a cup down there, Mirelle?"

"Yes."

Mirelle peered at her shadowy reflection in the clear windowpane. One look and she's going to know that I've been crying. And what'll I say? Oh why . . . Well, you *demanded* someone's presence. At least it's Sylvia.

High heels clacked on the bare space between hall carpeting and the stair tread. Mirelle, trying to smile, stepped back into the studio, shoulders braced for the inevitable question. But Sylvia's attention was focused on the tray she carried and didn't look at Mirelle.

"Oh, you're working on the Lucy again? That's good. I'm all for charitable works but in moderation."

"Not working. Just checking."

"Coming down with a cold? Your voice is rough."

Mirelle hastily cleared her throat. "No. Frog. Coffee'll help."

"Where's your cup? Ooops!" Sylvia filled it and handed it back to Mirelle, still without looking at her, being intent on not spilling the hot liquid. "You don't happen to have another of those silly pigs, do you? Like the ones you made for Tonia and Nick? Because I *have* to have something as an inconsequential birthday present and the pig would be sooo appropriate." Sylvia dropped her voice to a droll pitch to stress the fact that the recipient was unlikely to appreciate the obscure insult.

"I've two rough plaster ones, easily finished and glazed."

"On the shelf here?"

"Over more to the left, behind that plaque. Right there."

Sylvia stretched up, blindly but carefully feeling along the shelf with her hands. Then her fingers located the right shapes and brought both pigs down. She took them over to the window, turning them into the light and chuckling.

"You wouldn't mind, would you? I mean, if you're doing some serious work on the Lucy . . . "

"No, no. I don't mind at all. I'm sort of worked out at the moment, idling as it were."

"In that case, Madame da Vinci, I want the pig pink and polka-dotted. A raucous pink and a putrid purple for the dots. Could you possibly prostitute your art for little old me?" Sylvia swung round then, her eyes still on the bigger pig, her grin malicious. "How long will it take?"

"To glaze and fire? Two days at the most."

"Sure I'm not interrupting an important phase?" And Sylvia gestured at the Lucy.

"No. Not at all. I'd tell you. Here, drink your coffee and I'll put on the underglaze right now," Mirelle said. She could brush on a glaze without having to look directly at Sylvia.

Sylvia curled up on the couch, watching as Mirelle, with deft small strokes, applied the coating. She gave a shudder.

"I could never work that precisely. My stomach gets wrapped up in knots."

"You're the expansive type. That's why you can't be good with small motor movements and controlled gestures."

"You said it!" Sylvia sounded so unexpectedly bitter and caustic that Mirelle looked up. Her face was still averted but the coffee cup was shaking in her hand.

Mirelle suddenly realized that, if she had not wanted Sylvia's attention, Sylvia had been avoiding Mirelle in an adroit manner.

"Do you know what I was doing when you came this morning, Syl?" she asked, without thinking it over.

Sylvia ducked her head down and rubbed a forefinger on the rim of her cup. "No. What?"

"I was having a first class case of hysterics, praying to Almighty God to make the phone ring or let someone come to the door so I'd have to get hold of myself."

Slowly Sylvia met Mirelle's eyes. Her face, expressionless and almost ugly with its lack of animation, was sadly old. She'd no make-up on which, if Mirelle had not been so self-concerned, would have immediately indicated distress.

"If you could have seen me throwing cold water on my face, tearing clothes out of the dryer so you wouldn't catch me in my nightgown . . . " and Mirelle started to laugh at the inanity of it. "The two of us playing the same game . . . "

"Well, I'll be damned." She stared at Mirelle for one moment longer and then began to chuckle. Color came back into her face and the infection of Mirelle's giggles doubled hers. They sat across the room from each other, laughing at themselves.

"Okay, what were you hysterical about, Mirelle?" Sylvia finally asked, wiping her eyes.

Mirelle shook her head, as much at herself as to indicate an inability to answer.

"Oh, things just dumped on me all of a sudden. You?"

Sylvia grimaced. "All right, we'll play it coy a little while longer."

"Maybe if we both talked AT each other at the same time, neither of us would hear what the other said and our terrible confessions would remain secret?"

Sylvia gave Mirelle a long sideways glance. "I think you've got the right end of that stick, my friend. But," and she sighed deeply, "now that we've had a therapeutic laugh at each other, I do feel better." She cocked her head quizzically at Mirelle.

"I feel better, too."

"Good, then these two blind mice can fare forth anew to find that better mouse-trap."

Despite Sylvia's brisk rejoinder, Mirelle recognized that her friend had only the most tenuous grip on herself.

"I wonder if a better mouse-trap would do any good at all?" she said softly.

Sylvia glared at her. "You're nearly there," and she gestured dramatically at the Lucy. "Even this feckless thing," and she pointed angrily at the half-glazed pig, "is cuts above the usual twee gimcrackery. *You've* got an outlet. *You* create . . . " Sylvia broke off, her eyes filming with tears. Instead of giving way, she blinked furiously, knuckling her eyes with brusque strokes. "Can you produce a very very bad purple for the spots?" she asked in a wheedling tone.

Dutifully then, Mirelle took her bottles of coloring from the shelf and found a clean jar. She sprinkled in a few grains of red, blue, a bit of orange luminescent paint, and mixed. Sylvia didn't approve. They spent the next hour trying to extract from the pigments exactly the shade in Sylvia's mind.

"Of course, it'll fire darker, and more vitriolic," Mirelle said when an approximation of the vile shade had been achieved.

"This is going to be a horror," Sylvia said in triumph. "Honest, Mirelle, it's a shame to do this to such a *nice* pig," she added contritely.

"He should care. He does what I tell him."

"Can I come back tomorrow and see the damage?"

"With or without?" asked Mirelle coyly.

"What? Tears? Or laughter?" Sylvia grinned back, the shadows lifted from her fine eyes. "Thanks, Mirelle."

"Ha! If you hadn't come when you did . . . "

Sylvia's hand closed tightly on her arm for a moment and then she whirled off, striding up the stairs. Mirelle followed her to the door, waving as she drove off in her usual gear-grinding hurry.

She caught sight of her reflection in the hall mirror. With no make-up, she looked totally washed out. She was reaching for her purse to get her lipstick when the phone rang.

"Mirelle?" a very hoarse voice queried as she answered.

"Yes?"

"What is the name . . . hmmmm . . . of your doctor? Ahhhheemmm. I don't know one in this goddamned town."

"Jamie? You're sick?"

"As nearly as I can . . . ahhemm . . . decide, I died last

night only no one knows there's a corpse in my bed. I need a doctor!"

"I'll call Dr. Martin immediately."

"Nepotism?"

"What? No, he's not a relative."

"That's reassuring."

"Jamie, you'd joke on your death bed."

"And where do you think I am?"

"Oh, hang up so I can call the doctor. He's very good about coming on house calls."

"He'd better be." With that acid comment, Jamie hung up.

Will Martin actually answered her call. He couldn't make a house call to Jamie until mid-afternoon but he gave her the scant assurance that if the man were able to make a phone call, he'd be able to last until afternoon. He did promise to make Howell his first stop.

It was now 10:45 and Mirelle decided that Howell ought not to have to wait that long for succour. The hell with propriety. The man had no one else in town and Margaret's college was way up in Massachusetts.

She took eggs, milk, bread and some consomme, and made it to his development by 11:02. The front door was locked. She hesitated but she didn't want to rouse him out of bed if she could avoid it. She went around to the back door, which was also bolted tight. She stood by her car, trying to remember the layout of the house, and with sudden inspiration, raised the garage door. The kitchen door was unlocked, although the kitchen was a shambles of unwashed dishes and used pans. She walked through to the hall, which was neat except for the suitcase, hat and coat dumped in the middle of the entrance way. Several days' accumulation of mail had fallen through the door slot. She went upstairs. The first room she peered into had a rumpled bed but no occupant. The second room also had a used bed. The third bedroom, the smallest, was darkened and she didn't at first discern the figure in bed. She walked over, for one moment convinced that Jamie was motionless in death.

"I thought . . . ahhemm . . . you were the garbage man," he said in a painful rasp.

"They collect garbage on Thursday on this side of town."

"For all I know it is Thursday and has been . . . ahhhem . . . for five mortal long days. Did you call that doctor of yours? Or are you considering me for a death mask? Sorry. I'm indestructible. I've never had a sick day in my life."

Forgetting any lingering shyness, she put a hand on his forehead: he was burning with fever and his skin parched dry. She snapped on the bedside light and he waved irritably at her to turn it off. She saw enough in the brief instant: his eyes were bloodshot with fever, his face white and drawn, with several days' beard. She could hear the rales in his chest as he gathered wind in his lungs to speak.

"I absolutely detest women . . . "

"At this moment, James Howell, your likes are immaterial. I don't need Dr. Martin to tell me you are very sick. At the least, bronchitis; at the worst, lumbar pneumonia."

She automatically set about smoothing the untucked, disordered blankets and felt the dampness of the sheet. He'd been sweating profusely, which explained the musical beds.

"I'm going to change the bed in your own room. I'm going to get you clean pajamas," she said, walking back to the big room by the stairs. She opened dresser drawers until she found clean, laundry-packaged nightclothes. She scooped up the bathrobe that was crumpled on the floor, and returned to him. "You will get up and change. Quickly. And wash your face. By then, I'll have finished making your bed. If you haven't moved, I'll change and wash you myself."

She said the last as she was searching the linen closet for sheets and pillowcases. She heard him cursing as he lurched out of the bed, the exertion caused him to cough in tight barks that must have hurt his throat dreadfully from the sound of them. She heard further curses over the sound of running water as she stripped the bed and changed it quickly. She lowered the blinds against the brilliant morning sun and cleared the debris on the bedside table.

"Your bed's ready. I'm going to get you some hot soup," she called.

"You're a managing female," he said in a hoarse voice from the bathroom but, as she descended the stairs, he walked unsteadily down the hall.

While the soup was heating, she gathered up the dishes with congealed and hardened food and put them to soak in the sink. She made a pile of the first class mail, hung up his hat and coat and then carried the consomme and mail up to him.

He scowled at her when she entered the room, but it was a half-hearted attempt at disguising weakness.

"What's your daughter's college address?"

He put down the spoon half way to his mouth.

"That is enough meddling," he said with genuine anger.

"James Howell, you are very sick."

"Thank you, I'll wait for the doctor's diagnosis. I appreciate your phoning him and all this," he said, indicating the fresh linen and the soup, "but that is quite enough. Thank you!"

At that unqualified dismissal, he went back to his soup.

"You are insufferable, James Howell. How long have you been feverish? From the amount of dishes, I'd say you'd been able to feed yourself for at least four days of eggs and toast. The milk in your refrigerator is soured so it's at least a week old. You haven't picked up a newspaper from your front door for five days. And I don't see even aspirin in your medicine cabinet."

"You are also a prying woman."

But Mirelle could see that he was more sound than fury.

"Eat!"

"It's a liquid," he said with precise enunciation. "I'm drinking it."

"When did the fever start?" she asked, lowering her voice at his tacit capitulation.

He grimaced over the heat of the consomme.

"I started feeling lousy in Atlanta but we still had the Camellia circuit to do. I got off the plane Saturday at Philly and came straight home. Oh, look, call my agent. The number's in the red address book on my dresser. Dave'll have to get Heinrich to play at the Tuesday affair. He knows the repertoire. Ohh, hell!"

His hand was shaking enough to spill the soup from the spoon. Mirelle got a towel from the bathroom.

"You are not going to feed me," he said in an unequivocal tone.

"You're quite right. I might lose a finger. But I am going to put a towel where you can spill without drenching your last clean pair of pajamas."

She made the call to his agent, while he glowered at her, relaying the message.

"I'd wondered why I hadn't heard from Jamie," Dave Andorri said. "He's never sick. How sick is he?"

"The doctor's coming this afternoon but I'd say that he has bronchitis. Severely."

"I didn't give you permission to bandy my condition about," said Howell. "Tell Dave I'll be able to play for whosiwhatsis on the 18th as promised."

" 'Tell Dave that I'll be able to play for whosiwhatsis on the 18th as promised'," Mirelle dutifully quoted and was rewarded by a bark of protest from Howell who made an ineffectual grab for the telephone. Dave heard the protest and laughed, remarking that he sounded like he would recover.

"I'd appreciate it if you'd call me again after the doctor comes and let me know if there's anything I can do, Mrs. Martin," the agent said with genuine concern. "Jamie's not just one of the best accompanists in the business, he's a very good friend of mine."

Mirelle kept the little notebook hidden in her hand when she removed the tray. Howell slid down under the blankets wearily, announcing his intention to sleep until the doctor came. Mirelle went to the kitchen and immediately phoned Margaret at her college.

"I'll cut afternoon classes and fly down, Mrs. Martin. You know, I'd wondered why I hadn't heard from Dad. He usually calls me when he gets back home," Margaret said. "You sure he isn't . . . I mean . . . it's so unlike him to be sick."

"He *is* sick but he told me that I was a managing female, that he was really dead and no one had thought to lay out his corpse. Then he made me call his agent."

"Then he intends to live," said Margaret with a laugh of relief. "I'm sure he doesn't *mean* it . . . about your being managing, Mrs. Martin . . . " she added in earnest apology.

"Well, I am, because he has no idea that I have managed to call you. He wouldn't willingly give me your phone number."

"Well, I'm glad you did. Aren't men the living end?"

Mirelle agreed heartily and hung up.

By the time she had finished the dishes and thrown out the spoiled food in the refrigerator, she heard Howell's croaking voice calling. She got half way up the stairs before she understood that he would like ice water. Just as she passed the front door, the bell rang. After fumbling with the lock, she admitted Will Martin.

She felt a trifle silly introducing doctor to patient and retired from the room, ignoring Howell's fierce scowl. When Will came back downstairs to the kitchen, he was muttering under his breath about damned fools who insist they enjoy the best of health. He dialed the pharmacy and ordered several prescriptions sent over as soon as they could be made up.

"Not when Bart has had a coffee break," he added. Then he turned to Mirelle. "Good thing you called and insisted I see him, Mirelle. He's one step away from an oxygen tent. I'd fling him into the hospital right now only they're so crowded . . . "

"Is he that sick?" Mirelle was alarmed.

"It's nothing that medication and proper food and rest oughtn't to cure. He does have the constitution of an ox, as he boasts, but he needs someone with him in case that lung congestion . . . "

"I phoned his daughter at college. She hoped to catch the 3:00 plane."

"He said he didn't need anyone!" Will Martin snorted. "Hadn't taken so much as an aspirin. 'Never have any in the house'." Will did an excellent imitation of James Howell.

" 'I'm never sick!' Ha, well, he's sick right now and I've given him a massive dose of penicillin—where it'll remind him that he is. I'll drop in again tomorrow." He cocked his head inquiringly at Mirelle.

"I'll stay until Margaret comes."

"You know the routine to tell her, don't you? Plenty of liquid, not too cold, plenty of rest. I'll want to know if there is any increased difficulty in breathing, or a significant rise in temperature." Mirelle nodded acknowledgment. "Is she a level-headed girl?"

"Seems so."

Will frowned for a moment. "In any case, he's better off at home than in the hospital. No other relatives? No? Will you be looking in?"

"I certainly can," Mirelle assured him, and was then apprehensive.

"Oh, I'm just cautious, that's all, Mirelle. But he's the stubborn type and unless his daughter can keep him in bed, this could easily turn into full-fledged pneumonia."

Mirelle thought of the concert which Jamie intended to play on the 18th and smiled. "I've a lever for her blackmail."

"Okay, then. Give her my answering service number. Eckerd's is sending the prescriptions and a vaporizer. He's to start the tablets tomorrow morning, every four hours, and the codeine syrup ought to inhibit that cough. His throat is raw meat." Will gave another disgusted snort. "And he's never sick!"

"With more people like him, Will, you'd be out of business."

"D'you think I'd mind after this winter?" With a weary shake of his shoulders, Will buttoned up his coat and left.

Mirelle brought Howell his cool water. "On the doctor's orders I phoned Margaret," she said.

Howell narrowed his eyes. "You phoned her before he got here. I heard the click on the extension. Presumptuous female!"

"You know a lot of them, don't you?" she said, lobbing his address book at his chest.

"That's why I can make accurately odious comparisons," he said, his long fingers closing absently about the book. "And you have magnanimously agreed to stay by my deathbed until she comes?"

"I've my orders."

"Managing female!" There was no real malice in his voice, and not much strength. He buried his head in his pillow and closed his eyes.

Mirelle looked down at him for a few moments, thinking how illness brings out the boy in a man. Distracting to reflect that even a sophisticate like Jamie Howell must have been a nice little boy—from time to time. Then she went to change the other beds. She made a neat pile of the sheets. From the marks on them, they must go to a laundry. Margaret would know which one. With the kitchen cleaned and himself asleep, there was little to do now but wait for the drug store delivery and Margaret. She didn't feel that she could unpack his suitcase nor make noise vacuuming the house which was dusty. Nor did she feel as if she could intrude on his music room. The phone rang and she nearly fell over a chair trying to reach it before it could disturb the sleeper.

It was Margaret. She was at Logan Airport, having broken all records getting there, and would fly out on the 2:00 plane. She'd get a cab from the airport in Philadelphia which would get her to Wilmington about 4:00 but did her father have enough money in the house because she didn't have cab fare?

"If he doesn't, I do, Margaret. Just come." Mirelle gave her a slightly expurgated version of Will Martin's diagnosis.

"Imagine! Dad sick enough to ask for a doctor!" She hung up.

If Margaret couldn't reach Wilmington before 4:00, Mirelle wondered what to do about her children. If she flew home about 3:00 to collect Tonia, the boys would be all right by themselves but she didn't really wish to inflict Howell with Tonia. And ten to one, Tonia would drop one of her ambiguous comments at precisely the wrong moment. But, if she arranged for a baby-sitter, that would also be noteworthy . . .

Mirelle fumed. It wasn't as if she were doing anything wrong, helping a friend. It was ridiculous that she couldn't feel at liberty to stay here. With a sudden inspiration she dialed Sylvia.

"Are you busy from 3:00 to 5:00 this afternoon?"

"Now that YOU inquire, no. Why?"

Mirelle explained.

"Isn't that just like a man?" was Sylvia's comment. "Say, if you had to clean out the fridge, should I pick up a few essentials for the girl?"

"Would you? That would be a tremendous help." And between them they concocted a list of what might tempt an invalid that a daughter, probably unused to cooking, could prepare. Sylvia would drop the groceries off on the way to Mirelle's house.

While she waited for Sylvia, Mirelle mused again on how much she liked the woman. No coy questions, no arch suggestions about why Howell called Mirelle. And today, too, when Sylvia had been so depressed.

She answered Sylvia's soft knock on the front door and ushered her into the kitchen where they unpacked the shopping bags.

"My mother had a sovereign convalescent remedy," Sylvia said with a sour expression as she waggled a butcher's package about. "Where are the pots? I need a double boiler. Having beef tea prepared by my mother's own lily white hands was nearly an incentive for me to contract an illness. Ah, thank you." Mirelle discovered the double boiler. "We'll just put the beef in the top, water in the bottom, cover well, and leave for about half a hour." Sylvia followed her own directions. "Throw the meat out—he doesn't have a dog? Well, give that cat of yours a treat then—But the residual juice . . . hmmm, concentrated protein, easily digestible and it tastes incredibly good as well as being incredibly restorative to all those depleted red blood corpuscles. For that recipe I have forgiven my sainted mother some of her lesser transgressions."

Then the irrepressible Sylvia tiptoed out of the kitchen and essayed a brief exploratory tour of the lower floor.

"He must make a good bit of money tickling ivories while his canaries sing."

"Shush, Syl, he'll hear you."

"Nah!" Then she looked at her watch. "Ooops. I've got to dash."

"Wait! What will you tell the kids?"

Sylvia raised her eyebrows in mock innocence. "The truth! You're sitting up with a sick friend!" She drew her features into an exaggerated expression of noble piety.

"Who's that?" They could barely hear Howell's croak.

The pharmacy truck pulled in just as Sylvia sneaked out the door.

"Your medicine is here," Mirelle answered truthfully, taking the package from the boy.

"These'd choke a horse," Howell said, examining the tablets with suspicion. He sniffed the cough medicine and turned his nose away in revulsion.

"It's not how it smells, but how effective it is in relieving that cough," Mirelle said and poured him a spoonful. "Or are you that fond of hacking up your throat lining?" His teeth connected audibly with the spoon. "Don't eat it!"

"It smelled vile and tasted viler!" Jamie gave a histrionic shudder, then pointed a finger at her chest. "I heard females cackling in my kitchen."

Mirelle laid a quick hand on his forehead. "You're delirious!"

"I must be or I'd have you in bed with me."

Mirelle laughed, as much at the thought of anyone wanting her in bed, other than Steve, as at Jamie's rakishness in his present circumstances.

"It's no laughing matter to be invited to bed with me, young lady," he said, in a grand manner at variance with his unkempt appearance.

"Doubtless, but not prudent in your infectious state. I'd court respirating disaster as well as a scarlet letter."

Jamie gave her an odd glance and then flopped over onto his back, coughing at the slight exertion. He punched the pillow under his head to prop him up sufficiently to glower at her.

"Just what did that sawbones say was the matter with me?"

"A touch of bronchial pneumonia."

"A touch?" Howell was indignant. "I've sustained a knockout."

"So you admit that you're sick? Enjoy it while you may: you're due to recover with proper rest and nursing."

"Nursing? From Margaret? She's a baby herself."

Mirelle cocked her head at him. "So you'd prefer to go to the hospital?"

"No!" His explosive negative made him hack painfully.

"I have the feeling that Margaret will be quite capable of looking after your basic needs."

He glowered, plucking at the covers with petulant fingers as she left to check on the beef tea.

"What'n'hell's this?" he asked suspiciously as she returned with the steaming cup.

"It's good for you. Drink it. Slowly. It's hot."

He hadn't quite waited for her advice and must have burned his mouth with the first sip. Before he could complain, a look of pleasurable surprise crossed his face. "Hmm, it tastes good." He sipped more judiciously and with evident relish. "When is my junior Nightingale arriving?"

"About 4:30. Plane gets in at 3:15."

"Did she have enough money for the taxi?"

"Now that you mention it, no."

Howell chuckled. "I always buy a round-trip ticket for her. That way I know she'll be able to get home. But I've never known Mags to have cabfare. God knows she gets enough of an allowance from me."

"She'll earn it this time."

Howell started to snort in agreement but was seized with a violent spate of hard coughing. Mirelle handed him a box of Kleenex just as the phone rang. It was Dave Andorri.

"Does he need anything?" the agent asked solicitously when Mirelle had told him the diagnosis.

"Hmmm. Have you got a blonde," asked Mirelle, all innocence as she noticed Howell's fierce glare, "about 24, size 10?" She neatly ducked the pillow which was flung in her direction.

"He'll live then," Dave said with a chuckle. "But will he be well enough to play on the 18th? I've got a mighty particular primadonna who will raise an unholy stink if Howell isn't at the keyboard."

"I've told him that if he's a real good boy and obeys her, Margaret will let him up for that concert." She sidestepped the box of Kleenex which Jamie lobbed at her. The effort restarted the cough so she was saved his snide commentary.

"Is that him coughing like that? He is sick. But Margaret's a good kid. They've got a nice relationship."

"Even if he doesn't give her a decent allowance."

"I beg your pardon? Well, tell him I'll call tomorrow."

She hung up and gave Howell Dave's message.

"Mirelle . . . " Jamie began when he got his breath back, "you're a . . . "

"Managing female," she said, staring him down.

His glare dissolved unexpectedly into a smile. "A quality which I didn't suspect in you and which I appreciate, despite snide remarks to the contrary. What have you done with your children, oh devoted mother?"

"Sylvia's baby-sitting."

"Does she know you're holding the hand of a sick friend?"

"It was her suggestion, and her beef tea recipe." She reached for the empty cup, lying on the spread.

His hand, strong-fingered, closed about her wrist, jerking her off her feet and forcing her down to his level.

"Jamie!"

He held her eyes in an unfathomable gaze before he smiled oddly and deliberately rubbed the hand he held across his stubbly beard.

"Hey, your face is like sandpaper."

"I'll see to you another time, me proud beauty!" he said with one last baleful leer and then turned away from her.

Disturbed by the intensity of his expression and the unexpected strength in a man weakened by fever and coughing, Mirelle hurried down to the kitchen. His grip, angrily strong, had left white marks on her wrist. And why had he turned so abruptly violent? She had only been trying to lighten his illness with her teasing. Restless, she emptied the dried meat cubes out of the double boiler and put them into a sack to bring home to Tasso: that is, if he'd consider them fit to eat. She washed and tidied up the kitchen, delaying the time when she might be called up to Howell's room again. She was relieved to hear the noise of a car in the drive and opened the front door to see Margaret hurrying up the walk.

"I owe him a fortune," she told Mirelle breathlessly.

"Come and get it," called Howell from above and Margaret, with an apologetic smile at Mirelle, rushed up the stairs.

Mirelle could hear the obbligato of her greeting and questioning against his rasping counterbass. Then Margaret was clattering down the stairs again with a wallet in her hand. She paid the cabbie, retrieved a small case from the back seat and came flying back to the house, looking exceedingly pretty with her flushed cheeks and windblown hair. She looked not a bit like her father except for the jawline.

"I can't thank you enough, Mrs. Martin. Dad's said how you've browbeaten him with old maid nurses and beef teas, whatever they are, and he promises he'll behave for me."

Mirelle laughed and gave Margaret the doctor's instructions, adding that she'd be happy to do any shopping or fetching that might be necessary.

"Dad also said I'd better send you home now. Your children will be missing you."

"I'd better go, truly. Call me."

As Mirelle drove home, the hand which Jamie had rubbed against his unshaven cheek still tingled from that pressure. She could almost feel the strong fingers tightening again.

That night, at dinner, wondering why, she told the family all about Howell's distress call and waiting until his daughter arrived from college.

"Trying to keep that commission alive?" was Steve's query.

"I could hardly have left him alone in the condition he was in," Mirelle said. "He might not have lived to pay up."

"You aren't smart about charge accounts but you know how to handle your own art business," Steve said. "Speaking of which, is it absolutely necessary to buy seven pairs of underpants for Tonia at one time? Why did we buy that dryer?"

"The pants are special ones, each labelled with the day of the week . . . " Mirelle began to explain.

"Oh, for God's sake . . . "

" . . . and Susan Harper has them and Susie Miller and Karen Arnold . . . "

"So Antonia Martin, of course, has to have them?"

"Of course!"

CHAPTER TEN

THE NEXT MORNING when Mirelle called Margaret Howell, she was told that the invalid had been very restless during the night, constantly plagued by the racking cough. The vaporizer had had little noticeable effect and Jamie claimed the cough syrup was worthless. Mirelle told Margaret to confer with Will Martin.

Then she went down to the studio and finished Sylvia's pig. On inspiration, and because Howell was much on her mind, she took down the long-covered head.

The flaws in her execution were startlingly apparent and she spent nearly an hour making minute precise alterations.

"What? Not brewing calf's foot jelly?" was Sylvia's greeting. "Say, when did you do that?" she asked as she recognized the head. "Mirelle, how long HAVE you known James Howell?"

"I met him last May," Mirelle replied, hoping that a casual answer would inhibit Sylvia's curiosity.

"That's a mighty . . . ah . . . close study for a casual acquaintance."

"Is it?" Mirelle stared at the head as if seeing it objectively for the first time. "Not really. It's not at all finished."

"No, it isn't."

Exasperated by that droll remark, Mirelle turned on Sylvia. "What are you not saying?"

Sylvia returned the look with a sardonic expression and then, suddenly relenting, sighed, and headed for the stairs.

"Sylvia!"

"Well, it is an awfully perceptive study, until I remember that you worked the Lucy from a memory seven years dead, so forget about the sordid innuendo. Any idea how the invalid and his nurse are faring?"

"He had a restless night."

"Will she be able to cope?"

"I think so."

"Interesting type, Howell. I can see why his face caught your artistic eye."

"Go thou and make coffee."

Sylvia went with a show of alacrity. Mirelle stood back and eyed the plasticene model critically, beginning to experience some satisfaction in the result. The phone rang and Sylvia picked up the kitchen extension.

"It's Margaret," she called down to Mirelle. "He insists on beef tea and all but threw the boullion she made him in her face. Ha!"

Mirelle joined the conversation on the studio phone.

"There isn't any more beef in the house to make the tea. We can pick some up and be right over. D'you need anything else?"

"Yes, indeed, Mrs. Martin. Fruit juice. He drinks like there's no tomorrow. And Dr. Martin was calling Eckerd's to make up a new prescription for that cough. It's awful. My throat hurts just listening to him hack."

Mirelle and Sylvia entered by the kitchen door to prevent disturbing Howell. Sylvia started the beef tea while Mirelle took up the cough medicine. Margaret was sitting on her father's bed, reading letters to him. He looked, if anything, worse this morning. She still didn't have the dimensions of the forehead right. That would account for faulty positioning of the eye socket. No, she'd have to wait until he recovered from his illness. The bones in his skull were abnormally pronounced, his face drawn by fever and fatigue.

"Hi, Mrs. Martin."

Jamie opened his eyes slightly.

"There are females cackling in my kitchen again," he complained.

"Nonsense. You're hearing the rale in your chest."

"And another thing," Jamie opened one eye wider, "couldn't you at least have recommended a physician affluent enough to use sharp hypodermic needles? I've a bruise the size of a dinner plate on my butt."

"Couldn't get through the calluses on your tail bones from sitting on all those unpadded piano benches."

Margaret let out a whoop of laughter and Jamie kicked her off the bed, glaring at Mirelle.

"Will you kindly instruct this infant of mine in the proper recipe for that beef tea? She fed me a substitute, poured no doubt from last night's dishwater."

"Thy wish is our command, Effendi." Mirelle salaamed, and gave the necessary instructions.

"You see, I told you it was an essentially simple decoction," Jamie said with weary patience.

Margaret rolled her eyes expressively heavenwards. "You're saving my life."

Then Jamie caught sight of the bottle in Mirelle's hand. "Cackling females! Here I am, with a throat like a sandstorm, relief in sight," he pointed at the bottle, "and you two stand there exchanging inanities."

"Oh, dad," said Margaret contritely.

"Never mind him, Margaret. Here's the syrup and I hope it's more vile than yesterday's. I've got to go. The beef tea will be ready in half an hour. Don't forget." She gave Jamie a jaunty salute and left.

As she and Sylvia left, they could both hear Margaret upbraiding her father for resisting the new medicine "that Mrs. Martin was kind enough to collect."

"We're going to have to rescue that child," said Sylvia. "Once he's over the fever, he'll be impossible."

"Just like my Nick who was a terror," Mirelle said.

"Mirelle," began Sylvia, edging sideways into the Sprite's bucket seat, "where *did* you meet Howell?"

Mirelle chuckled.

"Now don't give me that bit about a flat tire. And the day that man steps into a Food Fair short of starvation . . . "

"To tell the truth and shame the devil . . . "

"By all means . . . "

"I won't say another word if you keep interrupting . . . "

"I'll behave . . . ."

"I got tossed from a horse last spring and as I turned onto the highway, the tire blew. He saw it and played Good Samaritan."

"I wouldn't have thought that piece was in his repertoire."

Mirelle gave Sylvia a stern look and she made a show of remorse.

"I'd wrenched my ankle in the toss and he said he decided to stop because he saw me limping."

"Where did the steak juice drop in?"

"That was later, in October."

"All right, if you insist on being coy . . . "

"Now, look, Sylvia," Mirelle began with a touch of anger in her voice, "don't go imagining a situation when one doesn't exist."

"I'm the slave of my romantic soul. That's a lot of good man going to waste."

"Howell? I doubt he allows any waste, the way he talks."

"It's so easy to talk a good game," and Sylvia's voice took on a caustic edge, "but when the time comes to produce . . . " She shrugged eloquently about such failures.

Though the words were glib, Mirelle began to wonder about the basis for such a cynical retort. She was reasonably certain that G.F. Esterhazy was the sort of man to take favors whenever offered them. It occurred to Mirelle that Sylvia would retaliate by finding extra-marital solace if the mood struck her. Mirelle had good reason to regard infidelity as a minor offense.

"Have you fallen silent in respect for my shrewd insights?" Sylvia asked Mirelle as she turned the Sprite into her development.

"I'm speechless, but only because I'm trying to figure out how to turn the wrath of El Howell from doting daughter."

"Shall we throw a wake?"

"And ask the corpse to play for it? That isn't done."

"I should like to hear him perform," and Sylvia's laugh was wicked with *double entendre*.

"My, we have an edge to our tongue today, don't we?"

"Pay no attention. This is 'I Hate Men Week.' Join me?"

"I'm not big on causes."

"At least that one? Well, that's a relief. I'd a notion things might be sticky in that department for you."

Mirelle smiled reassuringly. "There're always times."

"Hmmm," and the monosyllable was knowing as Mirelle brought the Sprite to a halt in the driveway. "I'll finish making coffee. I've only had one quart today."

Mirelle went back to her pig work and, when Sylvia brought down the coffee tray, they both admired her efforts.

"Now," said Sylvia with a drawl, cocking her head at the pig, "if it had jowls, an unshaven appearance and a more sardonic expression . . ."

"The very idea!" Mirelle leapt to the storage box and extracted a wad of clay. "To help Margaret, I'll make a Howell pig to remind him of how difficult he is."

"This I gotta watch."

"I used to make little animals for the children when they were sickabed. I developed a series of beasties, usually with obnoxious expressions, and just gave them hideous colors. Nick would be a blue mule when he wouldn't take his medicine. Roman was a yellow ostrich. He always burrowed under the sheets to avoid a shot."

"Can't say as I blame him. Nor would Howell."

Mirelle laughed, remembering his complaint. "The kids

would play with the animals in bed, before I broke down and permitted TV in the house."

"Are there any left?" Sylvia peered at the back of the storage shelves.

"No. They were just hardened clay and friable. In fact, the kids used to smash them in victory when they got well."

"How quickly can you work?" Sylvia asked, her eyes dancing.

"Depends . . . " and she lifted the pig explanatorily. "This will take only a few minutes but I used to do a lot of such things."

"Because . . . you know what you might do for your church booth? Turn out small busts of the children there. Could you do a rough one in say fifteen minutes?"

"Well, yes, I could," and Mirelle's admission was reluctance itself, "but that isn't the way I like to work."

"Work, schmurk," Sylvia said derisively. "You could charge . . . how much does the clay cost in a piece that size?"

"A few pennies only. Firing runs the price up."

"Don't fire. I'm sure you'd sell a lot. You probably wouldn't have time to pee. The previous minister at your church used to do quick charcoal sketches for a dollar a pose at the Bazaar and he could've had all the portrait work he could handle."

"Sylvia, I just don't work that way."

"I know, I know. But I was thinking that the exposure might lead to more commissions of the kind you do want. I just hate to see your light under a barrel."

Mirelle laid a light admonitory finger on Sylvia's hand.

"I appreciate your partisanship but kindly remember that I have placed sculpture in a few museums."

"So you've told me. But you'd better start doing more. Look, Mirelle," and Sylvia warmed to her subject, "your kids are growing up. Soon they'll not see you for small potatoes unless you yourself are something. They'll go off to college and you'll be left with nothing to do in this big house. You're not an organization type like June Treadway and you're not politically oriented like me. You're an artist and you're going to have to create a market for yourself and find an outlet . . . Oh, God in Heaven, where's my memory?" Sylvia slapped her forehead in exasperation. "If I were more dense. . . . "

"What are you talking about."

Sylvia leaned forward eagerly. "I haven't seen him for years, but Mason Galway and I were very friendly at one time. He now runs a very exclusive gallery in Philadelphia . . . "

"Sylvia, thanks, but there just isn't much demand for sculpture . . . "

"I keep telling you, you create your own demand. Make it a status symbol to own a Martin . . . " Sylvia noticed the change in Mirelle's expression. "What did I say now?"

"For one thing, I don't use Martin professionally."

"So?" Sylvia eyed her friend quizzically.

Mirelle got up and walked over to the window, scrubbing the adhered clay from her palms into a little scrap.

"Sylvia, one reason I don't aggressively seek commissions is because of the trouble it causes with my in-laws. Steve's parents."

"What trouble?" Sylvia's tone invited the full story, and Mirelle knew that evasions would not suffice.

"They don't understand about Ahrt, and they certainly have never understood my propensity for mucking about with kindergarten goo."

"All the more reason why a few respectable sales will make them change their tune. Nothing like money to sway the middleclass mind."

"It's not that, Sylvia. You see, I had established a little reputation as Mary Ellen LeBoyne and then my father died."

"Skeletons in your family closet?" Sylvia was delighted.

"Me."

"You?" Sylvia snorted. "You?" her tone was incredulous.

"My mother was an opera singer, Mary LeBoyne. She married a rich, if untitled, Englishman, Edward Barthan-More in 1920. She never gave up singing. In the spring of

1926, she sat for her portrait, as Tosca actually, for Lajos Neagu, an artist much in vogue in Vienna at the time. I was an unexpected bonus."

Sylvia's eyes widened dramatically in surprise at Mirelle's quiet disclosure.

"Barthan-More was terribly conscious of family honor and dignity . . . "

"Good old Victorian upbringing, no doubt."

"He permitted me to be raised as his child, although he never allowed Mother to have me baptised in the family church." Mirelle grimaced. Barthan-More's stricture had hurt Mary LeBoyne, a staunch Anglican. It had been one of the many mean little ways the man had had of revenging himself under the guise of magnanimity. "I was a blonde baby and there were blue eyes in the family. Unfortunately," and Mirelle tapped one cheekbone, "by the time I was six, it was painfully apparent that I was a . . . changeling."

Sylvia's face darkened with irritation for the unknown Barthan-More.

"In English families of his rank, no child is allowed out of the nursery so I was conveniently kept out of sight of the relatives. I was, however, permitted to accompany my mother when she sang on the Continent because it meant my Nanny had to go along." Mirelle could hear the change in her voice as she mentioned Nanny.

Sylvia caught the harshness. "How convenient to have an indispensable sort of spy."

"Yes, but despite her, Mother and I were very happy together. We could forget her at concerts and rehearsals. Nanny had no ear for music."

"A distinct handicap for an eavesdropper."

"Nothing to eavesdrop on." Mirelle shook her head sadly. "Mother never sought Neagu. Nor any other man."

"Pity!"

"I agree but I think she'd made a bargain with Barthan-More for my sake. At any rate, I never remember her speaking to anyone or of anyone. Backstage, she was known as the Untouchable, or the Icy Irishwoman."

"And all for one small fall from virtue." Sylvia let out a

dramatic sigh. "Thank God I saw the light of day in enlightened times. So what happened to part the charming twosome?"

"The war," Mirelle replied with a shrug, "and me growing old enough to attend public school."

"Looking more and more Hungarrrrian?"

"Yes, and Barthan-More getting nastier and meaner. When the bombing started, my mother's dearest friend and former dresser, Mary Murphy, wrote from the States, offering to take me. Mother accepted."

"And . . . "

"Barthan-More bought a one-way ticket."

"He would."

Mirelle broke the clay fragment in two pieces. "Thirteen months later, Mother was killed in an air raid, singing to the wounded."

She couldn't help the tears that welled up in her eyes. Sylvia's small square hand patted hers gently.

"So you spent the rest of your childhood happily in the States?"

"Yes, with Murph. Five wonderful years."

"How come you lost your English accent?" Sylvia asked in the silence.

"Why should I keep it?" Mirelle replied sourly. "I promised myself a completely new start in the new world, and I assumed my mother's name as a beginning."

"Then what's with the in-laws?" asked Sylvia exasperated.

"My father left me money."

"Father? Neagu, then, not Barthan-More. And what's wrong with money?"

"The *Times* which reported the terms of the will had me named as his 'natural daughter by the late opera singer, Mary LeBoyne.' "

Sylvia groaned. "Reporters! Anything to spice up copy. I can imagine how middleclass morality accepted that choice bit of news coverage."

Mirelle sighed at the memory of those distressing days of scenes and recriminations.

"Steve knew about my birth . . . "

"We are such idealists in the blush of love," Sylvia commented ruefully.

"There'd been no occasion to mention it to his parents."

"Until it was all over the local rag which probably elaborated on the story from the *Times*. So the in-laws were suitably shocked, shamed, appalled and acted in the best tradition of outraged middleclassery."

"I can't blame them. It was an awful shock to me, too. I didn't think that Neagu knew or cared about me."

"Well, he'd've known not to inquire of Barthan-More. What did Steve do?"

Mirelle flushed, not willing to discuss that.

"He didn't side with Mommie and Daddy, did he?"

"That isn't fair."

"Who to? You? His precious prude parents?" Sylvia flounced up out of the chair, furious. "And, for that kind of . . . " words failed her so she waved her arms about eloquently, "you've deliberately neglected your talents?"

"I haven't neglected them."

"Well, you sure haven't cultivated them."

"I don't want any notoriety, Sylvia. It makes my life too difficult."

"I'd never have taken you for a coward, Mirelle Martin." Sylvia flared up, the accusation flung out and then instantly retracted. "No, Mirelle Martin isn't but Mary LeBoyne sure isn't pushing. And I think it's downright asinine for you to stifle the contribution you could make because of an anachronistic irregularity of birth. Why must you be saddled with your parents' sin? Particularly in today's permissive society? For God's sake, as an artist, any sort of deviation is permitted. Encouraged!"

"That's part of it, too," Mirelle said, doggedly resisting.

Sylvia regarded her scornfully. "You mean, your dear in-laws are afraid that immersion in the artistic world would result in your descent into promiscuity? Hah! I got news for them. Most women don't need parental example to stray from the marital bed. It's so fashionable to be unfaithful." Sylvia fumed silently, waiting for Mirelle's response. "Well, are you going to wait until all the dear in-laws are six feet under before you walk out into the light of day? Or is it Steve you're afraid of?"

Mirelle eyed her levelly. "No, it's not Steve."

"Yourself, then? Do you fear your inherited tendencies?" Sylvia flung the sarcasm as a challenge.

Mirelle turned back to the little pig, needlessly smoothing the spine with her thumb. "No, it's a question of timing, Sylvia. I don't think this is the right time for me to start."

"Not the right time to start?" Sylvia gestured expansively from the Lucy to the Howell head and then the sick pig. "You've already started. You, inside you, is telling you to start with these! I'm disgusted with you, Mirelle. Lucy Farnoll would be, too. You don't deserve the right to sculpt her, not if that's your attitude. 'It's not the right time!' Ha!" Sylvia's acid scorn seared Mirelle.

"It's not that I wouldn't like to . . . particularly for Lucy," Mirelle began tentatively, "but I've children now. What if that story got repeated?"

"What story? Oh! That you're a bastard? Kids use that word so much on the playgrounds it's lost its original connotation. One of your in-laws' arguments no doubt." When Mirelle looked up troubled, Sylvia went on. "Thought so. Just what a petty narrow mind would spew out. Look, Mirelle," and Sylvia's manner changed abruptly to entreaty, "you've got a talent that I'd give my eyeteeth to possess. A genuine talent with a sensitivity and perception far superior to contemporary plaster hacks. Part of that sensitivity and perceptiveness is a result of that irregularity in birth, the drek you suffered as a child at Barthan-More's hands, even your arrival here in the States. I'll bet your father made that bequest to dare you to do something!"

"He never knew . . . "

Sylvia raised her eyebrows. "Want to bet on that? After all, he knew he had a daughter, and he must have known where you lived to have left you money in the will. Figure it out. And you have no right, do you understand, *no right*, to deny that gift. Besides, I doubt anyone in this decadent age would bother with a triviality like bastardy. If they do, make it work for you!" Sylvia chuckled maliciously, then returned to exhortations. "Look, Mirelle, I'll bug you until you do get work shown if only to get me off your back. Until you finish the Lucy and . . . hey, hey, what're the tears for?"

Bewildered by her own reaction, Mirelle felt the tears spilling onto her cheeks, her throat too tight for speech. Instantly Sylvia knelt beside her, a comforting arm across her shoulders.

"Honey, don't you see? If you were a half-baked pot thrower, it wouldn't matter. But when you can create a tribute like the Lucy, with so much love, you can't just ignore it. You can't. Not when you loved Lucy so much and when she wanted so much for you. Because that's what she said in that note to me. That she'd come across a really fine woman sculptor who needed to be cossetted and encouraged."

That made Mirelle cry harder into Sylvia's shoulder. She wept for her lonely mother, for the father she had never known, for all her early aspirations sublimated in childbearing and husband care, for all the terrible lonely hours when she had wished for success to compensate for scorn and neglect, for the emptiness and betrayal. Sylvia made no attempt to stop her crying until Mirelle looked up apologetically and saw, with amazement and surprise, that Sylvia had tears in her eyes.

"Why are you crying?"

"For you, you loon," and Sylvia smiled at Mirelle with great and fond affection, taking her by the shoulders and giving her a little shake. "And to think you've been squirming all this time on a bed of in-law nails!"

The vision projected made Mirelle laugh and she dried her eyes resolutely on a clay rag.

"You're a real sight now," was Sylvia's comment. "You wash your face and I'll hot up the coffee."

Mirelle washed her face in the laundry room, recalling that last time she'd done so.

"Confession is so good for the soul," said Sylvia, returning with the steaming pot. "I'd left the kettle on low so it didn't take long. Now, there's another minor detail which I feel I should impart to you as the ultimate in reassurances.

"As you may have noticed, G.F. is a great one for the skirts . . . however, we won't go into any detail today," and Sylvia took a long breath. "Suffice it to say, he is. However, tomcat though he may be, he also knows when not to press his luck with a gal. He also knows who's screwing whom, for he belongs to all the best clubs. If you think women are gossips, you should hear men!" Sylvia rolled her eyes. "It's G.F.'s informed opinion that you not only haven't, but won't. He heard all about it from Bill Townshend, Ed Eberhardt and Red Cargill."

Aghast, Mirelle stared at Sylvia. "I never told a soul . . . "

"Of course you didn't. But they did. When I told G.F. that you sculpted, well, guess what he said?" Dutifully Mirelle shook her head. "Well, he said, 'so that's where the fire goes?' " Sylvia's smile broadened as she watched the effect of her words on Mirelle. "Ah, honey, you got sold a lousy bill of goods. You're a big girl now. You're not minor, middleclass league. You can be big time stuff. You always were, so get with it. Show the Lucy and . . . show Lucy."

Mirelle listened with one sane rebuttal running like a descant around Sylvia's unexpectedly impassioned arguments.

"Sylvia, I'm never going to shake the world."

"So you're no da Vinci or Michelangelo, who cares?" Sylvia gave a massive shrug. "And the Lucy's no Pietà, just a good friend of mine, but your work is no bundle of wires tied together with perforated metal strips. It's not holey blobs of concrete that resemble tortured bookends. There's humor in that silly little pig: great love in the Lucy and in that study of Howell. There's something . . . I'm running out of words. At any rate, I think it's worth goosing you. And besides," she cocked her head cheerfully, "I'm fresh out of causes. You realize, Mirelle, that my only talent is causes!"

They were facing each other, Mirelle on her work stool, Sylvia on the chair she had drawn up, leaning towards Mirelle with only the work table and the half finished sickpig between them.

"Your talent is caring when others can't be bothered," Mirelle said. "You're like Lucy in that respect."

"If I were half the woman Lucy Farnoll was . . . " Sylvia began with a bitter edge to her voice. Then she slapped her knees to indicate a change of mood and pushed herself off the chair. "Well, promise me this, Mirelle, if Mason Galway, that gallery friend of mine, wants to exhibit your work, you'll agree?"

Mirelle decided that that was a safe enough promise.

Sylvia waggled a finger in her face. "You don't fool me, Mirelle. I know what you're thinking. That he won't buy. I bet he will. So there, too. Good God, it's nearly one o'clock. Goodbye!" And she dashed for the front door, slamming it behind her.

Mirelle sat still for a long moment, looking at the closed door, Sylvia's arguments reverberating in her head. She smiled, genuinely affected by such loyalty. Then she turned back to the sickpig. That night she dreamt of the hands for the first time.

CHAPTER ELEVEN

TWO DAYS LATER, Mirelle brought the finished pig, some chrysanthemums from her garden and a pan of butterscotch brownies over to the Howells. When she drove up, a black Mercedes 420 was parked in the driveway. She hesitated about intruding but she had cut the flowers and the brownies wouldn't last long if returned to her house.

Margaret, looking harried, answered the door and made an effusive gesture of relief.

"He's impossible," she said in a stage whisper, jerking her thumb towards the music room. "His agent is here, Dave Andorri, and Dad simply isn't well but he won't listen to me or Dave."

Mirelle exhibited the sickpig to Margaret and the girl let out a whoop of laughter, suppressing it quickly in her hand.

"Well, Margaret? Who's badgering me now?" demanded Jamie from the music room. Mirelle could hear the rumble of another male voice, evidently placating the sick man.

Mirelle gave Margaret the brownies and the flowers, and walked in. She had a quick glance at the heavy-headed, grey-haired man sitting on the couch and then marched up to

Howell who was slouched on the piano bench. He had shaved so part of the similarity between pig and man was eliminated. His expression of dissatisfaction, ill-health and gauntness, however, was perfectly captured in the porcine face. Jamie had risen from the piano bench as she entered. He sat down again as Mirelle placed the sickpig on the music rack of the grand piano. His eyes widened, his jaw fell open, and he began to sputter with indignation. The agent, who had also risen at Mirelle's entrance, had a view not only of the pig but of Howell's reaction. He burst into laughter, the contagious kind which can set off an entire room.

Howell, struggling against the infection of Andorri's laugh, his discomfiture and convalescent irritability, gave up and joined in wheezingly. Margaret, after watching apprehensively until she saw how her father was taking the joke, visibly relaxed.

"If you think, for one moment," Howell managed to say between wheezings, "that *this* is what I commissioned, you're crazy." He began to cough violently.

"Of course not," she replied blandly. "But when *my* children are ill and disagreeable, I found that if they had their 'sick' faces in front of them, they remembered to recover their good humor. The other nice thing about sickpigs is that they are breakable. It is so satisfying to temperamental patients to hear things shatter."

"Oh ho," said Andorri with a resonant crow, "she has you there, Jim. I'm Dave Andorri and you can only be Mirelle Martin," he went on, warmly shaking hands with her. "Your entrance couldn't have been better timed, Mrs. Martin. This idiot has been trying to prove to me that he's completely recovered. All he's succeeded in proving is how sick he still is."

Howell slithered around on the piano bench, the pig in one hand.

"The next time I'm ill-tempered, Margaret, just hand me my pig," he said, his long face repentant.

"Oh, you're all right, Dad. You just aren't as well as you think you are. I'm just scared you'll get sick again and not make the concert on the 18th. That's the important one, isn't it?"

When Howell graciously waved Mirelle to a seat, she could see that his hand was shaking and his complexion pasty.

"How about that tea you were threatening me with, Margaret? She makes a fair cuppa. Mirelle, will you join us?"

"If you promise to go back to bed immediately afterwards," Mirelle said, ruthlessly determined to extract that promise.

"But Dave just got here."

"And Dave can just go," the agent replied, getting to his feet, "unless you promise. Mrs. Martin is quite right. I'll stay for a cuppa to cheer me for the drive back to town. And we'll hear no more about how well you are. For that matter, I can get Nichols if I give Madame Nealy sufficient notice and enough rehearsal time."

"I've told you, Dave," Howell said, setting his mouth angrily, "that I'll be well enough to play for Madame Nealy on the 18th, but I simply cannot leave everything . . . "

"That's the last time we go round that argument, Jim," Dave replied with equal force. "Maggie, the tea!"

"I'd just brewed it," the girl said in Mirelle's direction, "and Mrs. Martin has brought us brownies to go with it," she added as she ran down the hall to the kitchen.

Howell glared at Mirelle. "How suburban! Brownies to the sick friend!" He appealed to the ceiling of the room.

"I wouldn't dream of forcing such suburbiana on you then," Mirelle said, blinking her eyes at him and turning to smile with exaggerated sweetness on the agent. "Mr. Andorri, Margaret and I will eat them all."

Margaret reappeared with the tray, depositing it on the music-strewn table.

"For God's sake, Margaret, watch what you're doing," Jamie said with sharp irritability.

"Don't be difficult," Mirelle suggested, motioning to Margaret to raise the tray so she could clear the music. "If you didn't spread out like an overweight rhino . . . "

When Howell opened his mouth to make a sharp reply, Mirelle pointed at the figure in his hand. He burst out laughing.

"You're right. I'm impossible. Forgive me, daughter dear. I must have been snapping your head off all day without realizing it."

"Well, not all day," Margaret said demurely and glanced up, surprised at the laughter from Mirelle and Dave. "As a matter of fact, this morning you had me wishing that you had been laid out as a corpse!" She made the confession with asperity and then, seeing his contrite expression, ran quickly around the table to plant an affectionate kiss on his cheek. "But you're never sick, Dad, so you've had no practice at being good and that cough would drive anyone up the wall."

She rumpled his hair, against his vociferous complaints, and then sat down, decorously, to pour the tea.

Howell fingercombed his hair down and settled his dressing robe over his shoulders. He snatched a brownie from the plate before Mirelle could carry out her threat and chewed it smugly as he eyed her.

"That cough's the worst aspect of this bronchial pneumonia," he admitted. "I feel as if the lining is coming out of my throat."

"He had a coughing fit just as you got here, Mrs. Martin. Brutal," said Dave sympathetically.

"Leaving me weak and wretched." Howell assumed a dramatically limp posture.

"Ha. Years of riotous living have caught up with you," Mirelle said with cool disdain. "Bucketing around the States from one concert hall after another."

"All of them drafty," and Howell jerked his thumb at Andorri. "He picks them especially for the drafts."

"What about long underwear? Or leg warmers?" Mirelle suggested with mock concern and Margaret giggled at the thought of her fashionable father wearing either.

"I can get my hands on a reliable portable heater," Dave made his contribution solicitously.

"You're cruel to a sick and ailing man," Howell said, hand to his forehead.

"Not at all," Mirelle and Dave said in unison. "Just trying to be helpful."

Howell snorted. Then Dave leaned over to examine the pig more closely, chuckling as he inspected it.

"That's delightful, Mrs. Martin. Would never have expected porkers in Jim's genealogy." Howell made an attempt to snatch it back.

"You might have used a more elegant animal," Howell told Mirelle when Dave returned it. "But it will remind me to maintain dignity at all times."

"Has Will Martin been in to see you recently?"

"Today," and Howell rubbed his hip.

"He came first thing," and Margaret giggled, "and warned Dad not to get up."

Dave was on his feet instantly. "If I'd known that, I wouldn't have allowed you downstairs, Jim."

"Don't be an ass, Dave."

"You're the ass," replied the agent with some heat. "I'm glad you spoke, Mags. I'm serious, Jim. You can't take any risks. Bronchial pneumonia is no joke."

"Is your fever down?" Mirelle asked for Jamie was beginning to frown at the harassment.

"Only yesterday," Margaret said when he didn't answer.

Dave took Howell's cup from his hand, gave it to Margaret and, firmly taking the sick man by the elbow, propelled him out of the music room and up the stairs.

"If I'm your manager, James Howell, I'm your manager. And I am managing you back into your bed, you pig-faced *espèce de canard!*"

Dave might be shorter than James Howell by several inches but he had considerably more bulk which he used to coerce his victim. Margaret sighed with relief as she saw the brute force was working where tact had not.

"Honest, Mrs. Martin, I don't think Dad realizes just how sick he's been. Of course, my opinion is a child's. Just at the wrong time he thinks I'm still nine. Well, I'm nineteen and old enough to take care of him now."

"Mirelle!" James Howell roared from his room and the effort started him coughing.

"Got any honey?" Mirelle asked Margaret as she pulled the girl to the kitchen. "Be right there, Jamie."

"He's got a cough mixture," the girl said.

"Well, it's not effective and this always works with my kids. It coats the throat tissue." She had put several teaspoons of honey in a glass, added lemon juice, and stirred. "Add some whiskey later on. That'll improve the taste."

Margaret was dubious but she followed Mirelle up the stairs. Andorri had got Howell back into bed, under the blankets and propped up against the pillows, but the invalid was still sulking.

"Here, try this. Always works," she said, sitting on the bed and giving him a spoonful.

"You are, my dear, a continual surprise package. Nostrums and sculpture?"

"Why not? Feeding sick cranky children requires the knack," she said, and when Jamie opened his mouth to protest, she tilted the spoon in so deftly, he had to swallow or choke, "very similar to plastering."

Dave Andorri guffawed loudly. "You've met your match, Jim."

"Ungrateful wench. Never again will I extend a helping hand to a female in distress," Howell said and then realized that his voice was less rasping. "Even more reprehensible is your distressing tendency to be right!" He reached behind him for a pillow to throw at Mirelle but she ran nimbly to the door, waving goodbye.

As she drove home, Mirelle was unexpectedly satisfied with the day, a state of mind which she'd not experienced in months. She'd been vaguely disoriented for so long that she couldn't quite pin down why her mood was improved. To be sure, she thoroughly enjoyed matching wits with Howell. He had such an atrocious sense of humor. She was pleased with the reception of the sickpig which should give Margaret a useful talisman. Everything contributed to her sense of euphoria.

She resolved to maintain the mood, even if the children

got to wrangling. Not even the sight of a letter from her in-laws put a damper on her exhilaration. As usual, the letter was addressed only to Steve. Not since the terrible fight in Allentown had she ever written directly to her mother-in-law. She propped the letter up on the hall table with a disdainful sniff. It couldn't prick her mood as she set about getting supper, an especially good supper.

When Steve's car turned in the drive, she paused long enough to check her hair and for any stray smudges on her face. She surprised herself by turning her cheek for Steve's home-coming kiss, a habit which lately he'd dropped.

"Say, what got into you?" he asked, hugging her.

"Oh, just a good day."

"Any reason it's a good day? More commissions or something?"

"No."

"God, you're coy," he said and swatted her proprietarily on the hip, his eyes still wary.

She laughed and rolled her eyes, and he echoed her laughter.

"It's good to see you like this, hon. You sure you aren't hiding something? Like an expensive new dress?"

She laughed again at that, for she was unlikely to buy expensive dresses at any time. Expensive art equipment, yes. "No," she told him, tolerant of his density, "just for a change, I feel right with the world."

"For a real change," Steve agreed. "Oh ho, mail from ma." He picked up the letter with an apprehensive glance at her.

"Not even that can erase the smile from my sunny face."

"Well, well." He slit the envelope and, as he read the contents, his hand slowly rose to rub the back of his neck.

That signified bad news, Mirelle knew, as she went to put dinner on the table.

The kids came clattering up from the TV room at her call and noisily forwarded the conversational ball at the dinner table. Steve joined in easily enough, so Mirelle decided that she must have been mistaken about the import of the letter.

In fact, she forgot all about it until after the children were in bed.

"What was on your mother's mind?" she asked as Steve fussed with his amplifier.

"Has one of the kids been fiddling with this?" he demanded irritably. "It's all off."

"I don't think so."

"What about the maid?"

"It was all right last night."

"You know how she dusts."

"She comes on Tuesday and this is Friday so it couldn't be Maria."

"Damn it!"

"So what was on your mother's mind?" Mirelle repeated, certain of the source of his aggravation.

Steve rocked back on his heels, still fiddling with the hi-fi settings. "We're getting a state visit."

"Oh no. When?"

"The 10th. They've decided to celebrate Dad's retirement by spending the winter in Orlando, Florida. You know, where the Randolphs went for so many years."

"Naturally it would be Orlando then," Mirelle replied blandly. The Randolphs were a stuffy, pompous family, important in Allentown. Mrs. Martin Senior quoted the Randolph authorized opinion on everything from Heinz ketchup to the state of the spring weather.

"Oh, come off it, Mirelle," Steve said in a sour tone of voice.

Mirelle shrugged. "How long will they be here? You know the Church Bazaar is the 12th and 13th. I have to be there."

"That's right," Steve said with a heartfelt groan. They sat quietly, deep in private thought for several long minutes. Then Steve shook his head. "I don't want you to renege on the Bazaar."

A wave of relief washed over Mirelle. It wasn't so much that she realized how much she had looked forward to participating in the affair as the fact that Steve was deliberately encouraging her in something they both knew that his mother would detest.

He unfolded the letter again. "She says 'a few days', so I guess that'll include the 12th and 13th." He got to his feet abruptly. "Damn it, Mary Ellen, things have been so much, . . . much better between us since I got off the road and you started this latest sculpting kick. I mean, like today, with you feeling a good mood over nothing." He leaned over her chair. "You're more like the girl I married than you've been since the kids started coming." He made a fist and gently pushed at her chin. "She's my mother and all, but hell, it's our life and our marriage."

Mirelle reached up to put her arms around his neck and drew his head down so that their foreheads touched.

"Steve, if you'll back me up this time, your mother won't be able to upset us the way she usually does."

Steve flushed and made a move to break her hold. She pulled him back.

"Steve, I've allowed your mother to crucify me and I've watched you standing squarely in the middle, not knowing which way to turn. You know that the only thing I've been able to do is shut up and put up. But I'm warning you, Steve. I'm not going to shut up this time, and I'm not going to put up."

Steve jerked away then.

"My birth may have been irregular," Mirelle went on resolutely, "but at least I spared us both another set of in-laws."

Steve whirled sharply, his mouth opened in angry surprise.

"Which is just as well," she continued calmly, rising from the chair, "because, as I remember my mother, she could outmanage yours any day. And I understand that my father's temper was usually at hurricane force. I really must be a throwback to a mild ancestor."

"You're one surprise after another today," Steve said, wonderingly.

"No, I just came to the conclusion that I've been existing in a vacuum for the last ten years. I'll be damned if I'll pull the hole in over my head again just because your mother's coming."

Steve blinked at her uncertainly. Then his face cleared. He encircled her waist, holding her tightly against him. As he began to kiss her with rough passion, she realized two things: he wasn't thinking of his mother and he wouldn't think about either the coming visit or Mirelle's threat. Only it wasn't a threat: it was a promise. How would Steve handle that? In bed?

That night, the hands came back into her dreams, more clearly, more insistently, with the tugging and clawing, the restless fingers nipping just short of her precarious perch, wherever that was, until one strong hand grabbed her shoulder out of the threateningly vague background. She was shaken and shaken until reality overthrew the miasma of dream and the hand, accompanied by Steve's urgent voice, woke her to the next morning.

CHAPTER TWELVE

THE DEPRESSION evoked by the nightmare stayed with her, intruding with uneasy flashbacks through the business of getting breakfast and shooing the children off to school.

Steve had come down in fine spirits, all set up after the previous night's passion. He called her a sleepyhead, cheerfully leered at her, and failed to notice her subdued mood. He kissed her a lingering goodbye, bopping her jaw tenderly, and left her, emitting an irritatingly gay whistle.

It hadn't been lack of satisfaction in sex last night, Mirelle thought, trying to counteract her depression. Steve had made rather inspired love and she had responded gladly. In fact, Mirelle told herself, she ought to be reassured by his passionate embraces, particularly on a day when he'd heard from his mother. Maybe, and it was just possible, this time he would align himself with his wife.

No, Mirelle decided, her depression stemmed from those damned nightmarish hands. Maybe she ought to get a book on dream interpretations, particularly since she had ones that played back all the time. She sighed and poured herself another cup of coffee.

Why couldn't Steve have been an orphan, too? In the early days of their marriage, before they'd made that disastrous move to Allentown, they'd been so happy and she'd be able to kid with him the way she could with Jamie.

Mirelle smiled to herself, remembering those courting days. She'd been doing display figures, models of Broadway stars for a music store window, advertising record albums of the popular hit shows. Scarcely the sculpting she'd intended to do, but, after Murph had died, there hadn't been any more money for training. She'd taken whatever work she could get, and was at least lucky to be doing some form of sculpting.

Wouldn't Murph have made mincemeat of Mother Martin? Mirelle snickered, imagining such a confrontation. Wow! would the sparks have flown! Mary Murphy, to quote herself, was 'knee high to a whiskey bottle and weaned on one.' She and Mary Margaret LeBoyne had been born and raised in Naas, had loved each other as only kindred souls could. They were as opposite as the supple birch and the hardy gorse, but they understood each other perfectly. When Mary Margaret LeBoyne had been launched in her music career, she'd sent for Mary Murphy to join her. Murph had stayed with Mary until they'd quarreled over Mary's marriage to Edward Barthan-More.

"Your mother made more than one mistake, m'dearie," Murph had once told Mirelle. "But she'd her heart that set on security! She'd seen the desperate mess others made of spending while the money rolled in, and dying in the gutter when the career vanished. Oh, I grant you, Edward was in love with her . . . like he was with all the things he owned. A greedy man was Edward and desperate greedy for Mary Margaret. He bound her to him in bands of his gold and respectability, you might say.

"Now mind, your mother wasn't the gilded cage sort. I think that's why your own father attracted her so. The free artistic spirit, I believe he would say," and while Murph had not approved of Edward Barthan-More, she was even more opposed to Lajos Neagu. "Still, Lou had that about him would have kept your mother free, and like as not, she'd've been singing till she died. Real singing, not that forced social stuff. The Red Lark of Ireland she was, darlin', and when she was happy, oh, how her voice would soar."

The oasis of calm and contentment with Murph had been shattered by Mary LeBoyne's death in an air raid. The news had come in a very curt note from Barthan-More's secretary, with a request that, as soon as Mary LeBoyne Barthan-More's personal estate had been settled, no further communication would be tolerated between the house of Barthan-More and his wife's irregular relation.

Murph had not been one for hiding from life's more callous blows and she had not shielded the teen-aged Mirelle from this one. Her indignation had been scathing and she had written a scorching reply to Barthan-More, announcing her intention of legally adopting Mary Ellen LeBoyne. A small packet of jewels and a bank draft eventually arrived with no accompanying note. After much deliberation and considerable thought, Murph and Mirelle decided to sell the more valuable pieces of jewelry, using the funds to put Mirelle through a good art school. And, when the war was over, perhaps additional training abroad.

Murph's terminal illness took the remainder of those savings. Mirelle was only sorry that she had spent so carelessly during her school days.

Despite her excellent intentions and repeated promises, Murph never did set in train the legal formalities of adoption. Mirelle was twenty-three when Steve Martin happened down Madison Avenue as she was arranging the display in the windows. He had stood watching her until his interested stare got on her nerves. His expression was a combination of hopeful boyishness and cynical pessimism. As he was a tall, attractive young man, she'd been flattered despite her annoyance. His attempts to attract her attention had also drawn the typical New York crowd of the bored curious.

When she had finally arranged the display according to the draft layout, he'd applauded loudly, and pressed his face against the glass, inviting her to coffee at the top of his lungs. She'd shaken her head disdainfully, all too aware of the delighted spectators. Steve had made a pantomine of a breaking heart, much like the male figure which she had just edged into a slightly more esthetic angle. Then Steve had dropped to one knee, in full sight of the amused audience. Horrified, Mirelle had motioned him frantically to get up and go away. To her surprise he did so, shoulders drooping, expression lugubrious with rejection. He'd been so funny. However, as she stepped out of the window in the store proper, there was Steve, leaning against the wall, grinning at his deceit.

She had absolutely no intention of doing more than drink a cup of coffee with him, but he'd left with her name and phone number. She had had no idea, either, of getting serious about anyone. She'd planned her life. She was going to amount to something. Marriage had stifled her mother's career. Marriage was not going to have a chance to ruin hers. Yes, Mirelle had had many plans, and not one of them included a phenomenon like Steven Martin. A year later they were married. While Steve went to college, Mirelle worked. She was five months pregnant with Roman when Steve, overwhelmed by his new responsibilities, took a job in his home-town.

Then things started to fall apart, reflected Mirelle. All in the name of mother-love.

Her previous contacts with Steve's family had been mercifully short, confined to long weekends when everyone had been delighted to meet Steve's stunning, if foreign-looking, wife who was so good about working to help Steve get his degree. There had been slight doubts whether or not Mirelle should have got pregnant so soon, 'with so many modern theories about', as Mother Martin sweetly put it. The crowning blow had been her inheritance and that had torn down the veil of hypocrisy. Mirelle was sourly informed that she had 'stolen' Steve away from Nancy Lou Randolph, (whose father owned the largest hardware store in town), who was everything a wife for a young up-and-coming salesman could be (particularly one who would work in papa's store).

Steve, insecure enough and wanting his parents' approval, had not known how to deal with his mother's unexpected reversals and accusations. He had been proud of Mirelle: viewed his imminent fatherhood as the outward display of his other achievements, and now Mirelle had brought shame on him and his family. He had tried to defend his wife at first, but his mother's strong personality, her infallible belief in her own judgments, and a long habit of obedience made him a poor advocate for Mirelle.

The estrangement that followed had not been all Steve's fault. Mirelle could see that now. Because of the guilt which she'd always been made to feel over her irregular birth in the Barthan-More nursery, Mirelle had acquiesced at just the time when she should have continued to fight. In the first place, she'd been stunned by the bequest, since she'd never had any communication with Lajos Neagu, though Mary Murphy had told her that he knew of her birth. She was sick with her first pregnancy and bitterly hurt by her parents-in-law's violent reaction to the 'notoriety'. Mirelle never did think that there'd been any more than the natural curiosity of people when they heard of someone inheriting money. The way Mother Martin had carried on suggested that Mirelle was going to be forced to wear a scarlet letter, or run out of Allentown on a rail.

Well, such thoughts were not clearing the breakfast table. Mirelle ruefully reflected that yesterday's lovely mood was completely dissipated. "Had I felt like that today, I'd've overthrown the shadows of five mothers-in-law," she muttered as she rose.

"Mothers-in-law?" asked Sylvia, whirling in the door. "Oh, you are lazy today. I expected to find you elbow deep in someone's head."

"No, I'm recovering from the shock of hearing that my in-laws arrive on the 10th."

"Eeek! What vile timing. And if your mother-in-law is anything like my mother . . . Really, I can't blame G.F.," Sylvia rattled on as she helped Mirelle stack the dishes. "Oh, dear," and she nearly dropped the cups she had just nested. "She's the one who doesn't want you artistic?"

Mirelle nodded, grimacing.

"And she'll be here during the Bazaar?" Sylvia made an

unhappy sound against her teeth. "Well, coffee is indicated and we'll kick this around a little."

"I know what I'd like to kick around."

"Naughty, naughty. Respect for the aged and decrepit, please. We will take steps. Yes. We will plan a campaign. Say, what was Steve's reaction to the impending invasion?"

"Well," and Mirelle could feel herself blushing as memories of the previous night's bedgames came to mind.

"That's using your head, gal," Sylvia said with a bawdy laugh. "You're one up on his mother right there."

"Sylvia, don't be so earthy."

"Why not? It gets me somewhere. At any rate, Mirelle, what was his reaction? To his mother's coming, I mean."

Mirelle explained.

"You said 'in-laws'. What about papa?"

"Oh, Dad Martin is very nice but he gave up struggling against Marian years ago."

"Course of least resistance? Did he take part in holding the bar sinister over your head?"

"No," Mirelle grudgingly admitted. On the other hand, Dad Martin hadn't said anything or done anything, just stood there in the dining room on the night of the worst vituperation, listening to his wife and daughter-in-law.

"This will be my Cause for December," said Sylvia, rubbing her hands together. "I've given up putting Christ back into Christmas. They were displaying Christmas wrappings in the drug store before Hallowe'en. That's the end!"

"Sylvia, I don't want you to do anything . . . " Mirelle stopped abruptly.

"Now, my dear, have you ever known me to do anything?" Sylvia began, all charm and guile.

"Yes."

"All right, all right. Look, I promise I'll be very circumspect but play along with me."

"Only if you tell me what you plan to do."

Sylvia regarded her with a deceptively innocent expression. " 'There are nine and sixty ways of constructing tribal lays, and every single one of them is right.' If I may quote Kipling?"

"Not in front of my mother-in-law. She's reactionary."

"I don't doubt it. Look, I can't stay any longer this morning. I've got an endless boring organizational meeting. Are you going to get in any work at all today?"

"No, I think I'll take the day off and get squared away for the coming invasion."

Sylvia dashed off, leaving Mirelle feeling not only slightly breathless but considerably dubious about any confrontation between her good friend and her bad mother-in-law. However, Sylvia's visit had dispelled the last of the nightmare's gloom, and Mirelle finished the necessary tidying. She took down the curtains in the boys' rooms to be cleaned for the state visit. She dropped them off in the dry cleaners on her way into town to the one fish market that she trusted and ran into a traffic jam. She took the first side street and drove back ways until she got out to the highway again.

Seeing that her route would not take her near Jamie's, she deflected to swing by and see how effective the sickpig was. She turned into a wooded area on a short leg of the triangle to Howell's house when she noticed a white Cadillac parked in a turn-off. She got a flash of two heads through the back window, kissing close. It wasn't until she was in Howell's driveway that she realized why the car had been familiar. It had been G.F. in that car, and the woman's head had not been Sylvia's. Mirelle slammed on the brakes in unaccustomed violence.

"Something your best friend doesn't tell you," she muttered, cursing whatever had prompted her to take that particular road at that particular time.

"Hi, Mrs. Martin, come join us for lunch," Margaret said in greeting.

"Oh, good heavens. I'd forgotten all about lunch. I'll come back later."

"Please don't do anything of the kind," Margaret said, quickly drawing her in. "I'm just setting the table."

"I'll help."

"You could tell Dad that his five minutes are up now. He's under the sun lamp. He wants to get rid of that pasty pig expression."

Mirelle stopped abruptly on the threshold of Jamie's bedroom. Howell was stripped to the waist, lying on his back under the glare of the sunlamp, pads protecting his eyes. His face, bleached further by the bright light, was in complete repose and the line of his mouth was sad. His hands, one across his waist, the other palm up on the pillow behind his head, looked strangely strengthless and lax. In contrast, the well developed pectoral muscles, the rounding of the bicep and forearm, the arch of his chest were those of an athlete, not a musician. His body looked considerably younger than his face. Mirelle experienced a curious disorientation looking at him. Quickly and quietly, she retreated a few steps from the door.

"Margaret says you've baked long enough on that side," she called as if making a first approach. "You'll be tasty for lunch." *I'm as bad as an old lady,* she told herself and was further dismayed to see that he only turned out the lamp at her warning. As she entered his room, he was removing the eye pads.

"I'm trying to approximate the coy shade of pink my sickpig wears," he said, reaching for his pajama top. Fascinated, Mirelle watched the play of muscles across the top of his arm as he slipped into a shirt.

"Anything is better than that underdone pasty effect you've been sporting," she said blithely. For heavens' sake, Steve has a better physique. Why should she get palpitations over Jamie's?

Jamie eyed her. "Actually I do feel better today. Your lemon-honey is a lot more effective than that $15.00 glue Martin prescribed. I slept all night." He shrugged into a dressing robe. "As a reward, Margaret is allowing me downstairs for lunch. Also to keep peace and support the legend that I am recovering." He slipped his hand under Mirelle's elbow and guided her downstairs. "You seem subdued this morning, not your usual caustic self."

Mirelle wrinkled her nose. "My mother-in-law is visiting us."

"Why didn't you marry an orphan? You did as much for

him. But I can see how it would dampen even the most normally merry temperament."

"Implying I am dour by nature?"

"Soured by nature, at any rate."

"Takes one to know one."

"Margaret," said Jamie very sweetly as he seated Mirelle at the table, "do serve Mirelle some of those mushrooms that killed the dog."

"You mean the ones you like so much?" asked his daughter in the same saccharine tone, as she placed a steaming pot roast on the table.

"You are all against me," Jamie said and then sniffed deeply. "So this is what has been tantalizing me all morning. The size of it I'll be eating pot roast for days."

"Exactly my plan," Margaret replied sunnily. "I've got to get back to college Sunday, Mrs. Martin, with midterms coming up. I've arranged for the cleaning lady to come in twice this week."

"You mean I've got to eat pot roast for a week?" Jamie was outraged.

"I'll supply you with calf's foot jelly."

"Thank you so much!"

Mirelle caught the unspoken request in Margaret's eyes and nodded reassuringly.

"Such devotion ought to please your egocentric soul, James Howell. Instead of which, you complain," she said, and took a bite. "Whereas you have no legitimate ones. This is very good and will be hot, cold or nine days old." Mirelle bowed elaborately to the cook.

Jamie had tentatively placed a morsel in his mouth and his expression altered to one of pleasure. "I haven't been favored with anything like this the whole time I've been ill."

"An invalid requires a suitable diet. How could you have tasted anything through that bronchitis," Mirelle said.

"I used a Family Circle recipe, Mrs. Martin, to be sure it would come out all right. I'm not a very good cook."

"Nonsense," Mirelle said in a tone to discourage further disclaimers. "I think the cook needs a raise."

Jamie choked on his mouthful and Margaret giggled, hiding her face in her napkin.

"I suspect collusion," Jamie said. "Nursing an ailing parent comes under the dutiful daughter clause in our relationship, Margaret, and this is the first time I've had occasion to exercise it."

However, he found it impossible to maintain his pretense of indignation with the two women smiling at him, so he changed the subject completely by asking Mirelle if he could still register to vote in next year's senatorial election.

"They've started early," Margaret told Mirelle. "We've already heard two sides of the story . . . "

"Both sounding remarkably similar to my apolitical ears," Jamie said cynically.

"Sylvia's involved in politics on the local level," Mirelle said and mentioned the referendum coming up in the Brandywine Hundred.

Time passed so quickly that it was half-past two before Mirelle realized it and hurriedly excused herself. Jamie saw her to the door as Margaret started to clear the table.

"Something else is bothering you, Mirelle, and I don't think it's the mother-in-law."

"Am I so transparent?"

Jamie eyed her keenly for a long moment. "I shouldn't have said 'bother'. 'Changed' is accurate. For the better."

"Just the other side of the worm." She ducked away before he could delay her. She waved as she backed out of the driveway but the sight of his Thunderbird reminded her of the white Cadillac and G.F. Esterhazy.

Mr. Howell is far too acute, Mirelle said to herself. I must remember to keep him away from my mother-in-law.

CHAPTER THIRTEEN

BETWEEN CLEANING her house and finishing the figurines for the bazaar, Mirelle kept herself too busy to worry about G.F. Esterhazy. Sylvia phoned several times for a quick chat because she had 'allowed' herself to be drafted into the major Referendum opposition group.

"If I spent half as much time opposing the damned thing as I do smarming people up, it'd be defeated hands down. There is no 'popular' mandate for this stupidity," and when she realized that Mirelle's remarks were mere courtesy, "but then political action is not your long suit so I'm boring you. Goodbye."

Before Mirelle could remonstrate, Sylvia had rung off and for a long moment, Mirelle worried whether or not to phone Sylvia back and apologize. She did dial the number but the line was busy. The next day Sylvia rang at her usual time with a crudely funny joke which she'd acquired and had to share with Mirelle. Combining a shopping expedition with a visit to Jamie, she found him snappish with convalescence but slowly regaining his strength.

Determined to leave nothing to chance, Mirelle organized every detail of the in-laws' visit. She decided to precut the small blocks of clay which she would need for modeling at the Bazaar. Most of her figures were glazed and ready, the remainder awaiting their turn in the kiln, so her mother-in-law would not see her 'wasting' so much time with her 'muck' in the studio.

The Bazaar was to run two days, Friday and Saturday, with a supper at the church on Friday night which all three generations of Martins could attend. Mother Martin fortunately was a firm believer in church work. Saturday night Steve had invited his current boss, Red Blackburn, and his wife Anne to dinner. He'd suggested that Mirelle invite G.F. and Sylvia. Mirelle had been torn between a desire for Sylvia's moral support and fear of what Sylvia might do to 'help' her. But there was a certain snobbism about inviting the Esterhazys: G.F. was a prominent lawyer, active in politics; Sylvia was Wilmington society; their presence was one way of proving to the in-laws that, despite Mirelle's background, the younger Martins were not social outcasts.

Sunday morning would be reserved for church and Sunday afternoon could be filled with a trip to the Longwood Gardens near Kennett Square. Monday, presumably, the senior Martins would depart for Florida. All should go well. Mirelle did not actually expect it to, but with so much to be done, there might not be time for the usual nastiness. And this Wilmington house was large, with several levels on which one could escape. The kids' noise from the gameroom was deadened by the acoustical tile so they wouldn't be a nuisance. Mother Martin made a special study in dominating conversations and any sound of off-stage enjoyment was promptly squelched if it interfered with her monologues.

The boys objected strenuously to camping in Tonia's room. But Mr. and Mrs. Martin did not share a bedroom in their own home and never considered sharing one when visiting either of their sons. Tripling up did not improve the kids' attitudes towards the impending visit.

"If they're going on to Florida, why don't they just go?" Nick asked sulkily. "I want to stay at the Bazaar all the time and watch you work. I could be a help instead of having to stay here and listen to Grandmother yak."

"Nicholas LeBoyne Martin, you will listen politely to your grandmother and you will be damned careful about what you say in her presence," Mirelle said repressively.

"You better, too, mother. 'Cause she don't stand for cussing."

"Doesn't, not don't, and I was emphasizing."

"You could of used 'darn'."

"That's exactly what I mean about being polite, Nick."

"Ahhh!"

"Nick?" Mirelle issued a blanket warning with that word.

Nick pouted and made a pattern in the rug with his sneaker toe.

Roman was more rebellious. His recollections of his grandparents were considerably more acute than his young brother's but he could be counted on to hold his peace when necessary. Mirelle prayed that Tonia's physical resemblance to her grandmother might be distraction enough. Tonia had no pre-conditioned opinions and looked forward with delight to the visit. However, Tonia's perceptions were sharper than her brothers' in the area of human relationships and, as her tongue was quick, no one was ever sure what the child might say next. In most circumstances, she could be amusing but, during such a critical period, she could as easily devastate all Mirelle's careful schemes.

And there was absolutely no way to safeguard against it, Mirelle sighed to herself Tuesday morning after breakfast. Her cleaning lady was coming on Wednesday this week, having obliged by shifting Tuesday lady with Wednesday lady. Overnight the house had a chance of staying neat for the Thursday arrival.

Mirelle ranged through the house again, trying to look at it with unfamiliar eyes, hoping to spot delinquencies. When Sylvia breezed in, she made her go over the house again before they sat down to coffee.

"If you'd warned me, I'd've brought white gloves," Sylvia said after she had reassured Mirelle for the fourth time that the house looked perfect. "I couldn't find so much as a spot of dried clay in the studio."

"Not that they'd bother looking in there."

"I see you vacuumed the crawlway. Honest to God, Mirelle, it's ridiculous . . . "

"It may seem so to you but you don't have my mother-in-law."

"I'll trade you my mother for her any day. In fact, there's still time for her to visit you. Mother'd spot your deficiencies as a housekeeper in short and scathing order. What I find reprehensible in you, Mirelle, is that you bother to conform to *her* standards. You don't like, you don't really care for her opinions . . . "

"Sylvia! Don't YOU houseclean like crazy before your mother visits?"

Sylvia's expression froze. "My mother lives with me. Or 'resides', to use her precise expression, when she is not bringing other relatives up to the mark." Sylvia sighed deeply but the sound was not all for effect. "She's been on an extended visit to her younger sister in Boston. Aunt Agatha is recently widowed and mother wished to be certain that she knows the new regulations of a relict. Can you imagine naming a child 'Agatha'? I'm afraid that Agatha will have learned all she needs to know very soon, unfortunately. The peace at home has been divine." Sylvia grinned impishly. "While the cat's away, the mice will play, you know." Then she leaned over and patted Mirelle's hand, smiling warmly. "So I know chapter and verse about maternal visitations, my dear. In fact, I have frequently thought of writing a book one day, 'Living With Mother' or 'Enduring In-laws'? Hmmm. Therefore I am A-Number-One qualified to appreciate, guard, defend . . . "

"Sylviaaaah!" Mirelle put her desperate plea into the elongation of the last syllable.

Sylvia cocked a sardonic eye at her. "All right. All right. I'll behave myself even though I'll be dying to tell the old bat off." She jumped almost as much as Mirelle when someone knocked at the door. "Expecting them today?"

Mirelle couldn't see the driveway and dashed nervously to the front door. "It's only Tuesday."

"I cannot force another morsel of pot roast down my throat and calf's foot jelly nauseates me. Lady, can you make an omelette?" It was James Howell, looking well tanned and himself again.

"Well, if that's your father-in-law . . . " drawled Sylvia from the dining room.

"You know perfectly well it isn't," Mirelle replied. "I don't think that you've met Sylvia Esterhazy before. This is James Howell."

"I see that the beef tea did you some good," Sylvia said, shaking hands.

"Ah ha, I was right. You were one of the cackling females in my kitchen," Jamie exclaimed in mock vindication.

"Pneumonia affected your hearing."

Mirelle brought another cup for him and noticed, as he lifted it, that the muscles in his hand were twitching. He noticed her glance. "Not weakness, my dear, from lack of a balanced diet but from a strenuous session of practise. Since Mahomet could not come to the mountain, and I do not exaggerate (he made a ballooning gesture out over his lean stomach), the mountain came to Mahomet."

Mirelle laughed, catching his reference, but Sylvia looked bewildered.

"I'm to accompany a rather famous soprano . . . "

"Who had best remain anonymous after that slighting description," said Mirelle.

" . . . In her Academy of the Arts recital, and due to my semi-convalescent state, she condescended to come to the wilds of Wilmington for a much needed rehearsal."

"When's the concert?" Sylvia asked, shooting Mirelle a glance.

"The eighteenth. By the way, Mirelle, I have tickets for you and your husband."

"The eighteenth? I think Steve has to be at a convention. Would you come with me, Sylvia?"

Sylvia professed herself to be delighted but she'd have to

check with her diary as she had so many political meetings right now.

"I'm a ward-heeler," she told Jamie, "and heeling the Referendum, over, preferably."

"I thought ward-heelers had to be rotund, rotten and male."

"Not in my party. Of course, if you've only encountered Republicans, I can see where such misconceptions might arise."

Jamie laughed. "Are you all atwitter?" he asked Mirelle.

She looked at him blankly, having missed the reference.

"Your mother-in-law, he means," Sylvia said. "You don't happen to have a pair of white gloves, do you, Jamie?"

"In my pocket," and Howell reached into his coat and flashed something white.

"It may seem silly to you, Sylvia," and Mirelle was piqued by her flippancy, "and to you, Jamie," she glared at him, "but there is nothing the least bit laughable about it."

"You need to change your perspective, that's all, Mirelle," Jamie said. "If what the old bitch said and thought made no difference to you or you could convince her that it didn't, she'd have no power to affect you."

"Me, yes. My husband, no. My children, no."

"You, my dear," and Jamie waggled a finger at her, "can still control the situation."

"That's a lot easier said than done."

"Sure, 'cause she's got you on edge already."

"She can do that all right," Mirelle admitted ruefully, "ever since the day . . . " and then she stopped.

"Ever since the day she felt she could make you kowtow by shaming you about your birth," Jamie continued.

Mirelle glared at Sylvia whose eyebrows raised with surprised innocence.

"I have accompanied singers who knew Mary LeBoyne, and Mirelle as a little girl," Jamie told Sylvia by way of explanation. "I have also seen some of Lajos Neagu's work. Mirelle has nothing to be ashamed of in either parent."

"Keep talking," urged Sylvia, winking maliciously at Mirelle.

"Mirelle, have you ever seen any of your father's paintings?"

"Only reproductions in portrait books. His work has never been publicly exhibited here. I'd've gone," she added defiantly. "So much of his output was portraiture and little of that is available for public viewing."

"You'll never guess who was done by Neagu," Sylvia was smirking with delight.

"I won't if you don't tell me," Mirelle answered caustically.

"G.F.'s mother. But he hasn't a clue where the portrait is now."

"Where's the infamous one he did of your mother, Mirelle?" Jamie asked her.

"I don't know. It was, after all, Barthan-More's. It used to hang in his bedroom but whether it survived the war or not . . . " Mirelle shrugged. She was less indifferent to the portrait's fate than she appeared, for her mother, as Tosca, vibrant, anguished, beautiful, in a brilliant blue costume with jewels and egret feathers in her elaborately dressed hair, had enchanted her the few times she had crept into the forbidden apartment to peek at it. "However, my father's fame is really not at issue."

"Just yours," said Sylvia pointedly.

"No, nor mine because it only points up what the Martins want to forget about their daughter-in-law."

James Howell snorted his contempt.

"So only your Dirty Dicks will go to the Bazaar?" Sylvia asked suddenly.

"The what?" Jamie demanded.

Mirelle explained.

"Are they on a par with my sickpig?"

"More or less."

"Tell me, Mirelle," Jamie began with an all too innocent expression on his face, "have you ever concocted a sickpig of your mother-in-law?"

Sylvia exploded with mirth and even Mirelle, gasping a denial, gave way to paroxysms of laughter.

"If we could but see ourselves as Mirelle sees us," Jamie said with unctuous solemnity.

"No," Sylvia said, wiping laugh tears from her eyes, "Mirelle couldn't do that woman. She sculpts with too much love. She's never done anything hateful. Even those Dirty Dicks and the sickpigs are done with tenderness and great affection."

"You wouldn't say that if you'd seen the face she put on that pig she gave me," Jamie said, affecting an injured expression, but his eyes were intent on Mirelle.

"I not only saw it, I encouraged her," Sylvia said. "Men who are never sick are incredible ogres when they finally succumb to physical discomfort."

Jamie waved his hands in defeat.

"Seriously, Mirelle, aren't you going to exhibit the soldier, or the horse, or even the Running Child? Or better yet, the Lucy."

"The Lucy's not finished and the others aren't for sale."

"Sale, schmale," Sylvia said in exasperation, "display them. Mark them sold or vacant but at least exhibit the quality of the real work you can do."

"That ought to be obvious in the . . . "

"Skeered of what your mother-in-law will say?" Jamie asked, one eyebrow raised challengingly.

Mirelle shut her mouth angrily, looking from Jamie's too bland face to Sylvia's earnest and determined expression.

"Not the Lucy," she said and to herself she sounded sullen.

"Now, then," Jamie said, briskly rubbing his hands together, "I'm a poor sick invalid who hasn't had . . . "

"Anything but delicious pot roast," Mirelle interrupted.

" . . . Nine days old," he finished, spacing the words with disgust.

"Do you think he deserves our culinary efforts?" Mirelle asked Sylvia.

"Hmmm," and Sylvia thoughtfully considered. "I'm a bit hungry myself."

The unscheduled luncheon successfully kept Mirelle from dwelling on Thursday's problems. The kind of remarks that passed between Jamie and Sylvia kept her laughing. She was delighted that her two friends liked each other.

"It's rude to eat and run," Sylvia said, consulting her watch.

" . . . Only for poisoners . . . " Jamie said.

" . . . but I've got to ward-heel," Sylvia continued. "It's evident from the number of Republicans voting in the primary that some returned from graves that had been their only residence for the past twenty years. I have endless records to check. After all, I only dropped in for a cup of coffee."

"It's been a pleasure, Sylvia," Jamie said, giving her a Continental click of the heels and a bow.

"Indeed!" Sylvia swirled out the door with a coquettish wink.

"You owe the beef tea to her," Mirelle said.

"Sensible as well as intelligent. How refreshing," and for once his banter annoyed Mirelle.

"Why are you always so . . . so . . . "

"Snide?" he suggested, overly helpful. "To hide a tender heart," and he placed one hand dramatically over his chest.

"Oh, you're never serious."

"It can be a disease." Then he dropped all pose, taking her by the shoulders and shaking her a little to make her look him in the eyes. "If you accept Sylvia's breeziness, as you seem to, you must accept my sarcasm, too. We're covering up something. Sylvia's a deeply troubled woman beneath that caustic wit. You, Mirelle, with your long silences and deep thoughts. Me with my rapier-like wit, my unfailing and devastating humor. We're all lonely people, Mirelle. I'll give that as a mutual bond. I'd also venture to say that it's because all three of us are out of step with our status in life. No, be quiet," and he put his finger to her lips to stop her protest. "Why are women so goddamned subjective? You were going to say, 'but I'm not out of step, I'm a happy housewife and mother' . . . " He had lightened his tone to a falsetto but there was nothing light about the expression in his eyes. "Bullshit, Mirelle. Bullshit. I've seen a change in you, a good one. You were beginning to sound like a functioning human being instead of a zombie. I don't want to see you lose the progress you've made." Then his eyebrow twitched and rose sardonically as he grinned with pure malice. "Not that either the Esterhazy woman or I will let you. In spite of the virago, Madame Martin."

"Between the two of you, my peace is destroyed," Mirelle exclaimed passionately.

"I intend to destroy it more thoroughly one of these days," Jamie said with quiet intent and left.

CHAPTER FOURTEEN

BY FRIDAY EVENING, Mirelle wished devoutly to return to being a non-feeling, non-thinking zombie again. At first, when the senior Martins arrived late Thursday evening, just in time for dinner, Mirelle had hopefully entertained the notion that perhaps this visit wouldn't be too bad after all.

Although Allentown was a scant two-hour drive from Wilmington and the Martins had planned to arrive by lunchtime, a series of ridiculous incidents had combined to delay them. Since a recital of turning back to the house before reaching the highway to make sure that the cellar windows were locked, et cetera, kept the dinner table breathless and the children squirming, it also prevented Marian Martin from latching immediately onto the shortcomings of either Mirelle or Steve. So exhausted by these untoward events was Mother Martin that she retired early, allowing Dad Martin to have a comfortable chat with Steve and Mirelle.

Steve showed his father the house and the garden while Mirelle tidied the kitchen, and made the final preparations for the Bazaar the next afternoon. The men ended up in the studio watching her pack the cut blocks of clay into plastic bags.

"I do kinda wish that Mirelle wasn't going to be so busy," Dad Martin began gently. "We get so little chance for a nice talk. Christmas and Thanksgiving are so hectic."

Mirelle looked at Steve quickly and then back to her work.

"I explained that in my letter, Dad. Mirelle had promised the church a long time ago that she would do the booth and there's been a lot of excitement about it," Steve said, though there was a note of entreaty in his voice. "A very nice mention in the paper, too, with the announcement of the Bazaar."

Mirelle winced inwardly and Dad Martin immediately picked up on the reference to publicity.

"In the papers? Is that wise?"

"Mirelle was referred to as Mrs. Steven Martin, Dad, not Mary Ellen LeBoyne."

Dad Martin looked at his son silently for a few moments, then shrugged his shoulders diffidently.

"If it's for the church, people oughtn't to need their names in the paper," he said mildly.

"Don't worry, Dad Martin. There are four other Steve Martins in Wilmington," Mirelle said.

"No need to be that way," Dad Martin said with a sniff and left the studio.

Mirelle looked pointedly at Steve, who gave his head a weary shake before following his father in to the gameroom where they watched TV together.

Friday was overcast and cold. Mirelle, tense and tired, woke groggily from a repeat of her hand nightmare. She could smell the aroma of coffee and thought how considerate of Steve. Then she heard him noisily showering. Mother Martin was also an early riser. Groaning, Mirelle barged into the bathroom to wash sleep from her face. She dressed hurriedly since she knew that the sight of one of her filmy negligees would irritate her mother-in-law. She got downstairs to find the dining room table all set for a formal breakfast.

Grimly she tried to dispel her sleepiness and jump into alert status without her usual gradual routine.

"How very kind of you, Mother Martin," she said, briskly entering the kitchen, "and you must have been tired last night."

"I just can't seem to sleep late after so many years of getting up to be sure that the boys and Arthur started the day off with a proper meal," her mother-in-law said, primly separating the edges of the eggs she was frying.

Mirelle suppressed the desire to scream and, noticing that the one thing the set table lacked was milk, she went to the refrigerator.

"Oh, I'd wait, Mary Ellen, to put the milk on. My boys always complained if the milk was warm."

Mirelle shut the refrigerator carefully, determined to keep her temper. But she wanted to remind the woman that she, Mirelle, had established routines with her children which were in no way dependent on Steve's memories of his childhood. Instead she sat down at the table and poured herself coffee, gritting her teeth when she saw how weak it was.

"Such good coffee, and such a treat to have it all made," she said, trying to sound sincere.

"I see you use the Food Fair and I think they put just too much chicory in their house blend. Doesn't Steve want the A & P he used to insist I buy?"

"He doesn't complain," Mirelle replied.

"Well, do take a little tip then, and get him what he wants," said Mother Martin, sitting down in Steve's accustomed place directly across from Mirelle. She passed the platter of eggs and bacon to Mirelle. "Help yourself."

"Thank you. I usually eat after the kids are gone," Mirelle said, shifting the focus of her eyes from the staring yolks. It had taken her years to be able to make eggs in the morning for Steve. Her early Continental training had imbued in her a desire to break her fast gently with coffee and bread.

"Roman, Nick, Tonia, breakfast's ready," she called as a diversionary tactic.

"Father's still asleep," her mother-in-law said, suitably lowering her voice.

"Nick's room is off to one side."

"Father's such a light sleeper though."

Mirelle got up and went to the stairwell, called again, intensifying her tone without raising the volume.

Roman and Nick came thundering down the stairs, despite her hissed warning.

"Have you forgotten that we have guests in this house who might still be sleeping?"

"Aw, Grandmother's up," Nick said. "I heard her slamming the kitchen cabinets."

Mirelle covered his mouth warningly and Roman dug his brother in the ribs. Nick grimaced contritely and then walked into the dining room with exaggerated stealth.

"No cereal?" he complained in his normal bellow when he saw the platter of eggs.

"That's not brainfood, Nicholas," his grandmother said sweetly.

"No one has any fun commercials about eggs," Nick grumbled.

"Eggs are just fine," Roman said distinctly and heaped two on his plate with several rashers of bacon. He'd have reached for more bacon but Mirelle managed to catch his eye. He retracted his hand hastily.

"Mom, can't I have cereal?" Nick asked. "I always have cereal."

"Grandmother's eggs are special, Nick. Do try them!"

Roman must have kicked his brother because Nick suddenly extended his hand for the platter. He ate without any show of delight.

Steve had hurried Tonia up and they came down together, Tonia subdued. Fried eggs were her favorite breakfast food and she turned cheerful as she helped herself to three.

"No, dear, that's too many for a little girl like you," her grandmother said, and Tonia looked in questioning surprise at her mother.

"I always eat three," she said. "At least!"

"Really she does," Mirelle said, laughing lightly. "Steve is of the opinion that her breakfast lasts her the entire day."

"It doesn't seem sensible to overdo it." Mother Martin pursed her mouth in disapproval.

"I like eggs," repeated Tonia, eating quickly and, to Mirelle's relief, neatly. "You cook eggs better than Mom," she added brightly, "but you don't use enough salt. Please pass the salt, Nick."

"Is so much salt wise?"

"She grows on it, Mother," Steve said, reaching for the coffee. "Hey, is this tea?" he asked Mirelle, frowning at the weak color.

"They're saying that chicory might be a cause of cancer. The Food Fair brand Mirelle uses has just too much chicory," Mother Martin said firmly.

"Oh, Mom, come off it. You just like weak coffee," Steve said with a chuckle.

I am not going to survive the day, Mirelle thought as she poured more weak coffee.

"If it's so weak, can I have some, Mom?" Nick asked hopefully.

"Coffee's not for growing boys. It'd stunt your growth," Mother Martin said before Mirelle could speak.

"Not if it's as weak as you say it is," Nick pointed out reasonably.

Mother Martin pursed her lips again.

"Nick!" Steve intervened.

"But Mom lets me have coffee and she said she used to have it when she was even younger'n Tonia." Nick didn't give up easily.

Mirelle tried to catch his eye. Dear Nick, she thought, putting my feet in my mouth!

"Your mother's background was very different from your father's, dear." The deft barb sweetly rammed home.

"The schoolbus," Mirelle announced in relief, noticing the time.

The boys dove for their books and coats, racing out the door with their snow jackets flapping.

"Come back here, boys. Let me fasten your coats. You'll

catch terrible cold," Mother Martin called shrilly after them from the front door.

"No, they won't," Steve said with a laugh. "But you will, Ma, standing in that draught."

She closed the door and came back to the table, shaking her head, making no attempt to hide the fact that she thought her grandsons were entirely without manners or supervision.

"I just don't understand it. I always buttoned you boys up properly before I'd let you step an inch outside."

"Yeah, I remember."

"Steven Martin!"

"Sorry, Ma, gotta go to work. Want to button my coat for me? For old times' sake?"

"I'll do no such thing. You're old enough to take care of yourself now."

He gave her a hug and a kiss.

Tonia had finished her eggs and, as she often did, took her plate out to the kitchen. She got into her snowpants and jacket and would have done her own zippering if her grandmother hadn't spotted her.

"Here, love. Let me do that."

"I know how," Tonia answered her grandmother, a little surprised at being thought incapable. She glanced over at her mother. Mirelle nodded imperceptibly and Tonia obediently submitted to her grandmother.

"How do you like kindergarten, dear?"

"Kindergarten? I'm in second grade. I'm no baby."

"You're so small though, lovey," her grandmother said, laughing to cover her mistake. "I've got five grandchildren to keep straight. Grandmother just forgot."

Tonia wasn't pleased that details about her could be forgotten.

"Thank you, Grandmother, for helping me," she said politely enough and then pointed wildly out the window. "It's snowing. It's snowing."

"Good heavens!" Mother Martin whirled to peer out the window. "This early?"

"It's not so early," Mirelle said. "December's half over.

There's your bus, Tonia. Now remember, you walk over to Nick's room and then you both come to the church together. Now scoot."

" 'Bye, Mommie. 'Bye, Grandmother."

Tonia danced off, trying to catch the snowflakes in her gloves, spinning around underneath the soft fall, her face upturned.

"Do you mean to tell me that you're going to let those children walk to the church by themselves?"

"Certainly." Mirelle turned to her mother-in-law in surprise. "They've done it before. It's not all that far from their school and there's sidewalk all the way."

"Why, Tonia's only . . . what? seven? And Nick is just eleven?"

"Well, they're both capable youngsters and it's completely suburban . . . "

"Why, I never let either Steve or Ralph go anywhere unaccompanied until they were . . . "

"Boy Scouts and the other boys . . . " Mirelle broke off, thankful that Dad Martin's timely arrival interrupted her before she had blurted out what Steve had once told her: that the other Scouts had teased him and his brother unmercifully because either his father or mother walked them the five blocks to the meetings.

"Mary Ellen tells me that she allows those two little children to walk all the way from school to church," said Mother Martin, incensed and looking for support.

"Why not?" replied her husband, a little surprised. "Always did think you coddled those boys of ours too much."

"Arthur Martin!"

Mirelle regarded her father-in-law with new respect.

"Coffee, Dad?" she asked, breaking the stunned surprise.

Dad Martin looked skeptically at the weak solution in his cup.

"Mirelle, perhaps you'd make a new pot for me?"

"Arthur Martin, what's got into you?"

"Marian, you know I like coffee with some guts to it.

Awfully glad when instant coffee came out, Mary Ellen," he said as Mirelle took his cup and the pot back to the kitchen. "Then I could make mine strong if Ma wanted hers weak."

Between getting her husband's breakfast in irritated silence and bustling about to iron the packing creases from her dress for the afternoon bazaar, Mother Martin kept pretty much out of Mirelle's way that morning. Mirelle loaded the Sprite with the last of her supplies, got the house picked up and a load of wash started.

"I don't know why you won't let me cook us a nice family supper here at home," Mother Martin began when she cornered Mirelle in the kitchen fixing a light lunch.

"What? Ask you to cook on your first day of holiday? No, the children have looked forward to the church dinner. Roman is acting as busboy and Nick is being allowed to put around bread and butters and set the tables between servings." Mirelle kept her voice light.

"I should think they'd be glad to sit down with their grandparents, they see us so seldom." Mother Martin gave an aggrieved sniff.

"Steve thought it would be a chance for you to meet more of our friends than we could have in the house at one time," Mirelle said, trying not to sound defensive.

"Hmmm, what's in this casserole?" asked Dad Martin, smacking his lips.

"One of my by-guess and by-gosh concoctions."

"Your cooking's as good as ever, Mirelle."

Mother Martin looked displeased, but Mirelle could think of nothing placatory.

"Children get hot lunches at school?" her father-in-law asked.

"Very good ones, too. For some of the students, it's the best meal of the day," Mirelle said, elaborating to keep conversation on a safe topic.

"Hummph. I hope you haven't had to have your schools desegregated," Mother Martin said austerely.

"No," and Mirelle could answer truthfully for the Wilmington school which the children attended had always had a black enrollment. She knew perfectly well that there had been blacks in Steve's Allentown high school class so she felt slightly nauseated to hear borrowed phrases and secondhand opinions frothing out of the mouth of her mother-in-law. She listened patiently through a badly organized and trite solution to Allentown's problems of overpopulation, lack of business, school system and town managerial shortcomings, fully aware that the founts of such wisdom were the omniscient Randolphs.

If there were any real affection between us, Mirelle thought as her mother-in-law chanted the magic phrases, this sort of thing would be tolerable, like her well-meant actions this morning at breakfast. I could have teased her about the eggs, and the weak coffee, and we could have laughed about Dad Martin longing for a pot of strong coffee and . . . oh hell. She hates me. It wouldn't have mattered who Steve married! Even the paragon Nancy Lou Randolph. Her one talent in life was dominating and she lost two-thirds of that when her boys grew old enough to leave home and marry. Good thing she had no daughters. They'd never have escaped. And yet, no thoroughly bad person could have raised someone like Steve. Why can't I find the good in her?

When Mother Martin finally concluded her monologue, Mirelle stacked the dishes in the dishwasher and went to change her clothes for the Bazaar. June had had bright colorful smocks run up by the Women's Guild, and supplied floppy artist's bows. Mirelle had unearthed a beret from her English school days to complete the outfit.

"You aren't going to wear that outlandish get-up?" Mother Martin was shocked.

"Everyone manning booths at the Bazaar is wearing the same thing," Mirelle replied calmly.

"I think it's cute," said her father-in-law.

"I think it shows very bad taste under the circumstances," Mother Martin said.

"The circumstances are, Mother Martin, that this is the costume which the Bazaar chairwoman chose for us. She has absolutely no way of knowing that I'm the bastard of an artist."

"Mary Ellen!"

Mirelle wished the sharp retort unsaid the moment she saw her father-in-law's reaction and cursed herself for losing control. Dad Martin was not the staunchest ally but she had prejudiced him once more.

"I was only reminding you that that fact is not common knowledge here in Wilmington." She didn't think an oblique apology would be acceptable but for Steve's sake, she would try. "My costume is a sheer coincidence, not something which I planned as a personal affront to you. If you still want to attend the Bazaar, just turn right onto the main road in front of the development. Take the first lefthand turn, and you'll run right into the church parking lot. Steve will be joining us there when he leaves the office."

Still seething, Mirelle drove the Sprite as fast as she dared on the now slippery roads. She was astonished to see that the light snow was beginning to cover the ground with ominous rapidity. She hoped that it wouldn't limit attendance at the Bazaar. As the church drew most of its members from the nearby developments, the snow might just add to the occasion. Mirelle pulled the Sprite up on a gravelly bank which had been left over from driveway repairs. It meant a longer haul with her clay but it would also give her tires traction when it came time to go home later.

A good crowd of women was already wandering around the booths in the halls. Mirelle chuckled at the sight of the colorful smocks, bows and berets. Under the circumstances indeed! As she got to her booth, set in the far corner by the stage, Mirelle noticed that quite a few of the figures were already gone. The pretty young girl who was also working in her booth was busy wrapping a purchase. Would the Martins also consider her shameless?

"Hi, there Mirelle, your Dirty Dicks are a hit," Patsy greeted her. She leaned across the booth to the purchaser and said in a mock confidential tone, "This is the sculptress . . . or are you a sculptor, Mirelle?"

"Either," Mirelle replied, conjuring a smile for the customer.

"I'd've sworn you'd used my nephew as a model if I didn't know he was in California," the woman said, cradling the Dirty Dick carefully in her arm. "This is just him to the life."

"Which one did you choose?"

"The Sunday school clothes one. I'm sending it to my sister. That is," she added hastily, worried, "if it's safe to ship?"

"The figure's been hard-fired so it should be all right if you pack it in styrofoam. And label it 'fragile'."

"Are these more?" the woman asked curiously, noticing Mirelle stacking the blocks of clay.

"That's what the sign is all about," Patsy answered. She'd obviously just been waiting for an opening. "Mrs. Martin is going to do small busts of anyone who wants to sit for her."

"Really?" The woman was definitely interested. "I'd love to have one of my daughter. She's nine."

"At that age they can usually sit still . . . with some judicious bribery," Mirelle said, smiling.

"Do I make an appointment?"

"No, just bring the child in when you can."

"I might just do that very thing. After school. Oh, I'm so excited by the thought," and she walked off, murmuring to herself.

Such gushing could become wearing, Mirelle thought. Ah, well, all in the line of duty. She assembled her tools, put a block of clay on the board and sat down, looking about her, and realizing for the first time today that she was already tired by the emotional strain of dealing with the Martins.

Mirelle glanced up at the shadow-box shelves where her smaller finished pieces were displayed. She had acceded to the demands of Jamie and Sylvia. The yellow velvet did show off the horse, the latest pose of Tasso, the bronze pig borrowed from Tonia ("only to be shown, Mother, not sold or anything"), and on the top shelf, the face hidden by the shadow of the helmet, the Soldier. On a pedestal was the Running Child, backed by a vivid red velvet swag. Should she have risked the unfinished Lucy? No, but this assembly of her output for the last ten years didn't make much of a showing, no matter what the circumstances. Considered dispassionately, the head of James Howell and the Lucy were her most impressive work to date.

Patsy had ceased rearranging the displays of the Dirty Dicks, the Christmas creche animals and the mugs which Mirelle had thrown for the Bazaar. Now she stood, listening to the conversation on the Apron Line that was strung across the stage, perpendicular to their booth. For lack of something more constructive, Mirelle started to carve Patsy's features from the clay rectangle. She glanced at her watch to have a time check on sculpting a credible likeness.

"Do hold still, Patsy," she called as the girl started to turn.

"Ooo," Patsy squealed, "I'm being done."

"Patsy, just look back at Aprons. For a moment more. Fine. Now, if you'll just turn and let me have the full face . . . "

Mirelle was only peripherally aware that a small crowd had gathered. She could feel their presence and hear their muted whisperings.

"Oh, I'd no idea you were doing me, Mirelle. Oh, this is thrilling. I was just talking to Ann Mulholland in Aprons and when I started to move, Mirelle told me to stop."

Mirelle permitted a very small gentle sigh for Patsy's exuberant chatter but the work reabsorbed her and she forgot about the ceaseless babble that drifted harmlessly over her head, pausing only when Mirelle asked the girl to turn.

"Would a piano stool help?" June Treadway quietly asked at Mirelle's elbow.

"Indeed it would," and Mirelle gave her a quick smile of gratitude.

A moment later June installed a giggling Patsy on the claw-footed, swivel-topped stool. Mirelle could now reach over and turn the model whichever way was required. Finishing the little bust, Mirelle held it up for inspection.

"No, please don't handle it," Mirelle said, as Patsy reached eagerly for it. "The clay is still malleable. It'll need a chance to harden." She put it on one of the shadow box shelves and pulled a corner of the velvet behind it.

"Oh, that's so . . . so me," Patsy crowed, her pretty face glowing with pleasure. To Mirelle's astonishment, the girl hugged her in an excess of gratitude. "I'm just so thrilled. Wait til my Pete sees me." Then she turned to the watchers. "Now that you've seen what Madame Michelangelo can do, who'll be next?"

Mirelle smothered a laugh at the girl's instinctive salesmanship.

"I think I'd like my children done," said a woman, stepping forward from the crowd. "How long does it take?"

Mirelle made a face for forgetting to check the time. "About twenty minutes," she said in a quick approximation. "I don't like to work so quickly. I have to warn you, too, that there's a danger of losing the detail if the soft clay gets knocked about."

"For two dollars, it's all in a good cause."

"Could you do my baby?" A younger woman pushed through the crowd with an eighteen month old boy.

"If you can keep him still long enough," Mirelle replied, a little dubious. The child was already squirming in his mother's arms.

"I will!" the mother replied grimly and sat down on the stool.

Three people crowded the booth too much so the stool was placed between the stage and the booth and Mirelle proceeded with the sitting.

The baby wiggled, squirmed, bawled and fussed but Mirelle kept on doggedly, and though the result did not please her, the mother professed to be delighted. She readily agreed to leave the clay in the booth until it had hardened.

From then on, Mirelle was kept so busy that coffee brought to her turned lukewarm before she could take more than a sip. Though she could see gross flaws in the execution, everyone seemed so pleased, she abandoned self-deprecation.

Tonia arrived with Nick in tow and they both begged money for the food display and the Trade-a-Toy table. Roman rambled in later, quite willing to stand and watch her working. Nor was he in any way embarrassed for he announced to any cronies who wandered by that the lady sculpting was HIS mother.

Mirelle found that she was cutting her time down to 15 minutes with children. Then Patsy had an inspiration and gave out hastily printed numbers so that people could wander around to other booths until their number was called. If they didn't answer, one presumed they had gone home and she went on to the next number.

"We need more sculptures," Patsy said once to Mirelle in a fierce whisper. "I've sold nine of the Dirty Dicks and there's all of tomorrow to go as well as tonight. What'll we do if we run completely out?"

"Take orders."

"Now why didn't I think of that?" Then she sniffed hugely. "Doesn't that roast beef smell heavenly?"

"Now that you mention it, it does," and Mirelle paused to rub shoulders, stiff from her concentrated efforts. "I hadn't realized how hungry I was getting." As she rotated her shoulder blades to ease the muscles, she turned half towards the door and saw Steve entering with his parents. She bent to her table. She'd managed to forget all about that problem and resented its intrusion now.

"Hi, hon. Wow!" and Steve whistled appreciatively as he saw the many little heads in various stages of drying on the shelves. "They sure have been working you."

"You know Patsy McHugh, don't you, Steve?" And Steve shook hands with Patsy and introduced his parents.

"There I was, just talking to Ann in the Apron section," Patsy began effusively, "and I turned around to see Mrs. Martin working on a bust of ME. In two shakes of a lamb's tail, there I was," and she pointed triumphantly to the small replica. "I'm so excited. This is much more original than a charcoal sketch. Why, it's much more me!"

Except, thought Mirelle, somewhat appalled at her reaction, that the statue doesn't have its mouth open. Then she looked at her mother-in-law and saw her counting the number of busts. Probably adding up all the earnings.

"Yes," Dad Martin said slowly, "it is a good likeness. Of

a very pretty girl." He smiled at Patsy, who blushed with becoming modesty.

"Oh, Mr. Martin," she murmured without, Mirelle also noticed, a trace of coyness. Patsy was a nice child in spite of her garrulousness. "But it's really a crime for Mirelle to be doing a church bazaar," and her tone was scornful. "Why, she should be doing things for the Louvre."

Mirelle closed her eyes briefly. Patsy never knew when to stop, did she!

"I hardly believe that Mary Ellen considers herself that talented," Mother Martin said reprovingly.

"You can never tell, can you," Patsy babbled on. "All she really needs is someone to discover how talented she is."

"Mother," and Steve broke in diplomatically, taking his mother's arm, "come see the white elephant booth. I believe there's some china there with the exact pattern you've been collecting. Mirelle, are you joining us for dinner?"

"As soon as I finish Tommy here."

There was little time for family conversation at dinner. Many acquaintances came up to meet the senior Martins and, unfortunately, to speak to Mirelle about her sculpting. Before Mother Martin could feel her eminence eclipsed by that, Mirelle finished her dinner and excused herself.

Though she worked as fast as possible, there were still ten uncollected numbers at nine-thirty when the Bazaar was officially closing. Mirelle promised that, if the next-in-line arrived by ten the following morning when the Bazaar reopened, she would do him. Patsy was overjoyed with the success of their booth but Mirelle was so stiff and tired, that she wondered if she could make it home. Steve, the children and the grandparents had left after eight.

When Mirelle finally stepped out into the crisp air, she was amazed at the serene snowy scene. She stood in the doorway a moment, breathing deeply, enjoying the smell of snow and the quiet around her. The new fallen stuff was fluffy and still drifting down in fine dustings here and there. It was a wonderful sight and Mirelle dreaded going home.

Steve had left the station wagon in the driveway so that she could put the Sprite in the garage beside his father's

Buick. She appreciated the thoughtfulness and went in through the laundry room to be confronted by the sight of her parents-in-law and her husband gathered around the Lucy in her studio.

"Hi, Mirelle. Say, why didn't you put her on show instead of the Child?" Steve asked.

Her father-in-law was handling the unfinished bust of James Howell. Raging inwardly, Mirelle stood in the door, not trusting herself to speak. Steve turned around again.

"What's wrong, honey?" he asked. "Why didn't you bring over the Lucy? It's very good, you know, Dad," he told his father earnestly. "You never met Lucy Farnoll but she was wonderful to us when we were in Ashland."

Managing a tight smile at Dad Martin, Mirelle took the bust from him. The malleable plasticene had been handled and several lines blurred. Trembling inside her skin, Mirelle put the head back on its shelf and covered it.

"I'm the only one capable of judging what work I show," she said. She knew her voice was cold and expressionless. "The Lucy is not finished and to show rough plasticene is amateurish."

"Mirelle!" Steve began to realize how very angry she was.

"I'm very tired and I'm going to take a bath. Please excuse me. Good night." She left the room quickly, her steps jolting through her body.

"Mirelle!" Now Steve was annoyed.

"Now, son," Dad Martin said soothingly, "she was working at quite a pace there, you know. A good hot bath is just what she needs."

"I just don't understand your wife, Steve, try as I will . . . "

Mirelle heard her mother-in-law's condescending tones as the last indignity and it was with great effort that she kept from slamming the door behind her.

Steve came up after she had bathed and got into bed.

"What the hell did you mean by that show of temper, Mirelle?" he said in a taut voice as soon as he'd closed the door.

"Steven Martin, if you'd heard your mother talking to me at lunch . . . And to come home and find her pawing over my . . . "

"She wasn't pawing. I was showing her because she was interested."

"Don't raise your voice to me, Steve Martin. The only interest your mother could possibly have in my work is how much money I could make with it. I saw the way she counted those busts this afternoon."

"Mirelle!" Steve was taken aback by the suppressed savagery in her voice.

"Don't 'Mirelle' me. She wasn't even going to come to the Bazaar because I had the audacity to dress up in a smock. Like an artist. 'Outlandish get-up' was her phrase, I believe."

"Keep your voice down."

"You keep your mother down. Off my back. I will not have her patronizing me any more!"

"Mirelle?" Steve's temper was beginning to heat up as well.

"No, Steve, don't defend her to me. Defend me! Just this once," Mirelle said, softly, pleadingly.

Steve sat down on the bed, shaking his head slowly in his hands.

"Mirelle, she's my mother . . . "

"And that's the only reason I even try to be polite. I've taken two sleeping tablets. I'm very tired and I've got a lot to do tomorrow, and no time or energy for wrangling."

Steve combed his fingers through his hair, exhaling through his teeth. "All right, all right," but the edge of anger had left his voice. "What time do you have to be there?"

"Ten o'clock. I'll set the oven for the roast lamb for dinner tomorrow before I go, so leave the oven settings alone. Thank God for automation. The Bazaar is officially over at four and no one's coming until seven so I'll have a chance to rest before dinner. There's a movie in the basement of the church at 1:30 so you can get the kids out of your hair." She turned over, groaning at the tautness of her shoulders. "My aching back. Good night, dear."

Steve knelt by the side of the bed and kissed her cheek. Then he began to knead her shoulder muscles. She wondered as she lay there, relaxing under his ministrations, if she'd dream of the hands again.

CHAPTER FIFTEEN

THE SMELL OF COFFEE woke Mirelle but she lay, encased in a motionless body that apparently had no intention of responding to the stimuli. The desire for the coffee intensified and she managed to open one eye. She was lying on her stomach, her head turned towards the bedside table. Her favorite coffee mug loomed invitingly, steam rising lazily.

"That does it." As she flopped over and hauled herself up against the headboard, she heard Steve's chuckle. He was sitting in his bed, drinking coffee. "You made it," she said, half accusingly as she reached for the cup.

"You're damned right, all that chicory notwithstanding. How do you feel?"

"The way I look." Mirelle blinked violently to clear sleep from sticky eyes. Her shoulders were still stiff. Steve wadded up his quilt and put it behind her, nuzzling her neck affectionately. "I'll spill coffee on you."

"You're unromantic this morning."

"I'm unawake."

He sat on the edge of the bed, looking at her.

"You get prettier all the time."

"I age well . . . like cheese."

Steve burst out laughing.

If I can keep him in this frame of mind, Mirelle thought sleepily, Marian Martin hasn't a chance.

She put down her cup and beckoned coquettishly at Steve. His eyes widened and his grin broadened. He swiftly locked the door.

"The kids are glued to the TV," he said as he slipped under the sheets.

A knock on the door shattered the very nice mood they'd been creating. Someone turned the door knob. The vengeful side of Mirelle hoped that it was an in-law and not a child.

"Mary Ellen?" asked her mother-in-law, and Mirelle managed not to grin.

"Yes, Mother," Steve answered, his voice colorless but his face flushed. With anger or embarrassment, Mirelle wondered.

"Steven, isn't Mary Ellen awake yet?"

"Just," Steve replied with a baleful look on his face. "Come ON, hon, you've got to get up now."

She glared wickedly at him for such dissembling.

"There's a phone call for her," Mother Martin went on, "a Mrs. Ester- something." She sounded disapproving of such complicated names.

"I took the extension out last night," Steve said in a quick whisper.

"I'll be right there," Mirelle said. She gave Steve another lingering kiss and then grabbed his bathrobe.

"Mirelle, is there anything I can do for you for tonight's feast?"

"No thanks, Syl, but it's good of you to offer."

"You sound awful."

"I just got up."

"Now why didn't that woman just say you weren't up?"

"It's okay. My, God, it's 9:00 and I've got to be at the Bazaar at 10:00. Good thing you did call."

"How's it going?" Sylvia asked with dry sympathy.

"The Bazaar's going fine. Excellent attendance."

"You know I didn't mean the flipping Bazaar," Sylvia's voice dripped with sarcasm.

"I'm keeping the fine edge of the wedge in place," and then Mirelle giggled earthily.

"Well, your spirits are good. I gather there are large unfriendly ears in the vicinity?"

"That's right. Are you going to give us the benefit of your presence at the Bazaar?"

"Wouldn't miss that height of the social season for the world!"

"Goodbye!"

"Did you sleep well?" asked her mother-in-law as she came back through the dining room. "Isn't that the robe I gave Steven?"

"Yes. I'm always snitching it: it's so nice and warm," and Mirelle sped up the stairs to avoid further comment.

As she pulled on her smock, she noticed the clay-stained front. She'd planned to throw it in the washer last night and have it drying while she breakfasted. Oh, well, stage-dressing, she thought and went back downstairs.

"We're heading down to Florida not a moment too soon," Dad Martin was saying as Mirelle sat down at the table.

She looked out the window at the grey day and the snow-covered lawns. Black lines of tire marks marred the roads and tangential curves indicated the treacherous road surface. Mirelle wondered just what traction she'd get for the Sprite on the hill.

"Looks like more snow," Steve added, glancing at the sky.

"I just can't get pleased with snow," Mother Martin said in a plaintive voice. "It makes driving and parking so difficult. Now, if the road department would only get going the minute it starts, and make an effort to keep the roads clear . . ."

"In this state," Steve told her, "they always hope that it'll stop before they need to call out the plows."

"That's exactly what I mean. Why, with all the unemployment up here, those people could stay off relief rolls if they'd get put to work clearing snow. And our taxes would stay down."

"You forget," Steve said patiently, "that relief is only partially federal, Mother. But the road department is all State so the more people you put to work on snow disposal, the higher your State taxes."

"Why, that's ridiculous, Steve," his mother said, almost offended by his rebuttal. "Elliot Randolph says . . . "

"That old reactionary . . . "

Mother Martin stiffened in righteous indignation. "Why, Steven Martin, you know perfectly well that Elliot Randolph keeps abreast of every important political issue."

"Yeah, he keeps abreast of it," Steve said, grinning, "but he can't see his breast, his double chins get in the way."

"Arthur Martin, are you going to let your son talk about Elliot Randolph that way?"

"Why not?" Mirelle rather thought that Dad Martin was amused by Steve's remarks. "He's free, white and twenty-one."

Mirelle hastily swallowed the last of her toast and excused herself. She took the leg of lamb out of the refrigerator, inserted the garlic slices, seasoned it, plopped it in the large roasting pan, set the dials on the oven timer, and closed the door on the roast.

"Mother Martin, I've got the roast all ready and the oven set to start so we don't have a thing to do but the vegetables and the salad for dinner."

"But dinner's not till late."

"I know but, with the automatic electric oven, it won't matter if we're late from the Bazaar."

"How about lunch?" demanded Mother Martin.

"Chicken pot pies at church," Steve chimed in.

"Old Kentucky recipe?" asked Dad Martin slyly.

"No, new Girl Scout," Mirelle replied. "Goodbye all."

Her relief at being out in the crisp cold air was tremendous. She opened the garage door and carefully backed the Sprite out. She hoped that Steve would get out with Roman and Nick, and clear the drive against the chance of freezing weather tonight. She eased the Sprite onto the road and took the hill in second with little trouble.

There were quite a few cars already in the church parking

lot and some of the sand from her gravelly spot had been distributed to cut down on skidding. She was gratified to find the first four of last night's leftover number holders waiting for her. Patsy, by her greeting, had renewed her exuberance overnight.

"You know, it's funny," Patsy said as Mirelle settled her first subject down. "You're only doing children. Don't adults want to be done?"

"Adults are more apt to be self-conscious, posing in a busy place. But I suspect it's a case of parents being willing to spend on their children what they'd never dream of doing themselves."

"Guess that makes me not as grownup as I thought I was," Patsy said with giggling candor. "I sure didn't mind posing."

Mirelle was not sure that the fad of the bust would continue as it had started but she worked as quickly as possible. Children were easier to do than adults, their faces still more symmetrical than angular, fewer lines and odd features. The trick was getting the shape of the head right, and the hair pattern. Girls' ears were usually completely hidden by their hair, and a good percentage of the boys had simple long styles. Perhaps it was just as well that the majority of her subjects were young people. She was a trifle startled therefore when Reverend O'Dell slipped onto the stool.

"I assure you that this is not all vanity, Mirelle," said Ken O'Dell. "It's also the only way to get your attention. Your powers of concentration are formidable. I've spoken to you four times with no response. Oh no, I'm far from offended. On the contrary, you've provided an unusual excitement in what, I fear, is usually a rather tame event."

"Excitement?" Mirelle blinked in astonishment.

Ken O'Dell smiled at her. "Yes, my dear Mirelle. As I said, your powers of concentration are phenomenal." He leaned forward and spoke softly. "Glance casually around."

She did and saw a row of small faces, just able to clear the top of the booth, then a second row of curious observers and a rather surprising number of adults watching from the rear lines. She smiled nervously and turned hastily back to O'Dell.

"Oh, good Lord, how long has this been going on?" She felt exceedingly uncomfortable. Her back had been angled to the main part of the hall so that she'd only been conscious of the few children seated on the edge of the stage.

"I wouldn't know," O'Dell said with some delight. "I bought a ticket from Patsy at 10:30 and they'd begun to gather then."

"You're better than TV," Patsy added with a giggle.

Mirelle hunched her shoulders over her work and, in a few moments, was mercifully oblivious to the crowd. Kenneth O'Dell's face was far more interesting to her than all the youthful ones she'd done. To capture an adult in clay was to learn his individuality. As she began to draw the minister's features from the clay, she felt she was getting to know the man far better than she could have in years of casual encounters. Engrossed, she spent a far longer time on him.

"I always envied the unconnected heads of Cicero and Plato, and all those others who held court in the niches of my classrooms," Ken said when Mirelle allowed him to look at the bust. "I must be very vain to get such an inordinate pleasure out of seeing myself in similar noble immobility. And, from the number of relaxed countenances in my congregations on Sundays, I am, alas, no Cicero."

Mirelle put the model high up, regarding it with mixed satisfaction.

"I haven't done you justice, Ken. I'd like to do a life-size bust one day."

"You've done me far more justice than I deserve, Mirelle. Oh, I see your husband and his parents. I must go speak to them."

Mirelle reached out to touch his hand, about to ask him not to refer to her work. He regarded her expectantly, half smiling and then she shook her head, meaning that she had nothing of importance to say. His smile deepened and he patted her hand in a way that told her he had understood her unspoken message.

Countenanced and encouraged by their minister's example, two members of Sessions sat, each more or less amused and embarrassed by the gallery of observers. Mirelle found it necessary to talk to them as they posed and so their sittings took longer.

"Met your in-laws, Mirelle," said Ty Hopkins, who was church treasurer and the manager of the bank which she patronized. "Suggested that they look up my cousin, Will Tackman. He's a vice president of the First National in Orlando. Think they'll like it down there. Town's organized for retired people. Although, come to think about it, St. Cloud might be less expensive. It's smaller, of course. Your father-in-law was asking about investment property. I hope he's not the type to jump first, look later. There're some rather iffey retirement homes among the legitimate ones."

"Dad Martin's always been a good business man, in a small way, of course, but sound," Mirelle said but her mind had leaped on the notion that, if her in-laws did settle in Florida, it would be quite a blessing. "It was kind of you to give him advice."

"Kind?" Ty Hopkins grinned at her. "Not at all. Pure business. And speaking of pure business, have you ever thought of sculpting professionally?"

Mirelle stopped tooling the jawline and stared at Ty Hopkins.

"I've known you two years now, Mirelle, casually, I agree, but I've never heard you mention your work. I'd very much like to see you do something ambitious. You know the Bank's always showing paintings. No reason it can't show sculpture as well."

Mirelle murmured appropriate thanks, adding that she didn't think people in a bank were in the mood to buy art.

"Oh, don't think that," said Ty, raising his bushy eyebrows. He waggled a finger at her. "People DO notice what's displayed in the Bank. You'd be rather surprised at how many of the paintings we hang get sold right there. Humph," he added as she indicated the bust was finished, "my superiors will think I've got delusions of grandeur."

"Make a good paperweight," Mirelle said, keeping her face perfectly straight.

Ty's thick brows almost met over his nose as he feigned displeasure.

"Yes, now that would put me in the proper perspective. More than you know." There was such a bite to his words that Mirelle looked at him apprehensively. "No, no, Mirelle. No offense taken. Keep at it, girl, and when you have something to show, bring it in."

She watched him leave, still a little disturbed by his remarks, when she saw Sylvia and Jamie Howell advancing towards her corner.

"Whoever is next will have to wait twenty minutes while I eat. I'm starved," Mirelle said arbitrarily, ignoring a chorus of protests as she intercepted her friends.

"Next showing, 1:30," Patsy said and slipped out of the booth behind Mirelle.

"Quitter," Sylvia said, frowning with mock reproof.

"I never expected to see either of you here," Mirelle replied, shaking hands with Jamie. His sun lamp treatments were producing results.

"Wouldn't miss the da Vinci act for the world," Jamie said. "Actually we watched you immortalize the V-P. For a gal who works slowly, you've got quite a display." He gestured at the shelves full of drying busts. Then he shook his head deprecatingly. "I distinctly remember you informing me that you weren't the panther-on-the-mantel type: I was glad, happy for you. But now," and he clicked his tongue in disillusion. "I perceive that you are, in fact, of the bust-in-the-family-niche school. Deplorable!"

Sylvia was also shaking her head.

"If you're going to pick fault with an honest, charitable effort, you can both disappear," Mirelle said.

"Not when something smells as good as something does," Jamie replied, sniffing deeply and turning to locate the source.

"They're serving chicken pot pies in the kitchen."

"Chicken pot pies?" Jamie made his eyes wide with simulated excitement.

"Chicken pot pies NOT nine days old," Mirelle said with a laugh.

Jamie took each woman by the arm and propelled them vigorously towards the kitchen. As they entered the busy crowded room, Mirelle noticed with relief that neither Steve nor her in-laws were present. Jamie steered them to the nearest free table.

"I thought they'd outlawed child slavery in this state," he murmured as one of the Girl Scout waitresses bore down on their table.

"Oh, Mrs. Martin," the girl began breathlessly, "will you have time to do any of us? I mean, we're stuck here serving all day."

"Just catch Mrs. McHugh and tell her to give you a number."

"Oh wow! That's marvie. Pies all around?"

"Three for me," Jamie said in such a sepulchral voice that the little Scout eyed him nervously.

"He's been sick," Sylvia said with gentle solicitousness, laying a hand on Jamie's arm.

"I hope you're much better now," the girl said dutifully.

"I heroically revived, stimulated by the incredible aroma of those three chicken pot pies."

"Jamie!" Mirelle saw that the girl was unable to cope with such bantering.

"Coffee, tea, milk or Coke?" The Scout wrote down the orders and hurried off.

"They can certainly mobilize the resources of this church," Sylvia remarked, a trifle enviously. "Now at Greenvale . . . " she shook her head sadly.

"They conned Nick and Roman into being busboys," Mirelle said, pointing to Nick struggling pantrywards with a loaded tray.

"Odds he drops it," Jamie said.

"That wouldn't matter. The crockery here is designed to bounce," Mirelle told him.

Jamie began to shake his head, pityingly. "I never have figured out how organized religion can prevail on otherwise reasonable people to do service in the name of religion that they would begrudge doing for any other."

"What?" Mirelle wasn't certain that she'd heard aright and Sylvia was reduced to staring at him.

Fortunately the Girl Scout came with their lunches. Just as if he hadn't dropped an unsavory thought, Jamie forked open his pie and speared a generous portion of white meat chicken.

"Well, Christian charity for once is substantial." He took the first bite, still skeptical but his face was beatific as he began to chew. "And exactly as advertised. Delicious!"

"Well, I'm relieved to hear that," Mirelle said caustically.

Jamie eyed her, eyebrows raised. "Sorry, m'dear. I have always been somewhat nauseated by too much good done and doing. I distrust it intensely."

"Like beef tea?" Sylvia asked.

"I'm speaking of wholesale lots, not isolated incidents. For instance, I assume this Bazaar has some ostensible purpose?"

"Yes, the annual payment on the mortgage," Mirelle replied.

"Well, then, considering the hundreds and thousands of people starving, wouldn't it have been more Christian to spend the money on roofs over the heads that have none, than an additional roof over already well-covered heads? And . . . " Jamie cocked a finger at Mirelle, "it would be far more reasonable for you to apply the effort which you have expended here today in forwarding your own career instead of knocking out busts that will, I'm positive, be broken into so much dust in the next week or two."

"Hey," Sylvia knocked Jamie's arm to get his attention, "that's hitting below the belt."

"Perhaps," Jamie replied, returning her glance coolly. "But I find this an appalling waste of Mirelle's talent and time. It gets her nowhere . . . "

"That's for me to say," Mirelle put in, wondering why Jamie's unexpected opinion irritated her so much. "I wanted to do it. I did it. Furthermore, it may well have furthered my career. Ty Hopkins said that I may exhibit my sculpture in his bank."

"Yah!" Jamie was scornful.

"Oh, now wait a minute," Sylvia said, "banks are good show places."

"Mirelle's work exhibited with the mossy millstone school of murky watercolors?"

"The quality of hers will stand out all the more," Sylvia replied staunchly.

"Indeed? To what end? Who'll buy in a bank? Certainly not the advanced tradeschool characters who infest this town. They haven't the perception or wit to appreciate what she does. Which, dear ladies, is why I find this situation so revolting."

Sylvia leaned across the small table and put a light hand on Jamie's arm. "My dear Mr. Howell, whatever you may think of this Bazaar situation . . . " Her eyes crinkled as Jamie groaned over her pun, " . . . it has forced Mirelle to do some intensive work. I intend to see that she continues: that she starts showing in whatever bank, left, right, Wilmington or Delaware Trust, and sells. And works. I happen to know it's no easier to get into a good gallery than it is to play Carnegie Hall, but the point is she'll be working, showing and seen. Quite likely she'll also sell. Because it's odd but these tradeschool degree boys pull down damned high salaries. And they've suddenly discovered that they've been missing things while they studied isocyanates and polymers and they might just as well pay their money to Mirelle for her sculpture. Those little busts you so contemptuously dismiss are a starter. Small but a starter and they are commercial."

"I'm not sure," Jamie replied with a caustic edge on his voice, "if the bust-in-the-niche is any improvement over the panther-on-the-mantel."

"My dear sir, of course it is," Sylvia reassured him. "Each bust is of a different person but when you've seen one prowling panther, you've seen them all. Speaking of prowlers, how're things at the in-law infested mansion, Mirelle?"

"More or less," she answered and rose. "I've got to get commercial again. See you tonight, Sylvia. And Sylvia . . . "

"I know, I know," Sylvia said, nodding vehemently. "I'll behave myself."

Mirelle was considerably disturbed by Jamie's remarks. If he deplored how she was using her talent, why had he come to the church? Sylvia had the right of it: you started and used what facilities were available: there was nothing onerous about using a bank. Nothing. James Howell had no call to be so supercilious. Of course, she was using her time to do something other than the commission he'd asked of her. Maybe that was what was annoying him. She'd get right to work on it after the Bazaar was over. Sylvia was also correct when she said that the Bazaar had gotten Mirelle started.

Patsy was rolling her eyes in mock despair when Mirelle returned to the booth.

"There isn't a single thing left to sell. Not a plate, cup, mug, Dirty Dick or creche animal. I have this whole list of prepaid orders." She stressed the last two words triumphantly. "You'll be busting until midnight the way the numbers have been selling."

"I can't," said Mirelle with a groan. "I've a dinner party to give."

"What'll we do?" Patsy was wide-eyed with dismay.

"Just don't give out any more numbers. I'll try to arrange additional sittings for those I can't get done today. Next customer," she called out, sitting down at her table and reaching for yet another clay block.

It was 5:20 before she finished, having decided that the difficulties of arranging sittings far outweighed finishing up today, no matter how fatigued she was. She had a nagging ache between her shoulder blades.

As she left the church, Mirelle catalogued the things to be done once she got home and decided that a bath headed the list. A good hot one would soak the fatigue out of her bones. She could get Roman to set the table and Nick to vacuum the living room. Steve could set up drinks. When she got in the door, Tonia cannonaded into her legs, crying bitterly.

"What's wrong with you, miss?"

"I don't like Grandmother," Tonia sobbed.

Steve came up from the game room looking like a thundercloud.

"I thought you were going to be back at 4:00," he said.

"My popularity was overwhelming. Did you check the roast?"

"Roast? I've had these brats screaming all afternoon."

Mirelle's head began to ache. She went out into the kitchen and was met with no warmth, no aroma of roast lamb. She yanked open the oven door. Grimly fighting the desire to shriek, she saw that the important automatic timer had been shut off. She wrenched the dials about to get the oven started.

"I don't like Grandmother," Tonia continued to sob, having followed Mirelle into the kitchen.

"You won't like me either if you don't do exactly as I ask," Mirelle said roughly. "Get Roman in here on the double."

Tonia, still gulping her sobs, obeyed that tone without argument. Mirelle checked the dishwasher, vainly hoping that someone had thought to turn it on after breakfast.

No such luck. She mentally tossed a coin between the steaming bath for which she yearned and enough clean silver and dishes to serve her dinner. She filled the slot with powder and slammed in the control, listening masochistically to the damned thing filling up with all that hot water.

"Is there anything I can do to help you, Mary Ellen, now that you're home?" Mother Martin asked.

"I hate to ask you to do anything for a dinner party that is supposedly in your honor," Mirelle said, keeping her voice as colorless as possible.

"Whatchya want, ma?" Roman asked from the doorway.

"I want my table set and you know where all the good china and crystal are. Now, Mrs. Hollander told me that you were her most reliable helper yesterday, do the same for me."

"Why, let me do that, Mary Ellen."

"I can do it all myself," Roman said.

"Now you go on and watch TV," Mother Martin replied. "Table setting's no job for a boy, anyway."

"In this house it is," Mirelle said before she could stop herself. "Roman, is the living room clean?"

"I'll check," Roman mumbled, sourly.

"Steve will fix the cocktail tray," Mirelle said, looking into the liquor cabinet.

"Drinks?" Mother Martin asked, immediately alert.

It had been so long since Mirelle had entertained her in-laws in her own home that she had forgotten that they did not approve of anything stronger than sherry.

"Yes, drinks," Mirelle said, trying not to sound defiant. "The Esterhazys and the Blackburns drink, and so do the Martins."

"Why, Steve never touched anything stronger than sherry," his mother exclaimed indignantly, implying that it was Mirelle's influence which had caused this deplorable change.

"Steve has been drinking a lot more than sherry in the way of business for some years now," Mirelle said. "My good linen is in the second drawer of the dining room chest. I'd planned to use the pink cloth and napkins. The water gob-lets are on the third shelf. There are pink candles in the top drawer and the pewter candlesticks are in the closet. I think there's just enough hot water for me to have a quick wash."

She met Roman on her way to the stairs.

"It needs vacuuming, Ma. Tonia's been cutting paper dolls again."

"Roman, just vacuum. Don't boss Tonia! She's in a state and I have no time to pacify her. My guests are coming in barely an hour and I'm bushed."

"Okay, Ma," and Roman flashed his helpful smile at her appeal.

Mirelle started the water in the tub, and laid out her dress. She was about to throw off the clayey smock when Mother Martin called up the stairwell.

"Mary Ellen, I can't seem to find the cloth you want."

Mirelle went down and found the cloth and the napkins exactly where she had said they were.

"I thought you'd said white. I'm sorry."

Mirelle got back upstairs to find that the small supply of

hot water left from the dishwasher had cooled to tepid.

Savagely now she threw off her clothes and got into the tub. There was not much point in soaking because the water had neither the quantity nor quality for any therapy.

"Mary Ellen," called her mother-in-law in a shrill voice, "which goblets shall I use? You have so many."

Mirelle groaned. She called that she was coming, hastily toweled herself dry and, throwing on Steve's robe, tore downstairs.

This time she laid out everything that would be needed to set the table, wishing that she had insisted that Roman did it, and went back upstairs to lie down. But she was tense, waiting for the next complaining summons. Steve came in the room, still scowling.

"Who turned off the automatic timer?" she asked before he could voice the complaints she knew he was harboring.

"Hell, how should I know? What I want . . . "

"Your mother is going to object to your drinking," Mirelle cut in, disregarding him.

"The way I feel she can just object. I *need* a drink after today. God, how I wish you hadn't been involved in that Bazaar."

He was rubbing the back of his neck which, to Mirelle, was the surest sign that his mother had been needling him.

"I'm not sorry I was then, if that's the way the day went. What's wrong? Your mother's nose out of joint because the church took the onus from my art?"

Steve looked about to explode and then, utterly deflating, he sagged onto the bed beside her.

"That's just about the size of it, Mirelle," he said, pursing his lips angrily, nodding his head up and down. "No one was all that interested in their state visit to Florida. Great event, their joining the Randolphs in Orlando, a real social coup. No, everyone wanted to know about your work, wanted to talk about you."

"What happened to Tonia?" Mirelle asked, deliberately cutting off his recital.

"Tonia and her grandmother are not likely ever to agree, particularly over matters of hair styling and dress," Steve said, a trace of a smile tugging at his mouth. "Seems all well brought up young girls should have pigtails and pinafores."

"No pigtails with Tonia's face structure."

Roman barged in. "All neat as a whistle," he said and then carefully closed the door. "But Grandmother's setting the table all wrong," he added, his young face distorted with worry.

Mirelle sighed deeply and struggled out of the bed.

"Roman, fix the icebucket and the liquor on the tray, the silver one, while I dress," Steve said, peeling off his shirt.

"Righto," he said, delighted for assistant bartending was currently his favorite household task.

Mirelle was struggling into her dress when Roman came back, stamping down each foot.

"What's wrong with you? And please help me with my dress," she said, turning so he could pull up the zipper.

"Grandmother says I'm not to touch the bottles. What does she think I'll do? Take a snort when her back is turned?"

Mirelle took a very deep breath, as much to get the zipper moving as to control the unreasoning anger inside her.

"Roman, your grandmother has different ideas about bringing up children . . . "

"I'll say so," and her son sounded so much like Steve that the comparison startled Mirelle.

"Robert Marion," Mirelle said sternly, for it was unlike Roman to be rebellious.

"Aw, gee, a guy can't do anything around here suddenly without being treated like a baby!" He shifted his feet, digging his hands into his pockets and emphasizing his discontent with violent twitchings of his shoulders.

"I'm dressed, son. We'll fix it together," Steve said, coming in from the bathroom. He draped his tie around his neck and, arm about Roman's shoulders, the two walked out of the bedroom.

"In-laws." Mirelle ground out the words between gritted teeth. "God, does she always have to twist everything out of focus? Well, maybe this weekend, with her carping at our children all the time, will show Steve how to separate himself from the rest of the stupidities of his childhood."

She took a good look at herself in the mirror, to make sure her make-up hadn't smudged getting into the dress. Anger had brought color to her cheeks and fatigue blurred interesting shadows around her eyes so that Mirelle could objectively consider herself pretty tonight.

"The fringe benefits of in-laws," she muttered to her reflection, trying to grab a positive thought for comfort and morale.

Steve's voice had a decided edge to it as he and Roman finished their preparations in the kitchen.

"Make us a big bowl of popcorn, too, will you, Roman?" his father directed, picking up the tray. "What's wrong, Mirelle?"

"Roman said that Mother Martin has set the table wrong, but I can't tell how?" Mirelle said in weary exasperation.

Steve glanced at the table. "She's set all the serving pieces in front of her place, all the plates around and there are three extra settings, unless you intend cramming the children in with the adults after all."

Mirelle slapped her forehead with her hand and advanced on the table to correct it just as Mother Martin came bustling downstairs.

"Steven Martin, I want a word with you about Robert," she said at her most forbidding. "Imagine! Allowing a child to set up a cocktail tray!"

"He never forgets a thing, Mother," Steve said.

"But what if he should get the notion to drink something?" his mother demanded, shocked.

"He wouldn't because he's already done his sampling and he doesn't like the taste of liquor."

"He's tasted alcohol?"

"Yes, he has already tasted alcohol."

"Arthur Martin," she said, rounding fiercely on her husband as he entered. "Did you hear what your son said? He's allowed that child to have an alcoholic beverage."

"I also heard him say that Roman didn't like it," Dad

Martin reminded her. "Which, I think, makes much more sense than forcing the boy to sneak some in the garage."

"What do you mean, sneak some in the garage?"

"What Dad means, Mom," Steve replied with a glint in his eyes, "is that he caught Ralph and me with his Scotch in the garage one day when we were about Roman's age."

His mother clutched at a dining room chair for support at this new shock.

"When did that happen?" she demanded, regaining her composure.

"When I was eleven and Ralph was fourteen."

"And you never so much as breathed a word to me, Arthur Martin!"

"No," replied Dad Martin reasonably, "because I figured it was my business when my sons drank. We had a long talk and it turned out that the only reason they'd tried some was because they'd heard you talking so much against it. Steve and Ralph both have good heads for liquor. Get it from me, I guess. And you've never objected to my drinking."

"You're an adult," she began in defense of her stricture.

"Yes, and don't forget that your sons are, too. So I think, Marian, you'd better stop interfering with the way Steve is raising his kids."

Mother Martin looked in astonishment at her husband, for once unsure of herself. Then, as he started to fix himself a stiff drink, she lapsed into grieved and disapproving silence.

Mirelle overheard the whole conversation as she quietly reset her table, redistributing the serving pieces by the hot pads and gathering up the plates to put them to warm. She checked the roast. Then she noticed the expression on Roman's face and realized that he had also heard the exchange.

"Now, listen to me, Robert Marion," she said quietly, "habits in child-raising have changed since Mother Martin's day, but she brought your father up to be a fine man. It's the end result that matters, pal. So you just close your big ears and your big mouth."

"Aw, Mom, as if I'd go blabbing . . . "

"Especially not to Nick."

Roman started to shake the popcorn pan furiously.

Mirelle tested the roast and decided that dinner was going to be a good hour and a half late. She fixed the salad quickly and got the dressing out to *chambré*. She turned on the small broiler for heating the canapes. Just on the dot of 7:00, she heard the doorbell.

"I'll get it. I'll get it," roared Nick, charging up from the gameroom, scrambling to get to the door first. "Who're you?" he demanded in surprise.

"Nick!" Steve gave him a shocked reprimand. "Ann, Red, good evening. This young gangster is Nicholas. Nick, do you think you could prove to Mr. and Mrs. Blackburn that you have some manners?"

"Sure," Nick replied, unabashed. "Very pleased to meet you, Mrs. Blackburn. Let me have your coat. I'll take yours, too, sir. Isn't it a lovely evening?"

"That's better."

"Shoulda tol' me who was coming. I thought it was Aunt Sylvia," said Nick, charging upstairs with hats and coats.

Mirelle saw the back of him as she came into the hall to be presented to Steve's boss and his wife.

Red Blackburn was a tall, heavy-set man, in his mid-forties, with red, attractively greying hair. His wife, Ann, was a very handsome woman with frosted blonde hair, nearly as tall as her husband, and dressed simply but with great style. They greeted Mirelle with conventional warmth and guarded appraisal.

Mirelle knew then that she was on review and wished she'd realized this possibility before she had invited them on what was surely going to be a trying evening.

No sooner had the Blackburns been introduced to the senior Martins than Sylvia and G.F. arrived. G.F. did his usual courtly bow over Marian Martin's hand and lingered a noticeable pause longer over Ann Blackburn's. Roman arrived with the first of the hot canapes and passed them deftly around.

"The next time I need a butler, are you for hire?" Ann asked, smiling up at Roman.

"My rates are low and I guarantee satisfaction," Roman

replied in the accent affected by well-trained English butlers.

"Well," Ann exclaimed, delighted, "here's a live one!"

"Robert, don't be saucy," Mother Martin admonished.

"He's not the least bit saucy, Mrs. Martin, he's charming," Ann said. "I only wish my teenager could make an original statement to an adult without stuttering and blushing."

Roman flushed and barely saved himself from stumbling over his feet as he presented the tray to Sylvia.

"Why don't you ever flirt with me?" she asked in a loud stage whisper.

"Roman!" Steve's quiet word held a warning.

"That's an interesting nickname," Ann said.

"He was christened Robert Marion," Steve explained, handing Ann her drink. "But he couldn't say it and it came out 'Roman' which Mirelle preferred to the usual Bob or Rob."

"What's Mirelle short for?" asked Ann.

"Mary Ellen but my . . . " Mirelle hesitated because she caught Mother Martin's disapproving glance. The woman disliked any mention of Mirelle's past and particularly her European childhood. " . . . my tongue tripped, too, and it was contracted into Mirelle," and she damned herself for a coward, allowing Marion Martin's petty grievance to inhibit the truth.

"I always thought it was your French nursemaid who gave you that nickname," Steve said, and all Mirelle could do was smile.

"Oh, were you raised abroad, too?" Ann asked with real interest.

Mirelle saw Sylvia's raised eyebrows. "You were?"

"My father was in the diplomatic corps. As a child, I went all around the world."

"Ann's even been in prison," her husband added with a sly grin.

Mirelle saw Ann flush and was quick to note that, although Red might make a joke of it now, it had been no joke to Ann, then or now.

"Yes," she explained swiftly in a bright voice, "in China during the Japanese war in the late thirties. But we weren't held as long as some of our friends."

"Was your father ever posted in Vienna?" G.F. asked, into the brief silence.

"In a Japanese prison camp?" Mother Martin asked, startled into overriding G.F.'s tactful change.

"Yes." Ann replied in a flat voice that would have told anyone the least perceptive that she didn't wish to continue talking about the experience.

"You're Viennese, aren't you, G.F., and your family often entertained the diplomatic corps," Mirelle said brightly.

"But you must have been just a child," Marian Martin persisted.

Ann smiled with thin courtesy. "I was."

"It's such a mercy how easily children forget their unpleasant experiences and remember only the nice ones," Mother Martin said fatuously.

Mirelle saw the tightening of Ann's mouth and knew that she hadn't at all forgotten her unpleasant experiences.

"Yes, Mr. Esterhazy, my father was posted to Vienna," she said, determinedly looking beyond Mother Martin. "As a matter of fact, we were there when Hitler marched in. I remember that Mother was particularly furious because we had barely had time to get settled in the *schloss* before we had to leave," Ann's face darkened, "for the second time in rather a rush, leaving everything behind us."

"So many experiences are just wasted in children," Mother Martin went on, "when all you can remember about Vienna is being angry at leaving it. Now, Steve was there during and after the war and he's told us so much about Vienna. Of course, he was a grown man then and could appreciate the finer things."

G.F. turned to Steve. "You served in Austria?"

"Yes, with the occupation. I really love that city, even though the Viennese I met kept telling me that this wasn't the real Vienna, that the real Vienna would take years to bloom again. Then, just when I didn't want to, I was transferred home in '46. My points made me eligible for discharge."

"Steve had a brilliant war career," Mother Martin said, still fatuous. "Both my sons did and I'm sure Ralph would have been decorated, too, if he hadn't been wounded so terribly."

Mirelle looked sideways at Steve and saw the telltale jerk of his mouth at the mention of Ralph's wound. Something had happened then that Steve knew and his parents did not, something that still rankled deeply. In their early courtship days, Steve had drunk his army experiences out of his mind and his dreams. When they had first married, she'd often had to wake him out of 'killing nightmares' but, with time, the deep scars had healed.

"Steve was awarded the Bronze Star," his mother rambled on, directing her remarks to Red. "But he never would say why."

Red made a suitable rejoinder and then looked inquiringly at Steve who shrugged diffidently.

"Steve always says that they were handing them out with the C-rations that morning," Mirelle remarked when patently Steve remained silent.

"Mary Ellen, you shouldn't be so flippant about Steve's heroism."

"Steve is."

"You were infantry, Steve?" Red asked.

"Yes," and then he asked Red if he could freshen his drink.

"I've eaten all the cheese canapes," Sylvia announced, rising with the tray in her hand. "Mirelle, are there any more left in the kitchen? I'll buttle now."

"There are more because I have to warn everyone that dinner will be later than planned. My automatic oven failed me," Mirelle said with a light laugh.

"Mine does that, too," Ann said, chuckling, "but only when I am absolutely relying on it."

"Now, Mary Ellen, you mustn't tell a lie," Mother Martin said. "The truth is that she was so busy with her church Bazaar that she didn't get home in time to turn the oven on."

"All in a good cause," G.F. said, sliding neatly into the gaffe.

Mirelle, too, managed a tolerant chuckle as she and Sylvia made for the kitchen.

"Good God," Sylvia said *sotto voce* as they got out of earshot, "can't she say anything that isn't two-edged? At least my mother gives me a fair break at rebuttal."

"I'd give anything to know who fiddled with the setting," Mirelle said through gritted teeth.

"Why does she hate your guts?" Sylvia asked.

Mirelle sighed. "I appreciate your unbiased opinion. It's trite to say that she resents me marrying her precious son but that was the start of it. She also likes to dominate. That's her talent."

"She can have it. Your father-in-law seems nice. Also quiet."

"Sylvia, can you get the conversation around to Florida, please?"

"Sure, sure, Mirelle."

Roman came in for more ice.

"Grandmother unset the oven herself," he whispered to his mother. "I saw her."

"That's what I suspected," Mirelle said. "But why? I warned everyone that I'd preset it."

"Grandfather wanted some broiled bacon."

"Okay, okay. Leave it at that."

"But it isn't fair to you, Mother," Roman said in protest.

Mirelle kissed his cheek quickly to take the sting out of his resentment for her sake. "I'll live."

"Say, Mirelle," Sylvia said when Roman had left, "what's this with Ann Blackburn?"

"I just met her."

"Your precious mother-in-law's all wrong if she thinks that gal forgot any of her 'unpleasant childhood experiences.' "

"I know. I saw it too."

"Well, here goes Sylvia into the fray," and, hoisting the tray over her shoulder theatrically, Sylvia went out.

When Mirelle got back to the living room, conversation was well launched on the subject of Florida.

"My parents live in Kissimmee," Ann was saying.

"Miss me?" Mother Martin stumbled over the name.

"No, Kis-sim-mee," Ann explained. "It's an Indian name. Father bought out on Lake Bryant, three hundred feet on the lake front and the house has everything every one of our previous posts lacked."

"Three hundred lake front feet?" Dad Martin perked up with real interest.

"Dad Mergenthau is a great one for buying innocently just the right thing," Red said with a laugh. "We've spent a lot of our vacations there with the kids, camping by the lake. Are you interested in fishing, Mr. Martin?"

"Never had the time."

"You should try it. Go over Daytona way and do some night fishing on the Banana River," Red went on, leaning towards Arthur Martin to emphasize his recommendation.

"I could never fish," Marian Martin said with a shudder.

"Just what my mother said," Red replied with a chuckle. "My folks visited the Mergenthaus for the first time about four years ago and hell, if Mother didn't become so devoted a fisher by the end of the first summer that she made Dad promise to retire there. They bought a place outside Daytona but they only use it during the worst part of the winter. Dad is still quite active in business."

"I don't think I could ever fish," Marian Martin repeated.

"It's contagious," Ann said, "or do I mean infectious?"

"Your parents like it out at Lake Bryant?" Dad Martin asked, bringing the subject back to relevant matters.

Fortunately both Ann and Red had considerable knowledge about the area around Orlando and it was time for dinner to be served before the subject was exhausted. Dad Martin had taken notes, including the addresses of both sets of parents.

Mirelle hastily carved some lamb for the children, horrified that it was nearly 9:00 o'clock and they were still dinnerless. Roman brought the plates down to the gameroom, coming back for milk and to inform his mother that Tonia had fallen asleep in a puddle of Crispy Critters.

"The poor dear. Well, cover her up and for Pete's sake, sweep up the cereal."

Sylvia invaded the kitchen while Mirelle was serving up the vegetable and efficiently aided in carrying the dishes to the table. Mirelle called Steve in to carve.

"Thanks, Mother, just the same but you're guest of honor," Steve was saying over his shoulder as he came into the kitchen. Then he started to curse under his breath.

Sylvia looked at Mirelle as if to say 'she's riding him hard' and Mirelle shook her head imperceptibly. Sylvia shrugged and carried in the broccoli.

"Dinner's served at long last," Mirelle called out cheerfully. "Mother Martin, you're here at the head of the table. The rest of you space yourselves, only no husband can sit next to his wife."

Mother Martin then noticed that the serving spoons had been removed from her place but before she could comment on that, Steve came in with the roast. No sooner had her plate been passed than she found a new objection.

"Why, Mary Ellen, this meat isn't cooked. It's pink."

"Ah, then, the lamb is done just right, the European way," G.F. said appreciatively. "So few Americans understand that lamb must be treated tenderly, not cooked until there isn't any juice or sweetness left in the meat. Mrs. Martin, may I serve you some of this broccoli?"

Marian Martin was not immune to G.F.'s brand of flattering attention and Mirelle was deeply grateful for his suave intervention. Her mother-in-law was almost simpering with pleasure.

"What have you done to the broccoli?" asked Red. "It tastes good."

"He likes your broccoli?" Ann Blackburn looked up in exaggerated surprise. "I beg you, tell me what you've done. I haven't been able to serve it to him for ten years."

"Simple. Cooked with a little butter in a heavy iron saucepan, served with caraway seeds and plenty of butter."

"The Hungarian in Mirelle coming out in triumph," Sylvia said, with a bland smile.

Mother Martin cut herself short mid-sentence to G.F. and stared down the table.

"Is that where your marvelous bone structure comes from?" Ann asked. "You're so delightfully un-American-looking."

"Thank you," Mirelle said and hoped that would be the last from Sylvia along this line.

"My four kids, nice, healthy, are so exactly the American prototype that you couldn't pick them out of a crowd of kids the same age. But all three of yours," Ann went on while Mirelle tried to look pleased, "have an indefinable difference about them. They'll always be noticeable." She turned to Red. "Remember how crushed I was, Red, when Professor D'Alseigne called Jerry *'un vrai type américain'*?"

"You may have been crushed, but I was flattered. All that foreign living ruins a good American."

"I think Robert and Nicholas look exactly like their father," Mother Martin said in an unequivocal tone of voice.

"Yes, they do," Ann agreed warmly, "except for their eyes, and Roman's cheekbones which are wide and high, just like his mother's. Of course, Tonia is the spirit and image of you, Mrs. Martin, plus those magnificent eyes. Where did you get such an unusual shade of blue from, Mirelle?"

"My unlamented father," Mirelle said lightly.

"The Hungarian." Sylvia qualified her statement.

"Did you know, Mrs. Martin," G.F. said, smiling, "that my mother was painted by Mirelle's father? He was extremely successful at the time as well as extremely expensive." G.F. chuckled reminiscently. "If there were status symbols in those careless days, one was to have a portrait done by Lajos Neagu."

Mother Martin looked as if she were going to have a fit. Mirelle tried desperately to think of something to fill in the deathly still silence.

"Neagu . . . Neagu . . . " Ann murmured, trying to

make an association. "Oh, yes, of course!" Her eyes widened with astonished delight. "Was *he* your father?"

Helplessly, Mirelle nodded. She didn't dare look at anyone else. But she wanted to murder Sylvia and G.F. Couldn't they realize that accepting her bastardy so casually would only exacerbate the Martins' displeasure?

"You're so right, G.F., about a Neagu portrait being a status symbol," Ann went on. "I remember the Ambassador's wife . . . and she was the most awful bitch, too . . . paid a small fortune to be done by Neagu. He gave the most outrageous parties. How wonderful, Mirelle. Just wait till I tell Mother that I've met Neagu's daughter. Won't she be thrilled? Do be sure to tell Mother when you meet, Mrs. Martin, that your daughter-in-law is Lajos Neagu's daughter. She'll do anything to smooth your way then."

Mother Martin sat stiffly still in her chair, staring at Ann Blackburn with disbelief.

"Did you inherit any of the fabulous Neagu talent, Mirelle?" Ann was too excited to notice the reception of her remarks.

"Watch out, Mirelle," Red laughed indulgently for he had noticed the strained look, "Ann collects people the way others collect stamps."

"Oh, you!" Ann gave him a dirty look. "People are so fascinating. After all, you have to live with them and most of them are so dull and prosaic." She sighed. "I sometimes miss the diplomatic phase of my life. It could be very exciting."

"After being around the world six, or was it seven times, Wilmington is rather dull potatoes for my wife," Red said.

"It is not," she contradicted him with spirit. "There are interesting people all over the world *and* in Wilmington. Why, here are Mr. and Mrs. Martin about to remove themselves all the way to Florida."

Silently Mirelle blessed her for that.

"And Mirelle with a famous father," she continued, compounding her original errors. "Now, do you paint, Mirelle?"

"No, she sculpts," Steve said very distinctly. Mirelle stole a glance at him and saw that his teeth were tightly locked but she couldn't tell whether he was just angry or worried about the impression this conversation might be giving Red Blackburn.

"You should have seen her at the church bazaar," Sylvia said in her drawl. "Her booth was very popular. She worked small busts in clay right there."

"May I see some of your work?" Ann asked.

"Watch out, Mirelle," Red said, "she's a manager."

"Oh, you be quiet, Red Blackburn. For the first time in years you introduce me to one salesman's wife who isn't a complete and utter idiot."

"Ann!" Red exclaimed, a little startled.

"Oh, Mirelle's no dope, Arthur Blackburn," Ann said with a gay laugh. "She's been with the Company long enough to know the routine. Sales managers always contrive to meet the wives," and Ann rolled her eyes, "and then the sales managers' wives have to listen to what child got sick with what ailment at what age."

Sylvia laughed out loud. " 'Judy O'Grady . . . "

" 'And the Colonel's lady . . . ' " Ann picked it up jubilantly.

" . . . 'Are sisters under the skin!' " Mirelle capped the verse.

"You are all behaving outrageously," Red said.

"What a relief!" his wife replied. "Particularly if you like her broccoli."

"How long have you two been in Wilmington?" Sylvia wanted to know.

"Three years, and then five years in the southwest, and well, I've been travelling all my born days."

"We're more or less settled now, sweetheart," Red reassured his wife.

"I remember my father telling my mother that." Ann's attitude was distinctly skeptical.

"Didn't you say that they'd retired to Florida?" asked Dad Martin.

"I don't want to be seventy when we're *finally* settled," Ann answered tartly.

"Salesmen's wives of the world, unite!" Sylvia chanted,

raising one hand dramatically over her head. "We have nothing to lose but our husbands' jobs!"

"My wife will find a cause anywhere in the world," G.F. said with tolerant amusement.

"Ooops, sorry. I get carried away."

"Yes, don't you just?" Mirelle responded with some asperity.

"Always and only the very best causes," Sylvia said, grinning like a cheshire cat.

"Lost any lately?" asked Steve in a quiet voice.

"Touché!" G.F. said, and Sylvia had the grace to flush.

Ann and Red were aware of an undercurrent, aware, too, that the Martins had turned their entire attention to their plates.

"Didn't I see your name on a Democratic poster?" Ann asked Sylvia.

"Hmm, yes. I'm a ward-heeler. That's how I met Mirelle."

"Are you and G.F. both lawyers then?"

"Heavens, no." Sylvia was startled. "One cynic in the family is enough."

G.F. placed a hand on his heart in exaggerated hurt. "I am touched to the quick to think that my wife believes that my profession has made me cynical. Although it is true that I have seen the seamy side of life, I have been able to retain my naiveté and *joie de vivre*!"

"Also your pose as a *boulevardier*," Mirelle added and Ann laughed.

"Did you ever get to Paris, Steve?" Red asked.

"No, I was too busy liberating Vienna," he replied, "and from what I heard on the ship home, I think I pulled the better duty."

"Well, I've heard that Vienna has quite a reputation, but there was this place on the left bank," and Red launched into a well told and, from the slightly glazed expression on Ann's face, an oft-repeated humorous incident.

That set G.F. off with a story which had happened to him on his arrival in the States in the late 40's and the men dominated the conversation. Dinner finally ended and Mirelle served coffee and liqueurs in the living room.

When Sylvia volunteered to help Mirelle clear the table, Mirelle demanded an explanation of her leading remarks during dinner.

"I watched your mother-in-law, Mirelle, and it's perfectly obvious that anything socially important counts with her. She sure didn't like your popularity at the Bazaar, but when she saw how much more important she became as your mother-in-law, you'd've laughed yourself sick to hear how much credit she was willing to take for encouraging you!" Sylvia's low voice was fierce with anger. "So G.F. and I decided to mention your very socially acceptable father. Just luck that Ann Blackburn—she's a find; I'll collect her myself—had also heard of Lajos Neagu. Mother Martin may not like it but I'll bet you anything she's now willing to lump it. And make good use of the Neagu connection with Mrs. Mergenthau. You might also take note of the fact, my friend," and Sylvia became less fierce as she covered Mirelle's hand with hers, "that it was never mentioned that your father and your mother were not married to each other. And no one on this side of the Atlantic is going to know unless you tell them."

Some of Mirelle's anger with Sylvia dissipated when she was forced to admit that Sylvia's ploy was logical.

"Evil is in the mind of the beholder, hon," Sylvia went on. "Not that your mother-in-law would believe good of you under the best possible circumstances."

"Oh, Sylvia!"

"Don't 'Oh Sylvia' me. At least she makes no pretense of any affection. She's of the ignorance-is-bliss school and she sure tries to ignore your existence. Say, I hadn't realized just how much Tonia looks like her? And did you see her face flush when Ann commented on the resemblance?"

"Yes, because Tonia also inherited Mother Martin's sense of importance."

"And the importance of being Mother Martin requires no imitations?"

"I guess. When I got home tonight, Tonia was in tears,

and I haven't had a chance to find out from Steve what happened."

Steve came in at the moment to refill the coffee pot.

"How did you find out about Mirelle's father, Sylvia?" he asked in a blunt hard voice.

"With some skillful cross-examination, a technique which I use rather well, even on my husband." Sylvia rubbed her hands together, a smug expression on her face. "I found out her father was Lajos Neagu. I remembered the family portrait so of course I mentioned it to G.F."

"Clear as mud."

"Steve," Mirelle began, stumbling over the words, "nothing was said . . . about my mother . . . or her husband."

Steve regarded her with narrowed eyes for a moment. "Coffee!" He pointed to the furiously whistling kettle.

Mirelle made a fresh pot and brought it into the living room, returning to the kitchen for more cream. She leaned wearily against the refrigerator door until she felt Sylvia's arm across her shoulders.

"I'd say you won this battle hands down, hon."

"Possibly, but I don't want to lose the war." Mirelle took a deep breath and straightened her shoulders, turning to catch the anxious look on Sylvia's face.

"You won't, Mirelle."

"Steve's relationship with his parents was a very close one."

"He's a big boy now and that devoted mother stuff has ruined many men." Sylvia put a slight emphasis on 'men'. "Well, the Blackburns like you, and Steve has to work for a living."

"Yes, she's an unexpected ally."

"Not all bosses' wives are impossible. Just ninety-nine one-hundredths."

"Onward to the fray," said Mirelle and, arm in arm, the two friends joined the rest of the party.

Mirelle placed herself on the far end of the couch, in the shadows of the room, hoping that the conversation would not devolve onto her again. The rest of the evening however passed very pleasantly. Fortunately the Martins retired at eleven-thirty, using their advancing years as an excuse. The Esterhazys and Blackburns reluctantly departed at one in the morning.

Mirelle started to pick up the party debris, determined to leave the downstairs in order against any criticism the next morning. Steve followed her out to the kitchen with the drinks tray.

"What was Sylvia trying to do this evening?" he asked her, his chin jutting out stubbornly.

"A case of misplaced loyalty, I guess. Look, Steve, I'm far too tired to argue and you are far too upset. Let's not give your mother another excuse to criticize me . . . "

"Criticize you?" Steve exploded. "If you need a taste of criticism, you should have heard her this afternoon!"

Mirelle blinked at him, not sure she understood.

"Do you mean, she was criticizing you?"

"Yes, for letting you participate in the church bazaar, putting yourself in a vulgar limelight, for the lack of supervision of the children, for their manners, for Tonia's appearance, for . . . " Steve raised his arms heavenward in frustration.

"Nancy Lou Randolph would never have put herself in such a position, would she? And her mealy-mouthed children would never dare contradict Mother Martin."

Steve glared fiercely at Mirelle. "Are you jealous of Nancy Lou?"

"Me? Oh, good God, no. But I get her thrown up to me as THE criterion of wifely virtues." Mirelle bit her lip, took a deep breath and said in a restrained voice. "We'll be shrieking at each other in a minute, which is just what your mother wants. To split us apart."

"No, no." Steve shook his head in vehement denial. "She just wants to . . . she's only trying to . . . "

"To what? I can't take that 'mother knows best' bit anymore, Steve. I hope it's worn thin with you, too. Let's go to bed," and she dropped her voice to soft suggestion. Kissing his cheek, she tugged him to follow her.

CHAPTER SIXTEEN

MIRELLE WAS ROUSED from deep slumber with a suddenness which she immediately identified as alarm. She had had the experience twice before. She lay for a moment in bed, gathering her senses, aware first that it was early. She could see the whirling of snow outside the window and wondered if she had been deceived about the hour by the grey skies. Her watch read 4:30 but it had stopped. She looked for the alarm on Steve's bureau. It was gone. Then she realized that it must be Sunday and Roman would have taken the alarm clock to wake himself up for the morning papers.

She threw Steve's robe around her and went into the children's bedroom. Nick was fast asleep in the bed, Tonia was on the cot but Roman was gone. She closed the window and saw a figure pulling a sled, coming down the hill. She watched for a few seconds until she identified the walker as Roman.

He must be cold, she thought, *he's hugging himself.* She glanced over at the clock and saw that it was 8:30. She could go back to bed for maybe half an hour, but the feeling of uneasiness was too pronounced. She went downstairs to fix coffee for herself and was momentarily surprised to see Mother Martin already in the kitchen. For a few minutes she had forgotten that problem.

"Everyone is lazy this morning," her mother-in-law said in a somewhat pleasant voice.

"All except Roman. He's been out delivering papers."

"On a morning like this?" Her pleasantness deteriorated quickly.

"Certainly. Neither rain nor snow nor dark of night . . . "

"That's for postmen, not children."

"Roman's had that paper route for two years. He saves his money regularly and he's very responsible about serving his route on time."

"Well, I don't see that it's at all necessary for him to have a route."

"It isn't. But Roman wanted to do it and as he's always been an early riser, he might as well serve papers."

Mother Martin was unconverted.

Mirelle took her coffee into the dining room and was about to sit down when she saw that Roman had turned into the driveway. She couldn't imagine where he'd found that long red sock and why did he have on two different. . . .

Mirelle ran to the front door and threw it open.

"Are you badly hurt, Roman?" she called, trying to keep her voice calm.

"My leg's cut, Mom, and I think my arm's broken. I'm sorry about the pants," he said with equal calm.

Mirelle dashed down the steps now, disregarding the cold wind and the snow over the tops of her light houseshoes. She resisted the impulse to pick him up in her arms. Mother Martin had come to the front door and when she saw Roman, she started to scream. As Mirelle guided Roman into the hall, her mother-in-law was upstairs, pounding on Steve's door, on her husband's, incoherently shouting disaster.

Mirelle led Roman down to the studio, arranged him on the couch. She threw a blanket about him and smiled reassuringly.

"How did it happen? Before or after?"

"After," and Roman grinned despite his pain. "Started to sled down the big hill and skidded into a storm gutter." Then he grimaced, rolling his eyes at the volume of his grandmother's screams.

Mirelle eased the torn pants away from the gash in his leg: probably from the sled runner, long and nasty. The shin bone was visible. Steve and Dad Martin came clattering down the stairs as she tore the pants leg off at the thigh.

"Steve, call Will Martin. Possible fracture of the right arm, eight inch laceration, deep on the shin bone, from a sled runner. Dad Martin, please get me some towels, dish-towels, napkins, anything that's clean in the laundry. There may be sheets in the dryer."

"Oh, that poor child! That poor child!" Marian Martin's keening was a counterpoint to Mirelle's instruction. "Oh, this is what happens when you don't take proper care of your children. This is what happens . . . "

"If you can't stop that caterwauling immediately, please go to your room," Mirelle said, turning to look up the stairs at the distraught woman. "The boy will be all right but your hysterics are completely unnecessary!"

Dad Martin returned with several napkins and a large towel. Mirelle took them and folded the clean linen over the open wound, binding a second napkin as gently as possible to close the laceration. There was only a hiss of inhaled breath from her son.

"Did you hear how she spoke to me, Arthur?" gasped the outraged wife.

"There's no sense in upsetting the boy. He's the one should be crying, Marian, and I notice he isn't. You never could stand the sight of blood, you know."

"Am I bleeding much, Mom?" Roman asked, suddenly concerned.

"Like a stuck pig," Mirelle informed him.

Steve came back and watched Mirelle fold in a pressure bandage.

"Doc Martin's sending the ambulance for you, Roman."

"Ambulance?" wailed Mother Martin, clapping her

hand to her mouth, her eyes popping out of her head in terror.

"What's all the noise?" Nick demanded, slipping past his grandmother and thudding down the stairs. He looked at the cut incuriously and then brightened suddenly. "Hey, Roman, that's going to take lots of stitches. You should be ahead of Max Schneider then!" Nick was envious. "How'd you do it?"

"Oh, Nicholas," cried his grandmother, snatching him back from the couch. "Come away from there. You shouldn't see such things."

"Why not?" Nick was surprised. "What's wrong, Grandmother? You look kinda green."

"Nick, go watch for the ambulance," Steve said firmly.

Nick's eyes bulged with admiration and excitement. "Ambulance? Gee whiz!" He bounded up the stairs, nearly knocking Tonia down. Mirelle could hear him explaining to her and she went with him, shrieking with glee over the necessity of an ambulance coming to *their* house.

Steve began unfastening the heavy snowboots and chafing Roman's cold toes.

"Can you sit up, honey?" Mirelle asked. He nodded but winced as the movement jarred his arm. Steve helped and they began to remove his damp jacket. Working very carefully, they also got the sleeve off the injured arm without hurting him too much. Through the thinner fabric of the flannel shirt, Mirelle could see the bone disjointure of the forearm. Mastering a desire to be ill, she smiled at her white-faced son.

"What about a shot of bourbon?" Steve murmured to Mirelle. She nodded.

"Gee, Grandfather," Roman said, distracting himself as Mirelle rigged a sling for his arm, "I'm sorry to wreck your visit like this."

"That's all right, sonny," Dad Martin said, glancing reprovingly at his wife when she gasped. "I'm right proud of you. You just take it easy and don't give a moment's thought about wrecking our visit."

Steve came back with a shot glass and sat beside Roman.

"Let's see you knock this back, boy. Take the chill from your bones. It's the very best bourbon in the house so don't waste it."

"But you said not till I'm twenty-one," Roman protested.

"Medicinal," Steve replied. "The trick is in the wrist." He demonstrated.

"Steven Martin, are you giving that child liquor?" Mother Martin demanded, striding across the room.

"For shock, yes. Be quiet, Mother," Steve said without raising his voice. "Go ahead, Roman."

Roman took it down as if to the manner born.

"He's been practising?" Mirelle asked with a nervous laugh. She needed a jolt herself.

"You see 'em do it on TV," Roman said, also a little shaky. "That's strong stuff," he added, unable to keep from coughing but the color was coming back into his face. "It's warm all the way down."

"It does help," Mirelle said, settling him against a pillow, and then rose. "It won't take long for me to dress. Or would you rather have your father at the hospital with you?"

Roman looked anxiously from his mother to his father.

"Both of you go," suggested Dad Martin. "We'll tend the shop."

"Thanks, Dad," Steve said with obvious relief.

As he and Mirelle turned to go upstairs, they saw that Mother Martin had already absented herself. They heard Dad talking quietly to Roman.

"When's that ambulance coming?" demanded Nick, his nose pressed against the window.

"Soon, soon," Steve said. "Now look, Nick, Granddad and Grandmother will be staying with you while we take Ro to the hospital. You do everything you're told to, right smart. Understand?"

"Sure, Dad. Always glad to cooperate in an emergency," Nick said, all seriousness.

"Me, too," vowed Tonia promptly.

"What TV show does that come from?" Steve wanted to know, and there was an odd quaver in his voice.

Mirelle took his hand and dragged him into the kitchen

where she poured a stiff shot of bourbon for each of them.

They had barely finished dressing when they heard the ambulance siren. Nick had thrown open the front door and Tonia was jumping up and down from excitement when they got downstairs again.

"Right down to the gameroom, sirs," Nick said, directing the attendants.

"Thanks, son."

"Did you tangle with a mountain lion, boy?" the other man asked as he saw the scratches on Roman's face that Mirelle somehow hadn't noticed yet.

"I tangled, period," Roman agreed with a wry grin.

"Don't want to jar that arm, feller, so you just use your other hand to keep it steady, and we'll just llllliffft you over here. There now." They had deftly completed the maneuver before Roman could tense up.

"Only room for one of you two in the back, so flip a coin," the attendant told Steve and Mirelle.

"You go with him, Steve," Mirelle suggested, thinking that would be better for Roman's morale. Steve hesitated so briefly Mirelle was sure she was the only one who noticed. Then he smiled encouragingly down at his son in the stretcher.

"Us men, huh?"

"Thanks, Dad."

"I'll go right to Emergency?" Mirelle asked the ambulance men.

"That's right, lady, and watch the roads. They're dangerously slippery."

"I will," Mirelle said and watched the party leave the house.

She turned to Dad Martin then, who had a comforting arm about Nick and Tonia.

"I'll call as soon as we know what's what. I'm terribly sorry that this should've happened on top of everything else."

"We should have checked with you first, before we made our plans to drop in on such a busy weekend," Dad Martin said graciously. "But we old folks get a notion and just pack up and go, come what may."

"That's the way it should be, Dad. But we do so little work in the community and the church that . . . well, you do understand?"

"Yes, Mirelle, I do," he said earnestly and then patted her hand. "You've got a fine boy in Roman. Go on now. He'll want you as much as his father."

"Be good, you two." Mirelle fixed Nick and Tonia with a stern glare.

"Promise!" they chimed.

It wasn't until Mirelle was driving cautiously onto the main road that she realized Dad Martin had used 'Mirelle' for the first time.

CHAPTER SEVENTEEN

WILL MARTIN met them at the Emergency entrance and, after a cursory examination, sent Roman up to X-ray.

"Good job of first aid, Mirelle," he commented. "Has he had anything to eat today?"

"Not that I know of."

"He did have a slug of bourbon," Steve reminded them.

"He was so cold when he got in," Mirelle added.

"Won't hurt. I'll give him a general. Between the broken arm, stitches and shock, I think it'll be smarter. You better go make the admissions department happy and sign away a second mortgage."

Mirelle fumbled in her wallet for the hospitalization card.

"How long will he be in?"

"Day or two," said the doctor with a shrug and walked off to the nurse's station.

While waiting for the X-rays to be processed, Mirelle and Steve stayed with Roman, saw him comfortable in a hospital room on the adult side, Roman announced with pleasure.

Martin had ordered a pre-operative shot and Roman was shortly euphoric.

"The coffee shop's open," said the floor nurse hospitably when the operating room orderly had arrived to wheel Roman's bed away.

"Momma?" called Roman, craning his head around to see her.

"Yes, Ro?" Mirelle went quickly to his side.

"You'll be here when I wake up?" His eyes could barely focus on her.

"Right here," she assured him.

"Okay, then," he mumbled, relaxing again.

"Neither of us had any breakfast, Steve. Let's go eat."

"Any idea how long it'll take?" Steve asked the floor nurse.

She shrugged. "Not long, but I'll page you when he's brought down. Ordinarily he'd be sent to the recovery room a while but as today's Sunday, he'll come down to his room instead. Your husband looks green, Mrs. Martin. You'd better feed him," she added over her shoulder as she walked away.

Mirelle looked at Steve and agreed.

"Come on."

"She needn't have said that." Steve swallowed hard. "Hell, to think that the kid *walked* down the hill . . . Oh, God, Mirelle, with a broken arm and that leg wide open."

Mirelle stared at her trembling husband. She pulled him into the elevator and punched the coffee shop floor.

"You're over-reacting badly, Steve. And it's not just Roman. Does it have anything to do with Ralph?" she asked very gently.

His horrified look was all the answer she needed. She steered him into the coffee shop and ordered quickly from the waitress standing at the counter. The woman nodded and gestured towards the empty tables. Mirelle guided Steve to a secluded one by a window.

"You always look that way whenever Ralph's wound is mentioned. Now I know that Ralph couldn't have been so badly wounded, in spite of your mother's tale. So what is the real story?"

Steve took the arrival of coffee as an excuse to delay his answer. He sipped half a cup before he began to talk, but the intensity of that tightly controlled voice startled Mirelle. She'd never seen him this way.

"I'd always wanted a paper route, too, but my mother wouldn't let me have one. She was afraid of what might happen!" Steve's fist came down on the table in frustrated emphasis. "She was always afraid of this happening, or that occurring. And she damned near killed both her sons with *her* fears."

"She thought she was doing the right thing, Steve," Mirelle said softly, wondering why she was defending her mother-in-law. But Steve sounded so vicious, so totally unlike himself.

"She was. Only she did it the wrong way." Steve shrugged helplessly. "And there were both of us, unprotected when we needed protection the most and not enough sense to know how to get it."

"But, Steve, you must have got over it. You were decorated."

Steve made an impatient, vulgar noise. "So I carried a mortar up a cliff that couldn't have been scaled and pinned some krauts down . . . in full view of a general, as it happened," he looked at Mirelle and covered her hands with his, "but I wasn't the only guy doing unusual things, and I'd been in combat a long time by then. I'd learned, the hard way, all the things Roman can do now.

"I never told you about breaking my arm, did I? In basic training." He made a disgusted noise deep in his throat and his eyes looked out at some far distant point. "Yeah, I broke my arm and sat there, crying like a baby for my mother! I sat there for nearly four hours until it dawned on me that mother was not going to come help me this time. We were on maneuvers and for all I know I'd be sitting there yet but I had the good luck to be 'captured' by the 'enemy'. And when the medico asked me how long it'd been broken, I was so ashamed that I lied, and said I'd knocked myself out in the fall and only just come to before I got captured." There was deep disgust and bitterness in his face when he looked at Mirelle. "No, I could never have done what Roman did this morning: got up in the bitter cold and walked myself home."

"And Ralph?" Mirelle asked gently.

Steve let out a sour laugh. "Ralph got a flesh wound, a lousy little flesh wound in the arm. But he sat down and waited, too. For mother to come succour her little boy. And damned near died of frostbite and pneumonia. He could have walked two miles to the nearest town—we'd occupied it and it was French anyhow—and got help. But he lay there, among the dead, waiting until he was damned near a corpse, too."

Mirelle couldn't think of anything to say to ease Steve's bitterness or reassure him. She'd often thought that Ralph's injury had been minor, just as she'd known that Marian Martin had over-protected her children, but she hadn't realized how seriously the woman's attitude had handicapped her sons. It accounted for Steve's attitude toward injuries of any kind and the self-sufficiency that he'd insisted all three of his children develop. The latter was almost a mania with him.

The waitress appeared with the coffee pitcher and a sympathetic smile, and the second cups of coffee took up more time.

"I'll bet she's forgotten to call us," Steve said finally, anxiously glancing at his watch. "Let's get back to his room." He paid the check and they went.

"He's not down yet," the nurse told them.

"But it's over an hour," Steve said.

"Oh, don't worry, really," she said reassuringly and continued briskly on her rounds.

They had waited another fifteen anxious minutes before Roman was wheeled in. Will Martin, still in his surgical gown, entered right behind him.

"Nasty breaks, but they should heal well," Will said.

"They?" Steve asked.

"Sure, broke both bones in the forearm. I'm a little concerned about that open shin wound. It was mighty cold out there this morning. So I think we'll keep him here at least two days." Then Will caught sight of Steve's expression. "Oh, for God's sake, Steve. I'm not anticipating trouble, but I am a cautious bugger."

"How long before Roman's conscious?" Mirelle asked.

"Oh, he's been round once, but I've ordered sedation, so he won't be with us much today."

"I'll stick around a little while," Mirelle said, throwing her coat over the chair.

"I'll get on back to Mom and Dad," Steve said.

Responsibility flooded back to Mirelle. "Oh, Lord, Steve, and there's no dinner meat defrosted. Nothing ready."

"I'll take everyone out to eat," Steve reassured her.

"Please tell them how sorry I am that their visit's been spoiled."

"Hon, this isn't your fault," Steve said gently.

Will Martin snorted and, waving a hand in farewell, left the room. Steve kissed her, looked down at the still form of his son, and then resolutely he bent and kissed Roman's cheek. He left without a backward glance.

Mirelle yanked the one upholstered chair into a position where she could watch Roman's face and composed herself to wait.

Roman woke a half-hour later, long enough to satisfy himself that his mother was where she'd promised she'd be, and then he dropped off to sleep again. Mirelle waited another hour, thinking that he might not remember his first awakening and believe that she had neglected him. She was about to phone Steve to pick her up when Sylvia Esterhazy peered around the door.

"Up yet?" she asked, her face anxious.

"Not totally," Mirelle said in a soft voice.

Sylvia looked down at the sleeping boy.

"I called your house to thank you for the evening and Steve told me the gay tidings. Imagine that! Walking himself home! Steve's very proud of him. So I decided that his bravery merited a reward, and brought him some reading matter." Sylvia handed Mirelle a bundle in drug store wrapping.

"Comic books? Did you buy out the store?"

"One each of every title in stock," Sylvia said with a laugh. "I also came to take you home because hell hath broke loose there or I misread the omens."

"Which ones?"

"I don't know, Mir," and Sylvia was suddenly serious. "But Steve sounded as if he were choking on every word he said and he twice covered the phone to speak to someone. Then he asked me if I could pick you up."

Mirelle looked worriedly from her son to her friend, biting her lip indecisively.

"It's too much. It's just too much," she muttered resentfully. "I can only take so much!"

"From the look of him," said Sylvia as if Mirelle had said nothing, "I'd say that he was going to make this an all day affair. Probably easier on him. Have the nurse call you when he does wake. Or he can. He's got his own phone."

"It's not so much not wanting to leave Roman as it is not wanting to go home," Mirelle said candidly, looking away from Sylvia's sympathetic eyes.

Roman stirred and murmured, the fingers of his uninjured hand picking at the spread. He tried to lift his right arm and the awareness of weight roused him.

"Mom? Mom, I'm thirsty." Groggily he focused his eyes. "My arm's so heavy. I can't lift it." His complaint was almost incoherent.

Mirelle looked up to ask Sylvia to get the nurse but the door was already closing behind her.

"Mrs. Esterhazy's gone for something, Roman. D'you remember you're in the hospital?"

"Hospital? Why? I'm never sick." He tried to sit up and then sagged back down against the pillows as memory returned. "I really did break my arm?"

"Both bones, compound fracture," Mirelle assured him, trying to keep her voice light.

"How many stitches did I get?" Roman was awake to important details.

"Lord, I forgot to ask Will. You can when he comes in to see you tomorrow. He wants you to stay in the hospital for a couple of days, just to make sure the shin is okay."

"Is this a private room?"

"Yes," and Mirelle grinned at his awed reaction.

"My own phone, too?" for he'd spotted that now. "Is that my john? Or, gee, Mom, do I gotta ask a nurse for a bedpan?" His voice had dropped to an outraged whisper.

Mirelle had not thought of that aspect of this experience. Roman had a particular need for privacy which she had always respected.

"Honey, they're quite used to helping young men with such problems. And you'll find that you don't want to walk on that leg."

"But, gee, Mom, when a fella's gotta . . . Oh, Mom," and Roman was quite upset.

"Then ask for the male orderly. There's always one on the men's surgical ward. I'm sure of it." Mirelle just hoped that she was right for the relief it gave Roman.

"Can I call my friends?"

"You're here to rest, and you may find yourself sleepy most of the day . . . He's awake," she told the nurse who swung in the door, followed by Sylvia.

"Ginger ale, coke or orange juice, Mr. Martin?" asked the nurse who Mirelle now realized was young and pretty enough to demoralize Roman.

"Ginger ale, please. And, Mom, ask her . . . " Roman made the last four words into a stage whisper.

"Ask her what? Oh, yes, there is a male orderly on this floor, isn't there?"

The nurse glanced swiftly at the boy and then at the mother and assured her that this was so with only the faintest tug of a smile on her face before she left.

Sylvia deposited the bundle of comic books on the bed.

"Rewards for your exceptional valor," she said and, as if unaware of his impaired dexterity, opened the package with a flourish.

"Oh, gee, thanks, Mrs. Esterhazy. Say, how'd you know that I got hurt?"

"Snowbird," Sylvia replied, winking. "I'm taking your mother home now."

"Mom," began Roman anxiously, "you and Dad aren't mad at me for . . . I mean, things are kinda screwed up anyhow, with Grandmother getting so hysterical and all, and I sure didn't make things any better, did I?"

"Robert Marion Martin, there isn't anything for us to be mad at you for. Why, your father's so proud of you . . . oh, be quiet and read. One of us will be in to see you tonight," she said, swiftly hugging and kissing him fiercely for his bravery and his perception.

"Read every word now," called Sylvia in farewell, and the door closed on his repeated thanks to her. "That's a wonderful kid, Mirelle."

"He's worth nine of his goddamned grandmother."

"I like you better angry than despairing."

There was considerable ice under the snow and Sylvia drove slowly, without her customary verve. Mirelle was glad that Sylvia appreciated the value of silence: her presence was reassurance enough. Sylvia gave her a jaunty up-and-at-'em grin when she let Mirelle off at her drive.

The first thing Mirelle noticed was the absence of her in-laws' car. As she climbed the snowy steps to the front door, she wondered if they had all gone out to dinner in the one car but, as she opened the front door to the excited welcome of Nick and Tonia, she realized that the Martins had left.

"How's Roman?" "How many stitches?" "When can we see him?"

Steve came out of the kitchen with a drink in one hand and a big fork in the other.

"Steak," he announced. "Stiff one?" he asked, holding up his own glass inquiringly.

"Very!" She began to shed her coat and boots.

"Nick, set the table! Tonia, get glasses from the dishwasher and help your brother," Steve said in a tone of command from the kitchen. He returned with Mirelle's drink which he handed her before he went back to his cooking. Mirelle followed to see him peering in at the broiler.

"It'll take a little longer," he said, "but it will be dark on the outside, and good and rare on the inside, just the way you like it. Make a salad for me, will you?"

"There's some left over from last night."

"Fine. How's Roman?"

"Coping rather well with hospital routine once he found out that there was a male orderly on the floor."

Steve stared at her a moment, mystified, and then laughed.

"Sylvia had brought him half the comics in town so he is well supplied . . . at least for today," Mirelle continued.

"Sylvia has the right idea. Was he sick or anything from the anesthesia?"

"No. Only worried about upsetting everyone."

"Goddam," was Steve's vehement exclamation and, when Mirelle swung around, she saw him sucking a finger, burned on the hot rack. "When those Cub Scouts come around with hot pads, buy a dozen, will you, Mirelle? I can't find one without holes."

Mirelle shrugged, too relieved that he was not going to expand on his parents' premature departure to question him. There had been a storm in the house: that was all too apparent in Nick's ready cooperation and Tonia's unusual compliance. But Mirelle had no energy to absorb any more emotional shocks and was grateful for the omission.

By the time the steak was done, Mirelle's drink had taken effect and she ate in a kind of daze, not really attending to the children's chatter.

"Why doesn't *your* mother ever visit us, Mommy?" asked Tonia, apropos of nothing.

"What, honey?" Mirelle gathered her wits.

Tonia repeated the question.

"My mother died a long time before you were born."

"Well, that's too bad for I'm sure I would have liked her a lot more than my other grandmother."

Before Mirelle could reprimand her for impudence,

Steve reached across the table and slapped Tonia so hard that her chair nearly tipped over.

"Steve!" Mirelle was appalled by the viciousness of the discipline.

"You are never to speak disrespectfully of your grandmother," he cried in a bellow, his face suffused with blood . . . "Well, what do you say?"

Tonia, gulping back her sobs, was too frightened to speak. She just held her cheek and stared at her father.

"Well?" Steve demanded, his face white now with anger.

Tears overflowed Tonia's eyes and she tried to speak but only incoherent noises emerged, which increased Steve's fury.

"Really, Steve . . . "

"You shut up, Mirelle. I wear the pants in this family and it's about time that was understood."

"There is no need to pound the table. And there was no need to fetch Tonia such a clout for a . . . "

"If I choose to punish my daughter," Steve's anger was now directed at Mirelle, "I will!"

"If you punish, yes. But do not take your anger out on her."

"Don't intimidate me, Mirelle!"

She glared at him, daring him to strike her, too, but suddenly all the aggression drained out of him. She held out her hand to Tonia and led her to the kitchen, to bathe the child's face and help her control her sobbing. The marks of Steve's fingers stood out red and fierce against the creamy skin. Mirelle crushed ice in a towel, certain that Tonia would have a livid bruise by morning.

"You cannot speak without thinking, Antonia. Daddy loves his mother," Mirelle began in a quiet voice, hoping to calm the child.

"No, he doesn't," Tonia replied defiantly, her eyes sullen. "Not the way he was yelling at her this morning."

Mirelle put her fingers across the girl's mouth. "Be quiet." She tried to ignore Tonia's instinctive flinch.

When Mirelle returned to the dining room with Tonia,

Steve was gone. She and the children finished their dinners silently, Nick darting glances at his sister's face.

"You two go watch TV," Mirelle said, "unless, young man, you've got homework to finish."

"All done Friday afternoon, Mom," Nick said. "Honest!"

She heard the grate of the garage door rolling up and, looking out the window, saw Steve attacking the snow drift in the driveway. His shovelling was almost frenzied and she thought for a moment of warning him to take it easy. He wouldn't appreciate such gratuitous advice. Better to let him take his frustration and anger out on the snow. She wondered exactly what had happened before her in-laws left.

"Have I won the war, or lost another battle?" she asked herself and then went to pack a suitcase for Roman.

She fussed in the kitchen, tidying up the last of the disarrangements of her usual placement of pots, utensils and spices which invariably took place when Mother Martin visited. She made hot chocolate for Steve, timing it so that it was ready when he had finished shoveling. He came in through the laundry room, stamping snow from his boots.

"I'm bone cold," he said, gratefully accepting the steaming mug she handed him. "Can I see Ro any time or do I have to wait for visiting hours?"

"He's in a private room. You can go when you want. I packed the small blue bag with things he'll probably need or want."

"I'll change then and go see him."

She accepted his neutrality. At least he'd worked out his anger on the snow. She wondered if she'd ever find out . . . short of pumping Nick and Tonia . . . what happened when he got home from the hospital that morning.

'I wear the pants in the family.' 'Don't intimidate me, Mirelle.' The phrases, like gauntlets thrown in preface to a duel, ran through her mind. They were unlike Steve. Was he stating the difference between himself and his father? Mirelle shook her head. She gave the drainboard a final swipe with the sponge and then went down to the studio.

Nick peered at her from the gameroom door.

"Gonna do Roman a sickpig?" he asked hopefully.

"I ought to but I'm too tired to do it tonight, Nickie."

"It's only six. Walt Disney isn't even on yet."

"It might just as well be midnight the way I feel."

"Yeah, it's been a day!" And Nick rubbed the back of his neck in imitation of his father's gesture.

Mirelle tugged his hair affectionately and then pushed him back into the gameroom. Without volition she went to the Lucy and touched it tenderly, dispassionately admiring the line of the figure that seemed about to spring forward into life and movement. She could almost see Lucy completing the gesture of patting her hair in order. She turned the statue into profile and sat down on the couch, looking at it.

"Momma," complained Tonia's voice in her ear, and Mirelle woke with a start. "I wanna watch . . . "

"Mom, I keep telling her it's her bedtime now," Nick said.

Mirelle looked at her watch and realized that she'd fallen asleep. It was almost 9:00.

"No more TV. Both of you get to bed and on the double."

She shooed them upstairs and settled the argument as to who would sleep where. She checked Nick's closet to see if he had school clothes for the morning and found herself automatically checking Roman's room as well.

She saw them tucked into bed and, wondering where Steve could be, slowly undressed and got herself ready for bed. She tried to read a book but the print blurred, so she gave up, and reassuring herself that if Steve had been in an accident on the the slippery roads, she certainly would have had a call. She thought of Roman, she thought of her in-laws and tried not to imagine what the final scene had been like. She tried not to think at all and touched the pole of concern for Roman, swinging back to her concern for Steve until she forced the figure of Lucy into her mind. Comforted by the symbol, she managed to drift into unconsciousness.

CHAPTER EIGHTEEN

DREAM AND REALITY got interwoven together, with hands grasping for her, hands tremendously enlarged by the power of the dreaming mind: grotesque hands, with thick fingers, hairy knuckles and ragged nails; horny palms and blunt fingers; then spider leg long digits with Chinese-length nails waggling grey-green index fingers at her in reprimand; suddenly the path opened into the depths of the forest and, grateful for the cool of the green woods and the smell of the ferns, 'they' plunged into the shadows, leaving the redness of the orange desert and the merciless sun behind them. The ferns grew fingers and grabbed at her ankles; the vines grew arms and reached for her.

"Mirelle! Mirelle!" Steve was shaking her awake.

"Oh, God," she groaned, shaking her head to dispel the nightmare.

"I overslept. Make me some coffee and an egg."

Mirelle grabbed his robe and staggered downstairs, yawning at the growing daylight visible from the kitchen window. She snapped on the overhead light, the glare making her squint. She got coffee made and was frying an egg when Steve walked into the kitchen. He gulped down the coffee, half-swallowed the egg, and went out to the garage chewing a slice of toast. She stood stupidly in the center of the kitchen and finally realized that he hadn't kissed her goodbye. Not so much as a perfunctory peck. She heard the car tires scrunching on the brittle snow and ice of the driveway and then heard him gun the cold motor as he swung up the hill.

She got the children up and ready just in time for their usual buses when Nick noticed that the high school bus hadn't come yet.

"Whee, maybe we have a snow day," he cried, cheering.

Mirelle felt none of his jubilation and was relieved to see the first bus belatedly making its rounds. She made them eat breakfast then, since the buses were obviously behind schedule. And then she dug up spare gloves so they could snowfight while waiting as all the other kids were doing.

She was just about to sit down for coffee when Roman's newspaper route manager dropped by to ask how he was. She had to ask him in, out of courtesy, but he didn't stay long. Just asked her to see if Roman knew of a substitute to work the route. Mirelle promised, feeling slightly guilty because she'd completely forgotten about that obligation. Roman, it turned out, had phoned his manager from the hospital.

Then she was able to sit down quietly to a peaceful cup of coffee and her usual twice-over of the morning paper. Roman's horoscope advised extreme caution in attempting new projects. She snorted contemptuously, wondering what they'd advised for Sunday for Libra. Her birth sign promised a completion of projects underway and a favorable outlook for the start of new business.

She made toast and sat by the dining room window until all the snow-clowning figures had embarked on buses. There were huge marred areas on the snowy lawns now, the sunlight reflecting off the untouched patches and shadowing the uncompleted forts.

With false vigor she dressed, got the upstairs to rights

and had some of the weekend laundry started before 10:00. She found one sock belonging to Dad Martin and a pair of earrings Mrs. Martin had left in Roman's room under used Kleenex. At 10:00 she called Roman.

"Hi, Mom. Dr. Martin put in twenty-eight stitches," he reported in an awed voice.

"Does that make you top stitch man?"

"By three. And I'll bet that lousy Schneider will try and make it up. Mom," and his voice changed, "my arm aches something awful."

"Did you mention that to Dr. Martin?"

"Naw."

"Idiot. If it hurts, you need something, At least for the first few days. Now, don't be foolishly brave."

"Aw, I couldn't. I mean, Mom?"

"I understand. I'll bring the subject up . . . not," she hastily assured him, "as if you had complained or anything. What shall I bring you when I come in?"

"Didn't Dad give you the list when he got home?"

"I was asleep when your Dad got home."

"At 9:00?" Roman was incredulous. "Gee, I don't have to go to sleep till 10:00 and I get a pill. Whammy. They got me up at 6:00 . . . with a you-know-what," and his voice dropped again with embarrassment. Mirelle stifled the impulse to giggle. "Didn't Dad say anything this morning?"

"We overslept and it's a miracle that your father had coffee."

"Well . . . "

"Can you remember what you told him?"

"Oh, sure," and he promptly listed his wants.

"Is that all?" she asked when she had tallied nine urgent items.

"Well, do I get a sickpig this time?"

"I'd say you already had your weight in plaster on your arm."

"Aw, gee. I oughta get a special one with a broken arm and stitches, shouldn't I?"

Mirelle laughingly agreed, unable to tease him further. She told him about his route manager dropping by.

"Gee, Mom, do you think we can get Nick to pinch-hit? It's awful near Christmas."

"I'll certainly mention it to him, dear."

She no sooner hung up than the phone rang again.

"Do you have to sit on that line?" demanded Steve.

"Well, no."

"You've been blabbing for fifteen minutes."

"I was talking to Roman."

"I didn't give you the list of things he wants. Get a pencil."

"I've already got it from the horse's mouth," she said, determined not to let his surliness get under her skin. "That's why we talked for fifteen minutes."

"All right then," and he hung up without another comment.

Rebuffed, Mirelle looked down at the dead phone before replacing it. She had started to rise when again the phone rang. This time it was June Treadway, thanking her for contributing so much to the success of the Bazaar. Patsy McHugh called then with the news that a number of people had phoned her, asking if more of the creche figures and the Dirty Dicks were available. Mirelle could see her time to make Roman's sickpig whittled down to nothing.

She patiently took the information from Patsy without explaining any of the difficulties which came to mind as the girl prattled on. She finally invented a knock at the door so she could terminate the call. Resolutely she started down to the studio when there was a legitimate knock on the door.

"Completion of projects underway . . . " she growled to herself and wrenched open the door. Sylvia, unbalanced by trying to scrape snow from her boots, fell in.

Mirelle, immediately contrite, was all apologies and helped her in.

"I came over here for peace and quiet," Sylvia said, rubbing one hip as she handed Mirelle her coat, "and things *keep* happening."

"I know exactly what you mean."

"Do you cry first or do I?"

Mirelle looked thoughtfully at Sylvia. All the vivacity was drained from the woman's face and eyes: the sallowness of her skin was not entirely due to the lack of make-up. Her usually erect figure sagged from the shoulders into the waist as if she were withdrawing as much of her body from contact as possible, like a fighter avoiding another punishing body blow. A not unapt simile, Mirelle decided.

"I assume that coffee might still taste the same," Sylvia said as she walked heavily towards the kitchen, "although I wouldn't put it past circumstances to have changed that as well."

Mirelle waited a minute, wondering if she should stay with Sylvia but when the only sounds from the kitchen were preparations for coffee, Mirelle went down to the studio. She took a large blob of clay and, almost automatically, began to wrest a porcine outline from the mass. When Sylvia came down with the coffee, Mirelle was somewhat surprised to see that she had nearly finished it. The pig was sitting on its rump, one rear leg stretched out, one forepaw bandaged and slung in a kerchief, the pig's body improbably propped on the other foreleg, its expression surprised.

"Roman'll love it," Sylvia said, again in that flat voice. She poured coffee and left Mirelle's on the shelf beside her while she curled up on the couch, looking out at the snowy woods. "Heard from him today?"

"I've heard from everybody today," Mirelle exclaimed with considerable feeling, then bent to detail the pig's trotters.

"One day you must make me a sickpig. That is, of course, if they ever do decide what makes me sick."

Mirelle looked up, concerned. "Are you sick? You don't look well today at all."

"Yeah, sick," agreed Sylvia, tapping her temple. "Sick!

Sick! Sick! Didn't you realize?" and her tone was far too brittle, mocking, "I was sure you'd've guessed . . . I'm in analysis . . . that's how sick I am."

"No, I didn't guess," Mirelle said, carefully and wondered if Sylvia wanted more of a response from her. *But then,* Mirelle thought, *I've been rather too wrapped up in my own troubles.* And Sylvia just didn't seem the sort of person who couldn't handle matters, any matters, efficiently. It simply hadn't occurred to Mirelle that Sylvia's attitudes and poses were camouflage for more than the ordinary frustrations, or at the most, the humiliating awareness of G.F.'s infidelities.

Abruptly Sylvia swung off the couch, hugging her arms to her sides, striding up and down the length of the room with tautly controlled steps. She halted unexpectedly right by Mirelle, glaring down at the clay with an intensity that was almost hatred.

"You can pound out your frustrations in that stuff. You can shape beauty out of nothing, and I've never seen anything hateful come from your hands. But God in his infinite wisdom has given me no such tacit gifts: no redeeming acceptable talents or qualities."

Mirelle opened her mouth to protest, but Sylvia held up her hand, almost imperiously.

"No, Mirelle, no. Spare me specious reassurances. I don't deserve that from you." Then Sylvia's expression altered to one of terror. She grabbed at Mirelle's shoulder. "I couldn't be going crazy, and not know it? Please, Mirelle, you don't think I'm losing my mind."

Mirelle gripped her hand fiercely. "No, Sylvia, you're not mad, not losing your mind. But something has hurt you . . . "

Sylvia gave her a startled look.

"Hurt? Oh, yes, I've been hurt . . . " Sylvia looked off into a middle distance and Mirelle waited, half-resigned to hearing a recital of G.F.'s infidelities. "All my life she's hurt me."

It was Mirelle's turn to be astonished.

"If she even knew that I'd consulted a psychiatrist. . . . "

"Your mother?"

A bitter smile touched Sylvia's lips. "My ever-loving mother has returned to her ancestral home. Having wreaked havoc broadside, she has girded her loins and returned to do battle anew in her ancestral home, rectifying all sorts of minor infringements of Her Ways, and correcting the errors of mine. Did you know? It's no longer socially acceptable to be a Democrat?" Sylvia's eyes were bitter and mocking. "After all, the Kennedys are really one generation removed from Irish immigrants. And only think how they made their millions! Selling liquor. Oh, they have the millions, undeniably, but they haven't got breeding and family and position and . . . " Sylvia ended the sentence with a snort. Her breath was coming rapidly and Mirelle wondered if she were fighting back tears or anger. Her hands were clenching and unclenching, and then Mirelle realized that the woman was trembling.

Mirelle made a movement, instinctively wanting to hold her against the tremors. Sylvia stepped back, one hand raised in warning.

"Sympathy would kill me, Mirelle."

"Hadn't you better get in touch with your doctor then? I can't . . . "

Sylvia gave her head a little shake. "I called him when this hit me this morning but he can't see me until 3:00. I knew that if I stayed in that house another minute, I'd. . . . " Sylvia turned her back on Mirelle. "The problem is, she means well. She's operating according to her high standards . . . which died with the Treaty at Versailles, for God's sake. She's an Edwardian relic but she's so goddam strong . . . You don't know how lucky you are, Mirelle," Sylvia went on, her voice losing the shrillness of desperation, "to have had a rebel for a mother."

Mirelle blinked. "A rebel?"

"G.F. once said that he thought my mother would have made a superb courtesan. In fact, his exact words were 'what an empire builder she'd've made'."

"I never thought of my mother as a rebel."

Sylvia's smile was less forced, almost as if she were enjoying Mirelle's disorientation. "Didn't you? She was a concert and opera singer when that profession was just barely respectable. Then she had a flaming affair with the leading portrait painter of the decade, *and* a memento of the occasion . . . "

"Mother . . . "

"Ah ha." Sylvia was enjoying herself and Mirelle was torn between relief at seeing her in control of her emotions and a dislike of being teased. Then abruptly Sylvia's face resumed its mask of tragedy. "At least *she* had enough courage to follow her honest emotions."

"And paid for that the rest of her life."

"It's the sins of omission one regrets."

"Such as?"

Sylvia's face got even bleaker. "Matricide, for one."

There wasn't a speck of facetiousness in that remark: Sylvia was completely earnest. Mirelle knew that. But the laughter that bubbled out of her mouth was irrepressible.

"But, Sylvia, you know your mother wouldn't approve of that at all!"

The words were out before Mirelle could stop them, though she clapped horrified hands over her mouth in the next moment, desperately trying to figure out how she could redeem her gaffe, but just then Sylvia's sense of the ridiculous revived. She gave a short burst of harsh laughter.

"Not only disapprove but find some way to come back and haunt me. And *that* would be entirely insupportable."

The phone rang and Mirelle swore vehemently.

"Answer it, Mirelle. It might be Roman." Sylvia turned away to stare out the window.

Silently Mirelle cursed as she reached for the phone. Not that she had exhibited any unsuspected gift in easing her friend's mental distress but surely a sympathetic listener provided some sort of a safety valve.

"Is . . . Sylvia there by any chance?" G.F. asked casually.

"Yes, she is."

"Good. Would you tell her that Bert called and wants her to call him as soon as possible please? How's Roman?"

She responded politely to the last question and made no more effort to continue a conversation than G.F. did. She devoutly hoped that this Bert was the psychiatrist. How tactful G.F. was!

"G.F. says that Bert wants you to call immediately."

The relief in Sylvia's face confirmed Mirelle's wish. Sylvia almost grabbed the phone from her, her fingers shaking as she dialed with joint-twisting frenzy.

"Bert? You're free? Oh, thank God. I'll be right over."

She practically flung the phone back into its cradle, grabbing up coat and purse with clutching, fumbling hands. In the act of setting her foot on the first step, she whirled, her eyes alive in her still drained face.

"Mirelle, you did help. You said the right things. Thanks."

Then she was up the stairs and out of the house. The air pressure between the storm door and the inside one kept it from closing so Mirelle went to shut it properly. She saw Sylvia's car skidding in the snow on the hill and she worried that Sylvia's urgency might have disastrous results. But, as the car reached the crest of the hill, it slowed. Commonsense had come back to the driver.

Mirelle closed the door firmly, leaning back against it until she heard the latch click.

"My horoscope is wrong today, all wrong," she said, and then went to answer the phone again.

CHAPTER NINETEEN

THE SENSE OF UNREALITY lasted through the next day. Steve had come home and started to drink. He had been preoccupied all during dinner, but he had gone out to the hospital and spent an hour and a half with Roman. Mirelle had watched him quietly during dinner and had been waiting for him when he got back from the hospital. He hadn't paused in the living room to speak to her but had gone upstairs immediately. She heard him moving around in their room, the squeak of the louvered closet doors opening, the opening and closing of dresser drawers. To her sudden dismay, she realized that he was packing.

With great unconcern she went upstairs and dallied, checking the children's rooms before she entered theirs. He was packing the two-suiter, quietly and efficiently. He looked up as she came in.

"I doubt I'll be back before Sunday. And, if the situation in Cleveland hasn't changed, I may stop off there on Monday," he said.

The knot that had begun in the bottom of her stomach suddenly unwound. She had entirely forgotten about his convention. The only thing she had thought of when she'd heard him packing was that he was leaving her.

"I explained to Roman. He's a terrific kid, Mirelle. I forget that he's going on fifteen and growing so fast. I hate to leave him in the hospital, but he told me Dr. Martin says he can come home Wednesday."

"Yes, didn't I mention that at dinner?"

"I had my mind on the Cleveland thing," Steve said, but Mirelle knew where his mind had been and accepted the tactful lie. "I'll have to catch an early plane from Philly. I'll take the wagon and leave it at the airport. Easier all around."

Mirelle agreed, hearing all the while the words he wasn't saying. She undressed in that remoteness that had colored the entire day. She did, however, have the foresight to take two sleeping pills while she was in the bathroom. She heard Steve rattling in the medicine chest, too, for the same remedy. She hoped he'd hear the alarm in the morning.

She had managed to wake up sufficiently from her drugged sleep to get Nick and Tonia fed and off to school, but the phone rang three times with complaints about non-delivery of papers and that made Tuesday as wrong as Monday had been.

The only bright spot in the day was the overwhelming success of Roman's sickpig, which she took to cheer his morning. Every nurse on duty, the orderly, and Dr. Martin had to admire the silly thing. In a state of high glee, Roman showed her all the cards that had come. Dr. Martin confirmed his Wednesday discharge.

"As a matter of fact, send him back to school Thursday, Mirelle," Will Martin said. "He's more likely to be kept quiet there than at home. And think of the status he'll acquire."

Mirelle laughed.

"Say," Martin went on, "your Mr. Howell sent me a pair of tickets to that concert of his on Friday. I've half a mind to rip out the telephone plug and go to it. My wife sees me at breakfast if she's lucky. By dinner I've usually improved enough to be sociable, but inevitably some damn fool has an emergency so we never get a chance to enjoy an evening's leisure time." He snorted over his choice of phrase. "Are you going?"

"Steve's out of town." Mirelle knew she was temporizing.

"So what? Go by yourself. You need a break. You look worn out. And don't come in for a physical. I'm booked until April." He scowled at her. "You're in a rut. Jump out of it for an evening."

When she got home, the phone was ringing frantically and she dashed to answer it.

"Are you never home?" demanded James Howell.

"I just got in from the hospital."

"Anybody I know?"

"Roman."

"Good God! There I go again! Open mouth, A. Insert foot, B. Nothing serious?"

"No. He broke his arm and gashed his leg."

"Oh, no, nothing serious at all," Howell said in a mocking tone.

Mirelle heard herself giggling. "If you knew how he had counted coup with twenty-eight stitches over the present neighborhood record holder, you'd know it wasn't serious. Matter of fact, he was delivering the Sunday papers and indulged in a sled run on the way home. Only he tangled with the sled runners. D'you know that he picked himself up, broken arm, gashed leg, and all, and walked home?"

"He's your son, isn't he?" replied Howell, unimpressed by the heroism.

"He's only fourteen," Mirelle protested.

"So what? I'd never heard that heroism was limited to a special age group. Look, I called to tell you that I have a pair of tickets, obtained with much bribery and blackmail from the management, for my concert."

"I thought a soprano was the featured attraction."

"I'll hang up."

"It's really very kind of you, Jamie . . . "

"There isn't a kind bone in my body, Mary Ellen . . . "

" . . . But with Steve out of town on a convention, and Roman . . . "

"You just finished telling me that he is eminently capable of handling minor emergencies . . . "

"But . . . "

"You need a night out. Bring Sylvia or someone if you require a chaperone, but I really must insist on your presence. Margaret can't make it and I must have some claque there. Prestige, you know."

Mirelle choked back a nasty crack because, despite Jamie's flippancy, it was apparent that he very much wanted her in that audience.

"As a matter of fact, Will Martin told me that I should have a night out, too. By the way, it was very nice of you to send him tickets."

"He needs a night out more than you do, though I doubt he'll be able to come. And I must have my own claque. SHE always pads the audience." He was at his most arrogant, and Mirelle laughed.

"All right, I'll come. I'll come."

"Good." He sounded very pleased. "When does Roman leave the dubious land of Blue Cross?"

"Tomorrow."

"May I be of assistance? That's a lot of boy to maneuver in snow, cast and stitch."

"Well, as a matter of fact," she said as she remembered that Steve had taken the station wagon and the Sprite was not exactly designed to accommodate an invalid. The upshot was that Jamie chauffeured them both in the Thunderbird, dealing with the obstinacy of an officious floor supervisor, and hoisting him deftly from hospital wheelchair to the car. Once at the house, he ignored Roman's protests and, with a running line of patter that took the sting out of the boy's temporary helplessness, conveyed him safely up the icy walk and into the house. They all enjoyed a very pleasant, even hilarious lunch together, before Jamie had autocratically removed Roman to his room to rest.

"I can't thank you enough, Jamie," Mirelle said at the door as Howell took his leave. "I never could have coped alone."

"What? Miraculous Mirelle at a loss?" he laughed in

mock horror. "The tickets." He slapped them into her hand in one more theatrical gesture before he left.

She held the envelope thoughtfully, remembering what Will Martin had said the day before. She admitted to a good deal of curiosity about Jamie as a professional. She didn't question his competence but she wondered if his sardonic humor intruded in his accompaniments. He would be extremely handsome in formal wear, with the height to be distinguished as well.

Roman called to her and Mirelle realized that she couldn't leave him on Friday to go to any concert, no matter how much she might want to. Not with Steve away as well.

"Whatcha got, Mom?" Roman asked as she came into the room, still holding the little white envelope.

"Mr. Howell gave me tickets to his concert Friday," she said, casting them negligently onto the dresser.

"Gee, that'll be terrific, Mom. I'll bet he's good."

Mirelle looked at him in surprise. "But I'm not going, hon."

Roman was stunned. "Why not?"

"Well, your father's away and I would hardly leave . . . "

" . . . Leave my poor hurt boy alone?" Roman was disgusted. "You sound like Grandmother." Then he blushed. "I mean . . . "

Mirelle held up her hand. "You mean, you wouldn't mind my going?"

"If you think a little thing like a broken arm and twenty-eight stitches is enough to put me off for long, you're nuts."

Mirelle was touched by his attitude and ruffled his hair, but she was still undecided. It would be so nice to go to a concert in town—particularly this one. The kids would be cowed enough by Roman's injuries to obey him. He'd certainly proved that he could handle himself in an emergency, and she wouldn't have to leave until 7:00. She'd better call Sylvia. Chaperone, indeed, she snorted to herself.

G.F. answered the phone: Sylvia was out and would not be back until late. There was no opening for Mirelle to ask G.F. how Sylvia was feeling. His courtesy was perfect, but his replies were framed to supply no additional information.

It was like talking to a super-efficient, idiot secretary, Mirelle thought, irritated by his deference. She hung up, disturbed. Why was he home at such an hour anyway?

After dinner, during which both Tonia and Nick, still awed by their brother's heroics, promised explicit obedience on Friday, Mirelle was clearing the kitchen when the phone rang. Juggling dirty glasses in one hand, she picked up the phone, hoping the caller was Sylvia.

"This is Long Distance, person to person to Mr. Steven Martin." The operator's southern drawl struck Mirelle with a premonition of disaster.

"He's in Chicago." She managed to set the glasses on the table before they slipped from her nerveless fingers.

"When is he expected back, please?"

"Not until Monday." Mirelle strained to hear what voice prompted these questions. The first time the operator had closed the circuit. The second time she kept it open.

"Will you speak with anyone else, sir?"

Something must have happened to Mother Martin, Mirelle thought, *and I shall have it on my conscience forever.*

"Is that Mrs. Martin?" a vaguely familiar male voice asked.

"Yes, it is."

"It's all right, operator. Murry Ellin," and there was only one person who pronounced her name that way, her brother-in-law, Ralph Martin. It also explained the southern operator, since Ralph and his wife lived in Greenville, S. C.

"Murry Ellin, what on earth did you do to Mother?" he asked, concerned but pleasant enough.

"Ralph, you scared me."

"What happened?" His voice took on an impatient edge.

"Ralph, I did nothing to your mother. Roman had an accident in the snow and by the time I got back from the hospital, your mother and father had left."

"Well, what did Steve have to say? Mother goes into hysterics if anyone looks in her direction. And . . . "

"I'm sorry about that, Ralph . . . "

"Sorry about that? Is that all you have to say?" Ralph lost all restraint. "My mother is not the hysterical type . . . "

"On the contrary, Ralph, she most certainly is. She took one look at Roman and started shrieking. He was hurt but he had walked home on his own and you'd have thought he was half dead the way she carried on."

"According to Mother, he was, and you took it as casually as if he'd had a splinter in his finger."

Mirelle closed her eyes and took a deep breath.

"Ralph, we did not take it casually. We rushed him right to the hospital. However, there was no point in creating a scene when he was doing his damnedest to act brave."

"Mother said you forced liquor down his throat."

"Forced is not the right word. He needed a quick stimulant because of the cold and the doctor approved of the bourbon. Ralph, you know how narrow-minded your mother is about drink . . . "

"I did not call you to discuss alcoholism . . . "

"I'm not discussing it. I'm telling you what happened and your mother's hysterical reaction to an emergency. Anything beyond that you will have to discuss with your brother. He knows what happened prior to your parents' departure. I do not. Nor do I care what happened. But I will say this. MY son could get up off his face and walk home for help when he was injured. And I'm very proud of him."

She slammed the phone back onto the receiver, trembling, hurt and humiliated. Ralph knew as well as anyone else how unreasonable his mother could be. His wife certainly spared no details of the naggings, bickerings and pettiness that ensued during her state visits in Greenville. But then, Ralph was the favored older son and would presume to call his younger brother to task.

But how could she have been cruel enough to make even an oblique reference to Ralph's unfortunate experience! She doubted that Ralph would ever speak to her again, and right then she didn't care. She'd had enough of the Martins' suffocating righteousness and social pretensions. Damn it! She'd been a good wife. A good mother! What more was expected of her? So what if she'd been illegitimate! That had not been her fault. At least she'd not paraded either her parents or her bastardy in plain sight, as they'd marshalled their second-hand opinions and miserable prejudices.

Mirelle was shaking so violently that she lurched to the cabinet and, not taking time to find a glass, swallowed a stiff jolt of bourbon, glaring her defiance at the silent phone.

"Mother," Tonia said in a whine, running into the kitchen, "Nickie and Roman won't . . . "

"If you can't be quiet, you can go to bed!"

"But, Mommie, it's my turn . . . "

"Go to bed! Now! No back talk or I'll slap you." Mirelle was startled by the savagery in her voice as well as the terrified look on Tonia's face. Weeping in earnest, Tonia dashed out of the kitchen and pounded upstairs, slamming her bedroom door behind her.

Mirelle buried her face in her hands, recognizing that she had lashed out at the child just as Steve had: pure fury looking for the nearest victim.

The phone rang again, and Mirelle regarded it with loathing. It couldn't be Ralph, back for another go at her. Could it be Steve? Neither of whom she wished to speak with. But this time it might be Sylvia. The phone rang stridently, its demand cutting into her subsiding anger and returning anxiety. If she answered the phone, she'd be required to control herself, and that was preferable to this terrible internal violence.

"Mirelle? G.F. just told me you'd called," Sylvia said with brittle brightness.

"SOS," Mirelle replied with matching false cheerfulness.

"Oh?" Sylvia's answer came out in a long drawl. "I'm not sure, dearie, if I have proper lifesavers on hand."

"But you promised you'd come to Howell's concert with me Friday, and he actually came up with the tickets."

"Concert?" Sylvia's voice settled to a more normal level. "Do you require a chaperone, dear?" Now she purred with amused malice.

"Don't be silly. But I'd like company. And I thought you wanted to hear Jamie play." Mirelle had the notion that her request met a vacuum.

"Friday," Sylvia said at length. "To be candid I forgot the date of the concert, but I have to be in Philly during the day. I expect we can meet. Why don't we have dinner together, somewhere?"

"Well, I'm leaving Roman to baby-sit."

"That cast should be just perfect for subduing restless elements."

"I didn't want to leave until 7:00."

"Not long enough for a decent dinner, then." There was a long pause on the other end. "I'll meet you at the Concert Hall. Why don't you take the train? I'll have the car."

Something about the quality of Sylvia's voice disturbed Mirelle when she hung up. She had the distinct feeling that Sylvia had been speaking for someone else's benefit. It must be her imagination. All her nerves were a-jangle.

Mirelle got out a Coke as a weak peace offering for Tonia. When she opened the girl's door, she was relieved to see that the resilient Tonia was dressing her Barbie dolls.

CHAPTER TWENTY

FRIDAY STARTED as a cold crisp morning, brilliant with sunlight on the snow. The novelty of Roman's injury had not worn off and he was helped solicitously onto the bus by classmates. The driver winked goodnatured reassurance at Mirelle before she trudged back to the house. She heard the phone as she reached the front walk and ran, slipping on the walk where ice had formed in the night. *Never will understand why the phone has to be answered,* she thought to herself. She slithered past the dining room table, arm outstretched to flip the instrument off the hook before the caller gave up.

"What took you so long?" Steve demanded.

"Loading Roman on the bus. Ice on the walk." She got the answer out in spurts.

"What did you say to Ralph?"

"Ralph?"

"Yes, Ralph Martin, my brother," Steve said acidly. "He tracked me down, hotel by hotel, until he found the right convention. Got me up at 12:30. Out of a sound sleep, I might add."

"He didn't ask me which hotel. He was upset." Mirelle resolved to keep her temper.

"I know that! I want to know what you said to him."

"He wanted to know what had upset his mother, because she was being hysterical, and then he tried to tell me that she isn't the hysterical type . . . " Despite her resolve, Mirelle felt her anger rising. "So I told him what happened when Roman got home, and then he said something about us treating the injury casually, and us forcing alcohol down Roman's throat."

"He said you called Mother hysterical and narrow-minded."

"Oh, Steve, do I have to defend myself to you, too? You were there! I'm not ashamed of giving Roman a shot of bourbon when he needed the stimulant. Nor are we an insensitive and alcoholic household. And I'm so proud that our son could get up and walk himself home . . . "

"That's it! Is that what you said to Ralph?"

"Steve, for God's sake . . . "

"Can't you imagine how that would make Ralph feel?"

"I don't care how Ralph feels. I know how I feel! Damned for doing the right thing at the right time in the right way! Do I have to use the same warped precepts your mother uses?"

"I didn't realize you hated my mother so." Steve's voice was low and bitter.

"I don't hate her, Steve," Mirelle said wearily. "I'm sorry for her, sorry that we're so different we can never be friends at all. But most of all, I'm sorry for us. Because every time she comes, she rips us wide open."

"I know, I know," Steve answered irritably but suddenly he wasn't fighting her anymore. "But damn it, Mirelle, you just don't tell your own mother that you don't want to see her again."

Mirelle stifled her surprise. Steve's remark had been more to himself than to her, but it clarified Ralph's attitude and his purpose in contacting Steve. She leaned a little weakly against the wall. She had won her long grim battle against the domineering Marian Martin. It gave her no sense of triumph, certainly no pride in having had to force the issue. And it would not be easy for Steve to live with his conscience, now that he had made his stand. Mirelle hoped that Dad Martin wouldn't become an enemy, as Ralph had. Surely the old man had seen and understood, even if he hadn't intervened.

"Mirelle? Are you still there?"

"Yes, Steve," she said, frantically wondering if there was anything she could say.

"How's Roman? What's this about his getting on the school bus?"

"Will Martin said he'd be kept quieter at school than if I tried to control him at home. He knows Roman."

"Yeah, he does. There's no danger of him slipping down those bus steps? The risers are steep."

"The driver said he'd carry him off to be sure."

"Okay. Look, Mirelle, I have to stop off in Cleveland on my way back. Don't expect me before Tuesday."

"We'll miss you, Steve."

"I've got to go."

The line went dead. Mirelle realized humorlessly that she had spent a lot of time lately, staring at silent phones. She started to hang it up and then, in an unexpected decision, left it off the hook.

"I shall have my coffee and read the paper in unbroken quiet."

She resolutely put all thought of the last phone call out of her mind and read with great concentration. Five minutes later, she couldn't recall a single sentence. She read the comics, the medical column, closed her eyes to the horoscope section, and went down the notices and the services columns in the classifieds. She had so firmly put the conversation out of her mind that it wasn't until she took the dress she planned to wear to the concert out of its plastic bag that she remembered she hadn't rehung the phone.

Suppose the school had been trying to reach her because Roman had slipped or hurt himself? She cradled the phone and calmed her fears. *They'd have called a neighbor or Will Martin,* she chided herself. She really shouldn't go to the concert, she thought wearily. *No matter what Roman says about being able to manage the kids. Steve's out of town and I just shouldn't go. Well, really, why not? When have you been to a concert recently? You used to go often with Steve: you both enjoyed it. Until . . . say it . . . until Allentown and Mother Martin's diabolical finger poked fun at her concert-going son. I will not think such thoughts! There is no harm in going to a concert with a friend. A chaperone!*

Thinking of whom, Mirelle dialed Sylvia's number, letting it ring and ring until she remembered that Sylvia had said that she had to be in Philly during the day. It was already 11:30. Sylvia would have left. So, Mirelle would have to go to the concert. She had the tickets and Sylvia would be waiting for her. In that case, she'd better take the train up to Philly. Sylvia always drove. Mirelle had also better taxi to the station. Oh, dear, is it worth all the trouble?

She held the black dress up to her, appraising her reflection in the mirror. The smell of the satin, the feel of it in her hands, the lingering scent of the perfume she usually wore clung to the gown, all evoking other festive occasions and exciting evenings. Yes, she needed the therapy of the concert badly. She needed to lose herself in music, in the passive participation of listening.

Mirelle whirled away from the mirror and hung the gown on her closet door. She went down to the kitchen to make brownies for dessert, iced brownies. She must remember to check if she had enough Coke for Roman to use as reward or threat.

I'm just unused to sheer dress fabrics, Mirelle told herself as she tried to wrap her coat more firmly around her and shut out the chill wind. *If I make my muscles relax, they won't shiver.* She forced her shoulders down and took a deep breath.

Another breeze found a minute opening and streaked up her backbone. She hopped around the corner, peering anxiously up and down the street for Sylvia. It was twenty past eight.

The nagging suspicion that somehow or other Sylvia was not going to join her grew stronger. But Sylvia had said she'd come, Mirelle insisted to herself, firmly, loyally. At twenty-five past the hour, Mirelle gave up all pretense and marched to the box office.

"My name is Martin. Was there any message left for me?"

She received a frown from the pear-shaped man in the box office as he peered at her over his glasses, pursing his lips in disapproval. He glanced over his shoulder at the plump man checking figures on an adding machine.

"Any calls for a Mrs. Martin?"

"Martin? Martin? Yeah, a Mrs. Eshazy called. She ain't coming." The plump party returned to his column of figures.

Mirelle was given a quelling stare. "No refunds, lady."

She turned quickly away to cover her disappointment. Hurriedly she fumbled for the tickets in her evening purse. Took one and handed it to the bored doorman. She went through the routine of being passed from usher to usher, and down the aisle to her row, nervously stepping over feet and muttering apologies until she reached her seat and could settle herself, and hopefully her emotions. What could have happened to Sylvia? And how was she to get home now? Why had Sylvia let her down? And why was the non-appearance so distressing?

The house lights dimmed and Jamie appeared, holding back one section of the curtains to allow the soloist to make an entrance. Then he followed her to stage center. Mirelle swallowed nervously and slid down a little in her seat. She righted herself, annoyed by seeing him so professionally aloof, so sure of himself. He was suddenly in a perspective that alienated him from her previous knowledge of him. He was a stranger in the complex and glamorous world of the performing artist: no longer the amusing stranger, the sick acquaintance, or Margaret's garrulous father.

The applause which had greeted the soprano's entrance died down as she gracefully acknowledged it and took her place in the curve of the grand piano. The concert spot narrowed, framing her in an island of light which spilled over onto Jamie's head and shoulders. Mirelle caught her breath as she fancied that Jamie looked for her, directly at her in the audience. To be sure, he must know her relative position from the numbers of the tickets he had given her, but that he wanted to make sure she had used them gave her a deep and unexpected satisfaction. He had seated himself now, and Mirelle realized that he had brought no music with him. Her respect for him, professionally, rose higher.

The audience quieted: the hall was completely dark. The soprano, her full figure elegantly gowned in rich garnet red, nodded to her accompanist and the chords of the first song filled the darkness.

Wide-eyed with shock, Mirelle gripped the arms of her seat. The notes of the Handel aria were so sweetly familiar: with this beautiful song Mary LeBoyne had opened the last concert which Mirelle heard her mother sing. Madame Nealy's voice compounded the anguish by having much the same timbre. Mirelle closed her eyes. She could see so clearly her mother's figure, standing on the makeshift stage in that awful little auditorium. The air had been cloying with the smell of the burnt, the burning, and antiseptic. The previous night's bombing had been heavy in the area and the stink of it was everywhere. Mirelle, about to be sent off to America for the duration, had accompanied her mother as a special treat. Self-conscious in her school gabardine, desperately shy, she had sat at the back of a hall filled with convalescent servicemen. She had been convinced, even then, that this was the last time she'd hear her mother sing.

The Mirelle of 1940 knew exactly why she was being sent to America: she was becoming too much of an embarrassment to Edward Barthan-More. And that afternoon, Mary Margaret LeBoyne had told Mirelle the circumstances of her birth, in a halting, embarrassed voice, flushing with the memory of humiliations at the hands of her vindictive husband. Half weeping, Mary Margaret had begged her daughter's forgiveness for the ignominies and slights which the child had suffered at her stepfather's hands. She apologized for being so selfish as to keep Mirelle by her when the girl might have had a happier childhood in some foster home where her irregular birth was no stigma to social acceptance. Embarrassed by her mother's anguish, Mirelle had fought the intense relief she had felt at knowing that she really wasn't the daughter of the cold autocratic vicious man whom she had come to hate for the many petty acts he was fond of committing against anyone subordinate to, or dependent on him. She had suffered agonies of mind because she was 'supposed to love her father' and couldn't. And she had hated him most because of the way he had treated her mother. To go to America to live with her mother's best friend, Mary Murphy, was no exile to Mirelle. It was paradise. And she knew, in her sudden maturity, that Edward Barthan-More would never give his wife permission to go to America once the war was over, to see her daughter. Her mother knew it, too, from the way she had clung to Mirelle that afternoon.

Mirelle was suddenly startled out of her reverie by the applause for Madame Nealy.

Somewhat bitterly, Mirelle wondered if there was any way Jamie could have known how much the woman sounded like Mary LeBoyne. But how could he? There were only a few recordings of her mother's voice, and they were on ancient 78 rpm discs. Jamie's contained face, dramatically highlighted in the spill of the spotlight, was intent on the soprano for her cue to begin the next song. Jamie wouldn't be so deliberately cruel, Mirelle told herself. She sat up in the seat, determined to put aside these painful memories and really listen to the performance.

Fortunately, the Gluck aria which was next held no painful connotations for Mirelle. She could appreciate the delicate balance between singer and accompanist, and she found herself unaccountably jealous of the hours of rehearsal necessary to achieve such rapport. Madame Nealy was an undeniably handsome woman but Mirelle could not picture Jamie as her lover. *Now why on earth would I think about that,* Mirelle wondered, *as if it made any difference to me at all whom James Howell had affairs with. Listen! Mirelle, you're here to listen!*

There was a brief intermission before the lieder section. Mirelle waited patiently, determined to hold her mind to the concert without further ruminations. Her knowledge and appreciation of lieder was good. She'd learned German as a small girl because her mother had been well received as a lieder singer in Germany. Mirelle's happiest childhood memories were the four tours on which she had accompanied her mother when Mary Margaret had been singing all over the Third Reich. That had been before Mary Margaret had become aware of the military build-up and the penetration of *Das Kultur* in all areas of German life.

It was impossible to stem the flow of memories: dust motes dancing on the beams of sunlight flooding a music room, her mother's patient repetition of "Die Ring an Meinem Finger", beyond the windows so bright from the attentions of the parlor maid that morning, the glittering sweep of the Neckar River.

Surrendering for the first time to the pull of associations, Mirelle leapt from one reminiscence to another: all of them centering around her mother and those four tours, though Mirelle hadn't been more than six on the first one. She remembered the starchy feel of her linen 'good' dress, the way her shoes had pinched her toes because Nanny would not tell Mother that the shoes were outgrown: the scent of her mother's cologne, the yeasty smell of buttered rolls, and the taste of well-milked coffee, a special treat in the mornings when she and her mother had breakfasted together in bed.

And never once, not even in that last painful interview, had her mother ever mentioned Lajos Neagu.

Once freed of her guilty hatred for the man she'd considered to be her father, Mirelle had nothing but contempt for Edward Barthan-More. Her hatred she had transferred to the father who had ignored her existence, and left her mother to endure the vindictive intolerance of her stepfather.

Tonight in the darkened auditorium, familiar lieder

melodies and words reinforcing associative memories, Mirelle could begin to appreciate her mother's silence; her father's apparent neglect. The long-held hatred dissipated and the bitter regret was absolved. Mirelle was limp with emotional strain by intermission and stumbled over feet with inordinate haste for the refuge of the sidewalk, chilly or not, and fresh air.

She could be relieved now that Sylvia had reneged. There would have been bright remarks and curious questions. Or perhaps, Mirelle pondered, she would not have switched to that train of thought in Sylvia's company. But where was Sylvia? The notion that Sylvia had arranged their meeting at the concert for someone else's benefit . . . as an alibi . . . reasserted itself. But surely if Sylvia had had no intention of keeping the appointment, why hadn't she had the decency to phone and warn Mirelle? It was only fair. Then Mirelle remembered leaving the phone off the hook all morning. She was partly to blame for her present situation, and she grimaced. The theatre lights blinked a warning.

Before the concert resumed, Mirelle had time to look at her program. Madame Nealy might have taken the selections from one of Mary LeBoyne's concerts. Even the arias had been in her mother's repertoire, and they were not the usual sopranic standbys, except "Pace! Pace!", the lovely old warhorse from *Forza del Destino!*

Peace, peace, Mirelle muttered under her breath. She could do with some of that, but if she immured herself in a hermit's cell, would she get as much done as she did now?

The lovely paean, "Il est doux" from *Herodiade* was next and, as the melody lifted, Mirelle found her eyes returning to Jamie. 'He is gentle, he is kind,' the aria said and Mirelle applied the adjectives to Jamie and found them suitable. 'I was suffering and alone, and my heart was calmed when I heard his voice. Oh, Prophet, so beloved, can I live without thee!'

That's enough of that, Mirelle told herself sternly. *This concert is an unqualified disaster. I should have stayed home with the children, where I belong.*

Nonsense, said the sane observer in her mind. *Tragedy is the catharsis of the soul. You've been denying your past and until you face up to it, it will distort the future.*

She had tried to submerge her background, wanting to eradicate anything that she owed to Barthan-More, and those English years, in her allegiance to her new country, and her love for Mary Murphy. And then, when her father's totally unexpected bequest had alienated the Martins, she had doubled her energies to camouflage her identity, to deny her parentage, and the talents that were her genetic legacy. But moulding herself on the pattern which she thought would please the Martins had not been successful. She'd become a shadow of a woman, and a shadow wife to Steve. Had she chosen Steve as a husband because he represented all she felt she'd missed? A happy home-coming father and a loving husband? Candidly Mirelle doubted that: hoped she had reason to doubt it or the last fifteen years had been a complete lie and she was crippling her children as subtly as she had been crippled in her childhood in the Barthan-More nursery.

Lucy, hand to her wayward hair, feet flying in an effort to stay in the same place, Lucy of the statue was superimposed on the other distressing images. Lucy who didn't apologize for her poetry or her housekeeping or her mistakes but kept on running, somewhere, anywhere so long as it was ahead. Lucy who had tried to pry open Mirelle's clamshell, mend the hurt and encourage her talent.

And Mirelle thought of Sylvia, bitter because she didn't have Mirelle's ability to sculpt. Sculpting, Mirelle thought sardonically, was a ready-made out, for sculpture is never very popular so that if she had filled a studio with her industry, she wouldn't sell very much anyhow. Only she sold as many of the creche figures and the Dirty Dicks as she could produce.

The applause snapped her out of those reflections and she found herself clapping violently just as her neighbors ceased. She slid down in her seat, so intensely embarrassed that she was separated completely from reflections.

Fortunately the final portion of the program was made

up of totally unfamiliar contemporary American art songs, devoid of any connotations with the past.

Madame Nealy was called back for two encores during which Mirelle gathered her shattered composure. Jamie, respectfully bowing the soprano through the curtains, looked directly at her as the houselights came on. A jerk of his head indicated that she should come backstage.

Rebelliously she waited as the audience cleared from the hall. She did not want Jamie's company. He was too perceptive. She dreaded his sly probes. But there wasn't a train until 3:00 a.m. Damn Sylvia! She was forced to go backstage and beg a ride from James Howell.

A bored usherette gave her directions and she found the green room crowded with elegantly dressed well-wishers. She hung on the fringe, knowing that she would simply have to wait, nervously wishing herself anywhere but in a crowd in her present state of mind.

She was pushed forward by a gaggle of newcomers and inadvertently found herself in line to congratulate Madame Nealy. She did so, trying not to sound perfunctory, when Jamie intervened.

"This is Mary LeBoyne's daughter, Mirelle Martin, Madame," Jamie said with cheerful helpfulness.

Madame Nealy was more commanding on stage than off, Mirelle thought. And right now the woman looked exhausted.

"That was a demanding program," Mirelle said, smiling, "but you made it sound so effortless, so buoyant."

"It's far easier to sing for an appreciative audience," the soprano replied kindly. "I had the pleasure of hearing your mother sing at the Albert Hall before the war. Such a lovely voice. Such a beautiful artist and a very gracious woman."

"I take after my father," Mirelle said, laughingly in answer to the question in Madame's eyes, and moved on to be grabbed by Jamie.

"No chaperone?"

"Sylvia didn't come. I don't know what happened."

"Need a ride home?"

"As a matter of fact, yes."

He looked at her a moment, his expression grave. "My pleasure," he said automatically. "Go sit down in a corner. You look as if you'd sung every note in the program."

"I feel as if I had."

As soon as the words were out of her mouth, Mirelle regretted them. Just the sort of thing that Jamie would pick up on the drive home. When only a few people remained, Madame Nealy came up to Mirelle and invited her to join them at supper.

"Madame," Jamie said as Mirelle was fumbling for a plausible excuse, "I rose from a sickbed to play and my doctor told me that I had to return to it immediately."

Madame looked from Mirelle to Jamie, eyebrows slightly raised.

" 'S'truth," Jamie swore, raising his right hand. He did, indeed, look tired.

"Yes, we're none of us as young as we once were, able to party into the early hours," she said with a smile. "I can't thank you enough anyhow, Jim, for tonight." She turned to Mirelle. "I always feel that I can just forget about everything but interpreting my music when Jim plays for me. He anticipates every retard, every nuance."

She kissed him warmly on both cheeks and then turned back to her guests. Quickly Jamie motioned to Mirelle. He gathered up his topcoat and hat, and headed her towards the door before anyone could stop them with further importunities.

"That's over," he sighed as they stepped into the cold night.

Mirelle couldn't agree more. His hand gripped her arm, guiding her towards his car. She could feel herself violently shivering as the wind whipped about them. Jamie unlocked his car, threw in his briefcase and settled her. He said nothing as he deftly maneuvered the big Thunderbird down the narrow streets, swinging at last onto the Schuylkill Expressway.

"There's a dirty dive a ways from here with the best steaks in town. I'm always ravenous after a concert," he said genially, "and I can't abide little snacks and champagne cup. I want meat, red meat."

"Do waitresses drip blood on you as they serve?" she asked brightly.

"You're lucky if that's all they drip when they serve."

Mirelle searched desperately for some way to continue the light conversation, anything to cover her growing unease. The tension in the car was palpable and yet she couldn't think of a way to tell Jamie what had upset her. She glanced nervously at him, but he was watching the road, both hands on the steering wheel. At first she thought it was a trick of the overhead lights, but then she realized that his hands were trembling.

"Playing a concert is exhausting," he said, noticing her intake of breath.

"You shouldn't have played such a demanding concert so soon after the pneumonia," she said, semi-scolding.

"Oh, then you did find my playing adequate?"

"Adequate?" She echoed the adjective in dismay. "You play magnificently."

"It's nice to hear you say so."

She caught her breath sharply at the unexpected cut, and found that she had to bite her lip to keep back the tears. But he was justified. She'd been exhibiting an appalling self-centeredness. But she didn't know how to redeem herself in his eyes.

Then Howell brought the car to a sudden stop. Mirelle saw that they had pulled off the Expressway onto a suburban street. He flicked off the lights, turned round to her purposefully.

"All right, what's the matter?"

"Matter?" The word came out as a blubber.

"Yes, matter. Perhaps it was selfish of me to want you to see me at my professional best, but I certainly didn't expect to be received by a dull thud. The least you could do was be courteous."

"I'm sorry. I'm sorry. I didn't mean to be rude, it's just that . . . " And she buried her face in her hands, sobbing uncontrollably.

"Mirelle! Mirelle darling." She felt herself pulled into his arms. His hands, warm and no longer trembling, were gentle and comforting. He held her close to him, her face on the soft camel-hair of his overcoat.

"The concert was like a nightmare for me, Jamie. It was Mother. Every song was one she'd sung . . . it was like old ghosts rising up to haunt me. I remembered hundreds of details about her that I hadn't thought of in years. And you played so beautifully. It wasn't your fault. I've just been upset all this week and everything had added to it. It wasn't Madame's fault that she has the same timbre in her voice as Mother. It wasn't yours. It's just me. I'm being self-centered and childish. And unmannerly and you wanted to give me a nice treat. And now I've spoiled the evening for you as well."

She looked up, trying to stop crying. He mopped the tears from her face with his handkerchief, his expression tender and concerned. Abruptly, she stopped crying. For the first time, the inner James Howell was visible to her. As she looked, their eyes met and he began to smile. Holding her face with his free hand, he lowered his head to kiss her, very slowly, very carefully, very thoroughly. Nor could she have gathered the strength of will to resist. His kiss, so expert, so loverly, was an anodyne to her torn emotions: like a benediction, she thought, and the music of the Herodiade aria sang through her.

"*Il est doux, il est bon,*" she whispered as he raised his head.

He let out a burst of laughter, hugging her tightly to him in surprise.

"I am no prophet," he crowed, looking down at her with a broad grin which faded as quickly as it came. "And I'm no saint," he added almost angrily.

This time he kissed her with no tenderness at all, his lips hard and bruising as his caresses awakened a passionate response which she was unable to control. He released her abruptly, almost flinging her to the other side of the front seat. Wrenching himself around, he gripped the wheel with both hands.

"Have you a little idea of how you affect me, Mirelle?" he asked hoarsely.

She sat, unable to speak, as he started the car and spun it onto the road. He drove with skillful speed, as silent as she, and Mirelle struggled to assess the impact of his declaration.

She paid no attention to the twists and turns of the road; instead she watched his hands on the wheel, the hands which had fascinated her for so long. Again she felt their strong grip on her ribs, her arms, her neck, like invisible burns. It had actually not occurred to her that more than friendship existed between them. She was certain that she had never encouraged anything more. How amazing that he had developed a *tendresse* for her. None of this shattering evening would have happened, she thought bitterly, if Sylvia had been along. Damn Sylvia! She had needed a chaperone. Oh, God, how she needed one!

Jamie braked, flicked off the lights and pocketed the key in one swift movement before Mirelle realized that they were in a garage. His garage.

"I want you, Mirelle. Christ, how I want you," he said softly, roughly, leaning towards her, his face a fierce shadow. His body pressed hers into the seat leather, his hands quick and expert, his lips searching and finding her sensitive places. He guided her out of the car and into the cold dark house. Thoroughly aroused by his seeking hands, she found herself undressing in his room as, somewhere in the dark, he cursed the folderol of dress clothes. Then his warm smooth skin was against hers and they were beside each other in the bed.

"What say you, my silence?" he asked in a whisper at her ear, his long body heavy against her as his restless expert fingers excited her.

"I need you, Jamie. Just now I need you very much."

"Thank God!"

Afterwards, lying in a lovely lassitude, Mirelle could not be sure if Jamie slept. Turning her head cautiously, she saw that, on the contrary, he was watching her intently. He lay on his side, barely touching her body, one hand propping up his head. As she turned, he tucked the blanket close about her, then let his hand rest lightly on her belly.

"The piano's not the only thing you play well," she said.

He chuckled softly, pulling her against him. She thought he sounded relieved, and, in the candid expansiveness of loving's aftermath, she asked him if he was.

"Yes, Mirelle, I am." He kissed her softly.

"Why?"

He looked down at her steadily. Her eyes were used to the darkness now and she met his gaze.

"I've taken a rascally advantage of your distress, my dear . . . "

"No, Jamie. I needed loving . . . your kind of loving . . . desperately."

He cocked his head slightly, his expression quizzical as he waited for her to continue. She ran her forefinger down the line of his face. He caught her hand and bit the finger. "No, Mirelle, no sculptor's pensive tracing now, please. This is between James Howell, man, and Mirelle LeBoyne, woman."

"Yes, that's who it's between, isn't it?"

He buried his face in her neck, kissing the line of her throat and she knew she had said the right thing, at last, in Jamie's presence. And she also knew why she'd phrased her answer that way.

So she pressed against him, inching her body closer to his, felt his legs overlap hers, his hips angling against her. He was strong, so strong and so the restraint with which he used her was all the more surprising. The difference between his and Steve's lovemaking was incredible yet she followed his lead as if they'd been lovers for a long time. Their bodies seemed to match, to fit, and he knew exactly how to draw out the tension before their climax to the precise and critical point of complete release. This second time she was unable to resist the need for sleep.

She woke, though, startled and immediately aware of the unfamiliar surroundings. The illuminated dial on his bureau alarm read 3:l0. She ought to be getting home but the thought of moving from his arms—his head pillowed against her shoulder—was unbearable. She could indulge herself this once. The children would all be safely asleep. No one need know where she was or how long she'd been gone. Even the late late train from Philadelphia didn't get in to Wilmington until close to 4:00.

She counted carefully. Nor would she get pregnant as a result. The reassurance amused her and the giggle got as far as her chest, which was far enough to rouse Jamie.

"And what amuses you, my love?" he asked, as flippant as ever.

"I won't get pregnant."

"That's a good girl. Oh, you mean, unlike your mother?" He propped his head up, unwillingly, she thought, for he kept the other arm draped over her, his hand on her breast.

"Mother did not have the advantages of modern science."

"She was quite a woman for all of that."

"Yes, indeed she was."

He gave her a long hard look. "You've forgiven her?"

"I guess I have, though I didn't know that I had to."

He stroked her face, his fingers idly dropping to her throat, her breast again. "And?"

She caught his hand, held it against her breast, feeling his fingers cupping the soft flesh, gently, possessively.

"Right now, I could even forgive my mother-in-law for her transgressions."

He laughed aloud, a vastly amused whoop of a laugh and rocked her into his arms, until her body was athwart his, her forehead pressing against his neck, his hands playing with her hair and caressing her back.

He was a marvelous lover, she thought, aware that love-making need not stop with the climax but could be, as Jamie proved, deliciously prolonged to ease the return to separate awareness. She did not want to leave this bed, disturb this mood . . .

"I've got to get you home, Mirelle," Jamie murmured with a groan of regret, and then began to kiss her face avidly. "But, God, how I hate to let you go."

"I hate to leave."

He held her from him a little so that he could see her face.

"Do you?"

She caught her breath, half afraid of what he might say next. "Yes, I do." She had to be honest with Jamie. "But I also have to go."

"I know you do, my silence." He was gentle again. No, not gentle, responsive. He understood what she meant. "Promise me one thing, Mirelle?"

"What?"

He grinned because she'd jerked her chin up defensively. He kissed her there. "Don't regret this evening. No, be quiet." His arm tightened to reinforce his order. "I damn well took deliberate advantage of your emotional state, but I've been trying to get you into my bed for some time. I'm not sorry I have. However, in the cold clear light of tomorrow, back in lower Suburbia, you may view the romantic nonsense of being swept into my bed as tawdry. I don't want that, Mirelle, not for you, and not for the way I feel about you. Lie still! You're a decent woman, Mirelle. You did nothing to lead me on so don't have that on your conscience tomorrow. And you're honest. At least you have been tonight in my arms. Don't turn plastic tomorrow. Or ever."

Mirelle ran her free hand up into his hair to pull his head down so she could kiss him deeply. "Thank you, Jamie." She couldn't find any other words but he held her tightly, so perhaps what she couldn't say was expressed properly.

Then, as if only a violent movement would suffice, Jamie threw back the covers and rose from the bed, his long frame silhouetted briefly in the moonlight. She rose, too, shivering in the chilly room, and they dressed in an easy silence.

CHAPTER TWENTY-ONE

HOWELL TOOK HER HOME, whipping through the deserted streets with deft speed.

"I've got make-up lessons tomorrow, or rather today, and a TV recital on Sunday. May I come leer at you on Monday?"

"If you're sure you can fit it in your overcrowded schedule," said Mirelle, grinning at him.

He grinned back for a moment, then turned uncharacteristically solemn. "Remember, tomorrow morning, what you promised me, Mirelle."

"I will, Jamie."

And because it was so painful to leave him, she did it as quickly as possible, with no farewell of any sort.

The children were, as she'd known, sound asleep. Roman had lost the pillow under his broken arm. She replaced it tenderly. Nick and Tonia were burrowed deep into their covers, warm little animals.

Roman had left a note on her pillow. "Everything here okay. Hope you had a good time."

She remembered her promise to Jamie and stifled an unworthy thought. In the bathroom mirror, she took a long look at her vivid face and then scrubbed until her skin tingled. She couldn't remove that well-loved look with soap or cold cream. Again, she suppressed a fleeting thought and then smiled at her reflection. She slipped into her nightgown, still smiling, and got in between the cold sheets, regretting the warm bed she had left.

Fatigue claimed her before she had had a chance to review any of the evening's unexpected developments. She was roused the next morning by Tonia's shriek of protest from the gameroom. She heard both Nick and Roman trying to shush their sister but the shrieks turned to wails and she knew that she'd have to referee the quarrel.

She had coffee started before the phone rang.

"My God, you sound alert," Jamie Howell said, disgusted.

"I can't be. I haven't had coffee yet."

"Mirelle?" His voice turned plaintively tender.

"I'm glad you called, Jamie," she said, answering as best she could the unspoken appeal.

"Then I may come on Monday?"

She giggled. He sounded like a boy expecting to be deprived of a promised treat. "Yes, of course."

"Good." His voice was brisk again as he said goodbye and hung up.

Mirelle was sipping her third cup of coffee and reading the newspaper for the second time when Roman hobbled upstairs.

"Did you have a good time, Mom?"

Mirelle swallowed, remembered her promise, and said that she had.

"Concert good?"

"Yes, it was, and the paper thinks so, too. Here's the review."

Roman rejected the offer. "Did you like Mr. Howell?"

Mirelle thought for one moment that she would burst into hysterical laughter but she caught herself and altered her thoughts. "He is a superb accompanist."

"What was the singer like?"

Mirelle regarded her son thoughtfully for a moment. He

was being so grown-up in his questions, so polite. She must simply ignore the other interpretations that sprang to her mind. No, it was not a guilty mind. She shouldn't read suspicion into a very natural question. Roman had wanted her to have a pleasant evening out; he had taken pains to see that she would; he was now inquiring politely for details.

"To be honest, the singer sounded a great deal like my mother, your grandmother LeBoyne. In fact, some of the songs were ones that my mother sang in the last concert she gave."

"Your mother was a singer?"

"I'm sure I've mentioned that." Mirelle was ashamed of the sharpness in her voice.

"You don't talk about *your* mother much," Roman said a little wistfully.

"No, I guess I haven't, have I?"

"Oh, that's all right," Roman said more briskly. "I figured it made you sad to talk about her."

"Yes, it did. But last night . . . well, sometimes you have to talk the sadness out." Now there was a fancy bit of rationalization, thought Mirelle.

"Sadness out? Of what?" Nick demanded, arriving just then.

"Shut up!" Roman said affably.

"Why? What did I say?" Nick regarded his brother with total innocence.

"Roman! Nick! No bickering!" Then Mirelle called Tonia upstairs and began to tell all three about the concert, the memories that it had evoked of her mother, of the tours in Germany, even of that last war-time concert. She had tears in her eyes when she finished, and Roman's uninjured hand crept into hers.

"Why'd you never tell us we had a nice grandmother?" Tonia asked into the silence that fell when Mirelle's reminiscing ceased.

"Do I slap your face the way your father did?" Mirelle asked sharply.

Tonia's hand crept to her cheek and her eyes widened with fear. She shook her head vehemently.

"Then don't say such things," Mirelle advised. "Grandmother Martin is a fine woman. And I don't know that my mother wouldn't be just as annoyed with you children. You can be selfish, mannerless creatures sometimes."

"Is my other grandfather alive?" Nick wanted to know.

"No. He died just before Roman was born."

"What was he like?"

"I never knew him."

"Why not?" Nick was shocked. Then he looked up at his mother from under his brows, his voice dropping to a whisper. "You mean, your parents were . . . divorced . . . like the Bellows kids'?"

Mirelle nodded. This small untruth was surely permissible.

"What was he like? Did you ever find out?"

"He was a portrait painter."

Nick was skeptical about the merits of that occupation but Tonia perked up noticeably.

"Was he as good as Mr. Robinson?" She had been impressed by a neighbor's landscape paintings.

"Well, some of his portraits hang in European museums."

"In museums?" Nick and Tonia were awestruck.

"Gosh, Mom, how come you never told us you have famous parents?" Nick asked.

"Because our other grandmother wouldn't have liked it," replied Tonia, setting her mouth just the way that Marian Martin did when stating an unpleasant truth.

"Antonia!" Mirelle felt obliged to reprimand her but then, with three pairs of rebellious eyes on her, she had to temper that rebuke. "My parents are both dead. No one in America ever heard of them, so there didn't seem much point in . . . well . . . " Mirelle shrugged.

"You got a picture of your mother. D'you have one of your father, too?" Roman asked.

Mirelle could no longer deny the presence of that unopened package in the attic. She might as well make a clean sweep of her ghosts. Hiding them had done no good.

The package was not only dusty but exceedingly well

wrapped. It took time and patience to penetrate the protective coverings. No one was more surprised than Nick when his grandfather's face was finally revealed.

"Hey, he looks just like me!"

"You mean, you look like him!" Roman corrected his brother, but he was staring at Mirelle.

The portrait wasn't large, 24" by 24", but the handsome Slavic face would have dominated any room. Nothing modest about Lajos Neagu, thought Mirelle, and nothing ordinary. He'd not flattered himself, certainly. The lines of dissipation and disillusion were carefully limned, the crook in the nose which marred its aristocratic length, the pits in the skin. But there was sardonic humor in the quirk of the lips, echoed in the intensely blue eyes, as if Lajos were amused at the notion of painting a portrait for the daughter he would never meet.

Mirelle liked the directness of that gaze, the strength of the face that overcame the dissolution. As she admired the honesty and the artistic technique, she realized that she had also forgiven her father the sin of begetting her. In fact, she experienced profound regret that she'd never met him. Deeper ran a secondary impression: Lajos Neagu with Mary LeBoyne beside him. They'd have made a magnificent couple! Why had her mother returned to colorless, autocratic, vindictive Edward Barthan-More?

"Gee, Ma, he's great," Roman said softly.

"Yeah, he sure is," Nick echoed with a shy grin.

"Can I tell people he's my other grandfather?" Tonia asked, glaring resentfully at Nick because she obviously didn't share his resemblance to this magnificent man.

Mirelle had intended to wrap the portrait up again and put it safely back in the attic. Now she knew that was impossible.

"Yes, you can, Tonia. You can say that he painted it for me, and for you, his grandchildren, to have. So you'd know what he looked like."

"I'll get the hammer and nails," Roman said.

"No, I will!" Nick was adamant. "He looks like me!"

Mirelle caught Roman's eyes and held them. He made a face but he let Nick run the errand.

"How come he didn't paint a picture of your mother?" Tonia wanted to know, eyeing her newfound grandfather thoughtfully.

"As a matter of fact, he did. But I think the painting was destroyed during the bombing in London."

"Gee whiz," Tonia was crushed. "All you got of her is just that tiny little picture on your dresser?"

"And lots of memories."

The children wanted to hang the portrait prominently between the windows in the living room. It was the best place, certainly. And she and Steve had often talked of getting a good picture for that spot. Lajos Neagu was shortly dominating the room. The rug, the drapes, the gold slip covers all seemed to take on added warmth as his personality blazed from the canvas. As it seemed unlikely to Mirelle that her parents-in-law would be gracing their home any time soon, they couldn't construe the portrait as an affront to their sensibilities. As far as friends and neighbors were concerned, Nick had innocently suggested the proper line: her parents had been divorced. No one knew about the Barthan-More part of her life, and to hell with the narrow-minded Martins.

She'd shooed the children off to pick up their rooms when the phone rang.

"How was the concert?" Sylvia asked, her words slurred.

"Just great, but where were you yesterday?"

"Your line was busy, my dear, for three hours." Sylvia was speaking slowly and her enunciation was very precise.

"Sorry about that. I had so many calls first thing that I finally took the phone off the hook. Besides, you had no intention of coming to the concert, did you?"

"Let us say, a conflict. I hoped that I'd be free in the evening. I was rather curious about Howell, the professional ivory-tickler. Tell me," and Sylvia's characteristic chuckle was remarkably unrepentant, "did he drive you home?"

Mirelle checked herself. She had been thinking only in terms of Sylvia using the concert as a cover-up for some activity of her own, not that Sylvia might be deliberately throwing her into Howell's company.

"Sylvia! You're meddling!"

"You're damned right I am. Have a little fun in life, honey," and the slurring was worse than ever, "before it's too late. Before it's much too late."

"Sylvia, what's wrong? You don't sound like yourself."

"Nothing's wrong. I'm insulated against the slings and arrows of outrageous fortune. I'm wrapped in cotton wool. God's in his heaven, all's right with the world. Pippa passes."

Abruptly the connection was cut. Sylvia couldn't be drunk at 10:30 in the morning, thought Mirelle, glancing at her watch. She started to dial Sylvia's number but, at that point, Nick and Tonia started some kind of a full-fledged, object-throwing brawl on the landing and what with one thing and another, she had no chance to call Sylvia back until noontime—when there was no answer. It was quite likely that Sylvia was busy with Saturday errands but Mirelle was strangely uneasy about her friend.

She did her own shopping, took the children to a movie which had been enthusiastically plugged on TV, ironed, cleaned, and cooked until the children went to bed. Then she purposefully entered the workshop.

She took down the bust of Jamie. She knew, in a glance now, where she had erred and corrected the faults with quick careful strokes. Then she sat for a long time in contemplative regard of her craftsmanship.

Yes, she had been drawn to James Howell, amused and stimulated by his quick, sardonic humor, his ruthless attitudes, and his contradictory sensitivities. She wondered if sleeping with him had been the necessary catalyst to capturing the elusive quality of the man. God, she couldn't go around sleeping with every man she wanted to sculpt. Reverend O'Dell would be shocked! She giggled at her irreverence and then wished she could tell Jamie. And that amused her further.

Was that why, she wondered, her father had been so successful a portrait painter? Certainly he had been with her mother's portrait. Was that why Edward Barthan-More had kept the portrait in his bedroom? It had too much of a hint of the bedroom to be hung with the staider family portraits. She privately didn't give her stepfather such perceptiveness but it made an interesting conundrum. Obviously Lajos Neagu had used that research technique often. But it was one thing for a man . . . and quite another for a woman.

Mirelle hugged her knees to her chest and rocked in a silent excess of amusement. What was the matter with her? Genetic traits making belated appearances? Well, adultery was a family custom, wasn't it? She ought to be scandalized and appalled by her behavior, by her outrageous thoughts and yet, they all seemed natural. Just as the course of events which had started the day the Sprite's tire blew was inevitable, right into Jamie Howell's bed. Were all the major changes of life heralded by such trivia? For-want-of-a-nail-the-shoe-was-lost kind of sequence?

Boots' toss had started an upheaval both subtle and violent. Well, since she was dealing in clichés, she must also believe that an ill wind blew some good.

She had, after all, done the Lucy statue; she had this very creditable bust of Howell *and damn the research which provided the final insight*; the little soldier. She'd caused Steve to throw off his mother's domination, and she had finally come to terms with her bastardy. (Though she reversed the cliché, the child acknowledged the father.) Well, she couldn't leave the metamorphosis half finished. As soon as the Christmas rush was over, she'd get in touch with Ty Hopkins at the bank and see about a showing. She'd even find out if Sylvia had contacted that gallery friend of hers in Philadelphia. She might even advertise her Dirty Dicks in one of those Shopping Columns in magazines.

The house was chilling off; it was past 11:00 and fatigue stiffened her muscles. She mixed a blue plaster and coated the bust. It was, to her eyes, too naked an admission of intimacy. Had her father felt that way when he gazed at his finished portrait of Mary LeBoyne? She couldn't imagine that father of hers regretting anything he'd *done!* God, half her adult life had been wasted in worrying about the things she hadn't done. Ye gods, the times Steve had apparently envisioned her in bed with another man! Just this once she would permit herself to stray. Just once? Like mother, like daughter? Mirelle was too weary to pursue the analogy further. In fact, she almost dared not.

That night she dreamt again of the hands, with one difference. She no longer feared them and eluded their grasping talons with ease, because the Lucy statue was running beside her, only it never seemed to change its feet, but sort of hopped along on the one toe, a technique which irritated the dreamer profoundly.

When she woke to the bright Sunday sunshine, she wondered in the drowsy borderland between sleep and wakefulness, if the hands symbolized all her vain efforts to conform to Mother Martin's notions of the proper daughter-in-law? If so, what was the Lucy figure doing, traveling in that pogo-stick fashion?

There were a few minor problems with Roman's paper-route that morning. He had found a substitute to help Nick with the heavy Sunday deliveries, but the two boys had fallen to squabbling. Mirelle finally had to bundle the invalid into the Sprite and help him check out discrepancies.

When they got back a strange car was turning in the drive. Mirelle assumed it was about the paper deliveries until she saw the yellow telegram envelope in the driver's hand. Wordlessly the messenger handed over his clipboard for her to sign. She would have preferred not to read the telegram at all because it could only be bad news. It was the phrasing of the message which rocked her.

"What's the matter, Mother?" Roman asked.

"Grandfather Martin's had a heart attack. Your Uncle Ralph says he'll be all right but he'll have to go easy," she said slowly. She did not add the final sentence of Ralph's message: "Trust you are satisfied now."

"I must reach your father," she mumbled and raced up the stairs to the privacy of her room. She threw herself on the bed. Part of her wanted to curl into a ball while the sane observer remarked that this was ridiculous.

'Satisfied now'? How could Ralph? As if she, Mirelle,

could be to blame for a heart attack that had happened a week later and eighteen hundred miles away. And yet . . . it had happened when she, Mirelle, had been lolling in James Howell's arms. She pushed that from her mind.

Lord, she couldn't remember which hotel Steve was staying at, or if he'd have left for Cleveland, or what? But she had to reach him. She must make him understand, too, how wickedly cruel that accusation was. The ring of the phone stabbed like a knife through her mind to her roiling stomach.

"Mirelle, Dad's had a heart attack," Steve said with no preamble.

"I know. I just got a wire from Ralph."

"Well?"

"Well what? Or do you think it's my fault, too?"

"Your fault?" Steve sounded shocked and angry. "What on earth do you mean by that, Mirelle? How could it be your fault? But you might at least act sorry."

"I AM sorry! I like your father, even if your mother and I can never see eye to eye. But let me quote you Ralph's wire." And she did.

"That's ridiculous and I hope you realize it," Steve said, his tone gentler.

"How could Ralph think I'd be satisfied that a nice old man has had a heart attack?" Mirelle was close to tears.

"Honey, don't cry. Ralph's not rational but can't you see how he'd think that? Mother and Dad were upset by what happened here."

"You think I'm not? But was it my fault? Because Roman should never have been allowed to serve papers at all. Because he might possibly hurt himself and, of course, he did. After two years without so much as a fall off his bike . . . "

"Mirelle, get a hold of yourself. You've never flown off the handle like this before."

"I've never been so desperate before, Steve. And I've never been so unjustly accused before."

"Mirelle, please. Get a hold of yourself," Steve sounded upset now, too.

"It's not a bad stroke, is it? Your father'll be all right, won't he? I mean, did Ralph tell you any details?"

"Yes, he did. It's not a serious seizure: more of a warning. Dad told me that he'd been advised to take it easier. Get away from the heavy winters. That's why they went south. It's just unfortunate . . . Well, I don't imagine Mother helped matters any on the trip down. Or at Ralph's. Now look, Dad's at the Orange Memorial Hospital in Orlando. Send flowers, will you?"

"I will. I will. I'm sorry." While Steve had talked, she'd tried to calm herself but the viciousness of Ralph's accusation rankled too deeply.

"Mirelle, honey?"

"Yes, Steve."

"It'll all work out all right, believe me? Ralph was scared. You know he's much closer to Dad than I am."

"Oh, come home, Steve. Please come home to me."

"I will, Mirelle, I will."

He'll come home, he'll come home! The words did a gavotte in Mirelle's mind. Steve had to come home. And yes, he was right that Ralph would be scared. Ralph scared easily. He didn't have the guts that Steve did. Ralph certainly couldn't have told his mother to leave, that he never wanted to see her again. Maybe Marian Martin was afraid of her, too.

The notion consoled Mirelle tremendously and she chose not to weaken the idea with any qualifiers. People are afraid of people who are different, and she was certainly different from the girl Marian Martin had intended her precious second son to marry. Nancy Randolph indeed! Mirelle Martin scares Marian Martin! Mirelle chanted it to herself. Ralph Martin is also scared stiff of Mirelle Martin.

For Arthur Martin she felt pity. She'd always liked him. She picked up the phone and called the floral service, putting her name first when she gave the donors. She intended to keep the upper hand with her mother-in-law. Then she fixed dinner for the kids.

She tried again to reach Sylvia but the line was busy. That was an improvement on no answer.

She wandered into the studio, digging her fingers aimlessly into the plasticene in its barrel. Finally she scooped out a handful and slapped it on a plywood base. At random, she worked in more and more, globs here and there, formless. Then she began to shape what she gradually realized were hands, fingers, joints, messes of hands, grubby fingered, skeletal jointed, fat palms, stiff thumbs, crooked fingers, the hands of her nightmares—masses of fingerlike snakes and jagged claw-nails.

Although she was absorbed by the process of creation, she didn't at all like what she was doing. The hands and disjointed fingers were repellent, disgusting, verging on the obscene. She raised her fist purposefully to smash this tangible form of the nightmare back into anonymity.

"You always sculpt with love," Sylvia had said.

"Not always," Mirelle said softly. And lowered her destroying hand for some obscure, perverse reason.

She covered the obscenity and shoved it up high on the shelf where the shadows would hide it. Then she went to bed. She worried about Dad Martin until she fell asleep.

CHAPTER TWENTY-TWO

MONDAY MORNING SHE forced herself to get her usual chores done before going to the studio. She'd put another color coat on the head first, she decided. Just then the door opened abruptly. For a fleeting, hopeful moment she thought it might be Sylvia and started to the stairwell, staring up at James Howell in surprise.

"Well, whom were you expecting?" he asked. "I even knocked."

"I thought . . . well, I'd half hoped it might be Sylvia," she said with devastating honesty, and giggled at the collapse of his haughty expression.

"Hah!" He recovered himself promptly. "Don't you remember giving me gracious permission to come leer at you on Monday? I thought I'd finally succeeded in making an impression on you. Now I find that you'd prefer the company of some mere female. I'm leaving."

"Oh, Jamie, no, please!" She ran up the steps, half convinced that he was really offended. "I didn't forget you were coming. But you didn't specify when, and you caromed in just the way Sylvia does. And I haven't heard from her. I'm worried. . . ."

She was level with him now and he put his hands on her shoulders and gave her a little shake to silence her.

"What else has been dumped on you, Mirelle?"

"Oh, Jamie, everything, I think." She leaned gratefully into his comforting embrace.

"All right then, I want to hear the whole miserable saga," he said, leading her by the hand to the couch in the studio. He sat at the other end, prepared to listen.

The incidents around Roman's accident came tumbling out, including Steve's disclosure at the hospital.

"Petty, petty, petty," Jamie said in a growl, when Mirelle recounted Ralph's call and the telegram.

"I'm sorry to unload on you, Jamie," she felt obliged to say. "But it all goes round and round in my mind, and I can't set things into any sort of perspective."

"That's why confession is so good for the soul."

"You're not the father confessor type."

He grinned at her. "No, I'm not. And ordinarily I would eschew the confessional as I would the plague. But the sort of trivia that's been dumped on you is best out in the air, shaken and thrown away for the sheer dross that it is." His tone was fierce, startling her, but his expression was half-amused, as he regarded her through half-closed eyes. "I have the strong urge, my dear, to take you on my lap and cuddle you, the way I used to do with Margaret when she was hurt."

"I've not been hurt . . . "

"Not physically, no. However," he went on briskly, "my intentions towards you are not the least bit paternal . . . "

"I can't imagine you ever cuddling Margaret," Mirelle said in a tart tone because she wanted to evade the reason for Jamie's visit as long as possible.

"No?" he asked, his expressive eyebrows raised. "I made a lousy husband, I know, but I've been a most exemplary father. Margaret tells me so repeatedly. She compares notes with her college friends, and they'd all prefer me ten to one."

Mirelle laughed at his smug expression before she realized that he had been subtly prodding her out of her self-pity.

"Seriously though, Mirelle," he went on, rising suddenly and beginning to pace about, "you don't deserve such treatment from your in-laws."

"I came to the self-preserving conclusion that Marian Martin is afraid of me . . . "

"And you're probably quite right. Oh yes, Mirelle," and he made a sound of utter disgust, "you're right because you're not cast from the Barbie-doll mold. It's been a source of never-ending irritation to me that the human race descends to the level of barnyard fowls the moment something new is introduced to them. Let poultry see a hen with different or more brilliant plumage and they either peck the creature from their circle or pluck out its distinguishing feathers. Which was what your mother-in-law was doing to you by ridiculing your parentage and denying you the exercise of your birthright. So hang on to that premise and let the truth make you free . . . of all the middle-class shit you've been smothered in."

He stopped his pacing a moment to glare at her. "You're a very different woman from the nervous little housewife whose flat tire I changed. Don't think I haven't been aware of what it has cost you. When I remember your statue smashed on the floor, I feel actively nauseous. Oh, I know he said it was an accident. That didn't erase all the damage it did . . . " he broke off and stared at her. "No, I take that back. I think that's exactly what you needed. A jolt: the symbolism of seeing your friend squashed flat . . . as much by middle-class mores as anything else."

"Oh, for Pete's sake," Mirelle broke in, irritated by his analysis. "I don't need an amateur psychiatrist."

"No," and Jamie's eyes were flashing, "*you* need a kick in the pants. From what you've told me, Lucy Farnoll pried you loose from your comfortable martyr's hole and made you take a good look around you. She died and you didn't have her skirts to run to when things got tough so you played pussy in the corner, and hoped that no one would notice you. Going to hide behind her skirts again?" And he gestured dramatically at the draped Lucy.

"I think you're a bit of a barnyard fowl, yourself, James

Howell. The rooster, in fact. All he has to do is crow and the good hen upends. Why can't you leave me alone?"

"Why?" The word erupted like an explosion from Jamie's lips. He reached out and whipped the sheet from the Lucy. "Why? Because of this! Because of that home-loving cat. Christ, Mirelle," and his voice changed to one of entreaty, "there is so little love in the world . . . real love . . . that kind that speaks through clay and paint and metal. There's a helluva lot of shoddy stuff exhibited that professes to portray the ages of man, the loves of man, the struggles of man! Shit!" He dismissed these travesties with a sidewise slice of one hand. "Love stirs in you and you create a Lucy. You make a head of a man you barely know and it is done with love. Did you realize that? Did you realize that you were already drawn to me when you fashioned that?" He started to gesture towards the bust and then whirled around, staring at the amorphous bulk of blue-coated plaster. "What have you done? Covered me with woad?" he demanded indignantly.

A sudden vision of his splendid lean naked body covered in the battle dye of an ancient Briton convulsed Mirelle with laughter. She was helpless with mirth until Howell's indignation turned to crestfallen amusement and he, too, began to chuckle.

"May I add, m'dear, that you'd've been a sight yourself had I worn woad Friday night?" He struggled to be dignified. "Why, in the name of all the Medes and Persians, did you have to do that to me? I'd rather looked forward to examining the head closely, you know. I've had to sneak my looks surreptitiously."

"I finished it up Saturday night."

That pleased him. "Then why the woad? Didn't you ever intend to let me see it?"

She couldn't meet his eyes. "That might be asking for it, Jamie."

He leaned closer to her, tipped up her chin. His eyes were tender.

"You can't deny . . . "

She covered his mouth quickly with her fingers and, with a swift gesture, he imprisoned her hand.

"I was so afraid, Mirelle, that the plastic coating had reached your soul, too. That you'd be afraid to give yourself . . . "

"I needed you, Jamie. I told you that. And I was wrong a moment ago. I've needed the kicks and the prods you and Sylvia . . . and my mother-in-law . . . have been dealing me. I've been afraid and . . . well, I find I'm allergic to plastic. Come."

She took him by the hand and led him to the living room, turning him so he saw the newly hung portrait. Howell gave her a look of startled delight before he studied the painting.

"Well," he said with a snort, "he didn't spare himself, did he?"

"I think I admire him the more for that."

Jamie looked down at her. "Yes, you would." Then his expression turned sardonic. "And what will the husband think when he sees his infamous father-in-law ensconced on his hallowed middle-class walls?"

Mirelle shrugged. "In his present mood, he might even give a rousing cheer. I think the portrait will stay where it is. Coffee?"

"Yes, indeed. All this exhortation has left me dry."

Howell followed her out to the kitchen and draped himself on the stool. She started the kettle and fixed the pot. Then she turned to face him.

"I don't want to have an affair with you, Jamie," she said firmly, looking him in the eye. To her surprise he smiled as if he'd expected her words. It made her stammer as she continued. "And don't say it's women's magazine morality." She had a flashing recollection of G.F. and that unknown woman in the back of a white Cadillac. She shook her head. "What happened between us the other night was a lovely experience: just right for both of us. But I'm not in love with you, Jamie Howell, though you are mighty attractive to me. I've a husband and children. Yes, yes, you know things aren't going too well with my marriage but that's because I couldn't face what I am. Because I was trying to be what

I couldn't be. Steve had to make a terrible choice recently, and he chose me. I couldn't desert him now even if I were madly, passionately in love with you. And I'm not." At the look in Jamie's eyes, she could almost wish she were. She turned from him, her eyes falling to the floor. "I don't always sculpt with love either, Jamie."

She motioned him to follow her back to the studio where she took down the Hands. She whisked the cloth away and stood back, watching him closely. He sucked in his breath, shooting a concerned glance at her before he examined the plaque closely.

"Yes, I see what you mean," he said at length. "And yet . . . " He gave his head a begrudging twist of approval, "There is something compelling about it. I don't *like* the goddamned thing but it's powerful." He gave her a rueful half-grin, his eyes thoughtful. "I've felt that way," and he made a pulling motion with both hands. Then he put his hands on her shoulders, drawing her close to him. He kissed her very gently on the lips, held her close for a moment before he released her. "I wish, Mirelle, that we'd met before you married, before I encountered Margaret's mother but . . . " and he made an open-handed gesture of regret and stepped back, smiling slightly.

She returned the smile, profoundly grateful for his acquiescence.

"I met you, Jamie, when I most needed to."

"Such magnanimous self-sacrifice on my part does not mean, however," he said in his usual crisp bantering tone, "that I will leave you alone to the tender mercies of invidious Fate." He waggled a long finger at her. "You are not going to stop sculpting, are you?"

"I've rather got to continue, Jamie, haven't I? Isn't that what this is all about?"

"Then stop that bloody kettle's screeching and make me some coffee."

As she raced to the kitchen, she wondered that he hadn't protested more. She hadn't realized herself, until the words came out, what her decision would be. But it was the only one she could make. She was not temperamentally suited to conducting an affair; despite the estrangement, she was very much married to Steve. And the estrangement had been due as much to the fact that she had evaded a confrontation between her mother-in-law and herself as any other single factor. There were other forms of infidelity worse than sexual. She had been denying Steve her complete self because she was denying it to herself as well: not because she resented an invasion of her private self, as she'd once thought.

"Did you ever find out what happened to Sylvia?" Jamie asked as she brought the coffee back to the studio.

"Not exactly, and I'm worried about her. I can't reach her by phone and on Saturday, when she called, she sounded as if she had a mouth full of cotton."

"Drunk?" Jamie cocked his right eyebrow cynically.

"Not at 10:30 in the morning."

"Oh?"

"Yes, 'oh'."

"Don't bristle so, Mirelle," and Jamie held up a hand in mock protection. "You realize that Sylvia's a mightily disturbed woman, don't you?"

Mirelle felt herself flush. "I didn't until recently. She's so breezy, so self-confident . . . "

"Hmm, yes, the bright facade to hide the bleeding heart . . . "

"You can be so cynical." Mirelle felt a surge of ire for him.

"No, Mirelle, I'm not actually," he said, quickly covering his hand with hers, all mockery gone. "But I find that armor suffices me best." He made a show of squaring his shoulders. "It's in keeping with my professional image. Speaking of which," and again he switched moods abruptly, "I met Madame de Courcy, Sylvia's maternal parent . . . at yesterday's recital. She is, one instantly apprehends, a major patroness of the Ahrts, with a very short list of acceptable composers of which my students played no compositions at all."

Jamie had drawn his features in such a supercilious expression of disdain that Mirelle clearly saw the grand dame he was imitating.

"If that's who Sylvia contends with, I sympathize deeply. Formidable woman!"

Sylvia's comments anent her mother problem had all been surface stuff, except for that embittered 'All my life she's hurt me'.

"I also deduce that Sylvia is not at home," Jamie went on. " 'My daughter is indisposed' was the euphemism given for her absence."

"How can you deduce that from that?"

"The knowing glance with which that information was received."

"Oh, Jamie!"

"Yes, it is a tragedy. Sylvia struck me as being rather a good sort. Consider yourself lucky indeed, Mirelle, that you're an orphaned bastard." He rose then. "I really have to go. I noticed this morning that it's the twenty-first day of December, and nearly noon at that, and there are but four more shopping days till Christmas. I'm so used to its intent from October on that I've become inured to its imminence. Margaret comes down on Wednesday and I've no Christmas trinkets for that little charmer. I must see what Woolworth's is featuring this year."

"Jamie! You wouldn't?" Then she caught his expression. "Well, if they have nothing at the price you're willing to pay, Wanamaker's has a good budget shop. And there's always Goodwill."

At the door, he searched her face a moment.

"I still want an original LeBoyne, you know."

"I know, Jamie."

"I'd take that bust in a flash if I could escape the accusation of overweening conceit. No, I will not accept it as a token of your esteem for myself. But you might try to sell it to the Music School." His eyes brimmed with laughter. "There's an empty niche in the hall next to Mozart which I'd grace elegantly."

"James Howell, you are insufferable!"

"Am I not? Merry Christmas, Mary Ellen LeBoyne, and a prosperous New Year."

She watched him drive out of the development before she

turned from the window to other concerns. She tried first to reach Sylvia and got no answer. Certainly Sylvia's daughters would be home from college by now, or that odious mother. Oh, they were all probably out shopping like everyone else.

The thought of the stores today defeated Mirelle so she compromised by baking Christmas cookies and worrying over Sylvia. She had only one more tray of cookies to finish when she remembered Sylvia wondering what sort of a sick-pig Mirelle would make for her.

What Sylvia needed was not a sickpig, but a talisman, Mirelle told herself. She could barely wait to get the cookies out of the oven before she was away to the studio and digging into the clay barrel.

With the almost finished model of the Lucy before her, it didn't take long to make a small replica. She worked steadily, absorbed, until the kids got home from school. She took a break then, because the concentrated effort made her head ache. But she had only the detailing to finish later before she could fire it. With any luck she'd have the finished statuette to present to Sylvia for Christmas. Mirelle couldn't explain why she knew it would be the perfect gift for Sylvia. Perhaps, hopefully, the miniature would be a catalyst for Sylvia, too.

CHAPTER TWENTY-THREE

STEVE DID NOT GET HOME that night. Nor did Mirelle hear from him. At the sight of his unused bed the next morning, a niggling half-fear, half-anger started in her belly. She called the office to see if he might have gone there straight from the airport. Steve'd been expected back, his secretary said, and left the question in her voice hanging expectantly. Mirelle mumbled some nonsense about a possible hold-up in Christmas air traffic and hung up.

That's what she told the children when they got home from school and began to notice their father's continued absence.

"We have to get our tree today," Nick said, frowning and looking exceedingly like his grandfather Neagu. "All the good ones'll be gone if we wait much longer."

"I think we can just get the tree. Daddy will understand," Mirelle said, unable to cope with imminent full-scale sulks.

Roman gave her an odd look for her unexpected capitulation. It was a long-standing family custom that Steve and the children bought the family tree and saw to its trimming.

They got a tree, full branched, 'a hen of a tree', as Nick styled it. She spent far more than she intended, or thought she should. Certainly more than Steve would, for he shopped the tree lots assiduously for the best bargain. She let the children set it up in the gameroom and get the ornaments out.

"We'll leave the creche until Daddy gets home or he will really hit the roof," Mirelle told them but she and Nick did position the creche board in the living room. Santa Claus reigned in the gameroom, and all the new toys and mess centered there. But the creche, with its landscape of Bethlehem, stable-cave, inn and fields, was traditionally in the living room, expressing the original meaning of the festival.

She made hamburgers for a quick supper, and to economize for the cost of the tree, and they ate as they decorated. Roman did his best to officiate but his manner, reminiscent of his father, provoked his sister.

"You're acting just like Daddy."

"Why not?" Roman asked. "He's not here and I am the oldest son."

"I think we should've waited for Daddy," and Tonia looked about to burst into tears.

"We've left the creche to do with Daddy," Mirelle said hastily. "He prefers it anyway. Remember? Now stick some more lights to the left there, Nick. It's awfully bare. Tonia, don't set those fairy lights in too deep. Keep them on the tips of the branches."

She had rather hoped that trimming the tree would take up the entire evening. Then Tonia started pawing through the creche box and found her favorite camel in pieces. The tears came in earnest. Mirelle managed to restore her daughter's humor by promising to fire up the kiln and replace any and all favorites that had failed to survive. With what she thought was true inspiration she suggested that they wrap their presents for their father. No one had shopped for parents yet. Roman got rather exercised because he hadn't been able to make newspaper collections and rake in the Christmas tip money out of which he bought his gifts.

Nick, with a great show of Christmas generosity, offered to collect without charging a cent for his services. In the next breath, he mentioned with heavy emphasis his longing for a wargame. Tonia, quick to recognize golden opportunity, insisted that she was just as capable of making collections as Nick, because she needed such a lot of new Barbie doll clothes. Seeing the makings of a battle royal, Mirelle decreed that both children would help Roman the very next morning, and sent them off to bed.

When she tucked Tonia in, the girl was still upset over having done the tree without her father. Mirelle managed to reassure her but, as she walked downstairs, she wasn't all that confident. Steve should be home. What could be holding him up in Cleveland? Particularly just before Christmas? Even major crises waited until after the Christmas parties.

Suddenly, with sickening certainty, she knew what had happened: he'd gone to Florida. His mother had got him to go to Florida because she couldn't cope with the emergency of his father's illness, and obviously Ralph was no help. How ironic! How too terribly, horribly ironic! Mirelle's laugh was silent and mirthless. She clutched herself about the ribs.

Here she'd renounced a lover, resolved to be a better wife, and her husband had decamped.

The sane observer shouted denial, accused her of self-pity, of wallowing in guilt. And she'd promised not to. Steve was only delayed in the holiday traffic: that was all. The weather was atrocious, storm warnings all across the country.

To get her mind off this insidious track, she turned to the damaged creche figures. She was disgusted with her first attempt at a new camel: it had no soul, no grace, even for a camel. Her fingers were clumsy. As she rose to get her file on animals, she saw the almost completed statuette and remembered that she still hadn't raised anyone at Sylvia's house. Surely by now, ten o'clock, someone would be home.

G.F. answered the phone.

"G.F., where is Sylvia?"

There was a brief pause.

"G.F., I've considered myself Sylvia's friend. She called me Saturday, sounding completely unlike herself. I haven't heard from her since, nor have I been able to get any answer during the day. Please tell me what's wrong."

"She called you on Saturday?" G.F. was surprised.

"Yes, and she talked as if her mouth was full of cotton. She hung up abruptly."

There was a weary sigh on the other end of the phone.

"Sylvia is in the Philadelphia Institute. She entered voluntarily on Friday."

"The Institute? Voluntarily?"

"Sylvia hasn't been well. I think you've realized that, Mirelle. She's undergoing a course of treatment which may help her get a grip on herself."

Mirelle found it difficult to grasp the significance of his stark words. Sylvia had admitted to being under psychiatric care, but that was a long step from entering a psychiatric hospital. Or was it? How could she, Mirelle, possibly gauge the condition of anyone's mind? She couldn't control her own wild thoughts and fancies. But Sylvia hadn't acted . . . psychotic. She'd sounded drunk.

"You mean, Sylvia's an alcoholic?" Mirelle wanted that to be the problem.

G.F. gave a wry snort. "That would be easier to treat. Sylvia is in mental distress, Mirelle. That's what they treat at the Institute."

"Oh, G.F., I'm so sorry. So terribly sorry."

"You shouldn't be, Mirelle. You've been a big help all this fall, you know."

"Me? I couldn't have been, G.F. . . . "

"I beg to differ." His voice dropped suddenly. "She'll be able to see you soon, I think, Mirelle." He spoke swiftly as if anxious not to be overheard. "In fact, you're the only one on the visitors' list. She stipulated that you had to bring a sick-pig when you came. Does that make any sense?" Plainly it made none to him.

"Yes, it does, G.F. . . . And tell her, if you're in touch, that I've got something along that line for her."

"I will, Mirelle. And Merry Christmas." That last was said in a normally cheerful tone.

"The same to you." Her response was automatic and

Mirelle gasped. How could she? With Sylvia hospitalized at Christmas! But G.F. had rung off.

How could she have been a big help to Sylvia this fall? Sylvia had spent so much time helping her. And Mirelle had called it meddling. How could she?

Mirelle reached for the small Lucy. If she was right, and this statuette could be a talisman for Sylvia, now was the time to finish it. She'd take her worries out on the clay—Sylvia had envied her that outlet—and put in the figure all the love and concern and hope, and believe that the messages would come across to the recipient. She was able to forget why the statue must be perfect in the process of perfecting. With a woad-blue, and smiling to herself at the recollection of Jamie's indignant spluttering, she covered the little Lucy. With luck, she'd get it dug out and cast tomorrow. And she'd make her luck.

Affectionately she looked across at the big statue. Lucy had been the catalyst for her twice now. It was a pleasant conceit to believe that the same magic might work for Sylvia.

She took up the little camel then and reworked it to her satisfaction. Before fatigue forced her to stop, she had replaced most of the broken animals. It was nearly 2:00 when she staggered to her room. She was too tired, suddenly, to undress, and just pulled the quilt over her.

She woke with a start as something brushed against her foot, cold from being outside the cover.

"Go back to sleep, honey. I just got in," Steve whispered. His hands were gentle as he picked her up and slid her under the blankets. He tucked her in and kissed her cheek. She smiled because he was so tender and fell deeply asleep.

The usual high-pitched shriek of protest from Tonia woke her next morning. She sat up in bed, instantly aware of the raucous snores from the next bed. Relief was almost a pain in her belly as she rose and flew from the room, determined to shut Tonia up and lay down strict silence. Steve must get his sleep.

Tonia, fortunately, retained enough of her previous week's inhibitions to comply with the threat of Daddy's continued displeasure. Nick was bribed to clear the walk of a light snow that had fallen during the night. Roman was already casting up his newspaper accounts so the kids could collect for him.

The office called about Steve's whereabouts at 9:30 and she promised that he'd call in as soon as he woke. His secretary was a little dismayed at her refusal to wake him but Mirelle was politely adamant. She got the children all out of the house, having suggested that Roman could sit on the sled and be taken about to supervise the collection process.

It wasn't until after she had put the creche replacements in the kiln for firing that she glanced into the living room. And saw that Steve had plunked down his bags there. He couldn't have missed the portrait.

She sighed deeply. He had come home. That was the first step. She was putting the second batch of figures in the kiln when she heard his steps. She met him on the landing. He was shaved and dressed for the office. He looked rested but there were lines of strain apparent in his face. He was suddenly very dear to her, as if she had to be threatened with his loss to appreciate how much he meant to her. She would have given anything for the right words to express her jumbled feelings.

"Office call?" he asked, as he gave her a hug and a kiss.

She wanted to believe that neither were perfunctory.

"Yes, indeed," she said in cheerful tones. "I said you'd got in very late and I was going to let you sleep. Miss Hayes was rather put out."

"Idiot woman. Any coffee?"

"Yes, I've been keeping it warm." She stepped past him to get the pot. "Did the Cleveland thing straighten out?"

"Naturally," he replied disdainfully. "A matter of proper briefing and a little blarney. Then I had to go on to Orlando."

She almost dropped the coffee. She'd been right. His mother had made him run to her. Her hand was trembling so much that she nearly spilled as much as she poured into his cup. He was glancing at the mail and didn't notice.

"I'm glad you went, Steve. You'd've worried all during Christmas if you hadn't." He had come back to her. He had come home.

Steve looked directly at her, then. "Ralph called me and insisted I had to come." He rubbed the back of his neck. "He's almost as bad as Mother, you know. Dad was all right, resting comfortably, and that pair was hanging crepe." He gave a mirthless snort of laughter. "In fact, the doctor had given orders for no visitors for Dad because Mother carried on so much she upset him. I got in touch with the Blackburns, you know, Red's parents, and they promised to divert Mother."

"Did our flowers get there?" That was surely safe to ask, Mirelle decided.

"Yes, the biggest poinsettia I've ever seen. Fix me a couple of eggs, will you, Mirelle?"

"Coming up." Maybe he hadn't seen the portrait last night.

He stood in the doorway between the kitchen and the dining room, sipping his coffee while she fried his eggs.

"Where're the kids?"

"I sent them all out to help Roman collect his Christmas loot."

"Roman's out?" Steve frowned.

"Oh, he's ensconced on the sled with Tonia and Nick as his willing steeds."

"Nick looks a good deal like his grandfather, doesn't he?"

"Yes, he does," and Mirelle hazarded a quick glance at Steve. To her astonishment, he began to chuckle, ducking his head to smooth the hair on his neck.

"God, your father looks like he'd been everywhere and done everything. You don't suppose Nick will take after him?"

"Good Lord, I hope not. One rake is enough for any family."

She flipped the eggs on the plate and retrieved the toast which had just popped up.

"Tree looks great," Steve said, pulling out his chair. "Who supervised?"

"Roman. We did everything except the creche."

Steve caught her hand as she put his plate down and looked up at her, his eyes dark, troubled and pleading.

"I'll do that tonight with you, won't I, Mirelle?"

Mirelle ran her hand through his crisp hair, resting it lightly on the back of his strong neck.

"Yes, Steve. We'll do that together tonight. After all, it's a tradition in our family!"

Wilmington, Delaware and Sea Cliff, Long Island, USA
Mount Merrion and Dundrum, Ireland

DISCARD
F
McCaffrey,
The y
DATE D
MR 19 '8
MR 23 '8
21
DISCARD